IN BLOOD WE TRUST

By
F.D. Davis

Other Titles
The Critic
Another Man's Baby
Many Shades of Gray
In The Beginning—F.D. Davis
Two Sides to Every Story
Forever And A Day
Let's Get It On
Misty Blue
The Wedding Gown
The Color of Trouble
The Lotus Blossoms Chronicles II (November 2008)
To Live Again (July 2009)

ISIS is an imprint of Parker Publishing LLC.

Copyright © 2008 by Dyanne Davis
Published by Parker Publishing LLC
12523 Limonite Avenue, Suite #440-438
Mira Loma, California 91752
www.parker-publishing.com

This book is a work of fiction. Characters, names, locations, events and incidents (in either a contemporary and/or historical setting) are products of the author's imagination and are being used in an imaginative manner as a part of this work of fiction. Any resemblance to actual events, locations, settings, or persons, living or dead, is entirely coincidental.

ISBN: 978-1-60043-041-1
First Edition

Manufactured in the United States of America
Printed by Bang Printing, Brainerd MN
Distributed by BookMasters, Inc. 1-800-537-6727
Cover Design by JaxadoraDesigns.com

Cover Design by Jaxadora Designs

Dedication

ADAM OMEGA'S DEDICATION

F. D. Davis has asked me to write a dedication . (LOL) Mortals! Is she seriously thinking that I will thank her for penning this tale? Her endless questions of: Mr. Omega what does blood taste like? Mr. Omega do you feel guilty when you kill? Mr. Omega this and Mr. Omega that. The woman is lucky to still be alive to pester me. So I dedicate this book to, ADAM OMEGA VAMPIRE, for having the patience of a saint in dealing with mortals.

Adam Omega
Vampire

F.D. DAVIS'S DEDICATION

I dedicate this book with much love and admiration to Brenda Willis. Brenda, Adam truly appreciates all that you do to make his site a place where he can call home. (smile) I'm proud to have you as one of the human helpers that Adam loves to annoy.

And as F. D. Davis, Adam Omega's alter ego, there are no words to express my sincere appreciation for your doing and maintaining the www.dyannedavis.com website. It rocks and so do you. Of course I know you have more fun with Adam's site. www.adamomega.com. So from the entire cast I wish you well in your own endeavors and thank you from the bottom of my heart and theirs.

Acknowledgements

As always I give thanks to the creator. For whatever reason you've allowed me to live my dream and I humbly thank you.

To my sister, Jackqueline Toreas Jackson, Since you're not reading about Mr. Omega I started to ignore your demand that I include you in all acknowledgements. You should break open the book just so you'll know I'm putting all of your business in the streets. LOL. I love you and have resisted all of Mr. Omega's offers to bend you to his way of thinking.

To Sidney Rickman, thank you for continuing the journey with me.

Thank you Parker Publishing for the opportunity to bring the second story in this series to my readers.

To Viola Stephens Brown, many many thanks for reading the mss in-between editing and telling me when the mortal had gone astray in telling Mr. Omega's story. And I would be remiss in not relaying Mr. Omega's thanks

To Gwyneth Bolton, an Emma award winning author.. WOW!! Your review of, IN The Beginning, both pleased and scared me. You had set a high bar for me and I totally didn't want to disappoint. So I want to thank you also for reading the second installment of Mr. Omega between edits and giving me your honest input. I also thank you for the cover blurb.

To my family and friends thank you for your continued support.

To the readers thank you for your continued support of my work.

And bringing up the rear, the most important two people in my world. Bill, my love, my hero, my romance story comes to life, you are as always loved by me. Thank you for reminding me that "I'M NOT A VAMPIRE." I'm so sorry that the absolute perfect dedication to you was left out of the perfect book for it. Another Man's Baby. Since none of the books that are coming out fit what I wrote I'll just have to think of something else. In the meantime your dedication will remain posted on my website.

To our son Bill Jr. As always you continue to make me proud. May all of your dreams come true.

IN
BLOOD
WE TRUST

By
F.D. Davis

"Suffer me a little, and I will shew that I have yet to speak on God's behalf. I will fetch my knowledge from afar, and will ascribe righteousness to my maker. For truly my words shall not be false: he that is perfect in knowledge is with thee."

—*Job 16:1-4*

Chapter 1

"Damn you, Adam, let me out!"

He cocked his head to the side as Eve's angry voice reverberated through his body and closed his mind to her. She wasn't ready yet. And until she was he would content himself with replaying that moment of sweet release.

Adam smiled as the pull to his groin increased. *How many days had it been?* he wondered. He'd almost lost count. Eight, nine, ten? One moment he'd been sheathed by Eve's wet warmth, hearing her moaning his name, telling him that she loved him, and the next he had been bringing her into his world, making her into one of the creatures of the night, the thing she'd fought not to become.

He hadn't killed her. He'd made love to her and he hadn't killed her. In fact, the exact opposite was true. He'd saved her life. She should be grateful to him instead of bitching and complaining. Rolling his eyes in annoyance, he once again listened to Eve's thoughts.

"You arrogant bastard!"

Adam sighed in disbelief. How could any woman who'd lain in his arms and received his lovemaking, and his love, call him names? It was a mystery. Of course he was arrogant, he'd never denied that. Then again, he had reason to be. Why lie? His sexual prowess was unparalleled. He didn't doubt that for a moment. He'd employed every one of his vast skills in making love to Eve, not to mention that all the love he'd stored away in his undead heart had poured out into Eve's body. She belonged to him now, completely and forever.

With that thought, his erection swelled and every thrust replayed itself in his body. He shuddered, smelling Eve, tasting her, drowning in her desire.

"Yes," he moaned. Eve was definitely worth the wait. Once she came to her senses he'd release her. An errant thought attempted to claim him. And *what will you do with her then?*

Adam's eyes squeezed shut and he jerked with the memory induced orgasm. "I will love her," he whispered softly, touching himself and feeling her hands cover his tip. *I will find a way*, he thought as he gave in to the fast building release that followed close on the heels of the last. *I will find a way to love her.*

❖

A coffin. Eve couldn't believe she was lying in a coffin, paralyzed. She would have screamed had she been able, but she wasn't. The only option open to her was to plead with Adam telepathically to let her out. So far it wasn't working. Maybe if she could force herself to stop cursing him, he'd come. But every time she thought to do that anger overcame her and she mentally let loose with a string of expletives. He'd better hope like hell that she wouldn't have his strength because if she did she was definitely seeking big time payback. Damn him.

Not knowing what else to do she decided to try Adam's mind over matter theory. *I believe I can move. I believe it with all my heart.* Though Eve repeated the words in her mind over and over, she still couldn't move. Even her tear ducts were frozen. That was the only thing in this horrible nightmare that Eve was glad of. She knew Adam's tears were drops of bloods. She assumed since he'd turned her into one of the living dead hers would be also. That was one little treat she didn't need.

How had her life come to this? Nine months before she'd been a librarian living quietly and peacefully. All of the dreams she'd had were on the verge of coming true. Then out of the blue her life had changed—forever, it seemed.

Her life now, such as it was, she owed to Adam and his obsession. Nine months ago the idea that vampires existed had never crossed her mind. That they not only existed but could even go inside a church… The very thought had been laughable. That she would allow a vampire to feed from her in order to save her friends and family, that she would fall in love with said vampire, no way would that ever happen. But it had and now that same vampire she'd fallen in love with had imprisoned her in a coffin.

Why?

Because she preferred being mortal? Because she didn't want a life sucking blood from the veins of other humans? Pain sliced through her soul with the speed of light and Eve wondered why she could feel that.

"Adam," she tried again, but he wasn't answering.

Emotions swirled through her like the winds, anger, confusion, back to anger, then fear. And at last, a moment before submission, she thought of someone else who might be able to help her.

"Sullivan," Eve called out to the cosmos. "Sullivan, help me, please." Eve didn't know how long it was before she picked up an answer, but to her it seemed forever. "Sullivan, I'm inside a coffin…" Even her thoughts halted. "Adam left me here and he won't answer."

"Why?"

God, thank you, she wanted to scream. "Sullivan, is that really you, or am I imagining things?"

"It's me. Why would you call me, Eve? How can you call me?"

"I don't know. I just know I need help. I'm freaking out."

"So he decided not to kill you?"

"Depends on how you look at it," Eve answered. "He turned me."

"Are you saying that Adam brought you over…that…"

"That I'm now one of the vampiric women Adam hates. Yes, that's exactly what I'm saying."

"Was that your punishment for betraying him?"

"Listen, Sullivan, I'm glad you answered, but can you…will you help me?"

"What about Adam?"

Eve felt desolate. "If you're worried about Adam I don't think he will know you've helped me. He still thinks you're dead. He won't know, he's closed his mind to me."

For a long moment she didn't feel Sullivan in her mind. When his voice came there was no ignoring the hurt in it.

"That wasn't why I asked, not out of fear. I assumed if Adam left you there, he will return for you when whatever game he's playing is over. You won't be able to hide from him. I wasn't thinking about myself, but you."

"I don't give a damn what Adam thinks." Eve attempted to convey her anguish. "I've been here for days. What if Adam doesn't come for me?"

"I don't understand. You have Adam's blood, you're a vampire. You have the strength to open the coffin yourself."

Eve couldn't believe it; she was debating with the only being who was answering her as to why she was stuck in a coffin. Why the heck couldn't he just come to her rescue? Then she remembered their last time together and cringed. Well, he might have a reason for not helping her. Once Adam had gotten it into his head that she was his reincarnated wife, Eyanna, and had begun abusing Eve because she'd rejected him, she'd been more than happy to have Sullivan in her corner. That was after she'd gotten over the shock that vampires did exist. Visits to countless psychics, along with dreams of Eyanna, had finally convinced Eve that she was a healer, that she was Adam's reincarnated wife. So she'd experimented with healing potions and used crystals to keep Adam out of her thoughts and her home. Who wouldn't have taken the deal Sullivan had offered? If it worked it meant Eve would live the rest of her life in an Adam free zone. She'd promised to help Sullivan render Adam harmless. He'd given her money to buy the ingredients for her potions. But when that little maggot of a vampire, Uriel, had bitten into Adam in an attempt to gain Adam's powers something in her had snapped. Her love for Adam had overridden every other emotion and she'd gone after the entire group of vampires armed with water she'd gotten from the kitchen sink and prayed over. It had worked. She'd killed four vampires that night with what she'd told them was holy water. She thought of Sullivan catching the crystal and the bottled potion she'd thrown to him. Sullivan was a good man. He'd tried to protect her and Adam from Uriel, yet she'd betrayed him the same as she'd betrayed Adam.

"I don't think you betrayed me, Eve. You just couldn't get over your love for Adam. It was too strong."

Thank God Sullivan had not broken the connection. "Sullivan, will you help me?"

"You didn't answer my question. Why can't you help yourself?"

Now Eve was back to being angry. "Okay, if you must know, I took the same potion that I gave Adam. I'm paralyzed and I have been now for seven days, maybe eight, I don't know, I've lost count. Are you going to help me or not?"

"Of course I am," Sullivan answered and Eve felt a whoosh of air as the lid was lifted.

"You came," she whispered in her mind.

"Of course I came." He lifted her in his arms and grinned. "I bet you wish you had left with me now, don't you? Don't worry, Eve, I brought something for you." He put the amber bottle to her lips and allowed the liquid to fall into her mouth. "I had a feeling I should keep some of this handy. I'm not sure how long it takes for the potion to work. Since this is your potion, do you have any idea how long it will take?" Sullivan smiled.

"I'm hoping it works quickly."

"Eve, seems like you have a choice to make. I assume since you asked me to release you that you don't like the accommodations Adam chose. I have only one other place to take you. I remember your earlier objections to entering my home."

He could feel the thumping of her heart. "I have no other place, Eve. I'm sorry but it is your choice."

"Not much of a choice," Eve said, then amended her hasty words. "I'm sorry, but if the choices are being in a coffin or in the home of a vampire, which would you choose?"

"You lived with Adam."

"That was…"

"That was what, different? You were in love with him? What? Tell me. You're the same as I am now. It wasn't me who did this to you. It was Adam who turned you, remember that. Of course I could just leave the lid off and put you back where I found you." He laid her back in the coffin and stared down at her. "You can stay where you are if you like. You won't be alone."

"There are other…other…beings here?"

"Yes, there are others here," Sullivan answered. "They will not harm you. They would be too afraid. You still belong to Adam and they will not forget that. Didn't you feel them around you?"

Eve would have to admit she had not only felt the presence of the others but heard murmurings. She'd been afraid that at any moment, because she'd killed four vampires, she would be targeted for revenge.

"I don't belong to anyone. Now will you get me the hell out of here?" Once again she felt herself being lifted and found comfort in Sullivan's arm. If Eve could have, she would have thrown her arms around him and given him the biggest hug he'd received in eight-hundred years. Instead, she repeated telepathically, 'Thank you,' over and over.

"So where do you want to go?" He looked into her eyes. "Shall I take you home, Eve?"

She could swear he was laughing at her. Just a few weeks ago she'd sworn she'd never set foot in another vampire's home. Now, as long as she wasn't in a coffin she didn't care. She might live to regret it but she agreed to go.

Then it hit her. She was no longer alive, not in any human sense. Damn Adam anyway. He should have done as she asked and let her die.

"You were dying, Eve?"

She'd almost forgotten Sullivan. "Please, no more questions until the potion kicks in. I don't want to be in your head and I don't want you in mine."

"It seems that was exactly what you wanted when you contacted me."

Eve didn't have an answer for that. All she could do was ignore him and hope for the best.

She should have known hoping for the best wasn't going to work. "Sullivan." Eve choked on the name. "I feel so dirty. I need to feel clean. No sooner had she spoken the words than her soiled clothing was changed.

"Sullivan, please, I don't know how to ask you this but I need water on my body." She paused. "Even if I can't feel it at the moment, I still want it. You have to listen to me and try to understand. I need water on my body. Real water and lots of soap. I would have scrubbed myself clean before all of this. I'm fighting for my sanity. I want to believe I'm normal, human, mortal, whatever. I need to know I'm alive." Within moments Sullivan was doing as she'd asked. Tears ran unchecked down her cheeks.

If she wasn't already dead, she would have died of embarrassment as Sullivan cleansed her body. He talked to her to take her mind off the intimacy of what he was doing, but it did little to help. At one point she wanted to tell him to stop but the knowledge that she was lying in his bed, on white satin sheets, and that she'd asked him to do it stopped her. She wanted to be clean. Somewhere part of her brain recognized that, but knowing Sullivan's hands were roaming over her body filled her with dread.

When he was done he refused to meet her eyes, just gave her more of the antidote, turned off the lights and drew the curtains. Eve could hear him outside the door. The familiar sound of a chair scraping across bare wood alerted her to his intentions. *So he's guarding me. Against what?* she wondered and fell asleep.

❖

Adam frowned and stood perfectly still. For the past days he'd been monitoring Eve's heartbeat. The muffled beat that came through the thick inlaid mother of pearl had its own distinct sound. He'd smiled to himself as Eve screamed his name, her anger telling him she wasn't ready for him to release her. No, she needed more time to become pliable to his wishes, to know that it was fated for the two of them to spend eternity together.

As he'd listened to her cries turn fearful, he'd almost thought to release her. But he was going for control. When he released Eve he wanted her to be grateful not to be in the coffin. He wanted her to remember her first life as Eyanna, his wife. He wanted her to remember that he'd given up his life for her. And he wanted her to remember how much pleasure he'd given her before turning her. Then he wanted her to beg him to forgive her for all the pain she'd caused him and pledge to love him for the rest of eternity. Adam wanted Eve to remember that she loved him.

"Eve," Adam called out and felt nothing, not a block keeping his thoughts out, not a heartbeat. There was nothing to tell him she was safe. If she were a mere mortal he would think her dead. The thought filled him with dread and without hesitation he found himself in the catacombs beneath the city, rushing toward the pearl coffin he'd commissioned especially for Eve.

He ripped the lid from the hinges, not bothering with subtlety. Adam's heart skipped a beat as he looked into the empty coffin. *Where the hell was Eve?* he wondered. He shouted her name and felt a shiver that must have come from her soul.

Blood calling to blood. He'd made her; he would always be able to find her. Still, he felt the resistance. She didn't want him to know where she was. Too bad. He knew and he was going to retrieve her.

❖

When she woke, Eve knew immediately the antidote was working. She no longer had to fight to keep her eyes open. She tried to move her mouth and could just a bit. She felt the stiffness followed by pain as she stretched muscles. An intense pain seared her brain and Eve moaned inwardly. Adam was calling to her, his voice anxious and filled with fear. She wasn't going to answer him. He'd not answered her. Her insides felt on fire as though each cell in her body was determined to betray her by revealing her whereabouts to Adam. *No*, she thought repeatedly, *I can keep him from knowing*.

She heard his voice again, louder this time, angrier and a bit baffled. *Serves him right*, she thought. Once again heat poured through her body. It took every ounce of concentration not to answer. Her nerve endings tingled with the knowledge that Adam knew where she was.

"Sullivan," Eve croaked, surprised when she actually heard the words come from her mouth. She felt liquid slid from the corner or her eye, saw the redness, and more followed. She couldn't stop crying at the sight of the blood tears. "Sullivan," she moaned. Then, "Oh God, Adam, what have you done to me?"

"Eve, don't cry."

It was Sullivan standing by the bed. She'd not heard him.

"What's wrong?"

"Look at me," she said and continued to cry.

He gazed at her sadly. "Oh, the tears. They're always the hardest thing to get used to. The more you cry, the more they come and the sadder it makes you." He attempted to smile. "You see, it's a vicious cycle. Now you know why no one in their right mind would wish for this or visit it upon another soul," he said disgustedly. "I wish Adam had killed you," he finished angrily, and looked at her.

"Then do it now, Sullivan. Kill me before Adam finds me, please."

"I can't."

"Why can't you?"

"Eve, I've never killed anyone intentionally. Well, at least not someone I considered a friend."

"But you wanted Adam dead."

"I know." Sullivan shivered and Eve looked at him.

"You mean you've never turned anyone into a vampire?"

"Of course not. I told you this life was a curse, not a blessing."

"Then why haven't you ended it, for yourself, I mean?"

"I guess I'm too much of a coward."

"I don't think you're a coward."

"That's not what you thought not so long ago."

"I was wrong."

Sullivan smiled but didn't answer.

"Thank you for helping me," Eve said.

Once again Sullivan didn't answer.

"What's wrong?"

"Adam, he knows you're not where he left you."

"I know and I don't care."

"He does."

Their gazes connected. Eve didn't want to ask, didn't want to seem ungrateful to Sullivan. She didn't want him to think she was waiting for Adam, but still she had to know. "How, Sullivan? Tell me how he knows where I am?"

"The blood. He made you. Adam will always know where you are. You won't be able to hide from him."

"Maybe not, but I don't have to be with him." Eve shivered. "I can return to my own apartment."

"You may stay here with me if you'd like." He held out the crystal she'd given him. "I'm not sure if this crystal and the potion you gave me is what now gives me immunity from the sun or my believing that it does. Either way it doesn't matter. You gave me the courage to try. I'll protect you with my life. I owe that to you for showing me that if a mere mortal could show such courage, then an eight-hundred years plus vampire could do no less."

Now Eve understood. She closed Sullivan's hand, leaving the crystal inside. "I'm sorry I couldn't help you bind Adam."

"Me too." Sullivan studied her. "But I knew it was a gamble from the moment I contacted you. I can't blame you for deciding to protect Adam."

Eve once again felt moisture on her cheek. "I couldn't let that little weasel suck Adam's blood. Uriel is disgusting."

"He was disgusting. Adam killed him."

"Do you blame me for that?"

"No. I blame Uriel. He should have known better. The plan was never to allow Uriel or any of us to turn into Adam. And I do apologize for Uriel hitting you. He should have never done that. I don't blame Adam for killing him, not one bit.

"None of this…none of you are what you seem. If it wasn't for the fact that I know you're a vampire, I would think you're human."

Sullivan laughed, a great booming sound. "Even Uriel?"

"No, he's the exception. He must have been a horrible mortal because as a vampire he was a lousy…" Eve suddenly felt Adam's presence and saw the hair on the back of Sullivan's hand stand on end. He'd felt it too. For a moment she thought he was afraid until he moved in front of her and spread his arms in a protective stance. She couldn't believe it; he was protecting her from Adam.

Chapter 2

Adam materialized and stood in the center of the room for a long moment, unsmiling, taking in the sight before him. He blinked twice, then cocked his head to the left to better observe the two.

"Sullivan, this is a surprise. I thought you were dead."

"I was already dead, Adam."

Adam laughed. "Yes, I forgot. Still, you know what I mean. I thought I'd seen the last of you when you walked into the sun."

"I'm immortal or did you forget that the sun can not hurt me any more than it can hurt you?"

"I'd be careful if I were you, Sullivan. Does this sudden bravado you're feeling have something to do with my wife?" He peeped around Sullivan and stared at Eve, not speaking to her but instead to Sullivan.

"Why is she here in your home, in your bed?" His voice was low, leaving no doubt of the warning.

"She called me and I answered."

Adam ignored Sullivan standing guard with his arms outstretched in an attempt to protect Eve. No one would ever be able to keep him from her, not Sullivan and not Eve herself. He glared in Sullivan's direction before walking to the bed and climbing in. He leaned down to look at Eve.

"I see that vile potion is wearing off." He didn't miss the way Eve's eyes flickered nor that she glanced at Sullivan.

"The two of you have a secret I should know about?" Adam asked, trying hard to sound undisturbed. Finding Sullivan was alive had been a surprise, but finding the woman he loved in the vampire's bed...well, it was a bit more than a shock. It was not going to continue, not a moment longer.

"I think it's time that we leave, Eve, don't you?"

"I'm not going anywhere with you."

"You're going." Adam smiled. "You don't belong here."

"I don't belong anywhere anymore but I'm definitely not going with the person who did this to me."

Adam swallowed. *Defiant to the end.* That was his Eve, the woman he'd fallen in love with more than a thousand years ago. Only then she'd been called

Eyanna and had not been nearly as defiant. Okay, so he'd turned Eve. So what? She had been trying to kill herself. He couldn't allow that to happen, not when he had the power to prevent it. He'd done what any self-respecting vampire would've done. He'd saved his wife.

"You're coming with me, Eve." He stood and put his arms beneath her body, but before he could lift her, Sullivan, her appointed guardian, was shoving him away. What crazy universe had Adam fallen into? Eve he understood, but Sullivan? He'd never shown an ounce of courage in the six hundred plus years that he'd known him.

Adam's grip loosened from the folds of Eve's gown and he glanced briefly at the flimsy material. It wasn't what she'd been wearing when'd he'd left her in the coffin. Very slowly Adam gazed around the room. His blood boiled on sighting the blue flowered antique bowl and water pitcher. He spotted the snow white washcloth and looked to the left at the folded white bath sheet. Sullivan had touched her, changed her clothes and maybe…

Rage enveloped Adam at the thought. His eyelids flickered as he readjusted his vision, accommodating for the blood that pooled in his eyes. He reached out for Sullivan and racked his fingers over his throat before getting a firm grip. As his fingers closed tightly, Adam roared, "Don't you ever interfere with my wife and me." With that he threw Sullivan across the room.

"You'll have to find something more than that. I'm not going to let you take her. She's under my protection and you have no rights here."

"No rights?" Adam snapped his fingers and Eve disappeared.

Sullivan's voice was filled with rage. "You had no right to turn her, Adam. She didn't ask for this; we both knew she didn't want it. But like always, the rules exist to be broken by you. Well, guess what? Not this time. I will not allow you to harm Eve any further."

"Are you challenging me?" Adam asked, dumbfounded. "You can't win. You and I both know that."

"Do we know it, Adam? I'm alive and you thought I had perished in the sun. Do we really know that I can't stop you?" He snapped his fingers and Eve reappeared. Sullivan moved closer to the bed. He pressed the small amber bottle into Eve's hand.

"What did you give her?" Adam glanced first toward Eve, then Sullivan. Anger filled him but he attempted to bring it under control before bringing his gaze back to rest on Eve.

"I gave her the means to free herself."

"You want her to die?" In disbelief Adam glared at Sullivan. "You'd give her a potion to end her life?" Before he could stop himself he'd lifted Sullivan into the air with but a thought. "You keep screwing with me and I will end your vile existence the same way you want Eve to end hers." Without preamble he allowed Sullivan's body to hit the floor with a thud.

"You ended her life, Adam. I'm merely giving her the keys to free herself."

Adam moved toward where Sullivan laid on the floor. The vampire was putting up a brave front for Eve. Admirable, but not enough. Still, it was more spunk than he'd ever shown and for what? "You can't have her." Adam spoke softly. "I won't allow it."

"I thought we'd settled things, you and I. You said if I survived the sun I lived. What's wrong? You can't or won't keep your word? You, a vampire who takes such pride in his word of honor. You gave your word that if I lived after walking out into the sun that you would do nothing to change that. Are you going back on that now?"

"Adam." Eve spoke as loudly as she could while watching the drama unfolding before her in quiet shock. Sullivan protecting her had not been totally unexpected, but she was surprised at the intensity of his convictions. He feared Adam and the three of them were aware of it, yet, he'd gone up against him. For her.

She looked down at the bottle in her hand. Adam had misunderstood what Sullivan had given her. She brought the bottle to her lips, uncapped it and called out. She saw the pain in Adam's eyes as she held the bottle.

"Eve, don't," he pleaded.

"I won't if you won't," she answered. "Leave Sullivan alone and stop beaming me around as though I were a piece of furniture, both of you. We're not on *Star Trek*."

"But—"

"No buts. You had an agreement with him, honor it."

"Are you coming with me?"

"No more, Adam. No more blackmailing me in order for you to do the right thing. No, I'm not coming with you. Sullivan said I could remain here with him until I get my bearings and if that offer still stands, I would like to take him up on it."

"And if Sullivan's not around to offer you his hospitality?"

"Then I offer her my home," Sullivan cut in. "If something happens to me, Eve, you're welcome to live here forever," Sullivan said, and looked in her direction. "I leave all that I have to you."

For a moment, no more that that, Adam felt beaten. First, Eve had stood up to him, now Sullivan. And Adam knew neither of them cared what he did to them. They no longer feared death. Nor did they fear him. Not the way they had, not the way they should. Because of loving Eve he'd softened somewhat, he'd allowed himself to show mercy. He'd have to change his tactics.

Adam stalked over to the bed, took the bottle from Eve's hand and capped it before shoving it into his pocket. He lay on the bed next to Eve. "If you stay, then I stay."

"Sullivan didn't extend his hospitality to you."

"Well, Sullivan." Adam leaned in closer to Eve. "Do you have any objections to my staying here as long as you're playing host to my wife?"

"She's not your wife, Adam."

"I'm not your wife."

Both voices came at him at once. Adam closed his eyes and slid his left hand over to Eve. "I was coming back for you. You know that, don't you?"

"But you didn't come back and you didn't answer me."

"You called Sullivan. I wasn't aware that you could."

"Nor was I."

"I wasn't aware Sullivan was still with us." Adam pulled Eve toward him and rested her head on his chest. "But I suppose you knew."

"Yes."

"Will I ever be able to trust you?" Adam asked.

"Will I ever be able to trust you?" Eve mimicked. From the corner of her eye she caught Sullivan fidgeting. She'd almost forgotten she and Adam were not alone.

"Eve, if you want some privacy, if you're sure you feel safe, I'll leave now."

A quick glance upward at Adam and Eve frowned slightly. "Don't worry about me." She waited until Sullivan left before she unleashed her wrath on Adam.

"Who the hell do you think you are? Why would you condemn me to this life? Sullivan's correct. You had no right to do this to me. You can't go around doing just anything that pleases you."

"But I can," he answered, unfazed by the tone of her voice. "I couldn't let you go, Eve. I love you."

Disbelief made her pause. "I don't think you truly understand what love means."

Adam moved away just a bit, offended. This nonsense Eve was spouting he wouldn't take, even from her. The images were as fresh in his mind as they had been when they'd first happened. Eyanna, young, beautiful and smelling of lemons, coming to him thinking she was plagued by demons because she had visions and had a way with herbs and crystals, and could heal. Distressed by her healing abilities and her natural inclination to know about the hidden properties of herbs and crystals, she'd sought counsel from the church, from him, the priest.

She'd confessed many thought her a witch. Her countenance was anything but evil. In spite of his being a priest he'd fallen utterly, madly, in love with her. When the church had demanded that Adam stop helping her and that the young woman be expelled from the church he'd rebelled, disobeying the orders, and had been summarily dismissed.

Adam was what he was because of love. He'd loved her as Eyanna, and he loved her as Eve. Now Eve had the nerve to say he didn't know about love, that he wasn't capable of loving her. He took a deep breath and growled low in his throat. "Are you saying you don't think I'm capable of love?"

"I'm not saying that. I do believe in your own fashion you believe you love me. I think the habit began when I was Eyanna but it's now more of an obsession. Don't you understand that loving a person doesn't mean that you take away their choices, that you blackmail them with your might? That isn't love, Adam."

"Then why did you fall in love with me? Why did you beg me to make love to you?"

Eve's eyes widened in surprise. She'd thought it had all been a dream, a beautiful dream. She shivered with remembrance and renewed passion flooded her. "All the way?" she asked.

"All the way."

"I thought you couldn't make love all the way with a mortal, that you couldn't control taking all of their blood and killing them. Nothing happened to me." She grunted. "With the exception of the obvious of course."

"Something happened alright," Adam grinned, "but if you're asking why I didn't lose control, why I was able to make love to you, find my own release and not kill you, then I can only say it was love. No matter what I said, or what I wanted to do to you, I could never truly hurt you. Now, are you ready to come home with me?"

For a long moment Eve lay where she was. Adam had thought he'd only have to give her a few words, a touch of his hand and she would melt and accept passively the blood-sucking life he'd condemned her to.

"I don't think I'll be going," Eve answered at last. "I think I will remain here with Sullivan for a couple of days." She ignored the jealous twitch in Adam's jaw and looked at his eyes. She watched in amused fascination as the red of his eyes obliterated the purple.

"What is it with the two of you?" Adam growled.

"What do you think? He came and got me out of a coffin, a coffin that you put me in, I might add."

"I will not leave you here with Sullivan." Adam's hand touched the flimsy fabric that she wore. "You allowed him to touch you, to change your clothes. He saw you naked."

"He took care of me. What do you want, Adam?" Without warning, pain traveled through Eve's spleen. If she weren't already dead the intensity would have killed her. Her head snapped back and her body yielded to the mattress beneath her.

"I feel sick and weak. I can't do this with you right now." The human need to retch overcame her and she looked into Adam's eyes just before her body convulsed and emptied. "I'm sorry," she murmured.

"I don't believe you are." Adam touched a hand to Eve's brow and glared slightly at her. "Every time you have to do this, it's me you do it on." He waved a finger over the mess and cleaned them both. He watched her reaction, saw the weakness as she fell backward onto the pillow, barely able to swipe her mouth with the back of her hand.

"What's happening to me?" Eve asked.

"You need to feed." He brought his gaze up to her eyes and saw the panic, the fear. "Sullivan didn't tell you? He didn't allow you to feed?" The last Adam said with relief. The last thing in the world he wanted was to have Eve feed on the blood of another vampire. Adam had made her, and he meant her blood bond to be with him and no other.

"What will happen if I don't?" Eve asked, searching Adam's eyes for the truth. "Will I be able to end this?"

"It doesn't work like that, Eve. A vampire cannot starve; believe me, I tried, as did most others. The cravings will become unbearable and eventually you will drink, whether from someone who's willing and you take just a sip, or someone who isn't and you ravish them."

"I won't do it."

"You won't have a choice. It's who you are. But for now you can feed from me," Adam said softly as he used a fingernail to make a tiny gash in his wrist and offered it to Eve.

For an instant time stood still as her guts twisted and a different desire threatened to consume her. A tremble started at the top of her spine and snaked downward. Her eyes remained glued to the red liquid oozing from Adam's veins and she wanted to taste it. It wouldn't be the first time. "Adam, I don't want this," she moaned. "I want to be human. Don't make me do this."

"It's the only way, Eve, trust me. I'll take care of you, my love. We'll be together forever."

"Sullivan," Eve screamed as she pushed Adam's arm away. "Sullivan," she screamed again, retching once more as he burst into the room. She could see him take in the situation.

"I'll take care of you," he announced softly, rummaging through the dresser in the center of the room and filling his arms swiftly with clean linen and a clean gown. It was then Eve noticed Adam glaring at the pan of water on a stand in the corner of the room. She shifted as he did toward the bundle of towels. The way Sullivan rushed to her aid, it was apparent he'd been expecting it. She shivered, knowing intuitively that he had known that as a newly made vampire she would go through this transformation.

"You will not touch her," Adam growled.

"Surely you don't expect me to let her lie in filth?" Sullivan asked in disgust.

"Give that to me." Adam narrowed his gaze and glared at Sullivan. "You're a vampire, Sullivan. You should have taken care of Eve as a vampire, not as a man. It was not necessary for you to touch my wife's body."

Adam snatched the linens and shoved Sullivan away. Before either Sullivan or Eve could protest, he'd thrown Sullivan from the room and begun to attend to Eve's needs himself, bathing her body the way Sullivan had done. He trembled as his hand came in contact with her flesh. Anger fueled him, knowing another vampire had touched her in this manner.

"You still need to eat," he whispered. "It will be better to do it from me. I'm willing and I can teach you." Her rejection of his blood burned like the fires of hell.

Adam growled, turning as he heard the light knock before the door opened once again.

He looked in disbelief at Sullivan as he wheeled in a pole. *I will kill him*, Adam thought when he noticed the bags in the vampire's hand.

"Eve, there is another way," Sullivan stated, ignoring Adam.

One glance and Eve grasped the situation. "A transfusion?" she asked.

"Yes, just for now."

"That isn't what she needs." Adam snapped.

"But maybe it's what she will accept," Sullivan snapped right back.

Eve just stared between Sullivan and Adam. "Where did you get it?" she asked at last.

"It's whole blood. All vampires keep a small stash in their homes for emergencies. It's your decision, Eve," Sullivan stated, looking directly at her.

"Do it, Sullivan," she replied, her eyes on Adam. She thrust her arm out and waited. "I don't want either of you having to take care of me. I'll take care of myself as I've always done. If a transfusion will enable me to do that, then that's what I want."

Within seconds the needle was inserted in Eve's arm and she watched as the blood flowed into her veins. It was true, she was a vampire. From now on she would need blood to live. A lot more blood than she'd previously required. Blood would be her source of nourishment.

Within moments Eve felt energy flood through her cells. She felt better. And with that knowledge came a thirst and a hunger she had never known. She looked from Adam to Sullivan. "Can I eat?" she asked.

Sullivan's head dipped and Adam glared at him. "You can do whatever your heart desires," Adam answered her. "You have no limitations, Eve. You have my blood in your veins. You can do what you want."

"Can I still work?"

"You don't have to," Adam cut in. "I will always take care of you."

"That wasn't the question. And like I said, I don't want you taking care of me, either of you. Adam, you've done quite enough for me, thank you. Now back to my question. Can I still work…in the daytime?"

"You don't have a job."

Eve turned pleading eyes toward Sullivan. "Will I be able to go out in the daylight? Will I be able to have lunch with my friends, without looking at their carotid arteries and wanting a drink?"

"Not for a while," Adam answered, daring Sullivan with his stance to challenge him. "It's best that way," he continued. "You have to learn to control the cravings, the urges. Otherwise they will take over your body and your mind, even your will to die. You will want to live at all cost and if you don't feed it will override every good intention you might have. When you look down on the still face of your victim, you will wish you had listened to me," Adam cautioned.

"I hate you for this, Adam. You should have just allowed me to die loving you. Now I never will."

"You can't turn love on and off."

Eve barely glanced in Adam's direction. Instead she turned her attention to Sullivan. "How long will it take before I'm able to safely be with my friends?"

"A hundred years, give or take a year or two."

Sullivan wasn't smiling. *Oh God.* Eve's hand twisted the sheet about her body. Sullivan wasn't kidding. "Everyone I know, everyone I love, are you saying I can't see them again?"

"It would be best."

"That's nonsense," Adam interrupted. "You can control your urges. You have my blood within you. This can be done quickly. I will teach you to feed, to take just a little, to take what you need and no more. Then when you can feed without killing, you can visit your friends."

Feed without killing. A shiver traveled through her body. "I don't feed, Adam. I eat, and when I do, it's bacon, eggs, cheesecake, fries, not blood."

First Sullivan glanced toward her, then Adam. Both of their gazes flicked on the needle in her arm. They looked at the blood suspended on a pole giving her the nutrients her body now craved. Neither bacon nor eggs were filling her veins. Eve's throat constricted.

"What have you done to me, Adam?" she asked softly. "What have you done? You had no right."

"You were dying."

"She's right, Adam, you had no right to turn her. You knew she didn't want this. You didn't do it for her. You did it for yourself."

The tone of the room changed. Eve could feel the anger emanating from Adam in waves, yet she didn't feel the fear she'd noticed in Sullivan when she'd still been human. Eve shuddered. She wanted to be human; she'd do her damnest to find a cure.

"Sullivan, what am I going to do?" Eve asked, bringing both of the vampires' attention to her. A slight twitch of Adam's lips warned Eve, but she was past being afraid of what Adam would do to either her or her friends. He'd already done the unthinkable. She would not give up another moment of her now cursed life to appease Adam or because she loved him. Her heart had turned to ice. Adam was dead to her; his pain was no longer hers.

"Exactly what are you asking me?" Sullivan said, bringing Eve's attention back to him.

"I have to do something. I have to have a job. I want to continue working on a cure. For that I will need to earn money."

"I will give you what you need," Sullivan answered.

A low growl came from Adam beside her. Eve ignored it and Adam. "No, I need to earn my own way. I need a place to live."

"I offered you my home. I would be honored to share it with you."

"What the hell do the two of you think you're doing? Have you forgotten that I'm standing right here?" Adam demanded.

"How could either of us forget that, your bloody majesty?" Eve sat up straighter on the pillows. "We don't care; you don't control us."

"You belong to me, you're my wife."

"You don't get it, do you, Adam? I don't care what you think," Eve snapped.

"What about the dreams, the visions? You know the things I've said are true. You know that you're Eyanna. Why do you fight me on this?"

"Because someone has to, Adam. You can't continue bullying people to get your way."

"You think that?"

"I'm not afraid of you," Eve whispered.

Adam turned toward Sullivan. Redness filled his eyes and he stared at Sullivan. "Are you afraid of me?" he asked.

"No," Sullivan answered.

"Are you sure?"

"I'm sure. I'm no longer afraid of you, Adam."

"And you still intend to offer asylum to my wife?"

"I didn't know she was a prisoner, but if that's what you consider her, then yes, I offer her asylum."

"And you will suffer whatever punishment I deem necessary?" Adam smiled a little, hunched his shoulders and turned to face Eve before glaring at Sullivan.

"You have a choice. Take back your offer to Eve now and you will not have to know the extent of my anger."

When Sullivan laughed, something in Adam cracked. He felt the beating of his undead heart and trembled in his wrath.

His aim laser sure, his eyes leveled on Sullivan.

Sullivan stood unflinching, until the flesh begin to melt from his hand. The bones in Sullivan's left hand became visible. Adam gave him credit; he didn't scream out initially, but as the smoke rose so did Sullivan's fear and his scream of agony followed.

"Stop it," Eve yelled, jumping from the bed and positioning herself between Sullivan and the lethal beam from Adam. She felt the heat and shuddered, but she didn't move.

"You've proven my point," Eve said as tears of blood slid down her cheek. "You're a bully."

"I'm a vampire!"

Eve pondered that for a moment. She thought over the events of the past months, the violence, the pain, the betrayal. Adam was right about only one thing. He was a vampire and knowing that, she had fallen in love with him, hoping somehow to save him. That little trick hadn't worked. Neither had her crystals or her potions.

Adam believed her soul was that of his wife Eyanna, dead for a thousand years, and somewhere in her spirit, Eve believed it also and had hoped that Eyanna would impart some knowledge to her of how to help Adam, how to save him and herself. But Eyanna hadn't helped; neither had the numerous visits to psychics who had all proclaimed that Eve had the power of healing. They were wrong, she'd tried. And now look at her. She was a vampire, a creature of the night. No, that was wrong. She had been turned by Adam, by his blood. She was not restricted to the night. She could and would do as Adam. She would live in the daylight. She could pretend she was still human.

A shudder filled her and Eve sighed, answering Adam at last. "You're a vampire but that doesn't excuse your actions, or the things that you've done to me. I no longer fear you, Adam."

"I never wanted you to. I only wanted you to love me."

Eve shrugged her shoulders. "Then you should not have made me a vampire. When I chose to die, I loved you. When I saved you from...," her eyes flicked over Sullivan, "from Uriel, I loved you. Now, Adam, you have successfully killed my love and I will remain here with Sullivan until he tires of me."

Adam moved slowly toward Eve and used the tip of one finger to caress her jawline. His hot breath covered her and he breathed in the heat of her anger. He'd erred, he could see that now. Still, he would not leave Eve to lie in a bed in the home of another vampire.

"Sullivan, you cannot have her," he said, reaching into the vampire's mind in order to keep the conversation private. He watched as Sullivan swiveled toward him.

"She is not your property, Adam."

"She is my wife."

"Not anymore, that was a thousand years ago."

"I married her for eternity."

"It is her choice, you can't force her."

"You cannot protect her."

"What can you do to me?"

Adam glanced down at Sullivan's mangled hand and gave a tiny smile.

"It will heal, Adam. I am immortal, just as you are. I will live forever. Isn't that what you've always preached to me?"

Damn it, what a time for Sullivan to suddenly grow some balls. All the power in Adam waited his command but he managed to control himself. He saw the slight smirk and the quiver of Sullivan's lips and became aware of the other vampire's game. Sullivan had won this round. If Adam destroyed him, his actions would not endear him to Eve. And if he backed down, he wondered, what then? Adam had no worry as a mortal man might of seeming to be a coward. That he was not. Eve was well aware of that fact. Perhaps he would gain her favor if he agreed to leave.

"Adam, go away." Eve's voice interrupted his thoughts. "Haven't you done enough to me already? Haven't you done enough to Sullivan? You're the most powerful vampire on the planet. Is that what you want to hear?"

It was like a stake going through his heart. Adam opened his mouth to speak but no sounds came out. He lifted his arm to embrace Eve but the cold fury shooting from her stopped him. He backed away. That much he would do, but still he would not leave her.

"Why are you here?" Eve asked, and Adam stared. The fire that usually accompanied her anger was dying out. He'd forgotten for a moment all of the ill effects a newly turned vampire suffered. She needed lots of blood now, preferably from him. If not, then at least from a living, breathing mortal. The blood from the blood bank that Sullivan was giving her would sustain her at this stage only for a short time. It didn't have the adrenaline that a new vampire needed. *Putting her in a coffin didn't help.* He decided to ignore the voice whispering in his mind. Now he needed to concentrate on Eve.

Her voice was weak, the same as a baby's. Adam saw her limbs tremble and falter. Sullivan caught her, lifted her in his arms and carried her back to the bed. For the second time Adam's hands closed around Sullivan's throat. "Don't test me," he warned.

"I feel weak," Eve whispered, her eyes frightened. "I can barely stand."

"It's normal," Adam answered her, though her question had been clearly aimed at Sullivan. He dropped his hands from the vampire's throat and turned his gaze to Eve. "It will pass in time. It will pass quicker if you feed from me," he offered again.

"Never, Eve whispered. Her eyes shuttered as he stood watching her and his closed as well. The knowledge that he'd done the wrong thing caused him to shudder.

For once Adam thought about what was best for Eve. She wouldn't get over the initial turning if she used her energy fighting with him. She would be weak, and he didn't want her to make her final decision from a weakened position. With that thought his decision was made and he was gone, unable to bear looking at her, unable to witness the decisive smirk on Sullivan's face. Besides, Eve wasn't saying never to feeding the need. The hunger would eventually take her there. She was saying never to loving him.

So, Eve thought she was unable to betray him into the hands of his enemies again. Didn't she realize that she just had? Didn't she know that shunning his love with Sullivan there in the room was worst than the hellfires he'd imagined for himself?

He could no longer torture Eve or hold her hostage as he tried to win her love. He had to try a new tactic. *And if it doesn't work?* his fevered brain asked. *In that case I will destroy them both. I made her. I gave her life and I will take it back.*

Chapter 3

Eve was determined to keep her eyes closed as long as possible. The tension in the room had been intensified by her new vampiric powers. She should be feeling only anger toward Adam, but once again his pain had blotted out her own emotions. He'd left believing she was betraying him again, that she was choosing Sullivan over him. And all because she'd allowed Sullivan to care for her needs and had not accepted his help. How could she? Adam was the reason she needed help.

"Leave me," Eve whispered to Sullivan. "I need to rest."

The moment she was alone she allowed the emotions to pour from her heart: the anger at Adam for what he'd done, the fear of what she'd become and the desire to live. The desire to live was amazing to Eve. She'd wanted to die, would have done anything to not become this creature that she now was. She'd professed her desire for death, had in fact attempted it. But now that the worst had happened, Eve did not want to die. Adam was right once again.

What did a newborn vampire do? Her body shook as images of baby bottles filled with blood entered her mind. She envisioned bottle upon bottle standing in a neat row, each holding the same vile red blood.

Eve screamed out in pain and fear. Her stomach was in knots, her throat dry and parched. With sudden clarity she took note of the new sensations swirling through her. She was thirsty and hunger filled her again. A scream tore from her throat and instantly Sullivan was back beside her bed.

She gazed into the vampire's eyes and saw his sympathy. It did nothing for her confusion. "Why the pain?" she asked. "Why the gnawing hunger, the thirst?"

"I'm not sure of the why. I just know that this is what happens."

"I'm dead. Why do I feel pain? Why do I hunger?"

Sullivan shrugged his shoulders the tiniest bit and his lips curled. Eve didn't know if he was smiling or sneering.

"If you don't mind, I have a few illusions left." Sullivan looked away for a moment, then turned back to Eve. "One of them, the one that keeps me sane, is that technically we're not dead. This is our life now. For better or for worse, we're alive. I have to believe that and so should you."

Eve thought about that for a moment, then thought of Adam. It seemed that her dying had released the barrier to her memories. She now remembered everything that had gone before, her life as Eyanna and her love for Adam. She remembered how she'd tried to save him in that lifetime as she had in this life. Her mortal life was also now in the past. She no longer had a life, did she?

"You're thinking of Adam," Sullivan stated casually and waited for confirmation.

"That's an easy assumption." Eve turned and found Sullivan staring at her. "Adam is the reason for every single thing that has happened to me in the past months. Adam is the reason I am forced to live like this. He's the reason for my pain, my hunger, my thirst."

"And your love?"

"Why the third degree? Why are you looking at me like that? Is it because you think I still love Adam? You don't have to worry about that. He killed any feelings I had for him when he made me into this," Eve said disgustedly, not apologizing.

"Eve, I am asking you this only because I have offered you my home. That offer still stands. But I want some honesty between us. Adam will not just go away. That we can both be sure of. Now you need to deal with that fact even before you deal with your feelings about him.

"I'm a vampire," Eve replied, with steel in her voice. "Adam doesn't care for vampiric women. We both know that."

"Yet he was here for you."

"To reclaim me as his property."

"As his wife."

"What difference does it make how Adam views this? I thought you agreed with me that it's what I think that's important."

"I do, and I did mean the words I said to Adam. I am grateful for what you've given me, Eve, learning that I can live in the sun." Sullivan stopped and smiled. "That is a gift I do not take lightly."

"So are you living in the sun?"

"Old habits die hard. After more than eight hundred years of waiting for the sun to go down, I can't convert in a day but I have made changes." Sullivan grinned. "You're trying to avoid the discussion."

"What discussion?"

"Your feelings for Adam."

"Oh that. I thought we were done."

"No, Eve, we're not done. I'm just being cautious. I trusted your words once because I wanted to believe you could help us, help me," he amended, "and in the end it was your love for Adam that led to the situation we have now. It was your feelings for Adam that made you a vampire." He held up his hand to stop Eve's protest.

"You could have stopped this, Eve. It was in your power. Adam was always in your power, just as he is now."

"What is this?" Eve protested. "I thought you hated Adam, that you believed as I do that he's an arrogant bastard."

"That we do agree on. He is an arrogant bastard and a danger to all of us. But still, you had power over him. He loved you, he loves you still. I just want to know if you're aware of that. I don't ask that you tell me words you think I might want to hear, that you no longer love him. I would much rather our new association be based on truths rather than lies."

"You lied to me also, Sullivan."

"I evaded." Again Sullivan stopped her. "I did what I had to do and you did what you had to do. I've already told you I hold no ill will against your betraying me. I understand you did it because you loved Adam. That was little more than a week ago, Eve."

"But a very long week, Sullivan. A lot has happened in this past week, things that would kill any love, no matter how powerful."

"It's been a long time since I've felt what you felt for Adam, but I still remember the all-encompassing, overwhelming thrill of it all. Adam's love for you has not waned. For now he's gone and we both know it's to figure out his next plan of attack. Who the hell knows what he's going to do? All I'm asking of you is for you to let me know where you stand. I would like to be your friend, put everything that happened in the past. I would like to trust you, especially if you're going to live in my home. Do you think you can give that to me?"

"Sullivan, I don't know why it's necessary for us to go through this again. I told you from the time we met my feelings on being made into this. My reason for joining forces with you was to cure Adam. Now I want to cure myself."

"But I thought I detected something for a moment between you and Adam, some energy. I saw you tremble when he touched you."

"Maybe I trembled out of fear."

"Do you fear Adam?"

Eve didn't have to think about that and she didn't want to lie. "No, I don't fear him."

"Then that tremble I saw would have been something else, love, lust, or both?"

"Maybe anger. You forget he left me for days in a coffin and wouldn't answer me."

"Yes, I saw the anger but there was something more."

Eve was becoming a bit annoyed. She was more than grateful that Sullivan had rescued her and cared for her and she would forever be indebted to him that he'd given her a transfusion and thus found a way for her to exist, but as for his probing around her heart, she was tiring of it.

"There was nothing more," she snapped. "Why?"

For a moment the pair stood staring at each other, neither giving ground. Suddenly Eve sensed something in Sullivan that had not been there before and she blinked.

Surely, he's not interested in me. Damn, damn and double damn. If he were, she would not be able to stay with him and she wanted to…badly.

"I am not lusting after you, Eve."

"How did you…?" She stopped. "I didn't feel you enter my mind."

"I didn't, the look on your face said it all. You're worried that I've developed a little crush on you and you won't believe anything but the truth so I will tell you. Yes, I have a little crush on you. Am I in love with you? No. You were such a brave human to work with us and I envied that, your courage, and in the end your love and loyalty to Adam. Yes, it was what caused our plans to fail but still I admire you."

She wanted badly to ask him if he were sure but something kept her from it. What a mess. One vampire who had not liked vampiric women and one who had not liked humans. Now the tables had been turned. She was no longer human and the vampire she might have wanted at one time she no longer wanted.

"I'm sorry if I've offended you." Eve bit her lip before sucking in a breath, not sure just how to continue. "I'm still tired, Sullivan. Please, just let me rest. I promise we will talk and I will be honest with you about my feelings about Adam."

"Just be honest with yourself," he said and smiled gently at her before turning to leave the room. Eve wondered for a moment why Sullivan never made the production out of leaving a room that Adam did. She could almost think he was human. Her throat closed and tears threaten to spill. Sullivan wanted more than anything to be human and so did she.

"Now I lay me down to sleep, I pray the Lord my soul to keep." The tears fell in red droplets down her cheek. *"If I should die before I wake, I pray the Lord my soul to take."*

Chapter 4

I pray the lord my soul to take. A stab of blinding pain filled Adam and he blinked to dislodge it. *Eve.* It was Eve's pain he was feeling.

For the third time since meeting Eve, Adam felt the urge to pray. *"Lord, what have I done?"* he moaned inwardly.

He took a deep breath, searching for Eve's scent on his body. It was faint, that human side of her. She no longer exuded the tantalizing aroma that was hers uniquely. He'd killed it. *And her*, his voice thundered in his brain.

Adam had not made another vampire in over seven hundred years. For the first three hundred years he'd turned others out of anger and revenge, then out of loneliness, and in the end he'd had to destroy them.

Yes, there were many ways to kill a vampire but he'd never tell.

But there was only one way to make one and that was mutual transference of blood. A simple procedure if one remembered to not drain their victim. Take so much blood and no more, then allow the victim to feed and repeat the process, each time taking a little more until the victim's body was fueled entirely by the mixture in the vampire's veins. It took longer if the victim was strong and in good shape. He'd figured that out from the moment he'd died.

Initially the blood had been forced down his throat after Tarasha had nearly drained him. She'd repeated the process, biting him, forcing him to drink of her blood until all of the fight had left his body and he'd drunk of her blood without resistance. When there was nothing of Adam's blood left in his body, he'd felt his spirit slip away. He'd reawakened with the taste of blood filling his throat. To his disgust, without coercion, he'd drunk hungrily from the woman who'd made him and he'd listened to the sound of her laughter. Even now her words rang in his ears.

"Adam, what do you think your precious wife would do if she could see you now, your pure Eyanna? Adam had felt strength flowing through his veins such as he'd never known and immediately sensed the power of Tarasha's blood.

He continued to feed, ignoring her cries to be gentle. She'd thought he was going to make love to her as he'd done throughout the night. Her fangs sinking into his flesh to force his body to join with hers had sickened him. Her threat that she'd kill Eyanna was all that had made it possible to even stomach her touch. From the moment he'd felt the inhuman strength fill him, he'd known that as long as he lived he would never again make love to a vampire. He'd taken her in a different manner. Instead of caressing her flesh he'd sunk his teeth into her jugular and held her in his steel embrace until he'd bled her dry. When he wiped away the blood, he'd felt the shape of his mouth changing to accommodate his new fangs.

When Adam looked at Tarasha's corpse, he'd been filled with rage. With his new strength he had ripped away a metal rod from her bed, then plunged it into her heart. He'd waited for hours to see if she was truly dead. When she didn't move, Adam had carried her outside and walked with her in his arms to the center of town, to the fire that was kept burning for witches.

He'd tossed her body in and stood watching until nothing remained. Then he'd turned and headed for his home, certain of Eyanna's love, certain that with her herbs and potions she would help him. Adam closed his eyes and trembled with the remembered pain.

If I should die… The words reverberated in his brain. *What have I done?* he thought. Eve did not deserve to pay for Eyanna's crimes. Eyanna had not truly loved him, had tried to kill him, but Eve had risked her life to save his, had fought off an entire team of powerful vampires and he'd repaid her by turning her into one of them. Eve had been so close to death that it hadn't taken much. She'd not put up a fight when he'd given her his blood mixed with his kisses. He'd given her pleasure and visions as he'd repeated the process. She hadn't had the strength to fight but she'd had the strength eventually to drink from him. And in that instant she'd crossed over into his world. She'd died as a mortal and was now one of the undead.

You could tell her the one sure way to kill a vampire, he thought. *You could end it for her*. But Adam knew that as strong as he was he didn't posses the kind of strength necessary to end Eve's life, not a second time.

He would endure her hatred. He would learn to overlook the non-human smell of her. He would do as he'd sworn never to do with a vampiric woman. He would love her. God help him, he would love her.

❖

When Eve woke she was not feeling as well as she had when she went to sleep. She didn't know if it was night or day. All she knew was that she felt as if she were dying. Again. The first death had been easy, gentle and peaceful. This time she felt pain such as she'd never known in life and with it came a great fear. Her thoughts were of surviving. Her lips were parched.

"Sullivan," Eve called, her voice little more than a rough rasp in her throat. "Sullivan, something's wrong."

Eve could barely open her eyes to see. When she sensed Sullivan in the room with her, she allowed her eyes to remain closed. She listened to the sounds he was making as he moved about her. She heard the wheels squeak on the IV pole and knew he was going to give her another transfusion. *How long will this one last?* she wondered as a cramp twisted her internal organs and she groaned aloud with the pain.

"It will be over soon, Eve." Sullivan inserted the needle into her vein and then started the flow of blood. He didn't want to look at her, didn't want to allow her to see that he had betrayed her.

Within moments he saw the change, saw the blood flowing, filling her with energy. This time he knew it would last longer than a few hours; he knew it would sustain her. Why wouldn't it? It was Adam's blood and it was what Eve needed. When Adam had returned and held several bags of blood out to him, he didn't have to ask whose. Adam had gone to the lab and had Dr. Meah take his blood so that Sullivan could give it to Eve without her knowledge. As much as he didn't want to admit it, it was true that Eve as a brand new fledgling needed blood with staying power. Adam's blood was a thousand times more potent than the blood from the blood bank that Sullivan had been giving her. Besides that, Adam had made her. Her body would always crave his life-giving blood.

"Eve, I have thought of a job for you." Again another lie, another betrayal. This was also not his idea.

"Where?" Eve asked, looking at last in Sullivan's direction.

"You can work for Adam."

"Adam? I don't want to work for him."

"Just think about it. You can work with the doctors who have developed a blood substitute."

"Did you give me a blood substitute?"

"No, I gave you whole blood. I told you that."

"Why didn't you give me some of the blood substitute?"

"We're still testing it. It may not be as safe as it should be and definitely not for a fledgling who's not had a chance to go through the transformation."

"What else are your doctors working on?"

"They're working on several new pill forms if you can believe that. The pills are used by all of us on occasion. They've worked well for us but we haven't had a fledgling to try them out on. You can help them. You can be their—"

"Their guinea pig?" Eve asked.

"That wasn't exactly how I meant it."

"Why do you think I would want to work with a group of vampires, vampires that hate me, I might add? I killed four of them. I betrayed you. Why would they want me there?"

"You're one of us now, Eve."

"That still doesn't stop them from hating me."

"You have nothing to fear from any of them."

"No."

"I will protect you, and so will he."

"Adam? Of course Adam will protect me. I'm his property."

"Do you want to work there?"

"Even if I wanted to, how do you know Adam will allow it?"

"I don't think there is anything you could ask of him that he would deny you."

Eve's lips curled upward into a snarl. "Unless I'm asking him to respect my wishes, to allow me to die, to not turn me into a vampire." She looked at the tubing that ran into her arm. If I had been able to ask anything of him this wouldn't be necessary."

"Call him, Eve."

"Why? I'm sure he's somewhere monitoring my conversation. What is it with you two? You hate each other but you've teamed up to…what?" She was truly flabbergasted until her gaze fell once again on the blood flowing through her veins. Eve felt the strength flooding her as she hadn't before. And then she knew. This was Adam's blood. She turned her gaze on Sullivan and swallowed. "Why would you want to help him?"

Sullivan smiled. "It's not Adam I'm intending to help, but you."

"Did you really think I would be so naïve or stupid that I wouldn't detect Adam's hand in this? You didn't give me his blood before, why now?" She reached to pull the tubing from her arm but Sullivan was faster.

"You need it."

"God, help me," Eve moaned before turning angry eyes on Sullivan. "Or am I not supposed to call on God anymore?"

"You can do whatever gives you comfort, Eve. Praying never worked for me, but maybe it will work for you."

Eve glared at Sullivan, wanting to hate him, but she couldn't. She was grateful for all he'd done. Even when she'd betrayed him and killed the vampires helping him, he'd still offered to help her, afraid that when the potions Eve had given Adam wore off, Adam would kill her. No, she couldn't hate Sullivan; he was her only friend.

"I *am* your friend, Eve."

"I know," she answered him, and sighed. Her eyes opened wide. "I didn't mean anything by the sigh; it just slipped out." She touched his hand. "It's hard to know this is what I am. And to know that Adam's blood can make me feel like this…there's so much power flowing through me now. Sullivan, I really did drink his blood when I was still mortal. Why didn't I feel the rush that I'm feeling now?"

"You weren't a vampire."

"Oh." Eve tilted her head and observed Sullivan. "Will I become as arrogant and uncaring as he is?"

"It's hard to know exactly what will happen to you. Adam has forbidden the making of new vampires for hundreds of years."

"No one defied him?"

"Of course they did, but the ones that did no longer exist nor do their creations." He shrugged his shoulder. "As far as I know, Eve, you are the first new vampire in many centuries in this country," he laughed, "who will be allowed to exist."

"What will happen to Adam because he made me?"

"Nothing."

"He makes me so angry. I wish I had let Uriel…"

Sullivan laughed, stopping her tirade. "No, you don't. Neither do I. You would do the same thing again and we both know it. You're angry at him, Eve. You may actually hate him, but in your soul, where it counts, you still love him. And as much as his actions disgust me, he's not uncaring. There are things Adam cares about and you're one of them."

He glanced at the now empty bag and removed the tubing from Eve's arm. "It doesn't matter if you don't like it, Eve, you're connected to Adam for eternity. You will have to find a way to deal with it."

"I suppose you mean by my taking his blood."

Sullivan smiled again but this time it was with sadness. "Adam will not allow you to do that for long, nor will he approve of your using the blood banks for your main source of sustenance."

"Then exactly what are you saying? What will I have to adjust to, besides the fact that I'm no longer mortal?"

"Adam. You will have to find a way to deal with him."

"Knowing that, why would you tell me to work for him?"

"You wanted a job and this seems made to order. Your life has changed, Eve. Like it or not, things are not the same for you. You are a vampire. You will have to learn to adjust to that. You need a job, Adam offered. All you have to do is accept."

"Do I have a choice in that?"

"To the degree that you have a choice. But if I were you, I would think it over."

"What about you? Are you still working for Adam?"

"No."

"Then neither will I."

"Don't be stupid, this isn't about me."

"You told me how much you liked working at the company. I know it's your life's work to try and find a way for vampires to live among mortals. Why can't you work there?"

At that Sullivan laughed. "Are you serious? You just yelled that you're neither stupid nor naïve but that question proves that you're both. There is no way in hell Adam will allow my returning to work there."

"Why not? You just helped him to deceive me."

"I wasn't trying to hurt you, Eve, and actually neither was Adam. You needed his blood and you wouldn't take it from him. For once Adam and I were in agreement. He didn't have to convince me to give you his blood."

"You didn't answer my question, Sullivan. Why won't Adam allow you to continue working there?"

"Did you forget so quickly that I attempted to bind him? I don't blame him, Eve. If the situation were reversed, I wouldn't allow him to work in my company either. It would make him look weak, diminish his control over those who work there and fear him."

"Because you didn't perish?"

"Precisely."

"But you told me before that Adam is so powerful that all in your world fear him."

"That's true. It's also true that it's your world now, Eve."

Eve sighed. "Thanks for reminding me. Do you really think Adam is that small?"

"Do you think he's not?" Sullivan touched the tubing that had held the blood. He smiled. "I see you still have a need to protect him."

For a long moment Eve said nothing. She wasn't aware of a need to protect Adam. Besides, he had no need for her protection.

"I'm stating a fact, not defending," Eve said at last. "If Adam wanted you dead I think you would be."

"You're blunt."

"You said you wanted the truth from me, so I'm giving it to you," Eve answered.

"And if I wanted Adam dead?"

Eve smiled in spite of herself. "Adam believes he's a true immortal and so do I. I believe he will come through any problem, maybe not unscathed, but I don't see him being easily defeated."

"And you see me as what? Someone who is?"

"No, but you don't have that something that Adam has, that total belief in yourself and your abilities."

"That might not be a good thing. You, my dear, were able to render him powerless with your potions because he believed he could trust you, that you were so afraid of him that you would never harm him, that we were so afraid that we would never attempt a coup. Who knows what might have happened to Adam had you not changed your mind."

"So you've decided to take off the gloves."

"It's true. We would have never had Adam had it not been for you. You never did tell me how you managed to do it, Eve."

For a second Eve stared at Sullivan as she remembered Adam learning of their plans and then making her bathe, him licking her body and waiting for Sullivan and the others to come. She could still see his look of pain at learning of her betrayal. She blinked, willing the picture away. "I don't think I want to talk about that."

"Why not? Are you ashamed of your actions?"

"Sullivan, why are we having his conversation?"

"So that things are clear between us. You lived with Adam and surrendered him into our hands. Will you do the same to me?"

"I thought you said you understood my reasons."

"And I do. But I want you to acknowledge that if we had gone through with our plan you would not be here in my home right now. You would not be a vampire if we had held Adam at the lab."

"We succeeded in capturing and binding him but I don't think we could have done much more. I think eventually Adam would have broken any bonds, including those made by me."

"And you don't love him still?"

"I don't have to love him to know the truth."

A long sigh escaped Sullivan before he spun from her to face the window. "Do you want the job?"

Did she want it? Of course she wanted it. "Only if you are allowed to come back," Eve said slowly.

"I will not ask Adam to return."

"I don't intend that you do. He will ask you."

❖

Adam sat nursing bourbon as he listened in on Eve and Sullivan. He had wondered how she would react to learning that she was receiving his blood. He smiled from time to time as he eavesdropped. Did Eve really think he would ask Sullivan to return, or offer him the protection he'd once enjoyed? The woman was mad, she had to be. The vampire had betrayed him, had used Adam's love for Eve to elicit her help in the betrayal.

The longer he listened to the conversation, the more annoyed Adam became. Both Eve and Sullivan were aware of his access to their conversation and yet neither talked as though they cared.

Adam growled low. A simmering vampiric rage waited at bay, but he refused to allow it to control him. He'd promised that he would look out for Eve, that he would love her as much now as he had before he'd turned her. He might as well start acting like it and put that nonsense about Sullivan's returning to the company out of her head at the same time.

Within seconds Adams materialized inside the room. He looked longingly for a moment at Eve, then walked toward her. His nostrils were slightly flared as he searched for something of the mortal woman he'd loved.

No, no smell. Her scent was no longer there. The ache began deep in his groin and traveled upwards. He reached out to touch her, smiled as she pulled back.

"You don't like what you made, do you?" Eve asked.

Adam studied her, knowing what she was thinking, what Sullivan was thinking, what he himself was thinking. Eve was a vampire and he had no use for vampiric women. He smiled slightly, closing his eyes as he thought of all they'd been through, all the women he'd been with in an effort to forget Eve. None had been able to make him stop wanting her.

And when he opened his eyes to look at Eve, Adam realized his mistake. His mind had still been connected with Eve's. She'd seen the women who had flashed through his mind. She'd taken his closing his eyes as a sign that he no longer loved her. He thought to tell her it didn't make a difference that she was now a vampire, that it no longer mattered, at least not where she was concerned.

But Adam knew she wouldn't believe him. She'd told him that she didn't want him, but she was hurting because he didn't want her. Allowing her brief foray into his mind had been a mistake. He stared at her, meaning to tell her the women in his bed had meant nothing, but then he stopped.

Maybe that would work to his advantage. There was nothing like a jealous woman. It would do Eve good to feel for once the contempt she'd heaped on him. Adam decided to go with it. He didn't answer. Let her think what she would, let her try and regain his attention, his love. If she didn't know by now that after a thousand years of yearning for her that she would never lose his love, then his saying it would not matter one little vampiric bit.

❖

Adam's turning away from her hurt. Eve had tried to mentally prepare herself for that, not sure when he saw her again what either of their reactions would be. Certain emotions were clear to her. She hated Adam for turning her and she was angry that he'd left her in a coffin.

She swallowed, closing her mind to Adam and Sullivan, trying to sort out the other emotions. She'd seen into Adam's thoughts and the knowledge of his couplings with others made her jealous. What did that mean? She wasn't sure.

She did acknowledge the pain when he turned away and wondered about that also. Could there be residual love left for Adam? Probably, but she would ignore it.

Then again, it could be just lust. She looked hard at Adam. Vampire or not, he was way past fine, from his neatly done locs to the huge amber ring he wore on his finger, the same color amber as the necklace he'd wanted her to wear. And his eyes... Eve had never seen a brother with purple eyes. Actually she'd never seen a man of any race with eyes that color. She wondered if Adam had been honest about the drinking of so much blood changing him. She wondered if that could really change basic DNA.

She brought her eyes up to face Adam's questioning look, realizing that she'd taken a moment too long appraising him. Sucking in a breath, she commanded her body to get over it. Lust or love, she would have to control it.

Eve glared at Adam, wishing as she did that she had the power to melt his skin from his bones as he'd done to Sullivan. Lacking such powers, glaring would have to do. She wondered about Adam's emotions when he'd first looked at her. She'd felt his love, his wanting her and then she'd seen the women.

Disgust was the only thing Eve had expected from Adam. Initially it had not been there and she'd wondered why. Must have been his leftover sentiment, maybe guilt. Eve wasn't sure but she'd seen the change that came over Adam, seen the truth in his eyes right before he'd shuttered them. She'd felt it when he turned away. She'd wanted it not to matter. She'd wanted not to give in to the pain. Eve heard her heartbeat pounding, then Adam's and Sullivan's. She'd almost forgotten Sullivan was still in the room. This was twice now that she'd forgotten Sullivan's presence.

For an eternity Eve didn't face Sullivan. He'd asked if she still loved Adam and she'd said no. She sighed low and made a wish she knew would not come true.

Sullivan would not believe her, she thought as she turned in his direction. Then again, why should he? She didn't believe her words anymore. Something was still there in her heart for Adam or she would not have felt pain. But she would be damned if she would ever allow him to know that. If she were now a vampire, so be it. If she had to live forever she would do it without Adam knowing she cared, if only a little.

"You've offered me work in your factory," Eve began. "If you want me, I want Sullivan."

Her heightened vampire sense told her both men were taking her words differently than she'd meant them. *Boys*, she thought, little boys who thought with other parts of their anatomy rather than their heads.

"Listen, Adam," Eve tried again. "If you want me to work at your company, then I want Sullivan to work there also. He wants the same thing that I do, to not be a vampire." She stopped and stared at Sullivan, holding his gaze.

"I can trust him," she said at last, releasing herself from the hypnotic hold Sullivan appeared to have over her and turning instead to face Adam.

You can trust him to get you both killed if you keep this up, Adam thought, meaning every word.

"Sullivan didn't make me into a vampire."

There, she'd said it. And her words had struck, Eve felt it. So the link worked both ways. Maybe Adam was privy to her pain, but she was also privy to his, and her remark had hurt. Good.

"Sullivan has no desire to be in my employ now that he's not afraid of the daylight. I'm sure he can find more meaningful work elsewhere."

Eve's head swiveled slightly in Sullivan's direction. "The work he was doing is meaningful. He wants to find a way to stop using mortals as human cattle. I'm all for that."

"Do you really think Sullivan doesn't drink human blood?" Adam asked with disgust coloring his voice. "Why don't you tell her, Sullivan?"

Silence. Never in all her life had Eve heard such a complete silence. She'd never thought about it, not when she was helping Sullivan to develop a potion that would bind Adam, not when she'd called him from her coffin to rescue her and not when she'd lain in his home helpless while he cared for her. He didn't have to do it.

As Eve sucked in a breath, her fingers toyed with the tubing.

"Did you really think that Sullivan would be able to stay so vital without frequent infusions of fresh blood?"

"I do use whole blood," Sullivan cut, in but his eyes would not meet Eve's.

"Exclusively?" Adam asked.

"I don't care," Eve shouted, sparing Sullivan the need to answer. "If you want me close, Adam, if you want me where you can keep an eye on me, then you ask Sullivan to come back. You tell him how much you need him, how much you value him or I won't be there working at your factory."

"What makes you think I care?"

"If you didn't care you wouldn't be here." Eve glared at Adam, not liking the way she was trembling inside.

"I don't have to beg you for anything, Eve, you're mine. I made you and I control you."

"You control me?" Her voice rose. "Am I now your puppet? Granted, you know a hell of a lot more about being a vampire than I do, but I do have your blood, remember? And I have my own will. I don't believe you control me."

Her voice rose with each word and she continued ignoring the push on her mind that Sullivan was sending her. It was a warning. Eve was aware of that but she no longer cared. What could Adam possibly do to her now? He'd taken her life, what more was left?

"You do not control me, Adam," Eve hissed.

"Would you like to see?"

"Go for it."

"Eve." Sullivan shook his head at her but Eve ignored him. "If you don't like shedding those blood tears don't do it, not now. You can't take Adam on, Eve."

Eve turned angrily to face Sullivan. "Do you also think I can be so easily controlled?" She watched as Sullivan turned his head from her, a pleading look in his eyes. She didn't know if that look was meant for her or for Adam. Then she knew. Sullivan was pleading with Adam not to exert his power over her. That made her angry, more so than Adam. She needed a friend but it wouldn't be Sullivan. She didn't need a friend who was afraid of his own shadow, afraid of Adam. Eve sucked in a deep breath, feeling her abdomen expand and contract as she let the breath out before facing Adam.

"Do it. If you think you can control me, Adam, then do it, damn it."

She braced herself, willing her body and her mind to remain under her control. She stared as the two men gazed at her. She saw the smile that played around Adam's mouth, noticed when the purple of his eyes turned to red and she shuddered.

"Are you sure this is what you want?" Adam challenged her.

"I'm positive."

Eve's feet began moving. She was about an inch from the floor, then another and another. This couldn't be happening. Her arms reached out for something to hold on to. The bed. She caught the bedposts as she ordered her mind and body to resist. She dug her nails into the wood until blood ran out and down her wrists. Her will was strong, just not strong enough. The moment Eve realized it, sticky substance flowed down her cheeks, those damn blood tears.

"Leave her alone."

Eve barely heard Sullivan's voice before she noticed his hands going around his throat, clawing at unseen hands. His long lean body twisted toward the floor. The look in Adam's eyes had changed.

The red was deeper, darker. Eve could sense the vibrations from Adam. There was anger involved with his tormenting of Sullivan that had not been there with her. Sullivan's body writhed on the floor for several seconds. Then he stilled as though dead.

Dead, Eve thought. How? He's already dead, we all are. There was no time to ponder the matter because Adam's attention returned to her and now some of the residual anger was directed toward her.

Her body felt as though it was being torn apart. Her arms left the bed posts and her body floated toward Adam. Nothing she could do stopped it, not her belief, not her will, nothing.

When she was chest to chest with him, her body rose even higher and Adam's hand reached out for her, sliding her down the length of him. She felt his hardness, his arousal, and closed her eyes. Instantly they were opened against her will. He smiled at her, wanting her to feel his power.

"So be it," Adam whispered, his breath hot on her face. "You wanted to resist me, to test me, and you have. Are you satisfied or would you like for me to show you what else I can have you do?" He grabbed her hand and placed it over his erection.

"I thought you didn't desire vampiric women."

"I don't, but I do desire you, my love. You are my wife and I do want you. I've wanted you for an eternity."

Eve thought of Sullivan lying there on the floor. This she didn't want. She didn't want to be defiled in front of him. Every muscle in her body ached. She was willing herself to move but couldn't. She blinked, unable to even talk. Adam's fingers trailed down the side of her face, his lips a fraction of an inch over hers while he used the tip of his tongue to tease her.

"Tell me, Eve, do you think I can control you?"

She refused to answer even in the face of his power. She watched as Adam turned again to face Sullivan. "Do you believe I can control him?" he asked. He grinned. "You may speak now." Adam grinned in spite of his inner turmoil. He pulled back his power in order for Eve to speak.

"Release him, Adam, release me. Now!" Eve shouted.

"Say please," Adam ordered.

"I will not," Eve retorted.

Adam hunched his shoulders and smiled. "Then I will not release you."

Clenching her teeth in frustration Eve groaned, wishing for some of the power that Adam possessed. He was crazy if he thought she didn't remember the powers she'd had a thousand years ago. She had every intention of regaining her powers and increasing them. For now all she could do was say, "I hate you, Adam."

"Do you think your hatred of me will prevent my ability to control you?"

"Why are you doing this?" Eve asked, wiping her hand on the side of the nightgown, soiling it once again. "Like I told you before, you're a bully, Adam. You don't want me, you just want to show me your strength. I'll ask you again: why are you doing this?"

"You're my wife."

"What does that mean? You have no responsibility to me. We both know the only woman you want in your arms is a human, something that I no longer am. I release you from whatever debt you think you owe me. All I want from you is a job for Sullivan and myself, for the two of us to be left in peace to live our lives. You do what you always do, go to Father Keller's church and find yourself a mortal woman, one with the smell of lemons on her skin." She held her arm toward him. "Do I have a scent, Adam?"

For a long moment Adam held Eve's gaze and then he allowed his anger to recede. Besides, he wasn't angry at Eve. It was never at Eve. All the things he'd done to her were so misdirected. For one brief moment he'd had her love. Would that have been enough if he'd allowed her to die? He backed away.

The thought of Eve's death riddled his mind and his heart. He glanced at Eve's outstretched arm. No, she no longer held that scent of humanity that he longed for. He wiped that memory from his mind.

Adam stared at Eve, wanting to shout, "It doesn't matter. I love you anyway." But the look on Eve's face told him she wouldn't believe it. Besides, he'd done nothing since he'd made her that would make her think that.

He glanced at Sullivan, his wife's champion, still motionless on the floor. What was it that made Sullivan challenge him, knowing he couldn't defeat him, that he could end his existence with but a thought? He felt Eve's worry for the vampire and once again his rage was stirred. He wanted to crush Sullivan, remove him from her life, but that would be another thing that would prevent her loving him. With that thought Adam groaned and released both Eve and Sullivan from his control. He walked slowly over to a chair and sat down, stretching his legs out in front of him, and exhaled hard.

"Now this is the way it will be," he began, watching as Sullivan rubbed at his throat, knowing he was making an even more bitter enemy of the vampire. Teamed with Eve, who knew what they would cook up to exact their revenge? Maybe it would be best if he allowed both of them to work in his company. At least there they would be unable to do anything without his knowledge.

"Sullivan, you may have your position back if you want it."

"That wasn't what I asked," Eve interrupted.

"Neither of you are in any position to bargain," Adam reminded Eve before a half groan, half laugh slipped from between his lips. "Do you want to come back, Sullivan?"

"Yes."

"And you, Eve, do you want to work with some of the finest minds in many centuries to find something that you want?"

Adam could tell Eve wanted to resist him, that she wanted things on her terms. And how he wanted to give her that but it seemed nothing had changed. He'd made love to her; he'd rediscovered his soul and her damn stubbornness was about to make him lose it again. Why couldn't she just come home with him where she belonged? Why had she set up house with his enemy?

The last thought angered Adam. "Well," he bellowed. "Make up your mind. Do you want a job or not?" He saw her still fighting it, saw Sullivan go toward her and Adam shot him a warning look. "You go any closer to her, you touch her and you die slowly and painfully."

This time Adam wasn't bluffing nor making sport. He'd tolerated a lot, but another man, or vampire, as the case was consoling his wife, being her champion in front of him, that he would not tolerate, not in this century or any other.

"Yes, I want the job," Eve spoke, interrupting the direction Adam's thoughts had taken.

"Good." Slowly Adam's attention went from Sullivan to his wife. "Good. Now I think you need to start learning about your new nature. I'm going to take you shopping. You're going to need new clothes."

"Why? Are there stores specializing in vampire attire? Am I supposed to dress all in black?"

Adam laughed. "Eve, you've had quite a bit of exposure to vampires, more than most mortals. And you've known whom you were dealing with. Have any of them dressed all in black?"

Adam waited for an answer, wondering as he'd done for almost a year now, how things had gone so wrong with Eve. Why wasn't he able to just tell her the truth, that he loved her, that he didn't give a damn that she was no longer mortal?

A stab of disgust claimed Adam. He couldn't tell her that because it wasn't quite true. Adam had spent almost a thousand years hating the touch of vampiric women. Why shouldn't he? His life had changed because of a vampiric woman.

Had the woman not threatened his wife, he would have never gone to her. Her primary goal had been to make him her eternal lover. Adam had not allowed that to happen. Even now the thought of killing Tarasha filled him with pleasure.

He glanced at Eve, the only woman he'd ever loved and his hatred for Tarasha was born anew. Would this be his hell, he wondered, not to be able to touch his wife the way he wanted?

Adam laughed aloud, ignoring the strange looks that Eve and Sullivan were throwing his way. They had reason to wonder if he'd gone mad. He knew he sure as hell wondered. He had the very being within his grasp that he'd longed for century after century.

'And yet the thought of making love to the woman he loved in the manner common to vampires filled him with revulsion. But he would not relinquish her to touch another, for his heart still belonged to her. Hell yes, finally there was something that had pierced him to the quick. Adam could even envision dying because of it.

Immortal? He was, or rather had been a true immortal until Eyanna returned and made him vulnerable. She was his weakness, his Achilles hell.

Adam blinked and brought his thoughts back to where they should be. "I thought you would want to blend in with the other vampires since you will be working with them."

"Don't lump me into a group, Adam. Don't refer to me as another vampire. I will never be *another* vampire. I will always search for a way to turn back."

"No one has been able to accomplish that, Eve."

"Then I will be the first."

"If anyone can do it I am sure you will. And you're right, I will never lump you with anyone else. Now, back to what I was saying. You are my wife, Eve, and like it or not, I cannot allow you to live with another man."

"You can't…"

At that Adam continued as though Eve had not spoken. "Without human blood you will feel weak. The need to feed will overcome you eventually and make you rash, not caring who you kill or why. You think you have control, but when the hunger overtakes you, and it will, you will not."

"I thought I could do whatever I pleased. After all, I do have your blood in my veins now."

"But you lack my discipline." For a moment he stared at her. "You may not like what I'm telling you, but ask your new champion. He will tell you I'm speaking the truth. It is the same for all of us."

"But you live like…like a human."

"I've had a thousand years of practice. You can do it, Eve, I don't doubt that. But first you must learn to control your new nature. If not, you will not know how to react when the blood that flows in the veins of mortals calls to you. You must learn when and how much to take." He paused. "You must learn how to not make more vampires, or perhaps how to make them. It will be your decision."

"I hate you, Adam."

"I know."

Adam took in a deep breath and gathered Eve in his arms to take her home where she belonged. The sting of Eve's hate filled him with hatred for his very nature, for his selfishness in turning her.

In seven hundred years he'd not created another vampire. He'd made it his mission to prevent more from being made, going so far as to kill the vampires who made them, as well as their children.

God forgive me, he thought, knowing there was no forgiveness for what he'd done. He'd been alone for so long, so unloved, that he'd forgotten that true love required real sacrifice. How could Eve love him? He didn't blame her. But he would do the things that he must to ensure her safety. He would teach her so that she could live without detection.

Chapter 5

Sunlight showed up as a dusty pale gold on the back of the heavy velour drapes. Eve saw it and made her way from the bed. "I want to see," she whispered to no one in particular. "I want to see if I am condemned for having loved something as vile as Adam."

She felt another's heartbeat slow and still before realizing that it was Sullivan, that she was connected to him in some obscure way.

"I'm sorry." Eve rubbed her hand over the base of her throat, knowing that she needed the crystal necklace until she learned to better block her thoughts. "I was thinking of Adam. It seems whenever I have horrible thoughts about vampires you're always somewhere around."

"Are you wishing I wasn't privy to your thoughts?"

"Just a little."

"What's going on, Eve? Is something wrong?" Sullivan asked, the worry for her coming through loud and clear.

"Just the usual," she answered.

"I don't blame you. I did and said a lot worse when I realized that I had become a vampire."

"Sullivan, why did Adam do it?"

"Only Adam can answer that."

"Sullivan?"

"You said you were dying. I can only assume Adam didn't want that to happen."

"I guess not," Eve sighed. "Tell me, how did he do it?"

"I would imagine he gave you a turn bite."

"A turn bite?"

"There are many kinds of bites, Eve. You will learn them all in time."

"I need to know. Adam warned that I could turn others into this. I never want that to happen. Just tell me, Sullivan."

"There is the exchange of blood."

Eve's heartbeat stilled and her eyebrow shot up. "Is there any other way?"

"Not that I'm aware of. But who really knows? As old as I am I'm sure I don't know all there is to know about vampires."

"If the exchange of blood is a sure way of making a vampire, then the vampire that did it would have to know it. That would have to be a deliberate act."

"Yes, that's why the influx of new vampires has been forbidden. How was your transformation done, Eve? How did Adam change you into a vampire? Surely you remember."

Eve swallowed. She wasn't exactly sure. They'd made love and he'd fed on her. He'd also forced his vile blood into her mouth and made her swallow repeatedly. "I don't know," she answered, despite the disbelief that she sensed in Sullivan's voice. "I'm not sure. I was almost dead when Adam found me and it's a blur."

She was aware that Sullivan didn't believe her but she found she didn't want to admit to him that as a mortal she'd allowed Adam to make love to her. He'd not had to threaten her or her friends.

Eve shivered. Not only had she allowed it, but she'd begged him with her confession of love. She wanted badly to cry. She felt the sting of tears but the thought of blood streaming down her cheeks held them at bay.

"Sullivan, thank you for all of your help. If...if...something happens to me know that I appreciated all that you've done.

"What are you going to do?" Sullivan asked.

"I'm going to open the drapes and feel the sun on my face," she answered.

"What if...?"

"Then it happens."

"I don't want you to die, Eve."

"I'm already dead. Besides, Adam held me out in the sun and nothing happened."

"Then why are you trying it again?"

"Just foolish, I guess. I'm wondering if my wanting it to happen will make it so."

"But you don't really want it to happen. I know. The urge to live is too strong in us."

Eve's hands trembled as her fingers touched the heavy material. She pushed away thoughts of family and friends. Briefly, thoughts of Adam filtered through her brain and landed on her tortured soul. She would not mourn him.

"Sullivan, you might want to leave my mind now," Eve said and sighed, turning to look at him as he materialized inside the room, his features contorted with pain. That stopped her for a moment as she wondered if the pain was for her. She didn't know. She looked toward the window and asked, "The sunlight, do you need to leave?"

He held out the crystal she'd given him and smiled. "Not any longer. I don't fear the sun nor do I run from it. That's why I came. If you're going to do this I want to stand with you."

"If Adam catches you here..."

"Why don't you leave worrying about Adam to me?"

Before she could answer him Sullivan had glided easily toward her and stood inches from her, not touching, not looking at her, merely giving her the comfort of his being there.

Eve shuddered once more and pulled the heavy drapes back with a force she didn't realize she had. For an infinitesimal amount of time she was afraid. It was fleeting but it was there. The thought crawled through her brain that she didn't want to die and shame followed on its heel. She should be embracing the thought of death, had claimed that she would seek it. But the truth was that she wanted to live. As brief as the thought was, it was there just the same. As the sun rose higher, pools of light filled the room and Eve turned away. Self preservation. She caught sight of the look on Sullivan's face, straightened her back and turned again to face the sun. The heat hit the glass, filling the room with light, warming her face, her body and her heart. She would not die. Again. She breathed a sigh of relief and stood with her eyes closed.

"It's okay." Sullivan's voice, soft and soothing, caressed her with warmth.

"What's okay?"

"Your feelings. Believe me, I know. For hundreds of years I prayed to die and immediately I followed it up with a prayer to live. It's only natural, Eve. It doesn't make you a bad or immoral person. Remember, self-preservation."

"Maybe not." Eve looked at him, grateful to have him there. Maybe not, but in that space of being afraid and wanting to live there had been one dominant thought that made her immoral. After everything that had happened, her last thought before she thought she would perish had been of Adam. A chill raced up her spine. He was telling the truth. He had made love to her and it had been exquisite. Adam had made her in every sense of the word. He'd made her fall in love with him and he'd made her into a vampire.

"What do I do now?" Eve asked.

"Learn to live with it."

"What about my family and my friends? How am I supposed to just cut off ties with them?"

"Didn't that happen in a way when you moved in with Adam?"

"I never moved in with him."

Sullivan smiled. "For all intents and purposes you did, and I know you left your friends behind."

"Were you following me?"

"Of course."

"Why?"

"There was a lot at stake, Eve. I had to be sure that you were as committed to the cause as I was."

"I was committed to stopping Adam."

"Maybe just not enough. Now maybe you'll have more of a reason to."

Eve stopped him. "Don't," she said glancing around the corners, then listening for Adam. "I'm not helping with any more of your plans. If you want to betray Adam, you do it alone."

"So you do still love him?"

"So what if I do?"

"You said—"

"Look, you can't keep interrogating me. I'm not going to do anything to Adam. All I want to do is find a way to return to my old life. If you want to help me, I'm all for it. As for Adam, forget it. Now I'm sorry, I really hate to be rude, but I think it's time you left."

"You're afraid for me, aren't you?" Sullivan asked, going up to Eve, touching her lightly on the wrists and turning her to face him. "You're afraid that's he's going to kill me."

"Sullivan, it didn't take you reading my mind to know that. Adam hates you. He hates the fact that you rescued me, that you brought me to your home and that you stood up against him. He hates that even after everything that happened we're friends. Yes, I'm afraid of what he will do to you, but I'm also afraid of what he will do to me if he comes home and finds you here."

"But you're a vampire now, Eve, you have his strength. Adam can't hurt you."

"Like he couldn't hurt you when he was choking the life out of you on the floor? Like he couldn't hurt me when he forced me against my will to come to him? He can hurt me, Sullivan. He can hurt both of us and I'm not going to give him any more reason than I have to."

"I thought you were not going to allow him to blackmail you, to control your life?"

"I'm not, but neither am I going to just taunt him and make him angry. He's not going to stop me from looking for a cure. He's allowing you to come back to work. No, I'm not going to deliberately pick a fight with him. And this time if you want you can call me a coward. I don't care. I'll bide my time until I know I can take him."

"I'd never call you a coward. You have never been that, not as a mortal, not as a vampire. I do understand what you're saying but for me nothing has changed. Adam is too powerful and he needs to be stopped."

Eve looked toward Sullivan, her gaze landing on his face. "Don't tell me your plans. I don't want to be involved." She hesitated. "Sullivan, can't you let it go?"

"I can if you can. Stop trying to find a way to undo that which Adam has done. You tell me that you're happy with this life and maybe I'll think about stopping."

"But Adam is not the one that made you…that made you what you are. You said so yourself. There has to be something else, something you're not telling me. There is more going on than the fact that Adam is powerful. You could be just as powerful if you wanted to. Adam has no special powers other than his mind. He believes and his thoughts are made manifest in his actions."

Eve stopped and stared at Sullivan, the look on his face more frightening than anything that had happened thus far. "What?" she asked softly.

"You're almost quoting scriptures. You sound just like Adam."

With that Sullivan disappeared and left Eve staring at the spot where he'd been.

❖

"So you think she sounds like me, do you?" Adam smiled to himself as he listened in on the conversation between Eve and Sullivan. Perhaps he'd given Eve more than his blood. It would be interesting to find out what other of his qualities his wife possessed.

"Adam, the new sample is ready."

Adam blinked, cutting off his mental connection with Eve and Sullivan. He turned toward the doctor. His nose wrinkled in disgust at the manufactured blood. "What is it you need from me?"

"You told me that you wanted to be the first to know of any new developments from now on. I thought that you wanted to…"

A harsh laugh broke across the tension. "You didn't think that I wanted to test the stuff? I still like my blood the old fashioned way." Adam stared at the man proudly holding the vile concoction.

"This is the best batch yet."

For the first time Adam noticed his heated brown skin. It was as though a furnace had been lit and the natural caramel coloring was imbued with a warmth, a fire. Adam frowned. It seemed that lately everyone had taken to disobeying his orders.

"You've tried it on yourself?" Adam watched as the vampire struggled to think of an answer. In a micro-second Adam made a decision to be magnanimous. "Well, how was it?" he asked, deciding not to reprimand the vampire.

He saw surprise fill the other vampire's eyes before pride at his accomplishment pushed it away.

"It was great, the best. It's exactly like human blood, the zest, the adrenaline rush, all of it, it's in here."

"And the sweetness?"

"Adam, this is what we've been looking for."

"When you take this can you see pictures in your mind? Can you see joys and sorrows? Can you pretend for a moment that your life is different?"

"You know it can't do that but it does ease the cravings to take all of the blood from a host. It makes it bearable to leave them after a feeding. Just think. We can have the best of all possible worlds. We can have many lifetimes and we don't have to rely on humans for our food source. There will be no need to make them into victims. We can end it. Isn't that the reason you started this research? Isn't that what you told me over two hundred years ago? We've been working toward that goal, Adam, and now it's here. What's holding you back?"

"Can you find a way to reverse what we are, to change us back into mortals?"

"You're older than I am, Adam. Have you ever known anyone to revert?"

There was a long moment of silence. The two vampires stared at each other until finally the silence was broken by the doctor.

"Do you want to be mortal, Adam?"

"No."

"Then who?"

"Sullivan is alive," Adam said instead, switching the conversation. "He will be returning to the company to help in your research."

"Sullivan's alive? How? The sun! We saw him, the others, they died."

"Sullivan didn't."

"How?"

"Faith."

Again a long silence.

"Sullivan is... I mean you're allowing him to return here to work with me?"
Adam smiled slightly at the thought. "Yes, I'm allowing him. Also, my wife
is going to be working closely with you. She wants to find a way to change
vampires into mortals."

"If you have a mortal working here there might be trouble."

"Do you think anyone here would dare harm my wife?" Anger flared in
Adam and he bellowed for everyone to assemble.

"Adam, I didn't mean—"

Adam glared at the vampire standing in front of him. "Doctor, I think you've
said enough." He felt the violet in his eyes changing to the hated red and
welcomed the change. When the entire company was assembled before him he
walked quietly before each vampire, allowing each to feel his power and his
anger. As he walked, papers began to blow about the room. He watched as his
underlings moved backwards from him.

"Sullivan will be returning to work here." He held up his hand to ward off
any questions. "You all know of my wife. I have no doubt that the word has
spread on that. She will also be working here." He heard a low mumble.

"Anyone who doesn't want to work with her is free to leave. Anyone who
stays, you're put on notice. This will be your only warning. If you so much as
look at Eve in an aggressive manner, you will regret it. You will treat her with
the utmost respect and you will defer to any orders that she might give you. Do
you understand that?"

"You want us to obey a mere mortal?"

"Not a mere mortal, my wife." Adam spun around and as he did the vampire
who had spoken was gasping for air. In a space of seconds Adam was holding
him with one hand and squeezing. His fangs descended and he bit into the
vampire's flesh. He twisted the vampire's head for all to see. The sound of the
head breaking from the bones and ligaments was the only sound heard. *Damn,
that felt good. I must be more stressed than I thought.* Adam gave a shrug then
continued with his warning.

"Hurt Eve and you will answer to me." With that he threw the vampire
across the room and used his eyes to set the limp body of the vampire on fire.
Within a matters of moments the vampire had been reduced to ash. With a glare
of satisfaction Adam stalked away, bellowing for the doctor to follow him,
wondering if his actions had assured Eve's safety or made her more unnecessary
enemies.

The thought crawled into his mind that he'd purposefully done what he'd
done in order to play the hero for Eve.

Nonsense. He shook the thought away. *Nonsense.* Why did this one woman
in a thousand years have this effect on him? Eve brought out the worst in him.
And the best, he had to concede, only now he was giving in to the worst.

Her hatred of him was too close to the surface, too raw. If he allowed himself
to show her just how much he loved her, he would be lost.

What Adam wanted most of all was to have Eve forget her resolve, to lose
herself in loving him, to forget the fact that he was no longer a mortal, that he'd
turned her into a being who was also not a mortal. He longed to have her love
him as he loved her, to lose control of her virtue and her morals and just love

him simply because she did.

For one brief moment she had but that didn't count. She'd been so close to death that her control had been literally taken from her. Adam no longer trusted that she'd given herself to him but that he'd taken her. He wanted more than anything for her to give herself to him freely and without reservation.

He was a vampire. He must not forget that or he would lose his edge and become soft. For a thousand years he'd lived with the power of his mind for comfort. He could not allow Eve to cause that power to slip, not even a fraction. He needed his power now more than ever. He needed it to protect Eve.

Chapter 6

Work. Eve was getting dressed for work. She'd showered just as she always had and she'd dressed, no difference. And she'd had a transfusion of blood administered by Adam.

Therein lay the difference. Before, she'd never had to have blood in order to function. Well, at least no more than God had put in her veins. Now blood was her breakfast. She'd tried to do without it but had become so lethargic that she'd felt as if she were slipping into a coma, if that was possible. And with her consent Adam had given her his life sustaining blood. The whole blood and packed cells from the blood bank that Sullivan had given her appeared to last only a few hours. Adam had given her a disappointed and disgusted look because she wouldn't just feed directly from him as she should. In the end they'd compromised and he'd given her his blood via transfusion. Along with that he'd delivered his lecture. She had to learn to feed properly.

With the infusion of Adam's blood, the pain that had been constant was receding, Eve realized as she walked to the door and peeped out. No, the sun didn't bother her, it wasn't even up. But there was something in her soul that screamed to her that she was different, that mortals would spot her. So far she'd not run into anyone she knew. Her cell had not rung even once in ten days. Eve had wondered in the beginning if Adam had stopped the calls. But with her heightened senses came the awareness that no one had cared enough to call.

For a moment Eve felt sadness. Her mortal friends appeared to have forgotten about her. Now she was in a world she didn't want to be in and didn't belong in and at the moment there didn't appear to be very much she could do about it.

"What's the matter?" Adam asked, coming up to her side. "The sunlight can't hurt you, and besides, it's not up."

"I feel strange."

"That's because this is your first time. You're like a virgin." He smiled and touched her. "Touched for the very first time. You'll do fine, Eve. I'll be with you."

"I don't know if that's wise."

"Are you worried about my behavior?"

"Always, but specifically about the reception. Adam, you're not well liked, it seems, and therefore I don't expect a bevy of approval."

"No one will harm you; they fear my reprisal."

"Fear and respect are two entirely different animals."

"Only if you're looking for friends." Adam's eyebrows rose. "Surely, Eve, you're not looking for friends, not among vampires? You hate them, remember? You want nothing to do with them."

She sighed and glanced toward Adam. He was doing his best to be charming. He loved her still, she could tell. But she could also tell he was afraid to linger near her for more than a few moments at a time. "I wish you hadn't done this, Adam," she said sadly.

His gaze landed on her, heated, sad. Then his hand reached out and he touched her, lifting her chin a tiny bit. "A thousand years of loneliness rendered me incapable of losing you yet again. Whether you believe this or not, I am sorry for the pain you're now in. With the passing of time you will accept this life. You will know it was the right thing for me to do."

"Your arrogance knows no bounds, does it?"

"What you call arrogance, I call truth. And I speak the truth, Eve."

"You think?"

"'My soul followeth hard after thee; thy right hand upholdeth me. Psalms 63:8'"

"Adam."

"'My soul shall be satisfied as with marrow and fatness; and my mouth shall praise thee with joyful lips. When I remember thee upon my bed, and mediate on thee in the night watches, because thou has been my help, therefore in the shadow of thy wings will I rejoice.' Psalm 63:5-7 I speak the truth, Eve, always to you. You are all that and more to me."

Their gazes held. Then Adam closed his eyes as he felt Eve's pain. He swallowed his hurt and hers.

"You're afraid of your feelings for me, aren't you, Adam?"

For a moment he didn't answer and then he lightly caressed the side of her face. He smiled slowly. "Yes, my love. I'm afraid."

❖

Eve walked beside Adam along the broad path. She stopped suddenly to look at the large brick building, the neatly manicured lawns and perfectly placed flowers of every color and variety. She couldn't believe the beauty or the trouble that Adam had gone to. "Adam, I will admit this is beautiful."

"Adam didn't order this."

Eve glanced at Adam before looking toward Sullivan. She'd have to get used to having vampires appear out of nowhere. Sullivan's voice was filled with loathing. She'd made a mistake. Naturally she'd assumed it had been Adam who had ordered it. After all, until now he had been the only one living in daylight, at least the only one that she knew of.

"Good morning, Sullivan. I meant no disrespect. It's just that I thought Adam was the only vampire who could have done this."

"There are others."

"Others what?" Eve glanced toward Sullivan, moving a bit closer to Adam as she heard his low growl. Sullivan was being foolish in baiting him.

"Others that live in daylight," Sullivan answered.

I have a lot to learn, Eve thought.

"Don't worry, you'll learn. I'll help you."

Blinking in surprise, Eve turned from Adam and stopped walking to stare at Sullivan. "You never could read my mind before I…before Adam changed me. Why is it that you can do it so easily now?"

"Because all vampires have a link. We can tune in if we choose to, and if we choose not, then we don't."

Eve felt Adam's annoyance at Sullivan's explanation. It was obvious he wanted to be the one to teach her these things. But to her it didn't matter. This was something she wanted to know now. As she looked toward Adam and her pulse quickened, she tuned in to the great line of communication that Sullivan spoke of and heard the mumbled thoughts. She was not welcomed here. Then the word *mortal* came to her, repeatedly. *Mortal.* Eve wondered why Adam had not bothered to tell the vampires what she was, what he'd done. She wondered if it would make it easier or harder for her. She wondered if they'd know the difference.

Before she could think it through, Adam's low growl intensified, as did his glare. He then shoved Sullivan in the chest, hard, clutched her hand and pulled her with him into the building.

❖.

"Everyone, this is my Eve, my wife."

A loud chorus of voices rang out. "Eve, welcome."

Adam peered through the throngs, searching each vampire's mind for any evil intent. Finding none, he glared in Sullivan's general direction, then back at those assembled. "By the way, since I hate groveling, begging and tears, I have decided to be generous and allow Sullivan to return to his prior position." Adam gave a cold smile while glancing at Sullivan. "'For verily I say unto you if ye have faith as a grain of mustard seed ye shall say unto this mountain remove hence to yonder place; and it shall remove; and nothing shall be impossible unto you.' Matthew 17:20. It's as I've always told you. You all need to have more faith in your own abilities.

He couldn't help smiling at Eve. Adam had heard her thoughts shouted at him. "You arrogant bastard," she'd said. "Temper, temper, dear wife," he'd whispered into her mind. To the vampires that watched him, he warned, "You will all make Eve welcome here." Then he vanished.

A feeling of dread worked its way to the forefront of Eve's mind as Adam left abruptly, leaving her to deal with a building filled with hostile beings who despite their words of welcome didn't want her there. She took a step toward Sullivan and looked at him. "So begins our day. It appears our new lord and master has taken credit for your survival."

"That I understood." Sullivan studied Eve for a moment. "He could have done a lot worse. I'm just glad to be back here. I meant it when I said I would watch out for you, be your friend." He gave her another look. "You look well. Did you allow Adam to give you his blood?"

Before she could answer and without warning and without her sensing him, Adam had reappeared by her side. Eve no longer wondered how he accomplished it. She only knew that he was never more than a breath away from her. No matter what, she couldn't run. She couldn't when she'd been a mortal and she couldn't now.

For a long moment Adam stared at her, his violet eyes hypnotic, his midnight locs tantalizing and his golden skin giving the appearance of life, of health, of love.

She shivered and sucked in a breath. It would be foolish and a lie to deny that she was unaffected by Adam. She had been from the first time she'd met him in St. Michael's church. She'd not known then what he was, only felt that he was evil and she'd been right.

Yet that knowledge had not prevented Eve from wanting him, from falling under his spell. Neither had it prevented her from falling in love with him on some mistaken idea that she could save him, turn him human. Now it was herself she needed to save, herself she needed to turn human.

Eve watched as Adam's lips curled upward slightly. Her heart thudded loudly as Adam's gaze filled with longing, then lust. In disbelief she sucked on her lip as she automatically reached out toward Adam before pulling away. As Eve pulled back, a feeling that she was falling filled her. She reached out to Sullivan for support. Her hand clutched his and she hung on, not liking the way Adam's presence affected her.

Sullivan's fingers twined with hers. Eve's heart stopped as the violet of Adam's eyes changed to liquid fire. She'd pushed him by reaching out to Sullivan and so had Sullivan by holding her hand. Now she waited for Adam to push back. To Eve's surprise, he didn't.

Adam waited as the remaining vampires he'd rounded up came and stood before him. "Everyone who doesn't know, this is Eve," Adam said loudly, "my wife. She will be working with Dr. Meah. Sullivan, thank you, but I will escort her now."

Adam's hand forcibly pried Eve from Sullivan's grasp. A little sound fell from Eve's lips and she glanced around. A bit more pressure was applied to her wrist, though it didn't hurt. It was a warning, Eve realized as Adam glared in Sullivan's direction.

"You keep forgetting that I'm a vampire, Eve. I don't ask for things. I take what I want. You will not do that again. Do not pit your champion against me. Ever! He will lose and it will be your fault. I gave him one chance at life. I will not give him another."

His words were spoken gently, his voice a soft whisper in her ear, meant only for her. She followed him down the hall, bristling at his usual arrogance, knowing that by going with him she was being branded. What difference did it make? She was branded as Adam's property no matter what she did.

"You're being unusually quiet and agreeable." Adam looked at her. "Why?"

Eve shrugged her shoulder.

"Do you care so much for Sullivan that you'd do anything to keep him safe?"

"Sullivan is a big boy. He can take care of himself. I will not kowtow again to you in order to save him. You will not have that leverage to use against me."

"I'm not trying to find things to use against you, Eve."

"Aren't you?"

"This is not a deal I'm trying to make or a contract I want you to sign. Things are how they are. You do not have to work here. You do not have to live with me, but I want to show you something."

"I want to see the lab."

"Later there will be time for that. Now you need to come with me."

Thoughts of complaining entered her mind but she was wrapped in Adam's arms and whisked away before she could speak. Within seconds they were in the heart of town, standing before the doors of a diner.

"What is this?" Eve asked."

"What does it look like?"

"I thought I was only permitted to drink blood."

Adam laughed. "I never told you that. You can do any damn thing you please. Do you want to eat?"

"No."

He pulled her hand toward the door. "Let's go inside, Eve. This will be your first lesson."

Eve watched silently while Adam flirted with the waitress, ordering coffee and sweet rolls for both of them. She felt nauseous, not knowing if she could eat. She hadn't in over a week. Sullivan had not offered her food. Surely if she could eat regular food he would have given it to her.

The smirk on Adam's face stopped her. She didn't know why, but she didn't want him reading her thoughts as she sat with him.

"Why are we here?"

"To teach you a lesson."

For five minutes Adam stared at her, his violet eyes intense and unblinking. Sounds filled Eve's ears, pushing all thoughts of Adam from her. She tried to figure out the source of the sound. It was as though a great ocean was filling the diner. The roar grew louder and louder until she wanted to scream. It coalesced into the body of the waitress when she returned with their order.

Eve rose from the seat, her eyes focused on the throbbing pulse of the woman's carotid artery. Her hands reached out to touch it. She felt compelled to touch the source of the ocean's pounding wave which resided in the waitress.

"No, Eve."

She heard Adam's voice in her mind, hard and commanding, but pushed him away.

"No, Eve."

This time the voice was louder, more forceful. There was a pull within Eve's body, she felt it, the war between listening to Adam and indulging her thirst. Her stomach knotted, the abdominal muscles pulling. Eve couldn't stop the groan that slid from her lips. The thirst was overpowering. She had to drink just a sip from the woman. She had so much blood in her body, surely a little sip would not harm her. As Eve's hand reached out toward the woman's neck, the puzzled, then frightened look of the woman did nothing to persuade her. The woman had blood, hot and fiercely pulsating. And Eve desperately needed it.

"Can I help you? Is there something you need," the waitress asked, fear making her voice tight. Eve's delicate control kept the woman rooted to the spot.

"Yes," Eve answered. "You have something I want and need. She pointed at the woman's neck. "I'm sorry," Eve whispered, "but your blood, I need your blood."

The woman paled, then as the blood seemed to drain from her face, turned white as a ghost.

Adam's strong hands forcibly pushed Eve into the seat she'd abandoned. "You have the part, Eve," he said, touching her, bringing her gaze to land on him. "I didn't believe you could do it but you did. You've convinced me, you have the part."

Understanding began to dawn on her. Her fingers trembling slightly, she held Adam's hand, squeezing his fingers with such force that had he been mortal, she would have broken them.

"What's going on?" the waitress asked. The fear was still in her voice, but hope flared in her eyes that maybe this was just a joke.

"I'm casting for a new vampire movie and this young lady was just trying to convince me she would be right for the lead. I didn't believe she would be. She's too innocent looking, too virginal. I didn't think she would be able to inject fear into movie goers. So we made a wager. She wanted to show me she was capable of striking fear in the hearts of…well, movie goers, like yourself."

"This was a joke?" the waitress asked, the fear now gone and annoyance replacing it.

"Not a joke, a lesson. A well learned lesson. Things are not always as they seem. We must learn our craft, whatever that might be. Don't you agree?"

Adam pulled his wallet from his pocket and extracted two hundred dollar bills from the thick wallet. He handed them both to the waitress.

"Thank you," he mumbled, "for helping me to teach Eve. He put another twenty down for the food they had yet to eat. "I don't think we're hungry anymore," he said. His hand wrapped firmly around Eve's as he led her from the restaurant.

Eve fought the urge to cover her ears. She now knew where the sounds of the ocean came from. It was the blood of all the patrons. Horrified, she realized she wanted their blood. She was indeed a vampire.

Her feet barely hit the pavement before darkness claimed her. From a knowing deep inside, she was aware of Adam's arms around her, clutching her to him, carrying her to his black Porsche where the little plastic vampire dangled from the mirror.

❖

"Why did you take me to that diner?" Eve asked, waking, not believing that she'd fainted. Did vampires actually faint? Apparently they did. She had.

"To give you your first lesson on why your old life is gone."

"But you live among humans."

"And I drink their blood."

"I won't, I won't do it." Eve repeated, holding her head in her hands. I will continue with the transfusions."

"Did I give you one this morning?"

"Yes."

"It's still morning, Eve. You're a fledgling. You need constant feeding. Even with my blood in you you'll need much more until the transformation is complete."

Eve peered around him to the clock in...in her bedroom, she suddenly realized. "You brought me home," she said, tears of gratitude filling her. She'd never thought she would see her apartment again.

"I brought you here to pack what things you need."

"I'll remain here."

"And what happens when the janitor come to your apartment, or your next door neighbor drops in for a cup of sugar. What happens when the doorman attempts to hail you a cab, and," he smiled, "what happens to the taxi driver? As much as I want you to accept your new nature, we can't have bodies filling up the morgue, now can we?"

"I hate you, Adam."

"I know but isn't it a good thing that I don't hate you? Now quickly, gather up your things."

Her things, her life, where did she start? Her crystals, her potions, Eve gathered those, then her books. Her tarot cards, wands and scrying mirror came next. She ignored the look of disgust Adam was shooting her way. She could read his thoughts plainly. She was a vampire. What did she need with such nonsense?

"I will not stay like this. I will find a way to turn back."

"That's debatable," Adam answered. "But in the meantime, you need to learn the proper way to feed. You have to learn moderation. You have to learn that you can't take blood from a victim in a crowded restaurant. Even I don't do that." He smirked.

"If you had not done what you did, it wouldn't be necessary for me to learn these lessons."

Adam sighed. "Please, Eve, just allow me to teach you the things you need to know in order to survive. I'm not asking you to let go of your hatred. In fact it's natural. Every new vampire hates the one who made them."

Eve turned angrily to glare at Adam. "Then why did you do it? Did you want my hatred?"

Their eyes locked, each in their own thoughts, before Adam broke the moment.

"What I wanted when I did it is no longer important. What's important now is that you need me."

"Not really." Eve frowned and looked around. "You're not the only one who can teach me."

"You're talking about Sullivan?"

"I now work in a world filled with vampires."

"And you think one of them will help you?" Adam laughed. "Eve, grow up, you're my wife. They hate me. Do you think they will be falling all over themselves to help you?"

"Is that why they all think I'm mortal? You want them to attack me?" Her brows rose. "So you can rush in and kill them for me, be my hero, have my love again, have me in your bed?" She saw the anger rising in him, saw it in his eyes, felt it in the air that crackled between them.

"Do you think I want you in my bed? It's only my duty I want to do with you. I told you before, Eve, I do not desire to make love to vampiric women."

For a long moment neither spoke. Anger and hurt spiked between them. Adam's words had been true. Still, he should not have said them.

Eve glared at Adam. Surely it had not been just a few days since she'd been consumed with love for Adam or since he'd lusted after her. Of course she'd known the truth all along, but still, she had not wanted to hear the words, not from his lips.

"You will not control me, Adam. I will learn from you the things I must, and yes, I will wear the title of your wife." She braced herself. If he could shoot his poisoned arrows so could she.

"I'm young," Eve continued, "and even as this thing you've created," she said with disgust, "I have need of love and I will fall in love eventually, Adam. I have no need to love a bully or a coward. I will be the one to choose the person to whom I will give my body and my heart. And I will choose my teacher."

"Only if you ask me nicely."

"Go to hell, Adam."

"That wasn't asking nicely. You belong to me."

"In name only."

"Ask me for what you want, Eve, and I will grant your request."

Her body trembling in anger she glared at Adam. "Why must you do this? I want Sullivan to teach me what I need to know. Can you not interfere?"

"Not exactly as I requested, but it will do. I will grant you this." At the look of triumph in Eve's eyes he amended his words. "We will both teach you."

Eve spat and walked away from him, shaking.

Adam stood where he was, glancing around Eve's apartment, looking at the bric-a-brac, the pictures of Eve's family. He had no such mementos. The only thing Adam had kept to remind him of a former life was the amber necklace he'd presented to Eyanna when he'd married her, a necklace that Eve refused to wear. He walked toward the shelf, picking up one photo after the next, ignoring the volcanic eruption in his body.

What had he done? Why was he behaving as though he hated Eve? Memories flashed back, pictures, Eyanna pushing him away, Tarasha's smile, her fangs distended as she prepared to bite him, her touch cold, her body stiff, unyielding, no warm womanly odor. He'd hated her, then himself, then every female vampire he'd come across in the past nine hundred plus yeas. The last smell he remembered of Eyanna had lingered in his senses, the lemony scent of her. He'd not found it again until he'd found Eve.

Adam's thoughts were irrational, he knew it. He'd taken away that smell from Eve. It had been his doing. He wanted to force himself to go to her, to hold her, cradle her, but he could not, too many years of hating. What a fool he'd been to think somehow he could make the transformation and nothing would change, that Eve's soft, sweet smelling body would remain just that and he would continue to love her for all eternity.

They now had nothing, no allegiance, no friendship, just this growing hatred between them. Maybe he should allow Sullivan to teach her all that she needed to know. He closed his eyes tightly, feeling the red haze of emotion that flowed through him.

How ironic. Sullivan had never been interested in human women. Now he would have no problem falling in love with Eve. She was beautiful, smart and everything that any male in his right mind wanted.

Too bad Adam was not in his right mind. He wanted the woman whose smell tantalized his senses, whose soft arms wrapped around his neck as she caressed him. He wanted the first woman he'd made love to in hundred and hundreds of years and had felt safe enough to spill his seed. He wanted Eve, but not the Eve he'd created.

Adam wanted the Eve she had been and no way in hell was that going to happen. Hatred for himself and his own actions filled him and spilled out on the woman he still loved.

Chapter 7

For two weeks Eve had been under Adam's tutelage, aversion therapy he'd called it. He'd had her sitting in the company of mortals until she could sit for a time without wanting to tear into them.

And he'd had her watch as he hypnotized the victims in the privacy of his home, or in the comfort of his little vampire car, until they themselves offered him their blood. And she'd watched as he'd fed.

With each new lesson something she didn't want to admit was made more apparent. As she watched Adam feed disgust filled her, more at herself than at Adam. As much as she didn't want to admit it, she found herself wanting to taste the blood. She could hear the ever insistent roar in her ears and knew it would ease the terrible ache she now carried within her soul. But with the disgust for herself came an intensified hatred for Adam.

Eve still refused to feed on mortals. Her only sustenance was the now twice daily intravenous feedings that either Adam or Sullivan administered.

It wasn't enough, it was never enough. She was constantly weak, always with the feeling of starvation and a great and unbearable thirst within made her throat dry and her lips parched.

"I know what you're thinking." Adam broke into her thoughts and turned from the front seat of his Porsche to smile at her as she sat in the back seat. His lips were covered in blood. Eve swallowed. Adam was being deliberately sloppy in his feeding to get her to…to…she didn't know. Eve's fingers gripped the back of the Porsche's leather seat. Her eyes fastened on Adam, on the way his tongue caressed the woman's neck. She watched as he drew in a deep breath of the woman's scent, his eyes closing dreamily. Eve's heart went cold.

"Is all of this necessary?"

"What exactly are you referring to?"

"You're taking pleasure in what you're doing, so much so that I have to wonder if it's not for my benefit."

"I always take pleasure in my eating. Does it disturb you?"

"Not in the way you mean." She would not give Adam the satisfaction of knowing that she was jealous. He'd told her plainly he didn't want her and she sure as hell didn't want him. What he was doing now in front of her was deliberately cruel. They had once meant something to each other and not so long ago.

"We still mean something to each other."

She watched as Adam slowly dragged his tongue across the small marks he'd made on the woman. Eve heard the woman's moan of delight.

"Get the hell out of my head," Eve hissed, horrified that she'd left herself open to Adam's probing. "School's out," she said, pulling at the handle of the door and getting out.

For several minutes Eve walked along the street, ignoring the hunger, the thirst and the anger. She refused to think about Adam. Instead, she concentrated on Sullivan. She knew she was calling him in order to annoy Adam but she also needed a friend and for now Sullivan was the only friend she could be around without being afraid she would kill them. Within moments Sullivan answered her call.

"Why can't I do like you and Adam, just think where I want to be and disappear?"

Sullivan laughed. "It will come in time. So tell me, Eve, what happened? Did Adam's teachings get to be a bit much?"

"A little." She smiled up at him. "Why is he doing this, Sullivan?" She watched as the corners of Sullivan's mouth pulled downward.

"He is right that you need to learn. I agree with him on that score."

"I think I was right in wanting just you to teach me. I didn't think it would be so damn hard."

"Watching Adam feed, or watching him romance another woman?" Sullivan smiled to let her know he was teasing.

Eve smiled in return. She couldn't believe how Sullivan had changed in so short a time. He was softer, braver and there was a bond that had not been between them initially. "Sullivan, you've been so busy being my friend and trying to help me that I think you're neglecting your own life. Is there someone special in your life?"

"There are lots of special someones in my life." He laughed at the puzzled frown on Eve's face. "Vampires are not monogamous, Eve. We may pair with a being for a period of time for companionship, but we don't allow jealousy or lust to rule us. Only the thirst for blood rules us. That is one thing that we can't control. In blood we trust."

"That's not true," Eve countered. "Adam was jealous."

"I'm talking about normal vampires."

Eve couldn't help grinning. She was beginning to like Sullivan more and more. "Do you attack unsuspecting victims?" she asked.

"There is no need for me to attack anyone. There are several mortals who allow me to drink freely of their blood."

"Do you drink from other vampires?"

"Some do, some don't. I do."

"Is there a difference?"

"There's not the same rush."

"Then why do it?" Eve waited while Sullivan smiled at her.

"I didn't say blood exchange with a vampire was a bad thing." He grinned.

"In fact it's the exact opposite. Humans, we feed on for nourishment, vampires for pleasure."

"Pleasure?"

"You have time to learn those lessons, Eve. Come, you're stalling. What bothered you more, that Adam was feeding or that he was romancing another woman in front of you?"

"You know, Sullivan, you're as annoying as Adam in your own way. How many times do I have to tell you that there's nothing left between Adam and myself except loathing? You told me yourself Adam doesn't desire vampire women. Did you forget that I am now one, that he made me one?"

"No, I didn't forget."

"Then why do you keep torturing me?"

"Once burned and all of that... I can't help remembering that I trusted your words before when you said you didn't have feelings for Adam, that you no longer loved him. That trust in your words got several of my friends killed and almost did the same for me."

"What am I supposed to do? I don't feel much like proving anything to you and I don't understand why you give a damn."

Sullivan shrugged his shoulder. "I am not Adam. I desire only vampiric women."

Eve stared at him for a nanosecond. "Are you telling me that you desire me?"

"You're beautiful."

"And not interested."

Sullivan laughed. "Do you have to make the idea sound so deplorable? I'm not the worst thing that could happen to you. And, Eve, eternity is a long time to go through alone."

"You seem to have done it with no problem."

"That's what you think."

"You mean you had someone?"

"Long ago."

"What happened?"

A wistful look came over Sullivan's features, and for the first time Eve saw his fangs. They glimmered in the moonlight. He took several deep breaths, hissing at no one in particular.

"I don't remember," he answered and took Eve's hand. "For now, I will be your servant, answering your call. I will be your friend and I will even play your paramour, make Adam jealous, if you will."

He stopped and before Eve could protest he had her in his arms, his lips covering hers, his tongue probing, his arms around her and his hand caressing. He laughed softly, holding her to him.

Eve glanced over his shoulder at the figure in the dark watching them. She held tighter to Sullivan, not wanting to allow the two vampires to go at it.

Something had come over Sullivan, something that had not a thing in the world to do with her. There was something personal between Adam and Sullivan. Eve realized that Sullivan was using her every bit as much she was using him. They both wanted to hurt Adam.

Adam stared across the street at Eve. He'd been watching her from the moment she left the car, having made quick work of the woman he'd picked up for Eve's education.

Yes, he'd known exactly what he was doing as he lapped at the woman's neck, smelling stale tobacco and liquor. The woman was not overly fastidious with her grooming and the thought of holding her sickened Adam. But he'd done it to see if it would bother Eve. Up till now she'd behaved as though she'd never loved him and he wanted to see how far he'd have to go before she pushed back.

Not far he saw. Within seconds Sullivan had appeared. She'd called him, that much was apparent. Adam stared in anger as Sullivan took her in his arms. He'd waited for Eve to fight him, to indicate that she needed help, that she didn't want the vampire's attention. But she hadn't done that. She'd slid as easily into Sullivan's arms as she had into his.

Blood filled him, stale, sweet, all mixing together and it filled him till he saw only the red haze. Only his well honed discipline kept him from tearing Sullivan apart.

Maybe he'd gone after this in the wrong way. Still, in such a short time how could it be possible that Eve no longer loved him, that she could find passion in another man's arms?

Adam stared at the pair until they both returned his glare. With every fiber of his being he was a vampire and for that reason alone he wanted to destroy both Eve and Sullivan. He growled deep in his throat. He crawled into Eve's mind and felt the fear chill her blood. It should, he thought, she was playing a very dangerous game. He didn't want her dead, he reminded himself. With that thought he disappeared. If he hadn't, he would have killed them both where they stood.

"Was it good for you?" Eve asked, staring up at Sullivan after Adam had disappeared.

"Probably better than it was for you," Sullivan answered.

"What was that all about?"

"You tell me. Are you asking about the kiss or the fact that Adam followed you here and saw? Or that you called to me? Or could it be," he smiled, "that you're wondering why he watched us and we're both still here breathing?"

Despite her apprehension, Eve couldn't prevent the smile, the first smile since she'd become what she now was. "Those are all good questions but the one I meant was the kiss. Why the kiss?"

"You're beautiful."

"I look the same as I always did."

"And you were always beautiful."

"But you never kissed me before."

"You were never a vampire before."

Eve turned away from Sullivan before finding the words. "No, I never was," she said at last. "But I lived in your home briefly, I've been working with you and you never kissed me before."

"You were a guest in my home. I didn't want to make you feel obligated."

"And now?"

"Now," Sullivan waved his hands expansively, "now you're not."

"Do you really want me, Sullivan, or do you just want to piss Adam off?"

"Do you really want me, Eve, or do you want to just piss Adam off?"

"You kissed me, remember?"

"And you kissed me back. Why?"

"Maybe because I need a friend."

"Maybe because you need a bit more."

"Do you…need a bit more?"

"I think we both do," Sullivan answered.

For a long moment Eve and Sullivan stood as they were, staring at each other. Eve felt the gentle wind as it rustled her hair and cooled her heated skin. She looked around. "Adam is no longer here; there is no longer any reason."

Sullivan stepped in closer. "No reason other than we both desire it."

Eve saw the look on his face change from slightly teasing to something else. Loneliness. That was it, that was what she'd sensed in him from the moment she'd met him, a great sadness. Sullivan was lonely and he wanted her to ease that ache. That was not a good enough reason for them to change the boundaries of their relationship.

"Was the kiss that bad?" Sullivan asked. "Is that the reason you're hesitating?"

"I'm not in love with you," Eve answered slowly. "I appreciate everything you've done for me but…"

"Damn it, stop! I don't want your gratitude. I don't do what I do for you hoping for something in return."

In a burst of injured male pride Sullivan was gone. Eve looked around the street, feeling as lonely as Sullivan. She wanted her mortal friends; she wanted her life back.

Chapter 8

Eve's fingers trembled as she dialed the phone. Such an innocent act, such a human one. If it weren't for the blood tears, she would cry from relief. Adam had warned her she wasn't ready, so had Sullivan. But she didn't believe them. It was now or never. She had to know.

"Chickie, I need to talk to someone. Any chance you can get away?"

The sun rose farther in the sky. The heat was burning Eve's arm, making her afraid. She winced, not knowing why. In three weeks there had not been the slightest hint that she would evaporate in the blazing sun, yet she still feared that she would. She could even now hear Adam laughing at her.

"You're immortal, Eve, start acting like it."

It wasn't that Eve didn't want to be immortal. Who wouldn't want to live forever? It was that Eve didn't like the price required to do it. She wanted her life back and calling Chickie was the first step toward doing that.

"Eve? What's up, Eve?"

"I need to talk." Eve shook her head, dislodging the memories of less than a year ago that had settled around her heart. What a different time that had been. And to think she'd ever complained about her life being boring. God, what she wouldn't give for boring right now.

"Are the others coming?"

"I got Wendy, Kelle, Ann and Lauren. I couldn't reach Barb. *Please just say yes*, Eve wanted to scream as the pounding of her friend's blood filled the phone line and came at her. Maybe this was a mistake. What if…

"Where do you want to meet?"

"Max and Erma, our usual place. Why? Did you have someplace else in mind?"

"I was thinking the Olive Garden. They have this new garlic special. It's in everything, maybe even the water. What do you think?"

Why not? Eve thought. She might as well go for it. She'd had nothing but blood for three weeks now. It was time to see what food and garlic would do to her.

Two hours later Eve found herself seated across from her friends. Even Barb had shown up. Eve wasn't sure how Chickie had reached her, but was grateful. She leaned into her seat and exhaled, watching her friends stare at her.

"We haven't heard from you in months," Ann began, "not since you moved in with Adam. Seems like you dumped us for the billionaire."

Eve barely managed a smile. If only it had been that simple. "I've missed you guys."

"Then why didn't you call?"

"I did, but you all backed off." Eve couldn't help noticing the movements of her friends, hearing their thoughts. She didn't want to but like their blood, their voices, were overwhelming.

"*You were talking nonsense.*"

"*You were beginning to believe in vampires.*"

"*You were scaring the hell out of us.*"

Eve moaned and shook her head. She didn't want to hear their thoughts, to learn that they believed she was crazy. She didn't want to be privy to their envy, to their thinking her life was filled with nothing but sleeping with a handsome billionaire. Little did they know that for the past few months she'd been nothing but a meal for Adam, that he'd fed on her brutally. Nor did they know that she'd almost been killed by vampires, or that she'd saved Adam. But even she wasn't sure what she'd saved Adam from. As he said, he was immortal, he couldn't die.

Eve shuddered at the memory of Adam, helpless, paralyzed by her potion, and Uriel's fangs biting into Adam's neck. Yes, she'd saved him and God help her, after all that had happened, she would do it again. Even her attempt to take her life, that she would also do again. Only she would do it before Adam had a chance to save her, to turn her into this.

She was shaking. Her body rocked from side to side and she wrapped her arms around her body. "Oh God," Eve moaned softly. "I don't want to fight with you guys, okay?" she said finally.

No one said a word but when Eve looked at them fear and concern showed on their faces. She wondered if the concern was for her or for their own safety. It was apparent they were all in agreement that she was losing her mind. Eve didn't blame them. She'd begged them to meet her for lunch, and now she was falling apart without any apparent reason.

She thought quickly. "Adam and I had a fight." She saw the instant relief that erased the furrowed brows of her friends. This they could handle, man problem, not vampire issues.

"Oh, I'm sorry," Ann said sympathetically. "What happened? Did you catch him with another woman?"

Eve forced a smile to her lips, wondering why it was that the first thing her friend would think was that she would not be holding Adam's attention. The reality of the situation jerked her up straighter. They were right. Adam was no longer interested in her. Dare she tell them the reason?

"Why would you say that?" Chickie piped in. "Eve didn't say there was another woman."

Good old Chickie, Eve could count oh her. Then Eve glanced up, noticing that despite her words, Chickie was also waiting for an answer. They all wanted to know what had happened to the billionaire that none of them had believed in the first place could be interested in Eve.

"Just a difference of opinion. No, I didn't catch him with another woman."
A sharp pang to her abdomen caused her to grip the edge of the table.

"You don't look good. Are you on something? Is that what's going on?
You're on drugs?"

If she hadn't felt so weak Eve would have laughed at Ann's bold question.
"I'm not on drugs, but I haven't been myself for a few weeks."

"Then why not see a doctor? They have a cure for everything."

Not for what I have, Eve thought. *No one has a cure for it*. Her head snapped
up and her spine followed. She was sitting straight, the weakness she constantly
fought at bay. She didn't have to feel weak. Here was a meal before her, a feast
that was hers for the taking.

The blood of her friends pulled at her, calling her name. Would she give in
for the first time since she'd been turned? Eve gave consideration to the
thought. What if it took away the hunger, the thirst? What if it satisfied the
cravings?

"Whatever it is, I'm glad you called," Lauren said.

Eve looked toward her, wondering what she'd been talking about. She didn't
know but she was sure she'd only caught the end. Then Chickie smiled at her
and like that, the spell was broken. Eve trembled. What had she been thinking?
They were her friends. She could not and would not drink their blood.

The decision cost her. She felt it in the marrow of her being. With the
rational thought, the beating of her friends' hearts became louder. She could see
the tiny veins and the larger arteries. She could see the blood filling and rushing
through the tiny tubular shapes. The knowledge that she couldn't have it filled
her with a numbing weakness.

Ants crawled over her skin. Eve wanted to brush them away but knew they
were not real, only a figment of her imagination. She attempted to laugh with
her friends, not keeping up with their chatter, unable to form more than a
syllable or two. She gave her order quickly to the waitress, wondering if she'd
even try to eat the food and what would happen to her when she did.

That thought didn't last for long. Eve had never known such prompt service.
Or was it? For a moment she had the feeling she was outside her body floating,
viewing what was happening to her and her friends in slow motion. Such a
strange sensation, she thought, but somehow it felt much safer to be on the
outside looking in.

She watched as her right hand lifted the fork of garlic chicken. Eve sniffed
from outside her body. The garlic was pungent, filling her pores. She observed
her body seated, twisting the pasta, also garlic laden, about the fork. Several
pine nuts covered in a rich creamy sauce clung to the tines of the fork.

Eve continued watching, saw herself put the pasta in her mouth. Instantly
she was yanked back into her body. The feel of the food was strange. She forced
it down her esophagus, imagining that she could see the journey in her own
body as well as she could picture the blood in her friends' bodies.

For a moment the food stuck, wouldn't go any farther, and Eve panicked,
looking wildly about. She reached for the water and drank. The water, too, felt
strange. It was like a burning acid in her throat, yet she continued, determined

to get the pasta down, not knowing why it had stuck. The cream laden noodles would have slid easily down her throat when she was human.

A gulp of relief came unbidden from Eve as at last the offending morsel went down. She didn't have to look up to know that six pairs of eyes were staring at her. She didn't blame them.

"I've had a sore throat," she offered. "Everything hurts."

"Pasta shouldn't hurt."

"It does, Ann. Trust me, it hurts."

"You sure it wasn't the garlic?"

What was Ann talking about? Eve wondered. She blinked. Surely she couldn't be. "I don't understand."

"All your talk about Adam being a vampire, maybe we haven't seen much of you because you're one now. Why should pasta hurt your throat? Let me see your neck, Eve."

For a moment Eve was filled with rage. She stared at Ann until she thought she could control the emotion but another equally as powerful took its place. She was downright insulted. For months her friends had deserted her, not returning her calls, not making any of their own. If Ann had truly thought she was in danger shouldn't she have tried to find her?

"Let me see," Ann ordered, this time in a firm voice.

"Let me see yours first," Eve countered, pushing the plate from her. When Ann bared her neck, Eve leaned into her. "If I am a vampire you've just taken your life into your hands. Do you have any idea right now how rich your blood would taste…if I were a vampire?"

She stuck out a finger and trailed it down Ann's carotid artery. She knew her friend wanted to move. In fact, Eve could feel her trembling, but she couldn't move away. Whatever it was that was now in Eve had commanded that Ann remain as she was. Eva laughed. Her tongue swiped her parched lips and she felt the convulsions begin. She needed blood and she needed it now.

"*Please, God*," she prayed, willing herself to move back in her seat. "*Please, God, don't let me do it. Adam*," she moaned inwardly. "*Help me. Sullivan, please I need, I need…*"

Eve's eyes lifted. She felt the sting of the blood tears as they slid down her cheeks. Her friends were like statutes, each of them. For a moment it frightened her until she turned and saw Adam and she knew he'd done it. He'd heard her. She glanced to her right and saw Sullivan. They'd both answered her call.

"Which one of you put them under?"

"Does it really matter?" Adam asked.

"No, I suppose it doesn't."

"Why are you here, Eve?"

"I wanted to have lunch with my friends. I wanted to be me, to live my life the way God intended."

"And now?"

"Now all I want to do is sink my teeth into their necks." She glanced from Sullivan to Adam. "God didn't intend that."

"You need to feed, Eve."

"I know, she answered, surprising herself and Adam. "Sullivan, can you help me?"

"I brought some of the new pills that Doctor Meah has been working on. Do you want to give them a try?" He started to move closer to her but Adam blocked his path.

"No, you have no way of knowing what those things will do to her."

"Not much, she's immortal."

"She needs to feed," Adam roared.

Eve covered her ears, grateful that the entire restaurant was in a trance. "I will not feed on my friends."

"Admit it, Eve, you want to. You want to know what their blood will taste like and you've imagined it. Besides, you have to resent their shabby treatment of you. Even now they think you're not good enough for me. Think what drinking their blood will feel like. Just think of them as a *Little Debbie* snack cake. It will be revenge of the sweetest kind."

"Why are you doing this to me?"

"Because once you start you will not be able to go back, you will be a vampire in every sense of the word, Eve," Sullivan interjected. "You'll be what Adam wants." He shrugged his shoulders.

"She already is," Adam spat out. "Now it's time she begins acting like it." Adam turned his palm upward choking Sullivan without touching him. "You will shut the hell up. And I do mean right now." Anger threatened his control but Adam refused to allow it and chose to take the conversation inside Sullivan's mind. "Do not toy with me. Do you think my love for Eve and my guilt for having turned her has made me into a wimp? Think again. I will kill your ass simply because I can, make no mistake about that. You're alive not because of my wife but because I gave my word. Keep testing me and all bets are off."

Adam applied a bit more pressure for good measure, then released Sullivan. Turning to Eve he repeated, "You need to feed.

"By drinking from my friends? I can't," Eve moaned as her will power slowly began to slip away. She found herself moving her hands across the table, feeling for Kelle's pulse, feeling the blood that flowed through Kelle's veins. Not Kelle, she thought, she's so kind. Who then? Chickie, Ann, Wendy, Lauren, Barb. She moved her hand away and covered her ears.

"Then drink from me." Adam went to her, pressed a nail against his smooth bronze skin and ripped open the flesh. He raised his arm in line with Eve's lips. "Drink from me, Eve."

Her head bent forward. The sight of Adam's blood excited her. She knew it was a thousand times more powerful than that of her friends. She rubbed his arm right above the font of blood; then her tongue snaked from her lips. She tasted Adam's blood and fire raged through her, filling her as always with strength as she pressed his wrist tighter to her hungry lips. She moaned in despair. Adam was right, blood was what she needed. His blood. *Oh God, please no*. The hunger overcame her and she drank her fill, feeling shame, allowing those awful tears to cascade down her cheek.

"Don't cry, my sweet Eve. Don't cry, my love. I will take care of you. You're famished. Drink more, my love, take all that you want." Her pain was killing him. Finally he'd done something since being a vampire that he regretted. As much as he didn't want to lose Eve, he'd give anything for her not to have to go through this. He caressed her hair, holding her to him, crooning as she drank. "It's going to be okay, Eve. I promise."

Adam's words gave her the strength to stop drinking. She stared into his eyes, guilt ridden, and filled with pain, and pulled away from the blood he was freely offering her. She'd had enough that the craving wasn't nearly as bad but not as much as she wanted.

"Thank you, Adam, but I think that will be enough. Sullivan," Eve called, her voice little more than a whisper. She was crying harder, trying with all of her might to break free from the hold Adam's blood was having on her. "Adam, stop." She pushed weakly at him. "I don't want this, I can't drink anymore. I don't want to drink blood."

"But you do," he crooned, stroking her hair, hating what he'd done to her. "You need to live," he said. *I need for you to live*, he thought.

"Give me the pills, Sullivan, now," she ordered. "Give me the damn pills."

Before Adam could stop him, Sullivan shoved several pills into Eve's mouth and then stood to her side. "This is her choice, let her do it her way."

"Sullivan, I warned you, now I'm going to kick your ass the old-fashioned way," Adam growled. He reached for Sullivan but Eve stepped between them.

"Don't, Adam," Eve whispered. Shaking her head she held Adam's angry glare. "He's right. Let me do this my way." She glanced at her friends, paused and glanced around the restaurant. "How long can you keep them like this?"

"As long as I want."

"Can you make them forget what I was doing right before?"

"You want me to erase their memories?"

"Just the fact that I was about to bite my friend." She shivered involuntarily. "Yes, I was going to do it," Eve admitted to both Adam and Sullivan. "Can you erase that?" She stared into his eyes, her lip trembling. "Please, Adam, erase that image. And while you're at it, maybe you can erase it from my mind as well."

"I can but maybe you'd better go in the bathroom and clean your face." He touched her lightly, his heart breaking when for the first time in weeks she didn't pull away from him. Now if only he could stop pulling away from her.

"Eve, go wash your face," Adam repeated, his gaze on her lips. He smiled at her. "I'm not going to hurt your friends."

"Adam, are you trying to get rid of me?"

"No, your face, it's covered in blood."

Eve blinked. She'd forgotten. Her hand touched her face and she felt the sticky remnants. "Thanks." She swallowed, unable to stop staring at her friends. She glanced at Adam. "Sullivan came because I called. Don't blame him for this. Thank you for coming, Adam." Without thinking, she reached up and caressed his cheek.

She turned to look at Sullivan. "Adam, don't do anything to him." She saw the muscle in Sullivan's jaw twitch and looked down. She should have used telepathy. Too late she did. "Don't hurt him, Adam," she said, making the mental connection. Then she went to wash her face.

❖

Don't hurt him, Adam. Eve's whispered words into his mind had the opposite effect of what she'd intended. She begged for mercy for Sullivan. Sullivan didn't deserve mercy. By all rights he should be dead. There was one thing and one thing only keeping the vamp alive and that was the fact that Adam had given his word. *Damn.* But he hadn't given his word about not kicking the vamp's ass. Surely he should have allowed himself that much pleasure. A sigh escaped. Adam hadn't given Sullivan a for real ass whipping because the vamp didn't fight back. What was the fun in that?

Adam gazed after Eve before turning his full attention to Sullivan. If he didn't kill Sullivan and soon, he was going to have to kill someone. This being passive was pissing him off big time. He didn't play nice. He didn't have to. He was Adam Omega.

"You know it's unwise to keep everybody here out for so long," Sullivan said. "If a customer comes in here and sees them like this…"

"No one is coming in." Adam turned his full attention to Sullivan and glared. "Tell me something. Why is it that you think I will not kill you?"

"Maybe I finally have it in my head what you've been saying for hundreds of years: I'm immortal, you can't kill me."

"But I can."

"Even if it's true, it doesn't concern me."

"It did before…" Adam's voice trailed off.

"Before what?" Sullivan roared. "Before Eve, before you made her into a vampire?"

"You know, Sullivan, you'd do well to worry about yourself." Adam smiled. "There are ways I can make you suffer and yet keep you alive."

"But the not quite forgotten priest in you won't allow it."

"Ah, so I see. That's the reason you feel that you can keep pushing." Adam laughed and shook his head. He supposed Sullivan was right about that.

"Isn't that the reason you do most of the crazy things you do, Adam? You give rules to others and you think they should be obeyed because you're what…God's right hand? Or have you risen above God?"

"What do you think?"

"I think you're nuts."

Adam shrugged. "Perhaps you're right but what can you do about it? I can still kill you," he gave a smirk, "or I can be generous and continue to allow you to live. Remember this, Sullivan. Even as a priest I did not obey blindly. I do take great pride in being a man of my word. And I am trying to honor that but you…you vex my spirit."

"Maybe I'll vex it even more. I too take great pride in keeping my word. I've pledged to be Eve's friend, to help her through this transformation. Who knows where our friendship might lead."

"You said you weren't in love with her."

"When she was mortal, I wasn't."

"And now?"

"It appears you're worried, Adam. It doesn't feel so good when it's on the other foot, does it?"

"That was centuries ago, man, let it go."

"I can't let it go. Could you let your love for her go?" he asked, jerking his head toward the opening Eve had disappeared through.

"What happened was not my doing," Adam said between clenched teeth.

"That's what you like telling yourself, that's how you sleep with your conscience untroubled. What do you tell yourself about Eve? She was your doing. How do you absolve yourself of that sin?"

"The sin she was committing was greater. You already know what she was attempting to do."

"But that was her choice, Adam. Now you've condemned her to a life she doesn't want, that none of us wanted. Even you, Adam. I don't believe you ever wanted this life."

"But it is the life I have. It's the life we all have and you're not helping Eve."

"Why are you so insistent on her learning to drink blood if the pills will work? The transfusions are keeping her—"

"Not enough," Adam interrupted. "She's needing them more often. You're making her weak and dependent." Adam's eyes narrowed. "Is that your plan, to make her dependent on you? I saw you kiss her."

"Did you also see her kissing me back?"

"Sullivan, I think you need to take a good look in that reality mirror you're always trying to shove in my face. You said I'm crazy and I say you are, and what I say has more authority. You're still pushing me and if I were you, I would not push."

"But you're not me. I've been through the worst that you could do to me and I came out unscathed."

"So that's it. You didn't burn in the sun and now you have some balls." Adam laughed cruelly. "Enjoy it."

"Believe me, I am. It's much more than I ever hoped for. I like being out in the daylight and feeling the sun on my face."

"Yet you still use the covered parking lot and you still work the night shift."

"Old habits are hard to break," Sullivan laughed. "Look at you, Adam. You are secretly glad that I survived the sun though you would never admit it. But that's another thing you can rub in my face, a fact that you tried for hundreds of years to get me to embrace. And I suppose in some way I owe my thanks to you for that. But you and I have been locked in a battle for many centuries. Even if we wanted to stop I don't know if I could. Can you, Adam?"

"I do agree with much of what you've said. As for our feud, I rather like it, though for the sake of Eve I've been trying to ignore my great urge to incinerate you and let your body fall as ash at her feet. I have done nothing to you and you have given me every reason to end your existence."

"I thought we'd come to an understanding about that. Our feud is over and yet you're constantly threatening me."

"Sullivan, I forgave your trying to bind me, for turning my wife against me, for using her in your plot to destroy me. I did not forgive you for trying to bed my wife."

A booming laugh burst forth. "Bed your wife? My God, man, you sound like some seventeenth century lord. If I make love to Eve, it will be her choice, and mine," Sullivan added. "You have no rights over Eve. Besides, you don't want her. Or should I say you want her but you can't get it up with her because you refuse to get over rules you set for yourself. Your priestly vow, as it were."

"You're wrong on that. I do want her. And I do get aroused for moments when she's near. Then my mind travels to how this all began." Adam shook his head and allowed his eyes to close as he remembered.

"Eve is not Tarasha. You would do well to remember that or you will lose her."

"It's been a thousand years, Sullivan. It's not that easy to let go of my memories."

"You're not physically incapable of making love to Eve. Forget your vow not to make love to a vampire. Forget what Tarasha did to you. If you truly love your wife and want her to remain as that, then you need to use the power of your mind and find a way."

"Why, Sullivan, I do believe after all of these centuries I've rubbed off on you. You sound like a priest giving me counsel. But I ask you, what if I touch Eve and can't complete the act. Wouldn't that hurt her more?"

"It was wrong of you to turn her and even more wrong for you to turn your back on her when she needs you the most. Sure, you offer her your blood. But what of your love, your body. She needs those also. Do you think she will live this immortal life you've given her alone? Do you think you're so terrific she will pine over you? She will eventually find someone who will take pleasure in making love to her."

"I will not allow it."

"You can't do anything about it unless you plan to kill the both of us. Are you planning that, Adam?" Sullivan glanced around the room. "I think you should release these people."

"Not until we get it straight between us about my reason for wanting Eve to do what she must." Adam looked toward the bathroom. "She's weak."

"Weak?" Sullivan muttered, surprised. "She's the bravest woman I know. She was brave as a mortal, and now as a vampire she's-"

"She's weak," Adam repeated. "She thinks like a mortal. Look at this," he said disgustedly. "She wants to have lunch with her friends as though nothing's happened."

"You dine quite often with mortals. Hell, you do everything as though you were. Why can't she?"

"Because she isn't me. She doesn't have the discipline. This I've learned over hundreds of years. She doesn't have my reasons for being ruthless. She still believes if she does good, good will come to her." Adam sucked in a breath. "I need to make sure she can take care of herself."

"Why?" Sullivan asked, this time in a much softer voice. "Why are you so worried about her?"

Adam winced, not wanting to reveal anything to the vampire. "There are those who would harm Eve to get to me. I have to make sure if I'm not around she can take care of herself. I have to make her strong enough to survive."

Sullivan opened his mouth and closed it without speaking. Adam said the words for him.

"You don't have to tell me," Adam said. "If I had allowed her to die, I wouldn't have to worry about her safety." His lashes fluttered and he closed his eyes, shutting away the brief moment of weakness. Damn Eve, he thought. She was, and always had been, his Achilles heel.

"Why don't you woo her with gentleness, Adam? This great love you have for her, why isn't it enough? It's obvious she loves you still. Beneath her anger lurks her love."

Something sparked behind Sullivan's eyes. "I know why you don't offer Eve the softness. Of course you would have to know she loves you. You can't stand her touch any longer, can you?" He laughed, then changed the subject. "Adam, it's been much too long. Bring these people out from under, now."

"Yes," Eve agreed, wondering why the raised voices. What were the two vampires talking about this time that they had not heard her coming? She'd stood behind them for a full two seconds.

"Shouldn't you take your seat first?" Adam asked, watching her, wondering how much she'd heard. He wished he'd answered Sullivan's allegations differently, told him that it didn't matter that Eve was a vampire, that she was Eve, his wife, the woman he loved.

Feeling a tightening in his chest, Adam wished it were in his groin, wished he could adequately show Eve the love he knew he had for her. Sullivan was right. Eve would not wait forever. Eventually he'd hurt her beyond forgiveness and she would seek her revenge in the arms of another simply to hurt him.

He watched as she slid into her seat. "How do you feel?" he asked. "Do you think you can finish this lunch or would you welcome a chance to leave?"

Eve gazed at Adam, then looked at the still faces of her friends. The hunger had receded, but not enough. She didn't trust that she would leave them as she'd found them.

"An interruption," she replied, ignoring the look on Sullivan's face. He was disappointed, thinking she'd chosen Adam's manipulating control over his friendship. It wasn't that she was choosing either one. It was just that as much as she wanted him not to be, Adam was right. Eve was not strong enough to handle being around mortals. She'd heard part of the conversation and had imagined the rest. Adam wanted her to become independent because he didn't want the burden of her safety.

"Adam, thank you," Eve almost whispered, not wanting to say it but knowing it needed to be said. "Your blood…" She looked at Sullivan. "The pills also helped," she said softly to Sullivan. "But I need to get out of here." She turned her head and looked toward Adam. "Do it," she said softly. "Erase their memory and replace it with something better, a time when we were friends, when they didn't ask to see my neck, or try to get me to eat garlic. Can you do that?" she asked softly.

"I can," Adam answered.

"Then do it."

Within moments her friends had come out of their trance and were laughing. Eve played along, not asking what they were laughing at. Adam had not informed her of the joke. She turned at the sound of Adam's voice calling her, surprised that Sullivan had stayed to assist him.

"Adam," Eve said rising, "you remember my friends. Chickie, Ann, Kelle, Wendy, Lauren, and Barb." Eve said, pointing at her friends. "This is Sullivan, he's—"

"My best man." Adam smiled at the women. "Eve and I are getting married and you're all invited."

"Married?" Ann burst out. "Eve, you said you two were fighting."

"We were, about a date. I want tomorrow, she wants to wait." Adam held his hand out to Eve.

So this is his interruption. Eve moved past her friends, her eyes fastened on Adam, not daring to look at Sullivan. For a moment she glimpsed the love Adam had felt for her, saw it clearly reflected in his eyes. Then he touched her and his look changed to one of revulsion. He closed his eyes and kissed her, drawing her close while his body trembled in disgust. She knew and hers trembled in regret. *God, don't let me cry, not in front of my friends.*

"We have to go," Adam said at last and produced business cards to the group with his home address. "The wedding's in three days, ladies, twelve sharp."

"Three days? Adam, we didn't agree to that," Eve said, looking at him."

"I think we did." He smiled. "Didn't we?"

She'd said she would put up with no more of his blackmail. It was clear Adam was using this situation to his advantage and now with her friends screaming in excitement Eve could only stare at Adam. She thought it over and agreed. She had her own reasons and Adam would soon find out what they were.

"I hope you can all come," Eve said softly. "Sorry for the short notice. It's going to be a really informal affair, casual, so come in jeans." She ignored Adam smirking at her.

"Enjoy lunch, ladies, it's on me. Sorry I have to steal Eve away but I need her. Believe me, she wants to remain here with you, but well…" He laughed. "That might be dangerous."

"What?"

Eve looked toward Chickie. "He's kidding. He always thinks when a group of women get together they're planning something. Well, thanks for coming, guys. I'll see you all in three days if you can make it."

She linked her hand through Adam's arm, not planning on hugging her friends. She couldn't yet take the risk. "I'll call you," she said, knowing she wouldn't. If they didn't show up for the impromptu wedding this would be her last time seeing them. Even if they showed up, she wouldn't see them after that. They would more than likely think she had become a snob because of Adam's riches. *Well, let them think it. Better that than for them to know the truth.*

She walked out of the restaurant arm in arm with Adam, knowing he hated her being so close. When they were outside she looked at Sullivan. Her decision had been made.

Chapter 9

"Adam, if your offer still stands, I want to take you up on it. I think it's time I learned all the things I need to know."

"Eve, I...I"— "

"It's not you, Sullivan, you've been a good friend to me."

"Then why?"

"Because Adam can give me what you can't. He's the only teacher I will need." She paused, snorted, and then shook her head. "I don't need kindness or affection right now. I need to learn to survive. I need to learn how not to kill my friends."

"Are you going to drink blood?"

"I'm going to do whatever is necessary. What better teacher to have than Adam?" She watched as Adam stilled at her words. "Do you know of anyone as cold-blooded and heartless as he is, who gives a damn for no one's needs but his own? Can you think of a better teacher for me?"

Eve turned and walked across the street to Adam's little vampire sports car. She closed her eyes, aware her remarks had stung but so had Adam's disgust for her. It had stung much more than she'd ever anticipated.

What better way to forget that once she'd loved him than to see the look in his eyes that condemned her to hell. He'd already driven the nail into her heart and left her wounded and bleeding. She wondered how much more blood she'd have to lose to drain all but the fast mounting hatred. She would feel for Adam what he felt for her, loathing and nothing more.

❖

"She's better off with me." Adam turned from staring across the street at Eve to look at Sullivan. "She will learn what she needs to learn."

"She will learn to harden her heart."

"Is that what worries you so, that when she becomes fully a vampire, the humanity you seek in her will not excite you, that you will also not want her?"

Sullivan looked ruefully at Adam. "But I never claimed to love her. I'm her friend. I can always be her friend." He straightened to his full height. "Besides, it's not me that Eve doubts."

Both men stared across the street, both knowing they would be unable to read her thoughts. She might not be fully a vampire but she'd brought along some of her traits from her old life. She was well aware they would be probing her, searching for clues. They were not surprised that she was giving nothing away.

❖

For two days Adam waited for Eve to ask him a question about the wedding plans. She didn't. She behaved as though she hated him and in a way Adam knew she did. She had every reason to. He hoped marrying her would soften the blows he'd already given her. "I'm going to perform the ceremony," he said in jest and waited for her response.

"Are you still a priest?"

"What?"

"Are you still a priest? Can you perform marriages?"

"I haven't since…since ours."

"Are we still married?"

"I guess," Adam answered, wondering what Eve was getting at.

"I don't want you guessing, Adam. I want to be your legal wife."

"Why?" Adam asked. "Two days ago you didn't want to be my wife, legal or otherwise. Why the change of heart?"

"Because of the protection."

"Whom do you need protection from?"

"You."

Adam was as curious as he'd been from the moment Eve had said she needed him and only him, and had stepped into his car. Sure, he'd wanted that when he'd made her. And from the moment he'd found her gone from the underground and living with Sullivan, he'd been working to get back in her heart.

But Eve wasn't marrying him out of any great love for him or need. If anything, he'd have to say it was more out of revenge. The way she was looking at him made his skin crawl. He'd first seen the look when they'd been in the restaurant and he'd kissed her. He had not intended to let her know his feelings but the revulsion came as it always did. He wondered what would happen if he told Eve the reason. He glanced at the hard look around her mouth. It wouldn't do a damn bit of good, she wasn't ready to listen to him. Thankfully she was ready to learn.

"You don't need protection from me."

Eve laughed. "What a joke. You stalked me, abused me, drank from me and blackmailed me. And then turned me into this and you say I have nothing to fear from you."

"But I do love you, Eve—"

"Don't you dare use those word to me ever again, Adam, I'm no longer listening."

"Eve, my reasons for not touching you, for not making love to you, have nothing to do with you. I promise I will try to put away my feelings."

"Adam, you're a real piece of work. You're certifiably insane. Do you know that? Do you think that even if you were making love to me that I could forget what you've done to me?"

"Eve, please. Just give me time, give us time. We will get past this."

"Will we get past the fact that I'm now a vampire? Will it no longer matter that the only time I feel alive is when I'm having an infusion of your blood? I'm grateful that you had sense enough to have Dr. Meah create the pills. They help."

"I don't really want you using them. You're a fledgling. I have no idea what they will do to you."

"Will they kill me?"

Adam winched. "I can't permit you to die, Eve." He held her gaze. "And I can't permit you to continue taking infusions forever. You need fresh blood from humans to be at your strongest. In time you won't need as much."

"You have no idea how much I hate you at this moment."

"I have an idea, Eve. I have a very good idea."

"Tell me something, Adam. Why does your blood affect me the way it does?"

"Because it is mine. I am Adam Omega. Vampire."

"Big damn deal."

"Trust me, Eve, it is a big deal. You will one day appreciate the fact that you were made by me."

For a long moment Eve could do nothing but glare at Adam. Finally her tongue loosened and she said, "I'll appreciate being a vampire when hell freezes over."

"Why did you agree to get rid of Sullivan, to have me teach you?" Adam was tiring of sparing with Eve. Yes, he'd done her a disservice and yes, he was doing her one still. But after a thousand years of being without her he didn't know if his actions made him selfish. *It was more like self-preservation. I need her*, he thought. "Why, Eve? Why did you want me to teach you?"

"Because I need a bastard to teach me how to be cunning and cold, to take what I want and not give a damn."

"Ouch, that hurt." He managed to smile. "Yes, I can teach you; you've come to the right place. I am a bastard and proud of it. What about your boyfriend, Sullivan?"

"You're evading the original question, Adam."

"Which was?"

"Are you still a priest?"

"I guess you could say that. I haven't thought about it one way or the other in hundreds of years."

"Am I your wife?"

"Yes, but I was kidding about performing the ceremony."

"I want you to marry us."

"Why not let Father Keller do it?"

"If you're not doing it find someone other than Father Keller."

"You want me to do this in one day?"

"You're the one that said three days, so I expect you to make sure this is legal."

"It will be legal."

"Good," Eve said, then sauntered out. "Call me when it's time."

❖

Eve stood by Adam's side. "Do you, Eve Moses take Adam Omega to be your lawfully wedded husband?"

Eve stared at the young minister. She'd not asked his name, only for his credentials. She wanted this ceremony to be legally binding. As soon as she answered the question it would be.

"I do," Eve answered. She barely listened to the rest of the words, knowing that in a moment Adam would kiss her, sealing them in marriage, knowing he would draw back as soon as possible.

It was done. They were now legally married. Adam had even managed to convince her friends that they would be out of the country for an extended amount of time.

Eve wasn't sure if they wanted to believe in fairytales, or if the diamond bracelets Adam had bought for them had blinded them to the truth. Adam should be mortal; he played the playboy billionaire with flair. But they both knew he didn't have what it took to make it as husband to her.

"We're legally married now, Eve. Do you feel more protected?"

"I will when you put my name on all of your accounts."

"If I didn't know better I would think you were a gold-digging mortal woman."

"But you do know better, don't you, Adam?"

"I will not be putting your name on anything. You're my wife, you're Mrs. Omega. That should be enough."

"Can I go in a store and buy something because I'm Mrs. Omega?"

"Of course you can. If anyone refuses you anything, give me their name and I will deal with them."

"That's all it takes, isn't it, Adam? If someone other than you harms me you will gladly stop their heart. I need my own money."

"You are still in no position to make demands on me. Perhaps after a time I will review the situation and if I feel changes are needed then I will institute them. Until that time, sign your name to what you want and I will pay the bills."

"Go to hell, Adam. I want my own money."

"By what right do you give me orders? Did you spend the last thousand years acquiring my wealth? You will do as you're told. I have already said you will want for nothing. Now stop acting like a mortal gold-digging bitch."

Adam studied Eve for a long moment. What had she expected? he wondered. He was still Adam. He had not changed. What had he done to give her the idea that he would? Then he knew. His apologies, his endless stream of '*I'm sorry*,' his guilt, his love. Well, to hell with all of that. When all was said and done he was still Adam Omega. He was still a vampire.

"When do you plan to give me your real reason for agreeing to marry me?" Adam asked, looking at Eve with suspicion.

Eve was tired of answering questions. She was the one who needed answers and now that part one was over she wanted them. "Do I have your strength?" she asked.

Adam shrugged his shoulders. "Why don't you test it out?"

Pow.

The words had barely left his mouth before Eve backhanded him and knocked him across the room. Adam stared at her, holding a hand to his jaw, feeling the drip of blood on his skin. "I guess you do, but I wouldn't keep attempting to prove it in that way. I do hit back."

"Just testing." Eve stood in front of him. "I'm taking the master suite," she announced. "By the way, congratulations, and I hope the honeymoon is everything you'd thought it would be."

"So, the vampire has teeth after all. Eve, this is my home and you will not give me orders."

"You're wrong, Adam, it's our home. You really do confuse me. Now that I'm in agreement with you that I'm your lawfully wedded wife, you balk. What's wrong, Adam? You don't like the arrangements?"

"I don't like that you're usurping my room."

"It's not yours any longer, nor are you welcome in it. But then again," Eve paused, "I'm not worried about your coming in there. We both know your feelings on that issue."

"What are Sullivan's views?"

She laughed. "Let's say what we have here, Adam, is an open marriage. I will sleep in your bed without you. I will use your funds and I will become the mistress of the vampire world. And I will do what I please with Sullivan."

"Are you planning to become stronger?"

"Yes."

"It will take blood to do that, fresh blood," he emphasized. "Neither the pills or transfusions will give you the strength that you desire or need."

"Doctors give transfusions all the time and it gets the job done."

"For mortals, my love, not for vampires. And definitely not for a newborn fledgling."

"Don't forget, Adam, I now remember what I was a thousand years ago. My powers might be rusty but with practice I will regain them. I was originally born into a family of witches." Eve laughed. "Don't look so surprised. What? Was I supposed to tell you, a priest, that I was a witch? I was and I am. One day my powers will be equal to yours. That much I can almost guarantee."

"And until that time?"

"Until that time I will do what's necessary." For what seemed an eternity Eve held Adam's gaze, knowing what she'd just agreed to, knowing she was not yet ready to use mortals for food. She didn't think she'd ever be ready for that.

"Good. Put your things away in your new bedroom. I will allow you to have it. And Eve, lessons will begin in an hour."

❖

"Think, Eve." Adam thunked his closed fist on the table, ignoring the splintering of the strong wood. It was built to take punishment but not built to withstand the annoyance of a vampire.

"I'm trying," Eve said, allowing her annoyance with Adam to seep through in her voice.

"You're not trying hard enough." He glared at her. "Besides, it shouldn't be that damn hard. You're a part of me. I made you, you have my blood in your veins."

"Maybe not enough of it," Eve snapped back. "Maybe your blood isn't as good as you think it is."

"And maybe you're doing this to piss me off."

"Why would I do that?"

Eve looked directly into Adam's purple gaze. For a span of a moment her heart caught in her throat at the sight of him, at his long black hair curling gently on his shoulders. She'd never seen anyone who looked a tenth as sexy as Adam. She blew out a breath as she took in the bronze skin shimmering in anger, the tapered waist and rippling muscles, the legs powerfully built and the violet eyes glaring at her.

She recognized the feelings she was having. For a moment she wished she could die. Why did she continue to allow Adam to have an effect on her like this? After a nano-second of chastisement, her eyes connected with Adam's. Their gazes locked and he blinked. Eve dropped her eyes.

That was all it took. Adam had her in his arms and was kissing her. She tried to not want him, to ignore the feelings that were attempting to rise to the surface, but she couldn't. His touch was electric, caressing the wanting from her soul, urging her to let go, to love him. He tasted of nothing she'd ever known except himself. Only Adam had ever been able to create this excitement in her blood.

He ran his hands down the side of her body, bent her over his arms and trailed hot kisses down her neck. She shivered as Adam moaned in lust. And she shivered again when she felt his hardness prodding her and the moisture flow from her body, wetting her legs, screaming an urgent need.

Another need was rising, one Eve had never known. Something more was happening to her. Her mouth was twisting, changing shape to accommodate her new fangs. The smell of blood called to her. Just a taste, a little taste. It wouldn't hurt, it was Adam. She loved him, he'd made her.

Eve sank her teeth into Adam and felt the blood flow over her tongue. When she swallowed, the electric feeling intensified and she held on. Ecstasy was just a little ways ahead, she could feel it. She wanted it with every fiber of her being. She needed it and so she drank and drank, quenching her thirst for all things in Adam's blood. She barely noticed that Adam's erection was no longer there. There was no longer that hardness pressing between her thighs, but still she drank.

"Eve, Adam can not make love to you while you drink from him. Stop now before he pushes you away. You're going to be hurt when he does." Not now she screamed. She didn't want or need to have Sullivan's voice in her head. But she couldn't ignore his words. His words made her aware of what she should have noticed. Adam's lust for her had abated. A second before she called a halt, Adam shoved her away. He was trembling, his hand on the spot she'd bitten. The look in his eyes terrified her.

"Did I hurt you?" she asked softly.

"I've never been bitten by a vampire since I was made. As much as I love you, Eve, I can't make love to you in this manner. I've not been bitten by anyone in all of these years except you. Once as a human now as…"

"As a female vamp. Go ahead and say it, Adam."

"I give you my pledge. I do love you, Eve, I would give you anything in my power to give, but to make love to you in the way of our nature, your new nature, this isn't in my power."

He turned from her and Eve died a thousands deaths. What a liar he was. Making love to her was in his power; he just didn't want to. What a fool she was, a stupid, stupid fool.

In the space of a breath that seemed to go on for infinity Adam felt a wrenching in his heart. "Eve," he moaned silently. "If I could I would. I do love you." He sent the unspoken words to her, saw her eyes lift as he thought them. There, she'd done it. She'd heard him.

The moment of victory was quickly followed by an eternity of regret at the look that came into Eve's eyes. He cringed, blinked, and moved away. He loved her with his whole heart, but he couldn't give her hope.

Anger flared within his soul. He'd spent a thousand years craving what he could no longer have. He flung his arm out, knocking objects from the table until he was planted in front of Eve. He used his thumb and forefinger to thump her head.

"Snap out of it and concentrate," he said disgustedly before stalking off. In a swirl Adam disappeared from the house.

Damn, she had been concentrating. She'd heard his thoughts. Now she knew his anger was not at her, but himself. He'd sensed the pain in her that his rejection caused and the immediate closing up of her heart. He'd lost her. Anger made his body shake. He was behaving like a mortal punk. That wasn't going to happen. He needed to blow off some steam, maybe kill a disobedient vamp. That shouldn't be too hard to do. He smiled while thinking of it and went in search of his prey.

❖

Eve licked her lips; her fingers caressed the area where Adam had tapped. It hurt, but she'd needed the pain to bring her out of it. For a moment she and Adam had been mesmerized by remembered feelings Adam no longer possessed. Love, she thought, what a tricky thing. For centuries that love had burned brightly for Adam, but now it was taking a dark turn.

What was Adam expecting of her, tears? No more tears, she thought. She'd cried all the bloody red things that she was going to, no more. Eve went to the bookcase and pulled out her witch's book of magic. If she couldn't do what Adam wanted, then she'd do it with magic.

Believe, she ordered her mind. *Believe you can do anything that you think you can. You're no different than Adam. If he can, so can you.* "You will stop loving Adam. He doesn't love you and you will not love him," she scolded herself aloud. Maybe she'd work on an anti-love potion.

Eve gazed at the splintered table and balled her hand into a fist, true a much smaller fist than Adam, but it would do. It would have to do. She brought her fist down with all the power that was in her and laughed as the wood groaned and gave way, falling to the floor in a heap. To hell with vampire power. She was a witch and her ancient power had done what Adam's blood couldn't do for her. "Is this good enough?" she asked and laughed.

"It will do. How did you know I had returned?"

"I'm a vampire, Adam, did you forget?" She had no plans on telling him exactly how she'd accomplished the feat.

"Eve…"

"I don't need anything from you, Adam. I'm not looking for love from you. You don't have to feel guilty."

"Let me explain."

"Just the lessons," Eve screamed, "that's all I want from you." She shoved her chair away. "That and your name and access to your money."

He came near her and before she could stop her hands were around his throat and she was choking him. She growled low in her throat, the sound guttural, like something from a horror movie.

"Eve."

"Eve what?" she growled. "Good job, Eve, you're giving in to your nature." A haze covered her eyes and for a moment Eve wondered if like Adam when he was angry her pupils were red. Her lips curled back and awareness filled her as she once again felt her mouth growing, opening wider for the fangs, fangs that until Adam's rejection had been retracted. She ran her tongue against the sharp enamel, then leaned into Adam. Why not? He'd done this to her, made her into a blood drinker.

The last time she'd bitten him in lust, but this was different. This time it was in anger. Her lips were pressed against his neck and she trembled, noticing he didn't move. There was no fear in him. She opened her mouth even wider, wanting to make him fear her, to shove her away in disgust as he'd done before. Still nothing. Her fangs pierced his skin and she bit down, feeling his blood fill her mouth.

"Do it, Eve, do it. Feed from me."

From out of nowhere a picture of Sullivan filled her brain. He was her unasked for guardian. She was going to have to speak to him about invading her privacy.

She pushed Adam from her, spitting out the blood, wishing she could swallow every drop. What had gone down was creating an electrical current within her body. She felt energized, as always since becoming a vampire and taking his blood. It didn't matter if it was via transfusion or if she drank from him, his blood was addictive, making her want more. Her eyes snapped open.

"What is it with your blood?"

"I don't know."

"You must," Eve insisted. "Why would only a drop or two make me feel…"

"Reborn," Adam finished. "Think what would have happened had you swallowed all of it. Why didn't you?

"I don't want your blood."

"You didn't spit it out before."

"That was different," Eve whispered, not finding the need to say she'd been so overcome with passion that the drinking of his blood filled a sexual need. "Why didn't you push me away like you did before?"

"I've decided I owe you at least my blood."

"Liar. You can stomach it when I touch you in anger." She studied him for a moment. "And you can stomach it when I'm in need, when you're helping me." She flashed back on him slashing his wrist and giving her his blood in the restaurant. It was beginning to dawn on her. "It's when...when we're filled with passion that you don't want me to have your blood, isn't it?"

"Let it go, Eve."

"You're supposed to be my teacher. Tell me. Am I correct?"

"Look at it this way. Regardless of the reason, I'm here and I'm willing to give you what you need."

"Out of guilt?"

"Still, it's blood and it's calling to you. I'm offering, Eve. Feed from me."

"No, I don't want to feed from you."

"But you do want blood?"

Eve didn't answer him. Yes, she wanted blood, her skin was crawling. All the blood she'd taken from Adam before had been but an appetizer. She wanted more, gallons more and she wanted it from Adam. Shame filled her and she cringed inwardly. She felt drugged. Something was pulling her under. Adam's voice came as though from inside a deep tunnel.

The potions she'd made weren't working, the pills weren't working. She was going to have to do a lot more research. But for now at least she needed a transfusion of real human blood. Surely that much wouldn't make her any more depraved than when as a mortal she had been given transfusions. Maybe that's how it had begun, the craving.

"Eve, are you listening to me?"

She swayed and her eyes closed and she fought to keep them open. She gave up and waited for the clunk of her body hitting the floor, and the pain that would accompany it. But that wasn't what happened. Instead, she felt Adam's arms close around her, heard his footsteps as he carried her, felt his caress as he laid her in the bed and heard his voice.

"My poor Eve," he crooned. "I have damned you as I am damned. This wasn't worth it." Her eyes shuttered, her heartbeat quieted and she went to sleep. The next thing she knew Adam was lifting her from the pillow.

"Wake up, Eve, this is Mark."

"Mark?" Eve did her best to lift her eyelids.

"Mark is here to help you," Adam explained.

"Help me how?"

"Mark's mortal."

Eve shrank back in disgust. "No, Adam. What have you done to him? Release him."

"I came on my own," Mark offered.

His words made her sit up straighter. "You came on your own to me? Why? Do you know why he brought you?"

"Yes," Mark answered. "You're a virgin, so to speak, and I would very much like to be your first."

"My first what?" Eve was totally alert now.

"Your first." He shrugged his shoulder. "Your lover, your feeding, whatever you need."

Her head twisted toward Adam. "You brought him here to make love to me?"

"Not exactly, but if that is what you want…"

Anger filled her belly and disgust quickly followed. It was one thing for Adam not to want her. It was another for him to procure lovers for her. She frowned. "I don't think so. I'm capable of handling my own needs." When Mark refused to move, she shoved him from her bed. "Don't mess with me," she muttered softly. "I'm not in the mood."

Mark sat on the floor where she'd shoved him. "Let me explain. I didn't know you didn't understand." He looked toward Adam for help. "I don't make love in the normal sense. I meant that when you feed on me I have an orgasm and sometimes the vamps have one also. That's what I meant."

"That's no less disgusting," Eve snarled and got up from the bed.

"He said you needed warm human blood," Mark whined. I'm here, I'm human and my blood is warm."

A knot twisted in Eve's belly. God, she couldn't believe that Adam had told the man what he was meant to do and he'd come willingly.

She'd been a vampire for a little over a month now and so far she'd managed to hang onto her resolve not to drink from mortals. It had been by a shred but still she had not willingly drunk blood except with Adam. Nor had she killed anyone. Now this man, Mark— standing before her, Eve wanted to smash his face against the door and watch as his blood stained the wood. She couldn't believe any mortal would willingly allow himself to be food for a vampire.

Yet, she'd done just that. She shuddered, remembering her own time as Adam's meal. She looked down at Mark in pity. She'd had her reasons; maybe Mark had his. Maybe Adam had forced him to; maybe Mark's life hung in the balance.

"Mark, why would you do this?" She had to ask. She needed to know.

"I get off on it," he shrugged. Mark stared first at Eve then turned his gaze to Adam.

Adam interrupted her thoughts. "Eve, it's time. It's either beginning right here and right now with a willing subject or allowing your hunger to overtake you. Which will it be?"

She glanced again at Mark. "Are you sure this is okay with you?"

"I'm sure," he grinned.

She looked him over. He wasn't anyone she would have chosen to touch when she'd been a mortal. And now even as a vampire she didn't really want to, but her pity for what could happen to him gave her pause.

Eve looked at Adam. "I don't want you here. I can do this alone."

"You have no idea how much blood to take. Too much and you can kill him."

For the first time Eve saw fear in Mark's eyes. *Good*, she thought, he should be more aware of what really waited for him behind the pretty faces.

She made the low growling sound again in her throat. "Are you afraid of me, Mark?" she asked, gliding to stand in front of him, not even aware that she knew how to glide.

"A little," he admitted.

"And you still want to go through with this?"

"Yes."

"What if your blood tastes so good to me," she paused to lick her lips and laugh a little, "that I can't stop myself?"

"Then it would have been an honor to die in your arms."

Eve's eyes closed and she shuddered. What nonsense, such dribble. "What if I make you into a vampire?" She saw the gleam in his eyes and knew immediately that was what he wanted, to be made a vampire. She smirked as she noticed Mark turning in Adam's direction.

"He's forbidden the making of vampires," Mark said.

"Adam doesn't control me."

"Others have tried," Mark confessed.

"And what happened?" Eve asked, bringing her gaze to rest on Adam instead of Mark.

"Adam killed the new vampires and their makers."

"I'm his wife," Eve offered.

"I don't think it matters." Mark looked from her to Adam.

Eve wondered why Mark was speaking so freely. Was this verbal lesson also part of Adam's plans? She glanced at him. Touché. Only she didn't plan to be taken down so easily.

"You may leave us now, Adam, I have this under control." To Mark, she asked, "Would you like a drink?"

"This is not a mortal date," Adam warned her. "Do what you have to do and call me when you're done."

"I'll do this my way." She stormed out of the room. "Mark, she screamed, "come along." Eve opened a brand new bottle of scotch and poured them both a drink. It was surprising how many things she had not done as a mortal that she was doing now.

She took a drink, expecting the burn. What she had not expected was to feel as though her tongue was going to be peeled from her mouth. She spit the liquid out, spewing it over Mark.

"How long?" Mark asked.

"A little over a month," she replied.

"Has it been rough?"

"Yes."

"Adam said I could answer any question you might ask that I know the answer to."

"So tell me why he gets to play God. Why he's allowed to make vampires and the others aren't."

"He's Adam."

"What difference does that make?"

"You're Eve."

Okay, now she could see what was going on. Adam had brought her a deranged man, someone who'd probably attack her and in order to defend herself she'd wind up killing him. She tried not to glare at Mark.

"I don't understand," Eve said, deciding to give Mark another chance to explain.

"Don't you? It's not hard."

"I don't get it," she repeated, getting annoyed.

"You're the parents, the chosen ones, Adam and Eve. Don't you get it?"

"Are you saying he can get away with this because of my name?"

"I don't know, not really," Mark smiled at her, "but it's what everyone thinks."

"Are you crazy?" Eve asked. The time for playing with this mortal was over.

"Some say it's your husband that's crazy, that you've made him that way."

"Aren't you afraid that I will hurt you?"

"Not really."

"Why?"

"Adam told me you wouldn't."

"And you believed him?"

"Yes."

"Why?"

"He doesn't lie."

"That's debatable." Eve stared at Mark. He was beginning to look just a little bit more appetizing. She smiled as his blood strummed through his veins. Here was someone sitting here waiting for her, ready to deliver to her what she needed. She thought of the drops of Adam's life-giving elixir that had recharged her. Surely the blood of this man sitting before her held no such power but she wanted to see, to taste it for herself.

"Don't do it, Eve."

Eve shook her head. Had Sullivan suddenly become the voice of her conscience?

"If you don't do it," Mark said, eyeing her warily, "you will only make problems for Adam."

"And you think I care if I make problems for him?"

"He's been shielding you from the community. No one knows that he's turned you. It is against the rules, you know."

"So what does everyone think I'm doing with him?"

"You're his wife, his mortal concubine. That's not a totally unheard of thing. Look at me. A lot of humans know about vampires. We consider it an honor to have a vamp drink from us. Did you think I was alone in doing this?"

Eve shivered, "I wish you were." Her brows knitted together as the obvious occurred to her. The man had too much information and was giving it too freely to not be… "Are you…does Adam…I mean, are you his lover?"

"In a manner of speaking yes, but not often. Adam prefers females. Besides, he never has to make do with me. It's only when I've done him a service; then it's his form of payment."

"Adam drinks your blood as payment?" Eve wanted to vomit, to throw the man from the house. But for the first time she was finally getting some answers. These were things Adam could have easily told her, even Sullivan. She wondered why neither had mentioned it. Again Eve shuddered at the horror presented before her.

"So you're here now, willing to deflower me, to allow me to drink from you in hope that Adam will reward you?"

"Yes."

The man said it so simply and without qualms. There was no shame in him.

"What if I don't drink from you?" For the first time since Adam had brought Mark into her bedroom, Eve saw fear snake across his face. She didn't ask what brought the fear. She didn't want to know. More than likely it was fear that Adam wouldn't use him as a meal. The entire business sickened her, making Eve more determined than ever to return to her human state. She would find a way to revert if it were the last thing she did.

"Please," Mark pleaded, "please don't send me away." He crawled to her, holding onto her legs, clinging tighter when she attempted to push him away.

"I'll do anything," he said, "anything at all."

"I don't want—"

"Don't send me away. I can be useful to you."

That rang a bell. He could be a friend perhaps, one who knew what she was, what she was capable of, but mortal nonetheless.

Eve watched as the man pulled his shirt from his neck and with his grimy hand wiped away the offending dirt and sweat.

Maybe not totally mortal, Eve amended her thoughts. What human in their right mind would do this? Again she remembered.

"Come along," she said to Mark. She picked up her half filled glass of scotch and brought it to her lips, taking a swig, forcing it to remain down. She would need this and a whole lot more.

Chapter 10

"No one has ever asked me to do this before," Mark laughed.

Eve stood in the door of the bathroom watching him shower. She tossed him shampoo and watched as he closed his eyes and lathered his hair.

Someone should have, she thought. She couldn't believe Adam would take blood from a man in his unkempt condition. She remembered how he'd behaved toward her when she'd attempted it. And she was the one he purported to love.

Suddenly it was as though a light bulb went on. Adam had not touched Mark, at least not in the manner that Mark thought. What Adam had done was implant memories. She laughed aloud.

"What's so funny?" Mark called out.

"Nothing much."

"You know, a man doesn't like to be in the buff and hear a woman laugh."

"I'm not laughing at you, Mark."

"Good."

Eve searched through Adam's bathroom drawers for a new toothbrush. For a vampire Adam sure made sure he kept a lot of mortal conveniences. "Here," she said to Mark as he climbed naked from the shower. "You can cover up," she said, reaching behind her for a towel. With the other hand she handed him the brush filled with an ample amount of toothpaste. "Here."

"You're strange."

"So are you, Mark, but if I'm willing to overlook it, then I suggest you do the same."

After leading him to her bedroom Eve pointed toward the bed, wondering if this was the way to do it, if all female vamps became deflowered in the bed they slept in. She shivered, thinking about Adam a couple of doors down waiting for her to do the deed.

Eve lay beside Mark, her muscles taut, the nerve endings dancing in anticipation. She was a vampire; this was her new nature. Blood, she needed blood. Eve could feel it calling to her. The thought of how it would revitalize her and make her stronger made her knees bend with the need.

She pierced Mark's skin with her fingernail and felt him jump, but he didn't move away. Damn, he was as nervous about this as she was.

"I believe I can do it," Eve whispered. "It's all in the mind."

She pressed her lips against Mark's now clean and sweet smelling flesh. *I believe.* She felt Mark trembling. "I believe," she said again as her teeth pierced his skin. She almost tasted his blood. Almost. "You can do it," she repeated to herself and moved, allowing the blood to dribble out and fall down her chin. "You can do it."

Eve closed her eyes, fighting against the hunger, the thirst. She could have him here, right now. He wanted it and so did she. She pressed Mark's skin, allowing blood to spill out. It was then Eve sent him image after image and watched in amazement as his body writhed in ecstasy.

She continued until she saw his hand move between his legs. She watched in fascination as he began to pump himself faster and faster. When Mark screeched in pleasure, shooting the thick liquid over his body, Eve sent him several more images until he fell asleep exhausted.

❖

Eve left the room with Mark asleep and went in search of Adam, entering his bedroom, surprised that he'd left. He'd told her he'd wait there until she was done with the deed.

When she couldn't find him there, she made her way to the den and sat in an overstuffed chair in the center of the room with her legs curled beneath her body. She fingered an untouched glass of scotch that she twisted from time to time just to know that it was there. The solid feel of the glass provided some comfort.

Then the tiredness came, a mind numbing sensation of being pulled underneath a current of need. If she didn't receive blood soon, Adam would know she'd not fed from Mark.

"Sullivan," she called. "You're the voice of my conscience. I hope you're listening now. I need to feed."

Within seconds Sullivan was standing in front of her holding a bag of blood in his hands. "Will this help?" he asked.

"Sullivan, were you in my head?"

"Yes, I made a connection with you. I couldn't help it, I wanted to look out for you." He smiled, then sobered. "I don't know if you can reverse this, Eve, but I want to help you for as long as possible."

"Why didn't I know you were in my head?"

"You did know it," he smiled again, "only you thought I was the voice of your conscience." He stared at Eve. "In a way I guess I was. I could sense the hunger in you, feel the emotions and then the power. It didn't take much figuring to know you'd drunk from Adam."

"Yeah, I drank from him twice. You kept telling me not to." Eve blanched, remembering when she'd fallen under Adam's spell and had kissed him with all the passion that was in her before she bit him. "Did you sense everything?" she asked.

"I wasn't spying on you, Eve."

Oh my God, she thought, *he knew*. She closed her eyes. "Sullivan, don't enter my mind without my permission, okay?"

"What did you do with Mark?" Sullivan asked without giving the promise.

"What Adam wanted me to."

Sullivan tilted his head. "Eve."

"You were there in my head. Don't you know what happened?"

"Not everything. When you started sending him images I lost the connection." He touched a finger to her chin. "But his blood is on you. You don't want to tell me if you had even a little sip?"

"I'm not going to tell you. You will know the same thing that I tell Adam. I fed on Mark, period. He has my stain on his throat. Now don't you think we'd better hurry before Adam returns?"

Within seconds the blood flowed into Eve's veins and she felt stronger, not the same power she'd received from Adam but stronger nonetheless. This blood was a new kind, packed with adrenaline. Not even Sullivan was aware that the blood he'd brought her was a new formula. She watched as Sullivan removed the needle from her arm and prepared to leave.

Eve put her hand on Sullivan's arm to stop him before he disappeared into mist. "Will you help me despite Adam's wishes?"

"There is no need to question me on that, Eve. I've made you a promise and I will keep it."

Sullivan smiled once more at Eve. "Anytime you tire of living here, come to me." With that he disappeared and Eve took *The Witches' Book of Spells* from the shelf and sat back to wait Adam's return.

She sensed Adam's heartbeat the instant he returned and sucked in a breath. Eve waited, wondering what their conversation would be. Would Adam know she'd faked it? Would he care?

"How do you feel?" Adam asked, peering intently at Eve.

"Stronger," Eve answered, not bothering to look at him. She closed her mind, felt him probing her and increased the amount of pressure she was using to keep him out.

"I'm going to check on Mark, make sure he's still alive."

Eve had expected as much. She tried not to smile at her ingenuity in actually piercing Mark's skin. Not doing so would have been telling. It was just as well she did not yet know how to sear the flesh with her tongue and cauterize the wounds. She needed Adam to see the holes her teeth had made. She shivered. Eve hated thinking about the fangs. She didn't want to have fangs. Suddenly she felt Adam's push on her mind and threw up every block she knew to prevent penetration.

"I don't want you in my mind, Adam."

"Why the secrecy?" Adam sat next to her, took her glass from her hand and drank hungrily. "You don't like scotch."

"There are a lot of things that I don't like, but I will do what I must to survive."

"Eve."

"Save it," she said. "I was waiting for you. I wanted you to know the deed is done. My soul is on the way to being as black as yours."

"And you blame me?"

Eve glared. Surely Adam was insane. Who the hell did he think had made her into a vampire? "You have to become independent. You can't depend on Sullivan to supply you with nourishment—"

For a moment Eve wondered if Adam knew she'd not fed on Mark, that Sullivan had just left after giving her a transfusion. She stared at him for a moment, deciding to play the story out without admitting to anything. She gave a short laugh before she answered. Then she said, "And I shouldn't become dependent on your blood either. Is that the rest of your little speech?"

Adam gave her a sad smile and continued as though she'd not spoken. "On occasion you can use other means but you have to know how to obtain food for yourself."

"I like Mark," she said unexpectedly. "I want him."

"Excuse me?" Adam moved the glass from his lips in disbelief.

"Does he belong to you?"

"Is there something you're trying to ask me, Eve?"

Eve laughed. "Adam, I could care less about whom you screw, Mark or anyone. I'm saying that I think for now Mark will be a good source for me. There will be others."

Adam felt a tremor at Eve's words. She was so cold, so calculating. She was more like that heartless bitch, Tarasha, the one who'd turned him, the reason why he'd made his vow. The reason why he wouldn't make love to Eve now as he wanted to. He'd never gone back on his word. He stared at Eve, hard. He didn't like her coldness. He glared at her.

For century after century he'd vowed never to touch a vampiric woman with anything akin to affection, to not make love to them and he hadn't, not even once, regardless of what Sullivan thought. His blood boiled in his veins. He should have set the vampire straight centuries ago, but he wouldn't have believed him. Besides that, Adam hadn't cared.

"I do not sleep with men," Adam said indignantly between clenched teeth.

"So what," Eve laughed, "neither do I, not anymore, right? If I make love it will be with a vampire." She laughed again, tilting her head and staring at Adam.

"What would happen if I made love to a mortal man? If I fell in love with one? Could that work?" She didn't wait for an answer before walking out of the door into the night. She'd already overplayed her hand.

Adam had sensed her getting stronger and she was. The new blood was much better. Adam would blow a gasket if he knew she was the guinea pig for its trial, but she cared little for what he thought. In time hopefully she would no longer need the transfusions or the pills. No one had bothered to tell her how long the transformation would take. And she'd not bothered to ask because frankly she didn't know if she wanted to know. She was treating the process as a virus, knowing that most ran their course in a matter of time. *And this too shall pass*, she thought.

As for Mark, he was her new mission. She intended to save him from himself and the vampires. Eve didn't debate whether brainwashing him was right or wrong. If she could plant pictures in his mind of wild lovemaking and her feeding on him, then surely she could give him pictures of what a normal life would be like.

She intended to try to make him value what he had, to leave behind the existence where he allowed her kind to feed on him. She shivered at the thought.

❖

"Are you sure that Adam will not be angry about your taking the new transfusions?"

"Why should he? He said to test them."

"I don't think he meant on you."

Eve's head snapped around. "Doctor, leave my husband to me."

"I can't help but worry. We've been given orders not to harm you. Eve, I have to tell you that I don't know all there is to know about the new blood yet. Of course I want it to work but I have to worry about it also. This batch is the newest one and I don't have any data yet. You're the only one who's even tried it. I really would like to study your body's reaction a bit more before proceeding."

"Are you having any luck with the pump I asked you to make?"

"Yes. But that's another thing. I think Adam would like to know about it."

"I thought Adam said you were to obey my orders without question." For a moment Eve's voice was distasteful to her own ears. Sullivan was right; she was beginning to sound too much like her husband.

"I'm sorry I snapped," she said. "It's just, well, you understand no one really wants me here. I've been sort of shoved down your throats and I'm searching for my own spot. I want to be useful."

"You have been. The suggestion that I use the insulin pump and make modification was brilliant, and the smaller base including the cooling system, that was a stroke of genius. Where do you carry it?"

Eve pulled the cosmetic bag holding the cooling system from her purse and handed it to the doctor. She joined him as he laughed at her.

"A cosmetic bag, with rhinestones no less?"

"Sure, why not?" Eve answered.

Eve watched as he unzipped the bag and tested the temperature. He smiled. "Perfect."

"Where do you keep yours?" Eve asked.

"I don't." He attempted to look away from her but her increased powers wouldn't permit it. There was something about Adam's blood.

Before fear could fill the vampire's eyes, Eve spoke. "I have no intention to tell Adam. Your secret is safe with me, just as my secret is safe with you. Not even Sullivan should know what I'm doing."

"How did you know?"

"I didn't," Eve smiled, "I guessed. I know if I had invented something like this I would want to try it out on myself. You're one of the few people to know what I am."

Eve saw the bemused expression. "What? Why are you looking at me like that?"

"You keep referring to us as people."

"I'm sorry."

"Don't be, I like it. And you're right. I had to know if I were right. I couldn't see testing this on you and not on myself." He smiled wider. "At least when

Adam finds out I can tell him that since I was using it I thought it would be safe for you."

"Why are you all so afraid for him?"

"He's not like us."

"But he is, he's a vampire."

"He's so much more than that. I wish I had a formula to find out what."

"Were you in on the plot?"

"To bind Adam? Are you kidding? I would have never been involved with anything so crazy. Besides, I like Adam. He's fair and he's generous. He has quirks like anyone and I think because he keeps to himself so much he's a bit eccentric but I still like him."

"When you've proved that your new blood works, then what?"

"It's not going to be that easy. It takes a long time to make and it's expensive. I've only received preliminary reports from the blood banks across the country. There are so many variables."

"Stop," Eve said, putting her hand on the vamp's arm to calm him down.

Embarrassed, the doctor moved away. "I'm a scientist. I think like one. There are too many variables. I have to be sure. I have to look out for the problems."

"You know money is not an issue."

"It never was."

"But what did you mean about the blood banks?"

"We always test on humans through the blood banks."

"You do what?"

"No harm has ever come to them."

"That's unethical."

"Was it ethical for us to become what we are? I'm not a murderer, Eve, but I have to know what effect the things I create will have on the public at large. We feed from humans. If the blood I create doesn't harm them, then in all probability it shouldn't harm us."

"Does Adam..." She stopped. Of course Adam knew. "Did he tell you to do it?" she asked instead.

For one long moment she thought the vampire wasn't going to answer her. Eve dropped her gaze. Looking toward the door, she frowned. "How can you be so loyal to him? What? Is Adam the master vampire?"

Dr. Meah laughed. "If we used such terms Adam would be the Grand Master, but he doesn't use those terms. He's simply Adam. He's the best. There is no need to place labels on him."

"But there are different levels?"

"Of course. As in anything these levels come with the power to control and maintain that which you've amassed. A lot of it is due to innate talents, a gift, if you will. Then there's skill that comes with age and experience. Experience comes by doing. As far as Adam goes, he's truly gifted. I have never seen a more powerful vampire. Others with his power would be corrupt. Not Adam. He's hard but he's not corrupt. He's trying to make things better."

"By tampering with the blood banks?"

"How else do I test? It has to be an exact match to human blood. If it's not compatible to humans it won't work for us."

"And what if it kills them?"

"It hasn't."

"What if it had? What if it still does? Why can't you just limit your test subjects to vampires?"

"Do you have any idea how hard it is to get vampires to agree to this?"

"Why?" Eva was truly curious. "What are the so-called immortals afraid of? Needles? I don't understand."

"There have been lots of moral—minded vampires through the centuries. Sullivan isn't the first. On the pretext of helping, these moral—minded creatures did the most immoral things. Vampires have been injected with many caustic fluids through the years. They've proven deadly."

"They died?"

"Some wished they had."

"Is that when you began testing on humans?"

"Let's say that's when Adam decided to clean house. I was brought in with several others and we began trying in earnest to find a new blood source."

"You make it sound like Adam is a Good Samaritan."

"We are not out to harm humans, not with the blood, Eve. We want it to work. That's why we're testing it."

He sighed, the anger he was feeling coming through his voice. "Besides, humans have attempted the very thing that we have. They've been trying for years to make something to use in the place of human blood. Who do you think they're testing it on? Don't judge us, Eve, until you have all of the facts. I'm not a monster; neither is Adam."

Instead of answering Eve went to the massive fridge and pushed through the colossal quantity of blood to get to the false back.

Once there Eve dug through the bags of blood that were placed there in case anyone found the false back. She dug until she came to the bite size containers. Eve dug out several of the bags, laughing at the name '*bite size*' she'd attached to them. She slipped the blood into the refrigerated pouch and slipped that into her purse.

"Let me check your Picc-line," Dr. Meah said, moving Eve's wide bracelet to check on the needle he'd inserted into her vein right above her wrist. He smiled at his own ingenuity. Now Eve could just attach the tubing and give herself the blood from her refrigerated pouch whenever she needed it. In fact the modified pump was so slender it could be hidden in her bra and the connecting tubing would easily be threaded through a long sleeve blouse without detection. Eve could receive continuous feedings if she so chose. It all depended on her needs. When he was done he replaced the bracelet. "You're all set," he smiled at her. "You didn't answer my question, Eve. Do you think we're monsters?"

"I'll see you later," she said, moving away. She had no answer as to whether or not she thought any of them were monsters.

Chapter 11

Eve walked confidently down the halls of the company, her company. She'd bought stock from Adam with his own money. He'd told her she was Mrs. Omega and all she had to do was sign her name to what she wanted so she'd done just that. Talk about being pissed when he found out…Adam was beyond pissed but what could he do. She'd beaten him at his own game. She now had the means to do what she'd set out to do months ago.

She would find a cure; she would not remain like this. If she'd known sooner that she would have more freedom, she would have moved in with Adam when he'd first demanded it. Eve shook her head and scraped her teeth over her lips. Lots of things had changed in the weeks since she'd taken over Adam's home.

They'd had a party, one where Adam had remained glued to her side, afraid that she would attack his guests, his mortal guests, and though she'd toyed with the idea, she had yet to take blood while it still flowed in the mortal donor.

Besides, Eve was remembering many talents she'd had in her previous incarnation and learning many more. Her work with her crystals and potions was paying off. She was getting stronger and that was due in part from her taking the crystal water she made. Since she'd been unable to find anything to cure what ailed her she'd decided that maybe as a vampire she needed something a bit different. Maybe the stones that were most toxic to mortals would be just the thing a fledging vampire needed. It appeared to be working. Her twice daily crystal energy drink was infusing her with almost as much energy as Adam's blood. She also believed it had something to do with the special energy net she'd fashioned for her bed. She smiled, knowing that the crystals that totally surrounded her bed from beneath kept the net charged. There was no doubt of that. She could feel the power of the crystals. She didn't know if Adam was aware of her actions and she didn't care. She'd promised him nothing more than that she would learn what she needed. She couldn't help noticing the difference in the way the other vampires treated her. Instead of indifference there was an inkling of respect.

Eve sensed Sullivan a moment before he appeared and wished she knew how to turn her body into mist and disappear. The one vampire she had been avoiding was Sullivan.

"Eve, I haven't seen much of you in the last few weeks," Sullivan said, walking to stand directly in front of her, blocking her path unless she wanted to be outwardly rude.

"Adam doesn't want me to have anything to do with you," Eve partially lied. While it was true that Adam would prefer Eve avoiding Sullivan, the decision had been Eve's alone.

"I thought Adam wasn't calling the shots with you anymore?"

"We're married."

"Not in this lifetime, Eve."

"We are."

"How? Did he do the same as he did with Eyanna? Did he perform the ceremony? He told me that he had. And you think that's legal?"

"Sullivan, are you insane? You know I would never allow Adam to perform the ceremony. If you had bothered to show up you would know. I did invite you."

"I am not human, Eve. I would never participate in holy services. I'm not Adam."

"I participated also."

"But you're part of him."

"Which parts are you blaming me for, Sullivan? For Adam having turned me, or for my having found a way to live with what I am? Or are you blaming me for marrying Adam? There is no need for you to worry, Sullivan, Adam does not desire me."

She looked at the pained expression that crossed Sullivan's face. "Excuse me. He desires me, Sullivan, he just won't act on that desire."

"Why Eve, why would you marry him? It was bad enough when he just considered you his wife. Now you truly are. I don't understand how you could do it."

She stopped and glared at Sullivan. "Because it makes me Mrs. Omega."

"Since when did that become important to you?"

"Since I found that being Mrs. Omega gives me power, financial power." Eve ignored the fact that Sullivan had moved away from her.

"You've been blocking me from your mind. Why?"

"Because I didn't want you there."

"Are you now feeding from Mark, Eve?"

"Yes," she hissed at him. "Adam brought him to me for that purpose."

A look of disillusionment invaded Sullivan's eyes and Eve winced inwardly. Sullivan had done nothing but befriend her. Now in her own way she was trying to do the same for him, keep him out of her deceit.

"You took him?" Sullivan asked, the skepticism showing clearly in his voice.

"I am alive, am I not? I'm not weak."

"You were alive when I was giving you transfusions and the pills."

"I can't depend on you, Sullivan. I have to take care of myself."

"You're so cold, so unlike the Eve I know." He reached out a hand to touch her and she moved away.

"Don't," Eve snapped.

"What happened to our being friends, being a team? There was a time I thought we were on the same wavelength. Now I'm not so sure. Your recent actions make me wonder. Eve, if you ever have to make a choice between my life and Adam's, whose will it be?"

"If betraying Adam, taking his life, was such an easy thing I would have done it myself. Look at me, Sullivan. You know how much I hate being this thing Adam turned me into. You know how I've struggled against it. I am not a woman of little reason or a mooing adolescent. I am not into being abused either mentally or physically and yet I want to survive. I've learned the rules. I know what it takes to live with Adam, to keep him off my back, what things make him flinch with guilt. I do what I must. So don't ask me that question if you don't want to hear the answer because I have no way of knowing whom I would chose, my husband or you. I hope I will never be faced with that test." Eve glared at Sullivan and marched away.

Sullivan stared after Eve. Something was not right; he'd sensed her nervousness. The anger seemed more an act than anything genuine. But she did have Adam's blood. Who knew what that would do to a person?

He closed his eyes, ignoring the stab of hurt. It had been different having Eve live with him, having someone to look after, having a friend.

Sullivan shook the feelings away. He'd known sooner or later her vampire nature would take over. Maybe that was the reason he hadn't wanted Eve to feed from a mortal. He'd wanted her to hang on to some part of her mortality for him. She'd been a symbol of hope. And Sullivan had not had any for over three hundred years, ever since Joanna's death.

He glanced in the direction Eve had gone and wondered how permanent anything was. After almost one thousand years Adam had found Eyanna again, so how permanent was death?

Sullivan walked into the lab and saw the same guilty nervousness in the face of the doctor that he'd seen in Eve. "What's going on?" Sullivan asked politely.

"Nothing."

The answer was a lie. Before the man had a chance to think of any way to further that lie, Sullivan was on him. "Are you testing your latest blood on Eve?"

"She asked me."

"Do you have any idea what Adam will do to you if he finds out?"

"He told us we're to obey her."

"Are you crazy?" Sullivan snarled. "Do you think he was angry with me for trying to overthrow him?" He shook his head. "You can't imagine what he will do to you if something happens to Eve."

Dr. Meah swallowed. "Eve ordered me. She wants to do this."

"How is she doing it? Surely she's not taking a chance on having you do it in here. Adam might come in. What are you doing?"

"She convinced me to invent a machine for her. It's sort of like an insulin pump. We modified it so that she can have continuous feedings if she needs them or she can just hook it up to the Picc-line I inserted and have a quick fix."

Sullivan grinned despite himself. "That's why she's looking so healthy."

"Yes."

He breathed a sigh of relief. So Eve had not turned completely. She was doing as she'd said.

"How can it work…I mean surely…that's great…" Sullivan couldn't help the fact that he was stammering. "Tell me how you're doing it." He watched as the vamp looked nervously around.

"Where is Adam?" Dr. Meah asked.

"Who knows? He could be here, or he could be anywhere. You're trying to hide something from Adam right under his nose in his own damn company. You're crazy. And Eve is going to bat those beautiful brown eyes of hers at you and get you killed."

"Calm down." Dr. Meah looked around the lab, listening with his vampiric senses, and for the first time it appeared, thinking of the danger he could possibly be in.

"Show me," Sullivan ordered and then watched in amazement as the doctor showed him the minuscule pump and the small cube sized bags of blood. "How does she keep the blood cool until she needs it?" he asked.

Questions and more questions. All answers just made for more questions. At the sight of the refrigerated bag that looked small enough to be concealed in a woman's makeup bag, Sullivan shook his head. "How long has she been using this?"

Dr. Meah shrugged his shoulders. "For a month now."

"No wonder she hasn't been asking me to transfuse her. I thought it was because Adam was giving transfusions to her." He shrugged. "What about the pills? I know she still has them. I've seen her with the pills."

"She carries them with her so Adam doesn't become suspicious and she dumps one out everyday. Then she returns it to the full bottle and…well, you get the drill."

"Yeah, you're right, I get the drill, and you're going to get the drill if anything happens to Eve."

"Nothing's going to happen. I've been monitoring her very closely. She's doing fine, mental alertness, everything. Even her strength has increased."

Sullivan thought of something else. "When did Eve tell you she was a vampire?"

"More than a month ago."

"Why?"

"We were talking and she just told me that she needed the pills and she wanted to be responsible for her own well being. She said she couldn't keep asking you to cover for her. I knew you had been taking extra pills. I had no idea they were for her. Why should I? I couldn't understand why she just didn't get them from Adam. But I didn't want any trouble with Adam, if I didn't do as she asked. I started giving her the pills and she started helping me in here. When she learned about the new formula I was working on, she wanted to try it."

Sullivan laughed aloud. Now he knew why Eve had stopped coming to him. He even understood why she was avoiding him. It wasn't because of any stupid orders from Adam, or that she no longer wanted to be friends. She was doing as she'd done since she'd become friends with him. She was trying to protect him.

Sullivan sure as hell hadn't believed that she was using a mortal for her blood supply, no way. Chances were she was trying to help Mark also.

That thought worried him. He needed to talk to Eve to warn her. There were many mortals so enamored with the vampire lifestyle that they longed to be turned. Many had formed weird clubs. He'd learned if any of the mortals hinted they wanted to leave the club they would be branded traitors and less scrupulous vampires soon made them disappear. There were a lot of things going on in the vampire world that Sullivan didn't approve of. But he couldn't control all of it. He did know that he didn't trust any of the mortals that wanted to be turned. He knew it was unwise for Eve to trust Mark. Sullivan knew Mark. Like most humans that hung around vampires, Mark wanted to be turned. Eve was playing a very dangerous game taking a mortal under her wing.

"Don't tell her that I know." Sullivan narrowed his eyes at Dr. Meah.

Confusion clouded the scientist's eyes and Sullivan frowned. "She may be beautiful, and you may have befriended her, but I can tell you now that if you tell her you will regret it."

Dr. Meah shoved past Sullivan. "I'm getting sick and tired of all of you, Adam, Eve and you. Do you forget that though I'm a scientist, I am also a vampire? I also have a vampire's nature."

"You're a scientist and vampire nature or not, violence is not in you."

"But you never…"

"I try to never use violence. But I have. I can and I will. If Eve wants to keep this a secret then you will do just that. You will keep it a secret and you'd better make sure to monitor her. The first sign it's harming her, you're to stop it immediately. I don't care what she says to you, or how fast she bats her pretty lashes at you."

"You sound like Adam. Are you in love with her?"

"She's my friend and I don't want her hurt. Besides, I'm doing you a favor by keeping you alive."

"I suppose you're going to blackmail me. You're going to tell Adam if I let on to Eve that you know."

Sullivan laughed for the first time ever, feeling what Adam must feel when he put fear into another being. "No, I will not tell Adam. I will take care of it myself."

He laughed again. Damn, it felt good. Since he'd taken that stroll into the sun a lot of things had changed. He had much to thank Eve for. For starters, he would continue looking out for her.

Sullivan walked from the lab. *What a world*, he thought. This was one of the best days of his immortal life. For some reason it pleased him that Eve was worried about him. Now he was going to go after her renewed friendship. He'd missed it and her.

❖

Eve felt a moment of hesitation. She missed Sullivan's friendship, having someone to talk over the things that were happening to her. She'd cut her family off completely and felt saddened that it had been easier than expected. With no siblings and her parents dead for several years Eve had only to worry about an uncle and a couple of cousins, none of whom ever called. As for her friends, the decision had already been made. She would drop out of their lives. Forever.

"Eve."

F.D. Davis

She turned, her hand twirling the newly replaced crystal necklace. It worked wonders on amplifying her powers and keeping others from probing her mind.

"Eve."

"Yes?"

"Would you go someplace with me? I want to talk with you."

"But, Sullivan, what about Adam…he…he…," Eve started to protest, then stopped. Why keep pretending. There was nothing between her and Adam. They barely spoke. From the moment he thought she'd taken Mark, he'd left her completely alone. She rarely saw Adam and for the first weeks she thought she wanted it that way.

But now she felt the pull of isolation. Mark was not the brightest light in the store. And he was constantly wanting her to bite him. He was proving more difficult than she'd expected.

There were many times Eve thought of just biting him and getting it over with. And if she were not having the constant infusions of blood she might have given into the desire.

But she had her safety net. She still had the desire but it wasn't that all encompassing need, the thought that if she didn't she would die. Now the sound of the ocean was more like the low murmur of a brook.

"Where are you?" Sullivan asked her.

"In my thoughts."

"Do you think you can come out of your thoughts long enough for us to have a private conversation?"

Eve glanced around.

"Please don't say Adam's name," Sullivan groaned.

Eve laughed, "Okay, Sullivan, just tell me the time and place."

"I was wondering if you would like to fly with me to Italy?"

"On a plane?"

"If you like."

"And if I don't?"

"Then I have other means."

"Tell me why I can't make myself disappear at will? Why I can't wish I were in Paris and be there?"

Sullivan smiled. "Would you be in Paris if you could?"

Eve stared at him for a long moment. "I think so. I would love to be able to think and be there."

"You can, you know. You just have to want to be someplace badly enough and poof, it happens. Don't worry, you'll get the hang of it. You're already coming along at an amazing rate. Until you learn how to bilocate, don't forget you have more conventional means of traveling and you won't have to deconstruct your atoms and reassemble them. Until then you have access to a private plane with a mortal pilot. You give the order and it's gassed up to go."

"How do—"

"Eve, you ask too many questions."

"How am I supposed to learn?"

"Everything is not necessary for your growth."

"You're keeping secrets."

Sullivan stopped smiling. "And you're not?" He was instantly aware the moment Eve began to shut him out, so he changed the direction of the things he wanted to say. "Yes, I never knew you had adjusted to this life. That's a tremendous secret to keep. It's not so bad, is it, given that we can't change it?"

"Well, I wouldn't go so far as that, but I have attempted to find my way."

"You're different, you're not afraid."

"What is there left to fear, Sullivan?" Eve said solemnly. "The worst has happened. What more can anyone do to me?"

"Why did you stop being my friend?"

"I thought it was better that you not be involved with me."

"Are you still fearing for my safety?"

Eve smiled.

"Don't worry about me, Eve."

"When you stop worrying about me, I'll stop worrying about you."

"I still want us to be friends," Sullivan said softly.

Eve could think of nothing to say, so she kept silent.

"Are you worried that I want more?" Sullivan asked.

"Yes, a little."

"The kiss?"

Eve peeked around Sullivan, a worried expression on her face.

"Don't look for Adam, he's not even in the country. Didn't you know that?"

"We don't do a lot of talking, not since I moved in with him." She ignored the curious look Sullivan was giving her.

"Before you ask, no, it doesn't bother me. I live with him because I want him to see every day what he's done to me. I want him to know and I spend his money because it's the only thing I can do." Her voice was hard, cold and clipped. She saw the way Sullivan winced as she talked, as though her words were somehow an insult to him.

"Sullivan, I want my life back." Eve looked at him. "I want to be human." She sighed and walked away. "I'll meet you in an hour outside the lab. I have a few things to do, then I need to talk with Dr. Meah for a couple of seconds."

"If there's something you need to pick up from the lab I'm going that way, I can get it for you."

For a moment their eyes met and held and Eve was aware that Sullivan either knew or was suspicious. She decided to go with suspicious. If he didn't ask she wasn't going to tell.

"Where do you want to meet?"

"How about my home? We can talk there and if your husband decides to join you, he will do that no matter where we are."

"He hasn't barged in on me in some time now."

"That's because you haven't been with me." Sullivan laughed. "I'll see you in an hour at my house."

❖

Adam stood in front of the Vatican for the longest time. He looked at nothing and no one before the priest caught his eye. The black robed figured marched by him as if he were not there, making Adam wonder if he'd gone invisible, but he hadn't. As he wondered what he was doing in Italy, the words "serving penance" drummed through him. Indeed, that was what he was doing.

Luckily he had no real feeding needs for he was afraid that in the state he'd been in for the past three months he would not be able to stop himself from draining his victim. He'd come close the last time, the night Eve had fed on Mark.

At first he had been unable to believe it, his skittish Eve drinking the blood she so needed to live, choosing instead to take her nourishment through IVs. But she had surprised him. The evidence of her feasting was in her bed. And Mark had not wanted anything to do with another vampire since Eve.

She was that good. Mark had a look of pure adoration on his face when he spoke of her and in Eve's eyes Adam had seen the loathing and self-hatred. How could he continue staying with her knowing she hated him?

One by one Adam walked up the steps of the Vatican. He'd requested an audience with the Pope but had been told the pontiff was booked solid. He'd thought of using a little mind control but decided against it. What could the man possibly tell him that Adam didn't already know, that not only was his soul condemned but that he'd forced Eve's to become condemned as well.

He felt the pull in his groin as his flesh jerked. Why could he so easily lengthen and harden when he was thousands of miles from Eve and thinking about her, but when near her only revulsion claimed him. That wasn't quite true. There had been times he'd become aroused in Eve's presence, times he'd actually thought he could relent and make love to her as he wanted. But nature won out each time.

A long weary sigh slipped out, for he knew the answer. The fangs and the intense mating need for blood during the act. That knowledge always took him back to Tarasha and Eyanna and his betrayal of his wife. As hard as he was working on getting over it, his vow had been a part of him for a thousand years. Hopefully it wouldn't take a thousand years for him to let it go.

Having climbed the last stair Adam now stood at the top and looked around St. Peter's square from his higher vantage point. A distant ache filled him, a long forgotten one, making him swallow his lifetimes of disappointment. His feet moved toward the massive doors and without wanting or meaning to, Adam was gliding, blood tears staining his cheeks. *Stop*, he commanded his body, *walk like a mortal man.*

Adam walked into the building, dipped a handkerchief in a fount and washed the red stains from his skin. He made his way through the onlookers, paying little attention to the ornate statues or the gold that lined every nook and cranny of the place. Enough gold, Adam thought, that the entire world could be fed if the gold were melted down and the money used to feed the hungry.

He looked around as he always did when he visited. He sent forth a small charge of energy toward the man bowed behind Adam's favorite kneeler. As he made his way there the man looked toward Adam, crossed himself and hurried away.

The power of prayer, Adam thought. The man had glimpsed who and what he was. In an hour or so Adam could sit across from him having lunch and the man would find nothing amiss. This building seemed to provide something akin to insight to those in prayer. Several of Adam's colleagues had warned Adam from constantly going into the building to challenge those inside. But it didn't worry Adam that occasionally his essence was glimpsed. Who would ever believe the ranting?

Adam knelt down and laughed softly. What negative comment could anyone make concerning him, especially since he himself knelt in prayer? Only Adam didn't pray, at least not in the usual sense. No, he always used this time for reflection, to keep alive a part of himself that he'd lost. Here in this building he let down his guard and his hatred for the church. Here the bigotry that had been shown toward Eyanna and her natural gifts receded, as well as false witness against Adam. The charge that he was a willing participant in Eyanna's supposed unholy doings had been the catalyst for Adam being cast out the church as priest. But here in this place, for a few moments it could be forgotten.

As always, Adam's mind turned toward Eve, Eve, the woman he'd loved more than life itself. He'd proven that for a thousand years. Eve, the woman who'd begged him to make love to her, who'd given him more than a glimpse of his soul. Eve, the wife who had redeemed him for a short time, and Eve the woman he'd turned into a vampire.

He shuddered deep in his soul for the wrong he'd done her, not her turning, but the fact that he'd failed her afterward. He should have been there for Eve, to help her overcome her fears, to teach her, to love her. He should be there with her now. He loved her and he'd left her at the mercy of... Adam's eyes opened. *Sullivan*. He'd almost forgotten Sullivan desired his wife.

"Eve." Adam tried to reach her, knowing it wouldn't work unless he used force. She'd long ago shut her mind off from him. "Eve," he tried again. "I do love you and one day soon I will show you that." Adam finished up and walked out, glancing one last time at the opulence. He laughed softly and moved his finger just the tinniest bit, aiming it at one of the golden figurines and melting it where it stood. *Hmm that felt good.* A sigh of satisfaction filled his chest and he made his way toward the door, lasering one of the founts of holy water and making it boil. This time real laughter fell from his lips as parishioners ran and chaos ensued. *This was a good day's work*, Adam thought and walked out of the doors. He didn't feel up to doing the tourist thing today, though a couple of bottles of wine made by the brothers would have been a treat. He decided he would get some later. Maybe he'd come back tomorrow. Maybe he'd find another artifact he wanted to destroy.

"So, Adam, how did it go this time?"

Adam looked at the vampire and smiled. If he had a friend, Evan was it. "I had one man look at me and make the sign of the cross. Oh, and I caused a little ruckus."

Evan laughed. "You do enjoy taking risks, don't you?"

"What risks?"

"A little ruckus, Adam? We both know the kind of damage you're capable of when you create a little ruckus. And what about the man you allowed to sense you?"

"It's not as though the man can harm me, now is it? Do you think I will allow anyone to keep me from where I want to be?"

"No one except yourself," Evan replied.

Adam glared at his friend, his meaning evident. "I am not here hiding, I'm here to visit."

"Right."

"Don't push it."

"Adam, we've been friends now for five hundred years. Were it not for you I would be cowering in the dark instead of living in the light. Were it not for you I would have never thought of amassing a fortune, picking up other skills along the way, I might add. But unlike the mortals you challenge, there is nothing you can do to me."

Adam cocked his head at his friend. "Do you think your powers match my own?"

"Are we going to get into our usual pissing contest?"

Adam grinned.

"Grow up. You want to challenge me to make yourself forget her. Why? She's all you've talked about for five hundred years."

"Sorry I've bored you."

Evan grinned. "You know it's not that but… Adam, you found her. Why are you here with me instead of with her? Surely if she loves you, you can find a way. My wife is mortal, so are my children."

"Children."

"Yes, children, in vitro. It's been way too long my friend." Evan gazed at his friend. "I haven't seen you in twelve years. I've been married ten years. I have two sons, seven and five."

"Does your wife know?"

"She knows I worship her and our boys. She knows I will never allow anything or anyone to harm them."

"How do you explain the fact that you don't age?"

"I don't."

"How do you manage to not bleed her out when you make love to her?"

"I feed before I touch my wife." He smiled a little to himself. "There have been occasions when I couldn't help myself and my fangs sank into her flesh and I tasted her sweet nectar but I always stopped."

"What if you couldn't? What if one day you went all the way? What if you drained her and then gave her your blood?"

"Then she would be a vampire and I would never allow that to happen."

"What if it were an accident?"

"I'd stake her."

"Just like that?"

"Just like that."

"What would you do if she were dying? Would you turn her to keep her with you?"

Evan looked appalled that Adam could even think to ask such a question. "Of course not. I would let her die. This is not the first mortal woman I've loved and married."

"How did I not know?"

"Adam, you knew."

Adam blinked and stared at Evan. "It doesn't matter what I knew before. I'm talking about your wife now. And I know I've never known you to have children. So just answer the question. Tell me what you would do to keep your wife by your side."

"I'd do nothing. What would you have me do? Condemn her to the life we lead, have her hunt fresh blood, all the while pretending to ourselves and to those around that we've evolved." Evan stopped short. "Adam, what have you done? Why are you here?"

Silence.

"Adam."

"Eve was dying."

"*Was dying*? Adam, what did you do?"

Adam turned away. "What do you think? I'm not you. You've loved many vampiric women and mortals alike. I've had no one."

"Not because they didn't want you. Women have always flocked to you."

"And I have never wanted them."

"Adam." Evan's voice was quaking with anger and disbelief. "Surely you didn't turn her?"

"Did you think I could stand by and see her die again?"

Evan groaned. "You should have."

"I couldn't."

"Now what?"

"I can't touch her. The thought of making love to her..." A shiver traveled the length of Adam's spine and back.

"Why, Adam? It's not as though there's anything physically keeping you from it. It's your vow. You made it, you can break it."

"I tried. I've held her in my arms. I've wanted her so badly that I thought I would burst from the wanting. I even became aroused."

"What happened?"

"What do you think happened? She's a fledging. She wanted me, wanted to have my blood as we mated. I tried. I really tried. I kissed her and felt the sharpness of her fangs. My thoughts went to Tarasha and I couldn't continue. As much as I wanted to make love to my wife I looked at her and remembered, And all I could see was that bitch that turned me."

"So, you turned her and then abandoned her?"

"I didn't abandon her. I remarried her. She lives in my home, works in my company. She's well cared for."

"You abandoned her, Adam. Did she know what you were before you took it upon yourself to play God? I don't believe you. I've heard rumors of what you were up to. No wonder your underlings seek to destroy you. You're impossible."

Adam had no answer.

"Answer me," Evan roared.

"You know you're one of the few people who could get away with talking to me in that manner."

"We're not playing any silly macho games. Yes, you can kick my ass but not without receiving an ass whipping in the process. My powers are nearly equal to yours, but at the moment that's not the point. Did the woman you've been mourning for a thousand years know what you are?"

"Yes."

"Did she love you, Adam?"

"Yes."

"And you did this to her?" Evan spat disgustedly.

"I couldn't save her before. I had the power to save her this time. I couldn't just let her die."

"And now what have you left her to do?"

"I've taught her how to take care of herself, how to feed. She has a human companion." Adam spoke softly. "And I've given orders that Eve is to be obeyed, that no harm is to come to her."

Evan eyed Adam thoughtfully. "Do you think that's all that she needs?"

"She hates me."

"Do you hate her, Adam?"

"I hate what she is."

"That's crazy, you made her into that."

"Don't you think I know it? Don't you think it kills me every time I look at her?"

For the first time since Adam had told his secret, his friend looked away, the smirk evident on his face. "So, that's why you're here? Frankenstein can not stand to look upon the face of his own monster. You hate her."

A shudder so deep that he shook in his seat ran through Adam, snaking up his spine, bending him as he'd never been and he moaned. The shame washed over him, the self-hatred, and the blood tears managed to squeeze past his tightly closed lids.

His hands twisted in his locs. Though not wanting to, he was finally able to speak the truth to someone.

"Some part of me hates her, but the greater part of me…" He trembled. "I love her, I'll always love her."

"If you had it to do over, if she were dying, would you intervene?"

"I know you think I should say no, but I can't say that. I don't think I could allow her to cease existing."

"Then you haven't learned your lesson."

"My lesson? What do you know about my lesson?"

"You think just because you were a priest you have all the answers. You don't."

"Well, I do in this case."

"How long has it been?"

"Six months."

"Six months? For six months you've allowed her to believe you didn't love her, that you couldn't stand the touch of her?" Evan whistled. "If she didn't hate you before, she does now."

"I'm going to make it right."

"How?"

"I'm going to get used to the touch of our women. I have to," Adam continued softly.

"You're sick, Adam, you need serious therapy."

"Have you heard of any of our kind practicing?"

"Matter of fact I have. We're into everything now."

"I don't need therapy." Adam laughed. "I know what I'm going to do. I'm going to bed so many vampiric women that it will be easy to make love to my wife."

"Has it worked so far?"

"No, I haven't been able to go through with it. But I'm determined to stay away from Eve until I can either hide my feelings or until it no longer matters."

"How long have you been away?"

"Three months."

"You haven't contacted her in three months?"

"No."

"And still you don't think you've abandoned her?"

"I left because I was hurting her. I'll return when I won't."

"By then it may no longer matter. Do you listen in on her thoughts, visit her dreams?"

"No, what's the use?"

"And you say you love her?"

"I love her."

"Who's looking out for her while you're away?"

"Sullivan," Adam said and waited for Evan's reaction.

"Sullivan. Wasn't he the one who led the rebellion, the same vampire who has hated you for centuries?"

"He doesn't hate me."

"But he is your enemy."

"Yes, and I believe in keeping my enemies close."

"With the history between you and Sullivan, you're taking an awful chance. He blames you for Joanna."

"Don't you think I know that?"

Evan sighed nosily, disgusted with Adam. "You could have cleared the entire matter up three centuries ago if you had only told Sullivan the truth."

"Do you think he wanted to hear the truth, Evan? He loved her, it was easier to blame me for her demise. That way he could carry the belief that she loved him."

"The ever noble Adam. Why don't you ever show this side to people, to Eve? It would make your life a hell of a lot safer."

"Safe is not what I'm after."

"I'm afraid what you're after you're not going to achieve. The vampires are too afraid to grant you your wish."

Adam stared at his friend, now the great philosopher. He'd saved Italy for last to see his one true friend who wouldn't bullshit him. "And why don't you tell me what my wish is."

"You're hoping that someone finds a way to kill you, the great Adam, and put you out of your misery."

Adam cringed. "That's nonsense."

"But true nevertheless. You're no more happy with your life than any of us."

"You're happy."

"I'm happy for now. Do you know how many people I've buried, how many women I've loved? And Adam, you aren't the only vampire who's been tempted; you're just the only one selfish enough to do what you did. And now you don't have the balls necessary to live with your decision. Do you know what you need, Adam? A slap upside your head would stop all of your melodramatic whining. Where the hell is the bad ass Adam? Snap out of it."

"You want to be the one to try and slap me upside my head in the mood I'm in?" After a moment of silence, Adam smirked, "I didn't think so."

"No, I won't attempt to touch you in the mood you're in. Just like your *little* ruckus in the Vatican, you're looking for an excuse to let off steam. I'm not going to give it to you. My words still stand. You damned her soul and you left her. You are one cold-hearted bastard."

In a swirl Evan was gone. Adam couldn't believe it. They'd never lied to each other and nothing Adam had done in five centuries had caused such a reaction. *Cold-hearted*? Evan had no idea what his being away from Eve was costing him. No, cold-hearted would be the last adjective Adam would use to describe himself. He thought of his vampire car left in the States and wondered if Eve was using it. He wished he had it now, but he didn't. Now he had to travel strictly on vampiric power.

In a swirl of mist Adam was gone as quickly as Evan. He would find what he needed on his own. He opened his mind and listened for the call of the vampires who dwelled in Rome. He wasn't disappointed. He heard them and followed the sound.

Chapter 12

"Adam, it's been a long time."

"Melvina, you're right. I thought you were...well, never mind what I thought. It's nice to se you."

"You do know this is a restricted club, don't you?"

Adam arched his brow without answering.

"There are no mortals here, Adam."

"Who said I was looking for one?"

"You didn't have to. We all know your tastes and we've given up trying to win your heart." Melvina laughed, "However, we have heard impossible news about you. There have been rumors that someone has finally won your heart."

"Rumors shouldn't be listened to." He stroked her arms.

Melvina's eyes went cold and she pulled back. "What do you want here?"

"To be among my own kind."

"Since when?"

"Are you saying you don't want me here?" Adam bristled. He was getting annoyed at the shabby treatment he was receiving. In the past year it seemed all vampires he knew had gotten considerably braver.

"It has nothing to do with bravery."

Adam couldn't believe he'd left himself open to be read so easily. A fledgling learned to avoid that straight away. Look at Eve. He'd been unable to read her for months.

"Who's Eve?"

Adam's hand clutched Melvina's wrist. "You will not enter my mind unless you're invited."

"You were open. I assumed it was an invitation."

"It wasn't." Adam frowned and his lips curled into a sneer. "I asked you a question. Am I not welcome here?"

"Did you come to start trouble?"

"Why would you ask that?"

"Because every time you grace us with your presence, something happens."

"I've never been here before."

"You know what I mean. We get a new meeting place and you show up and make it uncomfortable for everyone. No one comes back and the place closes down. Is that what you're after? I hear you're now richer than God. Why the hell can't you leave the rest of us alone? We're trying to survive, same as you."

Adam winced. Was he really the monster everyone thought he was? He shook his head. "Melvina, I didn't come here to start trouble. I came to be around my own kind, like I said."

"You're not looking for a woman to bed or to feed from?"

"Yes."

"Then you've come to the wrong place."

"No, I've come to the right place." Adam watched as Melvina's eyes narrowed.

"What's going on, Adam?"

"Nothing much." He grinned and reached to touch her again. "I had forgotten how beautiful you are. Sit and have a drink with me."

❖

Several hours later Adam had convinced Melvina to allow him to accompany her home and to share her bed. She was beautiful to look at, he thought, as she pulled the gown away from her flesh. He observed her breasts in all of their vampiric perfection, nibbles long and brown, hard with desire. His hand reached out to tweak them. He smiled as she arched her back, forcing her breasts into a more prominent position in his hands. Her moan of satisfaction drilled through his body and he moved to take her breast in his mouth.

His mind was closed to her. Adam thought of Eve. He would do this for his wife. He would make love to Melvina and he would find others until finally it was done. He would force himself to hunger for the touch of women of his kind. And when his desire became a burning need, he would return home to his wife and he would claim her.

If only he'd kept his eyes closed. If only he'd been able to make himself not see the fangs descend from Melvina's mouth, the incisors growing in length as she prepared to sink them into his flesh. He saw a spot of red drool around the corner of Melvina's lips. She was salivating with lust. The sight of the blood turned Adam stone cold. He could not sleep with her.

"Melvina, wait," he said, rising on one arm and leaning back on his elbow. "I rushed into this. I can't do this, I've changed my mind."

"Changed your mind?" Melvina panted. "What kind of game are you playing, Adam? You asked me, no, you begged me to allow you to come home with me. You knew I wanted to make love to you. I've always wanted you and now that you have me hot, you want me to do what, put my clothes back on?"

"If you don't mind."

"I do mind, you bastard." Melvina raked her nails across Adam's face, drawing blood. Then she fell on his chest and sank her fangs into his neck.

For a micro-second Adam was stunned, surprised at the violence in Melvina. Things had changed since he'd last seen her. As her sharp fangs pierced his skin he howled, more in anger than pain.

"What the hell do you think you're doing?" He flung Melvina away only to have her pounce on him several more times.

"Melvina, if you don't stop I'm going to slap you so hard you will sleep for a week." That stopped her. His voice held no emotion; it was flat and deadly serious. That was why people called him a cold-hearted bastard. He spoke the truth. That shouldn't have labeled him as cold but apparently it had.

"You have no feelings, do you, Adam? None whatsoever."

"I have feelings, Melvina, and what I'm feeling at the moment is that you're crazy if you think you can continue hitting me and not pay the consequences.

Melvina backed even farther away. "Why did you come to the club, Adam? The truth this time," she barked.

"I wanted to see if I could go through with it."

"Go through with it?"

"I wanted to try and make love to a vampiric woman."

"You were using me for some experiment?"

"Yes," Adam said calmly, watching Melvina closely. "Don't get any more ideas of hitting me. You asked for the truth and I'm telling you. What's wrong with everyone lately? You're a vampire, Melvina. Why are you behaving like a love struck mortal?"

"Because, unlike you, I do have feelings."

"Are you saying you're in love with me?" Adam frowned, narrowing his eyes at the vamp. "Since when?"

"Try for the last hundred years."

"Why?"

"Like you said, I must be crazy."

"Melvina, I've never given you any reason to think that your feelings were reciprocated."

"Do you think a person stops loving because the feelings aren't returned?"

His thoughts flew to Eve and he cringed inwardly, wondering if what Melvina was saying was true. Could it be possible that Eve still loved him after everything he'd done to her? But now wasn't the time to reflect on Eve. Melvina had a dangerous glint in her eyes and a woman scorned was nothing to play with. A vamp scorned was risking suicide. As it was, Melvina had pulled a surprise attack, knowing that Adam would think nothing about ending her stint as a vamp. Yet she'd done it just the same.

"Well, Adam, answer me," Melvina shrieked.

"They should," Adam said finally. "It's no fun to not have your love returned, it's painful. We're vampires, Melvina, not mortals." The last he said softly, wishing he'd not caused her pain. That had not been his intention. He'd only wanted to find a way to make love to Eve.

"I can see in your eyes that you're thinking of this woman. You got so angry when I spoke her name, as though I'm not good enough even for that. Eve," Melvina said boldly. "Tell me, Adam, is that the reason you've never allowed anyone to love you? You've been waiting for her, Eve, your unrequited love?"

"My love was never unrequited."

"Then what brought you here to my bed?"

"I told you I wanted to get over my…" He stopped, wondering if he should try to be gentle.

A cackle filled the air. "Are you going to try and spare my feelings after all?"

"I didn't intentionally hurt you, Melvina."

"Yet you did."

"I didn't lie. I do think you're beautiful and if I could desire vampiric women, you would definitely top that list."

"Gee, thanks."

"Now you're being sarcastic. I was attempting to pay you a compliment."

"Adam, why don't you get the hell out of here and allow me to sleep. My body is feeling heavy. I need to sleep and I don't want to do it with you here."

"I'm sorry, Melvina," Adam said, attempting to apologize.

"No, you're not, but you will be. You willingly came here to use me for your sick little experiment. When I wake I will spread the word. You will not bed any of our kind. The word will be out. Don't even try it. I was not the one for you to toy with, Adam. I truly hope you rot in hell."

"I'm sure I will, but I'm also certain you will be there beside me, rotting as well." Adam gave Melvina one more glance before he vanished into the mist.

❖

Adam lounged with Evan. Melvina had held true to her word. Now not only would the women not come near him but the male vampires bristled as well, taking Adam's actions as an insult to all the females. And in reality it was.

"What the hell am I suppose to do now?"

"You're asking me?" Evan laughed.

"You're the only person left here who's speaking to me."

"So what are you going to do?"

"There is no reason to remain here any longer. I found what I came for."

"And that is?"

"I can't make love to my wife. I tried. If Melvina did nothing to fire my jets, then I don't think anyone can."

"But you don't love Melvina."

"No, I don't."

"Then why don't you try and work out your problems at home with your wife, where you belong?"

Adam sighed. "Because I do love her, and I will not put her through the same things I put Melvina through."

"Then tell her, Adam. Tell her that it's no fault of hers that she has fangs, that she now requires blood with her loving."

Adam cringed as Evan's words hit home. "I didn't ask for sarcasm. If you have any genuine ideas I'm ready to hear them."

"There is one thing left to do, Adam. Tell her everything about Tarasha, how she made you feel. Tell her that you've transferred your hatred for Tarasha to all female vamps. She may very well understand."

"I believe I have told her of Tarasha."

"Did you tell her that you'd not held out, that you'd succumbed to Tarasha, that you'd betrayed Eyanna, betrayed her love, your marriage?"

"I can't."

"Then tell her or lose her love forever."

"I think that's already happened. But you do have a point. I may owe her that much, just so she doesn't think it's her."

"So you're going home?"

"Not immediately, but I will soon."

"You can't hide from yourself, Adam, no matter where you go. Remember that."

"I've allowed bullshit and self pity to occupy my mind for far too long. That's not my way. That's not who I am. My wife has me behaving like some kind of unbalanced mortal. What's the word for it? Bi-polar? Yes, I believe Eve may very well have hexed me." Adam frowned as he thought of the possibility. "Eve is coming into some of her old powers. She could very well have done something to me." He smiled. "She's pissed enough to do it."

"Can you blame her?" Evan asked.

Adam smiled again. He had the first real need to taste blood that he'd had in months. All other feedings had been done mechanically. Tonight, he needed it.

"I need to feed." He looked at Evan. "I'll see you later."

"It's been awhile since I fed. Maybe we could do it together," Evan offered.

"Are you attempting to baby-sit me?"

"Call it what you will, but I'm still a vampire, Adam. In order to keep my mortal wife alive and well, I must feed same as you. So why don't we do it together same as we did in the old days."

Adam grinned. "Except unlike the old days, this time we will ask permission." Both vampires laughed as they took off into the night to feed their hunger, to forget their pain, to pay heed to their nature.

Chapter 13

If he thought he'd been lonely for the past ten centuries, he was desolate now. Love was so close. The irony wasn't lost on Adam. The power of his mind was linked to his belief in himself, his speaking the truth, keeping his promise to himself, no matter the cost. For a thousand years Adam had not found the ultimate sexual pleasure that existed for those of his kind. As much as he might want to change now, it appeared he was unable to. His little experiment hadn't worked. Reverse aversion therapy, he called it. Well, he'd been gone from Eve for four months and his love had proven a constant ache in his heart.

Still, when he'd glimpsed her, Adam hadn't gone to Eve as he'd wanted to do. Instead, he'd materialized in the house unannounced, and now stood watching her as she kept her back turned away from him. Even if Eve didn't want to admit it, she had to have known he was there. Adam's blood would have conveyed that much.

Studying Eve, Adam noted the circle of crystals. He narrowed his eyes and frowned when he saw the sea salt. What the hell was Eve up to? He took another look around the room, saw books spread out over the counters, the table and the floor. He picked up a book with a black covering and the sign of a pentagram. *What the hell*, he thought again. A witchcraft bible? In his home? Had Eve gone insane? This was sacrilegious.

❖

Eve kept her guard up as she'd done for the past seven months. She'd been even more vigilant in the four months Adam had been gone, never knowing when he would return and find her not feeding on Mark but inserting one of the compact bags of blood into her pump.

Now he was back. She could feel his eyes on the back of her head. What did he expect, that she would rush into his arms so he could push her away?

Her blood sizzled in her veins at the realization that she was glad he was back. She wanted to look at him, to see the quick flash of love he always had for her before he masked it. She shuddered. This was stupid. She would not be a fool for his love, not as she'd been when a mortal. She was stronger now; it was time she started behaving like it. She was a vampire and if she couldn't do anything else, she could at least present a cold exterior to him.

Eve took a deep breath, then turned to face him. She looked into his eyes. Neither said a word. Eve moved toward the door, grateful that she actually had somewhere to go. Nighttime, hunting time, a time for her vampiric nature to be at its best. At least that was what Adam would think. In truth, she was going to hear a psychic give a lecture on harnessing one's psychic powers.

Adam spoke at last. He took a step toward the circle of crystals and held out the witch's bible toward her. "What the hell are you doing with this?"

"I'm reading it. Don't cross my circle. It's consecrated."

"For what?"

"For magic, what else?" Eve stared at him.

"A vampiric witch," Adam laughed. "Have you put a spell on me, Eve?"

This time it was Eve who laughed. "If I did it's not working very well. You're back."

"Touché, wife. You look well."

That stopped her. *I look well. To hell with him.* "Do I look well for a vampire, or for a mortal, Adam?" She saw the pain fill his violet eyes and changed her mind about leaving. There was some part of him that still felt and she wanted to make him hurt. She wanted to scream at him, to rant and rave, to ask him where the hell he'd been for the past four months.

"Why did you come back?"

"It was time."

Eve blinked. "Time for what?" She could barely remember a year ago when she would have given anything for Adam to be gone from her life. It seemed every time that she'd begun to heal he'd popped back up. This time she would not give Adam power over her. This time she would take it back.

She waited for him to speak, her hands clutched in the pockets of the long black coat she was wearing. Her nails poked into the material of the coat, growing longer. The hotness called to her as the blood flowed to her eyes, covering the brown with red. There was nothing she could do about either thing. Those physical changes were now a part of her, a part of her nature.

"Look what you've done to me," Eve said quietly. "You've turned me into a monster, Adam, and then you leave because you can't stand the sight of what you've done." Tears ran unabated down her cheeks. Nothing inside her could keep them from falling. It was as though someone had struck her with a red-hot poker.

"You're right," Adam said softly, going to her, reaching out to her.

"I…I…" She couldn't help the stutter. She'd expected Adam to argue with her, tell her she was wrong, but he hadn't done that.

"I should never have left you alone. I made you and you're my responsibility. I love you and even if I didn't you would still be my responsibility. Eve." He drew her to him with the sound of his voice. His gaze held her. "Tell me truthfully, wife, did you miss me?"

"No."

"No?"

"No," Eve repeated for the second time.

"I missed you," Adam continued. "I missed you every second of every day. You were not from my thoughts for even a second." He reached his hand out to touch Eve, cringing when she moved back. He moved closer. "It's not you, Eve."

"What," she asked blinking, "what isn't me?"

"My not making love to you. It's not you. I told you long ago that I don't like vampire women."

"Then why did you make me one? I begged you not to. I loved you so much, Adam. Why couldn't you let my love be enough?"

Adam moaned, crushing Eve to him. He could kill without thinking, torture with glee, but this damn woman was his weakness. She was making him insane, making him go against everything that made him who he was. He trailed his hands over her body. Each touch of her flesh sent flames of desire licking through his veins. They ignited and started a burn in his groin; his flesh jerked.

He couldn't believe it; knowing what she was, what would happen when they mated, he was once again aroused. His erection jutted outward, fueled by his needing to have her, to be inside her, inside her wetness, her hotness. He remembered the feel of her flesh against his own. Adam held Eve tighter, tremors of desire moving from him into her. He felt her tremble, then the slight hesitation as her arms wrapped around him. He heard her pull in a short breath and he tasted her regret.

"I'm not going to hurt you, baby. I just want to hold you and remember how good it was. Holding you like this, all I can think about is the night we made love." Adam dropped a kiss on her forehead. "You remember, too, Eve, don't lie. The way our bodies blended, the way your muscles contracted to keep me inside you."

He sighed heavy and deep as remembered heat bathed the two of them. He remembered the taste of her juices on his tongue and he wanted it and her right now. As his hand moved forward to her breast, he felt a hard object in her bra and felt her moan of desire slip. He caught it in her mind, the fear that he'd found out, but found out what?

If he could, Adam would have ignored the secret. For the first time he was holding Eve for longer than a second, fully aware where their vampire nature would take them, and with every intention to allow it. But now it was she pushing him away. He glared at her for a moment and pulled her back, relenting when she jerked away, nearly falling in her haste.

Adam moved away, not wanting this one moment of love between them to turn into something else. And if he stood too close to Eve, he would rip away her clothing and find the secret she was hiding.

"What do you have beneath your clothes?" he asked when he was sure he would be able to take what would undoubtedly be a flippant answer.

"What I have beneath my clothes is between me and the man I make love with."

He smiled. Flippant, just as he'd expected. "You're making love to someone?"

"That's none of your concern."

"You're my wife."

"But not your property."

"Now on that you're wrong. You are my property." Adam smiled, sensing the nervousness in Eve. For a moment it had been her pain he'd sensed. Now whatever she was hiding had blotted out the pain. It had to be an awfully big secret.

"Are you hiding something from me?" He allowed his eyes to rake over her body. "I can find out, you know. It wouldn't be that hard." He watched as Eve slowly buttoned the coat she was wearing, the better to conceal whatever it was that lay beneath. She was doing her best to ignore him.

"Where's Mark?" he asked.

"How should I know?"

"Isn't he your consort?"

"My consort or my..." Eve cocked her head. "What is he to me, Adam, my servant, my lover, my meal?" She watched as he flinched. "Who's your consort, Adam? Is that where you've been, visiting her?" Too late she regretted her last words. She would have rather cut out her tongue than spoken them.

"You have no reason to be jealous; you are the only one that I love. It has been that way for me too long for it to be any other."

"And yet..." This time the words didn't come out. Eve swallowed, knowing he was aware of her unspoken words.

"Eve."

"Don't, Adam, it's just your presence. I don't care, really."

"I thought you hated me."

"You're right, I do."

Adam smiled for the first time in months, feeling the joy wash through him. Eve wanted to hate him and in many ways she did, but he had looked deep into her eyes and into her heart. The love was still there.

"Would you like to know what I've been doing?" he asked, smiling at her. No answer.

"I've been visiting the beds of vampiric women." He saw her flinch, just barely, and continued. "Since the day I was made the hatred has been so deeply ingrained in my soul that it made me incapable of coupling with them." He brought her even closer, lifted her chin with a finger so that she could stare into his eyes and see the truth.

"I've never wanted to make love to a vampiric woman until you. Still, as much as I love you, as much as I remember our night of passion, as much as I wanted to make love to you, I couldn't forget the day I was made."

He touched a hand to her wrist, lightly trailing a fingernail down her hand. "I wanted to be with you." He trailed his hand back up her arm, felt her shiver, and it flowed into him, sending several electrical currents cascading down his back.

"I wanted to get over my aversion." He ignored the dangerous glint in Eve's eyes, ignored the red that was once again taking over. She was angry.

"I wanted to do this for you," Adam whispered softly. "I wanted to hold you in my arms again, to make love to you."

"I disgust you, Adam? You have an aversion to me? And you did what, tried aversion therapy? Tell me, did it work?" She glared through the red haze, placing her hands on her hips for effect.

"No. I couldn't make myself go through with it."

"What do you want from me, Adam?"

"I love you. I didn't love them, that's why it didn't work." Adam moved closer. "Don't be angry, Eve, work with me. In spite of everything, I know you love me. I want to try. Let me sleep in your bed."

"You want to try and see if you can stand the sight of me, the touch of my flesh against your own? Go to hell, Adam," Eve said as her hand slapped him across the face. With all the vampiric strength in her she slapped him again, this time sending him crashing into the wall.

"I deserved that, Eve," Adam said, approaching her. "I deserve everything you want to do to me. But it still won't stop your knowing that I love you, that I need you. You're in my soul. You're part of me and I'm part of you." She reached to strike him again but this time he was faster. He caught her hand and pulled her hard against his body.

"Enough hitting, Eve, just let me love you. I could force you to submit if I wanted. We both know that but that's not what I want. I've never had to force a woman to accept my loving and I won't now, not with my own wife." He lifted her in his arms and allowed his tears to drip over her. Her head was nuzzled into his neck and she was moaning softly.

"Adam, you'd better not turn away from me."

"It will be okay, you'll see." He walked with her up the stairs toward his old bedroom, resisting the urge to just materialize there. Walking was slower, more time to keep her in his arms. "Don't cry, Eve," he crooned. "We're going to make it work. I promise you, we're going to have an eternity together. We're going to make one hell of a powerful vampire couple."

He had her on the vampire bed. Adam smiled at the bats decorating the bed, remembering Eve's reaction the first time she'd glimpsed the bed. Then he lay beside her. He sniffed the air for the scent of lemons, then stopped himself. It wasn't important. It didn't matter that she no longer exuded the scent. "I love you," he moaned sinking down, removing her coat. He still felt the hardness beneath it but ignored it. "Give yourself to me, Eve."

"If you turn from me again, Adam, it will be the last time."

"I'm not going to turn from you." He reached for her, pressed her against his body and kissed her, feeling her pain, taking it into himself, giving her all the love that was in him.

This was what he wanted, Eve, his wife, the woman he'd waited ten centuries to find.

He ran his tongue inside her mouth, searching, tasting. This was Eve. He felt the baby fangs, no more than a half inch or so but still fangs nonetheless. They would grow longer in time with more blood. He was surprised they weren't already longer.

He pushed the thought out of his mind, ran his tongue over the sharp enamel and felt the point of one fang. It pierced his tongue and his blood dropped into Eve's mouth. He felt her shudder as the drops went into her. Her arms came around him pulling him closer and he tried. By everything that was holy and unholy he tried. His muscles strained with his trying. "No," he screamed out. "No, please." Adam held Eve so tightly he could hear her whimpers of pain, of knowing. He reached out one hand and wrapped it around the massive bedpost willing his body and mind to remain in the bed with Eve, his grip on the bedpost inhuman. Damn it. He was Adam Omega, the most powerful vampire in the world. He could do this. He could do any damn thing he wanted. He could feel the blood oozing from his fingers as he fought to stay where he was.

"Adam," she whimpered.

"Eve, I can do this. I can." He shuddered hard, opened up his eyes and saw the sense of betrayal in his wife's eyes. "I can do this, Eve, it just might take a bit of time." She moaned and closed her eyes and just like that Eve was gone. Adam sat there in shock, wondering when she'd learned how. Then his blood begin to boil in anger, knowing to whom she'd gone. He opened his mouth and bellowed and a resounding clap of thunder answered him back. He lifted both arms above his head and brought them slowly down breathing out as he did so. Eve had better be damn glad that he intended to conquer his aversion to vampiric women or he would kill her, end it for her, do as she'd asked. He breathed deeply. Why kill her? She'd probably welcome that. No, he'd allow her to live. In the end he would control her. He never lost. He just had to hit upon the right combination.

❖

Eve's eyes closed and when she opened them she found herself in Sullivan's home. How? she wondered a second before Sullivan and his female companion spoke.

"Is she…?"

"No, she's not," Sullivan said, staring at Eve, then at the female vamp sitting beside him. "I brought her here," Sullivan stated, ignoring the disbelief in the woman's eyes.

"Why?" she asked him.

"Because I wanted her here."

"Are you looking for a threesome or did you bring her for us to feed from?"

The revulsion on Eve's face was almost enough to make Sullivan laugh out loud. "Neither," he said. "I have business to attend to with her. As for you, my dear, I'll call you later." He gave the woman a kiss on her forehead, ignoring the way her nails came out, and sent her on her way a moment before she could think of attacking Eve.

"Eve, how did you get here?" Sullivan asked, rising and going to her.

"I wanted to see you and," she shrugged her shoulders, "here I am."

"You've wanted to see me before and it never happened. You always called me to you. Why didn't you call me this time?"

"Sullivan, I don't know how it happened. I just…would you rather I leave?"

"Of course not." A big grin covered his face. "I'm flattered. I'd be even more so if you told me you were here because you only wanted to see me, that you have no immediate problems."

"I don't," Eve answered, "have any problems, I mean. I just suddenly wanted to be with you." She saw the look in Sullivan eyes change from warmth and friendship to something more, lust. She took a deep breath, not moving away from it or from him, knowing what was coming next and giving her tacit permission for it to happen.

He stood in front of her, his smile genuine, his fondness for her coming off him in waves.

"You look beautiful," Sullivan said, moving his hand to brush away a strand of hair. "You're trembling," he said softly. "Tell me to back away and I will."

Eve licked her lips, suddenly feeling very dry.

"I'm looking for more than a kiss, Eve."

"I know."

As she stood trembling, waiting for him to touch her, she saw that he was waiting for the same thing. She smiled broadly and leaned into him, bringing her arms upwards to wind around him. She felt his lips on hers.

"Are you sure?" Sullivan asked.

"I'm sure," Eve answered, giving him the permission that he wanted. His lips closed over hers and for a brief moment Eve wondered how different it would be to make love as a vampire. The last time she'd made love she'd been a mortal.

"Now I'll show you just how much better it is and how much you've been missing."

Why bother wondering how? Sullivan had read her closed mind. She wanted him to show her what she'd been missing. She was lonely and so was he. Maybe together they could help soothe each other's pain.

"Sullivan, I need a moment." Eve held her hand to her side. "I need to have some privacy."

She walked toward his bathroom to disconnect and stash the pump. She pulled her bracelet from her pocket and covered the tiny needle embedded in her vein. This was one secret she still intended to keep, even from Sullivan. Maybe it was a good thing that Adam had been unable to make love to her. With him, she'd never thought to disconnect the pump, to hide the Picc line with her bracelet.

When she came out she knew exactly how this night would end. It was what she wanted, what they both wanted. He kissed her and she gave in to the heat, the desire and hope she sensed in Sullivan. She took in a breath and before she could release it she found herself lying in Sullivan's arms, in his bed, his breathing rapid, his eyes changing with the lust that had quickly filled him.

Eve clung to Sullivan, accepting his lovemaking, making love to him in return, realizing that in everything Sullivan had not exaggerated. *What a rush*, she thought, a thousand times better than making love as a mortal, with only one possible exception. *Making love with Adam.* Eve shivered in Sullivan's heated embrace. She would not think about it now. Adam would not enter her thoughts.

Before she knew what was happening she felt fangs piercing her skin and cried out. "No, Sullivan, please don't." He shuddered twice. She felt the steel in him as his incisors nipped away at her flesh, felt the battle going on inside him. He rocked back and forth for what seemed forever.

"Eve," Sullivan groaned out, "this is part of making love. This is how we find our supreme release."

"Not like that, Sullivan, I can't do it like that." She thought of Adam. Please, Sullivan, not like that."

"Don't cry, Eve. I'll respect your wishes. I'll never do anything to hurt you.

I'm not, Adam." He slid more firmly into her wetness, going as deep as he could and then pushing farther, riding her hard, wanting to drive away any thoughts of Adam she might have had, wanting to open her heart to receive him. And this time when his fangs descended several inches, he drove into her, but sank his fangs into the thick pillow, sending himself images of blood flowing freely down his throat, tasting it and imagining tasting Eve.

Sullivan came with force that had been denied for longer than he cared to remember. He held her to him, felt her shudders, felt her pain, knew she was thinking of Adam and though sated, he pumped into her several more times, each time sending her images of himself, anything to wipe out any traces of Adam.

"I want you, Eve. I want you for tonight and every night."

At last he felt the pictures taking hold. Eve's body tensed and her mind was cleared of all thoughts but him. He recognized she'd given him this gift, this knowing that he was the one she was thinking about. And for that he was grateful.

"Sullivan," Eve cried out in pleasure, her vampire nails racking his back as electricity twisted her inside and pleasure consumed her. She screamed out from the pleasure and her body trembled. She was alive and for the first time in seven months she was happy.

With their release came an awakening. Eve didn't know exactly how to describe it, a rebirth, a freeing. She only knew that what she'd experienced with Sullivan was akin to something sacred. As Sullivan held her tightly to his body, the blood tears inexplicably ran down her cheeks and Eve held him even tighter.

"Who are you crying for?" Sullivan asked gently. "You or him?"

"I'm crying for him. He has no idea how it can be."

"Are you crying for yourself as well?"

"I suppose so. You asked me my feelings for Adam and I lied. I didn't mean to," Eve said, looking into Sullivan's blue eyes, running her fingers over his heated skin while the blood tears continued to run down her cheeks.

"I love him, Sullivan. I know now that I always will. Adam is a sickness with me. That's why I believe him, why I don't think my memories of being Eyanna were planted by him. They're too vivid, my connection with him too powerful. Where Adam is concerned all my emotions concerning him are a million times stronger than they've ever been. When I'm angry with him I feel as though I could kill him and not think twice about it. And when he touches me, no matter how angry I am, I melt. Our souls are connected, Sullivan. There is little I can do about that. I hope you understand."

"I do understand. I almost had that once with a woman I loved, but it was never quite what you describe, though I always wanted it to be. He smiled at Eve and placed tiny kisses around the corners of her mouth.

"He's back."

"I know."

"How?" Eve asked.

"It's just something that happens in time and with age. Whenever a powerful energy is anywhere in the vicinity, the older ones know." He rolled over. "Is that why you're here, to get even with him?" He cocked his head and looked at her, the desire still there, the wanting, the need.

"I didn't come here to use you to make Adam jealous. I didn't consciously think about doing this, just that I wished I were anywhere but with Adam. I hate myself for allowing him to keep hurting me. For months he's been gone and then he whizzes in and touches me and I melt. And I hated the effect he had on me. When the pain became too intense I thought of you. And then I wished I were with you. I've never been able to do it and didn't try then. It just happened. When I saw your smile I was happy that I was here."

"And now?"

She grinned.

"What about Adam?"

"He doesn't want me, Sullivan. He loves me and I love him, but he doesn't want me." She looked at him. "Do you?"

"Yes, he said roughly. "I want you."

He proceeded to show her just how much he wanted her, making love to her until the sun rose high in the sky. For once he was grateful to Adam, grateful for his aversion that had now brought Eve to his bed. He thought briefly of the hundreds of years he'd spent the daytime hours sleeping. Now he would spend the time making love to Eve in the light of day.

❖

Adam sat alone in his home feeling more human than he had since he'd become a vampire. Human emotions swirled through him—rage, jealousy and envy. He didn't know Eve had learned to bilocate but it took little thought to know where she'd gone.

He imagined her in Sullivan's embrace with him touching her in her most intimate places, Sullivan making love to his wife and her moaning Sullivan's name when she reached orgasm.

He thought of bursting in on them, killing them both. Only the memory of the look in Eve's eyes stopped him. He'd thought he was being noble telling her of his wants, his needs, his love for her. He didn't understand why she had become so angry or hurt when he'd confessed to his whereabouts. It wasn't as though he'd gone looking for love. He'd gone in search of…a cure.

He laughed to himself. Adam wanted to be able to touch Eve beyond a quick embrace or a kiss on her forehead. He wanted to make love to her as Sullivan was doing now. His fangs came down inch after inch and the red haze filled him, robbing him of his senses. *Find her.* The words vibrated through him, strumming his nerves. *Kill her. Kill him.*

If he found Eve in the state he was in now, he would kill her, there was no doubt. It wouldn't matter if he found her in Sullivan's bed or sitting across from him. Adam would kill her and Sullivan because of the images in his mind.

He growled low and then the sound rose on the wind, getting higher. He called her name. "Eve!" Adam shook, hating that she was attempting to keep him out. Until now he'd respected that, but he could cross any boundary she'd made against him. Didn't she know that?

He'd made her with his blood. She was a part of him now. Every breath she took he knew about, and now when he could smell the scent of her sex rising on the air, he was enraged. There was no doubt about what she was doing.

Focus, Adam, bring it down a notch, he scolded himself. He let out his frustrations as he exhaled then he looked around his home. In the months he'd been gone Eve had made many changes. He turned on the new computer that was taking up most of the space in the den. A new desk, he noted, turning on the computer. He quickly scanned the sites Eve was visiting. They all seemed to have something to do with magic, crystals, witchcraft. What the hell was she attempting? He opened several of her files. She was working on healing potions, it seemed. He smiled. So she was doing as she'd said, looking for a cure. Good luck, he thought wondering if she found a cure if he wouldn't still at some point bring her back to this vampiric life. He really didn't know but he doubted if he'd allow her to find a cure, live a short mortal life and die, not while he held the power of life and death in his hands. He'd more than likely turn her again.

Sounds of Eve's pleasure washed over Adam and he grunted. Eve had no idea how close she was coming to pushing him to the breaking point. But he wouldn't be the one to break. She would. He'd see to that.

This is your fault, Adam. He shook the words from his mind and went out in search of a mortal woman to make love to. He would forget his inadequacies with his wife in the flesh of a mortal.

And his wife would live another night.

❖

When they were sated Sullivan put his arm around Eve. "I'm exhausted," he said.

She grinned and said, "So am I."

"I need to feed."

"I need to sleep," Eve answered. "Do you mind if I stay here?"

Sullivan knew what Eve wanted was for him to leave so she could reattach her pump. That was fine, he had important things to take care of.

❖

Sullivan sat at the bar waiting, knowing it wouldn't be long. He tapped his cigarette against the pack, ignoring the looks of those around him. He was radiating energy, he knew, dangerous energy.

"So, you've bedded my wife?"

Sullivan ignored Adam's crude comment. "You came back."

"Obviously."

"Where were you?"

"I went to live among our kind," Adam said quietly.

"For what?" Sullivan asked, startled. "That makes no sense."

"I went for Eve. I love her."

The speech Sullivan had planned was forgotten. Once upon a time he and Adam had been friends. He breathed deeply. He had not made love to Eve in order to hurt Adam. No, he'd made love to Eve because he'd wanted her. He sat quietly, waiting for whatever Adam was going to say. What he got was Adam's hands around his throat, crushing his windpipe.

"Adam, listen to me," he sent the urgent message telepathically while trying to remove Adam's fingers from around his throat. "Killing me will not solve your problems. There will be others Eve will make love to if I'm not here. If you don't love her someone will. Stop this and let's talk." He felt Adam's fingers loosen and Sullivan rubbed his throat.

"She loves me no matter what she says."

"I know that, Adam, I'm not a fool. Besides, she admitted to me that she loves you still."

"Then why?"

"You hurt her."

"I could do a lot worse to both of you," Adam said matter of factly.

"I know that but you won't."

"Tell me, Sullivan, what makes you so cocky? What makes you think I will continue to be lenient with you?"

"You owe me."

"I don't owe you my wife."

"You owe me for Joanna."

"I didn't take Joanna from you; she came to me."

"And you killed her."

"That was centuries ago."

"I have not forgotten."

"Sullivan, that was an accident. I'd made love to tens of thousands of mortal women. I lost control. Since that night I've never allowed it to happen again."

"Do you think that makes up for it?"

"Of course not, but that's the reason. What did Eve do to you? You're going to hurt her to get even with me? I won't allow that. I've hurt her enough for the both of us. I won't allow you to hurt her also. Come on, admit it, you're simply using my wife to get back at me for Joanna."

"I care for Eve, I'm not using her."

"But you don't love her."

"Maybe not at this moment but I can easily grow to love her, Adam. All I ever needed was to know there was a possibility that she felt the same.

"She doesn't, she loves me."

"That can change. In fact, I think it already has begun."

"Why, because she had sex with you?"

Sullivan looked hard at Adam. "We made love."

"Are you looking for me to kill you, Sullivan? I owed it to Eve not to barge in and kill the both of you as you lay in bed. But hear me and hear me well. She is my wife, and I will not give her up to you. I will kill you and stuff your ashes in the deepest well I can find." He glared at Sullivan. "Maybe I'll feed you to dogs."

"Killing me won't be that easy, Adam. I now have someone to live for." He tapped the cigarette once more on the pack. "Suppose you tell me what sent her to me in the first place."

Adam frowned, sighed and slouched into a seat beside Sullivan. "That's none of your damn business."

"I'd say since your wife came to my bed that makes it my business."

Adam laughed and shook his head. "Please do something to me, Sullivan, hit me, anything, do something to justify my killing you right here and right now. You are trying my patience beyond belief. Why you're not dead is a mystery to me. I want you dead, Sullivan, do you understand that? You're doing everything to make me make that happen. And yet here we sit and you're trying to get me to unburden my soul. What the hell has happened in the last few months? Since when did vampires start to question my authority? Evidently I've been too lax. Perhaps you think I've gone soft. He smiled as he took hold of Sullivan's heart and twisted. He felt Sullivan's erratic heartbeat and twisted some more.

"Have I gone too soft, Sullivan? Is that the problem?" Adam gave one more twist, then released the grip he held on Sullivan's heart.

"Now if you're still interested in what I told my wife," Adam continued as if Sullivan was not still gasping for breath and trying to gather his wits about him. "I tried to tell her why I'd been away, that I was trying to get over my revulsions, that I wanted to make love to her. I just-"

"You did what?" Sullivan laughed, ignoring the fangs that descended from Adam's mouth, ignoring his eyes turning blood red or the fact that Adam had damned near stopped his heart. "You stupid fool. You told a woman that you were repulsed by her and you wonder why she left you."

"I was being honest with her."

"That may not have been the wisest thing you've ever done."

Adam stared hard at Sullivan. "We're really not that different. Since Joanna's death you've been unable to so much as think of making love to a mortal woman and since I was turned into this, I can think of making love only to them. What are we going to do about Eve?"

"I'd say that's pretty much up to her. She's changed, Adam. She'd not intimidated by threats. She makes her own decisions, and lets the chips falls where they may. She's not looking for your protection or mine." Sullivan halted. "Everyone knows that she's a vampire, that you turned her."

"How? Who?"

"Eve, she lifted Thomas off the ground one day when he refused to obey the orders of a mortal woman. I was there and before I could intervene, she had a death grip on him and asked, 'Then do you have trouble obeying a vampire?' I swear it was almost as if your voice was coming from her. It was your strength that flowed through her veins and in that moment everyone knew it. When she tossed him to the ground and strutted away, I'd say she claimed her own respect."

"Why didn't you stop her?"

"She doesn't answer to me."

"Is Mark still alive?"

"He is, he's with her constantly. He's extremely loyal to her, he'd die for her. She's put out an order that no vampire is to feed from him. I'll tell you either she had this in her, or your blood gave her this coldness that she uses to her advantage. It's been nearly a year since you turned her. Eve will make her own choices, of that we can both be sure."

"And you think she will choose you?"

"I think she will choose someone who wants her and that would be me. I don't find her repugnant in the least. I find her beautiful and desirable."

"That is still my wife you're talking about."

"Adam, you're not a fool. What did you think was going to happen when you turned her? You knew she would hate you for this. No matter how much she loves you, she will never forgive you for turning her into one of us. Maybe you could have had some kind of life if you had been able to show her how much you love her but you can't. Even now, knowing that I want her, that she willingly came to me, you can't get over the aversion of making love to her. If you could, Adam, she would be yours."

"Why did you summon me?"

"For this, to let you know that I am not hiding my relationship with Eve. Neither your threats or your torture will stop me. If you intend to kill me I suggest you do it now. If not I will continue to see Eve as long as she wants to see me. It will be out in the open. I'm asking her to move back in with me."

"And if she doesn't?"

"Then I will still see her as long as she wants."

"I want you to know that if you follow your plan you are signing your death warrant and Eve's. I will not hesitate to kill either of you. Remember that, Sullivan. Eve's blood will be on your hands."

"No, Adam, whatever happens next, Eve's blood is on your hands, not mine. You're the one who turned her, remember?"

That was one reminder Adam didn't need. He was well aware of what he'd done. "You can never know what you'd do, Sullivan, until you're faced with the same situation that I was. I was the one there. I was the one who saw her dying before my eyes and I was the one who had the power to prevent it."

"I can't say what I would do, you're right. But I do know I have enough self-control to stop when Eve asks me to stop." His eyes flicked and he thought of the ultimate in their lovemaking and how she'd asked him to stop. "No, Adam, I don't think I would ever do anything to Eve that she didn't want."

"Maybe, maybe not," Adam answered, "but then again you've never loved anyone as much as I love Eve. The thought of her dying…" Adam shivered, unable to speak further on the subject, then abruptly changed the conversation.

A few more minutes of idle conversation and Adam took his leave, disappearing suddenly, knowing he'd left Sullivan there to the curious looks of the mortals surrounding him. Adam smiled to himself. It was the least he could do to the vampire for what he'd done to him. The thoughts of killing Sullivan were gone. Adam wanted Eve to be as happy as she could possibly be. Given the circumstances, he didn't believe he could make her happy. He accepted that now.

❖

Adam returned to his home, surprised to see Eve there. He stared at her, unable for a moment to speak. Once again he was amazed at the number of crystals that Eve had purchased. She had enough books on the occult that she could start her own bookstore. Something big was up and he didn't know if he liked it. So far none of Eve's potions or crystals had been to his liking.

"You never did tell me what you're working on."

"Different things," Eve answered.

"I kind of figured that one out for myself." He pointed to her consecrated circle. "Could you at least tell me as large as this house is why you decided to have all of this nonsense here?" he muttered in disgust, glaring at her paraphernalia. "Why couldn't you do this stuff in your quarters?"

"I didn't want to." Eve turned toward Adam and returned his glare. "Sullivan asked me to move in with him."

"Are you?" Adam asked, staring at her.

"No."

"Does he know?"

"He knows."

"Why aren't you?"

"Males tend to become territorial when living with a female. I think we will do better in our own space."

"I applaud you for using your brain to know that I would never allow you to do that."

"I'm getting sick and tired of your saying what you won't allow, my lord. It's my choice, not yours."

"Are you sure you're not staying here to turn the knife a little deeper?"

Eve shrugged her shoulder. "I'm not sure. I could change my mind, but for now I've decided to stay here."

"Eve, I know your opinion of me. You think me an arrogant bully. While those things are true it was not my intention to be insensitive to you. I wasn't attempting to hurt you. I wanted you to know that I had taken steps to rectify the situation, to change things."

Eve glared at Adam for several seconds before blinking her eyes and moving toward the kitchen. She began throwing crystals into spring water, then handfuls of herbs into pots, stirring, working off her anger.

"Adam, you knew before you did this to me that you wouldn't want me. I knew it. Hell, the whole damn vampire world knew it." She stopped, her hand shaking. "Tell me, please, why you did this, and don't for heaven's sake tell me it was because you loved me. You don't do things like this to someone you love."

Her voice had grown soft, the memory of their night together at the forefront of her mind. She wanted to let it go, she'd tried a million times. She lifted her chin and stared at Adam, at his beautiful eyes, his lush mouth. Her eyes fell on the amber ring that matched her necklace. A gift of love. She trembled. There was something about Adam's ring. If only she could remember what it was.

For a moment she resided in both the past and the present. She could plainly see the ring in her hand, hear herself saying words over it. Then the details became fuzzy.

She couldn't help remembering Adam as he had been then. His love was the one thing she'd been sure of. He had been her husband and her hero. She sighed, knowing that in his way he did love her, that much she knew, just as she knew she would forever love him. Time would never erase that love. At the thought that they were now bound for eternity, a tear slid from her eyes and ran down her cheek. She thought of what she'd read involving reincarnation. *The karmic debts one owes, or is owed, must sooner or later be individually paid by the debtor to the creditor*. She'd done something wrong to Adam in that incarnation. She was well aware of that fact. She owed Adam though she wasn't sure exactly how.

Eve softened her glare as she looked at Adam. How awful to have unrequited love for all of eternity. The irony turned into anger and Eve once again glared across the room at Adam as he stood there not answering her, as though he were only an innocent spectator. There was nothing innocent about him.

Adam didn't speak and Eve grew angrier. "Tell me, damn it. You owe me that much. Why did you turn me?"

"The only answer I have is the one you don't want to hear." Adam waved his hand nonchalantly, as though he were tipping his hat.

Eve flung the bottle of freshly made potions at Adam. "I will remain here and I will make your life a living hell."

"Do you think you have that much power over me, that I will allow you to get away with it? Do you think my guilt will allow you to sleep with another? No, Eve. Think again. Knowing that you're making love to another will eventually drive me mad. And when I am driven insane I will not be responsible for my actions. Retribution will eventually be required if you insist on continuing your little affair. I'm not going to permit it."

"I don't need your permission, Adam. I have your strength and I have your nature, your coldness. I am no longer human. I'm a vampire. My world revolves around the undead. There is no longer anything that you can harm me with. If you threaten my friends, I will ask you what friends? I don't care." Eve opened her mind. "Scan me, Adam, see if I'm lying."

He did as she asked, saddened at the coldness that had crept into her heart. Her soul was as dark as his own. She would do as she'd said, not care. "Eve," Adam started, then stopped. "You have no idea how much I want to hold you."

"And you have no idea how much I want to plunge a stake into your heart and end your existence."

Adam smiled slightly. "It wouldn't be that easy and it wouldn't end my life."

"I know," Eve replied. "That's why I haven't done it, but still, I want to, Adam. And you should be mindful of that fact."

"Maybe you should move in with Sullivan."

"No, I think you were right that you should keep your enemy close."

"I'm not your enemy, Eve."

"But I'm yours," she said and began sweeping the broken glass up and dumping it into the trashcan.

Adam watched her as she finished and reached for the phone to order more supplies. Eve was now a vampire with money, a female vampire in a rage. Who knew what she would do next?"

Chapter 14

Eve stood before the doors of Sanctuary Crystals, not caring that there were witches and psychics inside, people who would undoubtedly know her for what she was. What did it matter? She meant them no harm. If they did nothing to her she would do nothing to them.

Shoving the door open, she stood for a moment and looked around, smiling at the ground crystals that had been sprinkled at the front of the entrance to keep out evil. She almost laughed before going in, breathing in the incense, stepping over the charged crystal dust that was almost invisible. She watched as two sets of eyes turned toward her. Their mouths opened and she wondered if they would speak. She smiled, closing the door behind her, and proceeded farther into the shop. The crystal dust was to keep out evil. Eve was not evil.

"Hello," she said, going to the person behind the counter. "I want your strongest crystal."

"You have to have a specific reason so I will know what stone to give you."

"I want the ones that you keep in the back, not the ones that you used to charge your store. I need something more powerful, something that a healer would use."

"Are you a healer?"

"Of sorts."

"What sort?"

"Let's say I'm an extremely ancient and powerful healer and I'm in need of replenishing my tools."

"This might prove to be very expensive."

Eve laughed to herself. Money, it always boiled down to that. For money the man behind the counter would forget that she exuded some quality he couldn't name. He would not care that there was a dark cloud hanging over her head, or that her aura was black. The color green would erase everything else. Since marrying Adam she had lots of green, lots of plastic. She was now an extremely wealthy vampire.

Eve laughed aloud. "Money is not an obstacle," she said, wishing that she would find something expensive enough that Adam would question her purchase. Until now, he'd not said one word, not about her comings and goings, not about her spending his money as though it were water, not about the work she was doing with Dr. Meah and nothing more about her sleeping with Sullivan. She sighed, bringing her attention back to the present.

"Would you like to see the crystals?"

"Yes, I want every manner of crystal, every single stone you have that will heal and protect. I want the strongest that you have. And if you know of more and don't stock them I want you to order them for me."

"What specifically are you looking to do with them?"

With a smile Eve told the man honestly, "I plan to make amulets and healing potions. I need to work on reversing impossible things and I need to prevent psychic attacks."

"That's going to take an awful lot of stock. Why don't you just use quartz crystals?"

"I would consider it, depending on what you have. I'm not a novice in this. I know what I want and I can pay for it."

Eve stared at the shopkeeper, reading his thoughts with little trouble. He was planning on charging her double.

"I have some really large quartz in the back that a healer ordered but found the stones too expensive once they'd arrived. If you're not a novice you can probably feel the energy emanating around you from them. Would you be interested in seeing them?"

"Yes, let me see them. And get the thoughts out of your head about overcharging me. I will pay you for them and you will make a nice profit, but do not take me for a fool."

Eve felt the shift in the man, saw the nervous twitch and gave him a smile. Power surged through her, making her have a moment of pity for Adam. She thought she understood how hard it was for him to have cultivated this kind of power over centuries and not abuse it.

"Show me the stones." Eve walked quickly, wishing that lately all of her thoughts weren't of Adam. It was no longer any fun to hurt him.

Eve spent over seven thousand dollars on crystals and various stones. Three of the largest were column crystals so powerful that the energy emanating from them could be felt several feet away. Such crystals were used only by healers.

❖

When she reached home Adam eyed the crystals suspiciously. "Don't you have enough crystals? The entire house is bursting at the seams with them. Are you planning on making it so I can't return to my own home?" He stared at Eve, waiting for an answer.

"No."

"I know what you are capable of doing with stones. You used crystals to keep me out of your apartment before. And that damn crystal necklace you made to keep me out of your thoughts." He paused. "I know you're still wearing the necklace, Eve." He pointed at her new acquisitions. "And those particular crystals are so powerful I felt the energy before I entered."

Eve stopped what she was doing to turn and face Adam. "I have no need to worry about you, Adam. You don't concern me. I'm working on something."

"A reversal spell, or something to kill me?"

"Like I said, you are not my concern."

Adam appeared in front of her. "Are you in love with Sullivan?" he asked, using everything that was in him to keep the words from sticking in his throat.

"I'm not sure," Eve answered, shaking her head a little. "Why?"

"I know that you slept with him."

This time she merely stared, refusing to take the bait.

"I had a talk with him."

Eve was well aware that Adam was trying to make her angry, to frighten her. She'd long ago passed frightened. Now she wasn't even out for revenge. Her work with the crystals was simply her latent talents and desires coming alive again.

"Why, Adam? Why bother, why do you care?" The anger Eve fought to keep at bay struggled to come out. "I know that you're sleeping in the beds and arms of mortal women most nights."

"Yes," Adam said softly, "but how do you know I'm enjoying it?"

"If you're not enjoying it you shouldn't do it," Eve snapped. "I wouldn't. I'm doing nothing that I don't enjoy." She glared at Adam. "Now go, leave me alone, I'm busy."

"I never intended it to be like this."

"What did you intend? We both knew how this would play out." She frowned. "I don't think you did this to me because you loved me. If you truly loved me you would have respected my wishes," she said softly. "You would have allowed me to die. No, Adam, I think you did it to get revenge on me for the things I did when I was Eyanna. That was a thousand years ago, another incarnation. I'm a different person now but you still haven't forgiven me completely," She shrugged her shoulders. "You wanted revenge on me. Now you have it."

Suddenly and without warning Eve saw the pain her words inflicted. She was as privy to his feelings as she was to his thoughts. Her words had hurt him deeply, that she knew, as his emotions swirled through her. He loved her and he regretted what he'd done. Eve blinked and pulled away from Adam's feelings. Too little, too late. She returned her attention to the potions.

"That was not my reason and you damn well know it," Adam said angrily when Eve refused to answer or look at him. "I will rectify what I've done. I will give you the death you seek." He took her roughly by the shoulder. His fangs descended, but before he could bite her, she moved her head away and smashed the crystal that was in her hand against the side of his face.

Stunned, Adam withdrew, looking at the blood on his hand. Anguish filled him. "What have I done?" he asked softly. "Did I make you into this?"

"Yes," Eve answered. "Defending myself is now a part of my nature."

"And hating me, is that also a part of this new nature of yours?"

She connected to his feelings again. *Confusion.* He really didn't understand. "Adam." Eve spoke quietly, all of the fight gone from her. "For close to a year this has been my life, a life I never wanted. I will not lie now and tell you that I didn't love you. Despite all rational thought I loved you. In spite of the pain you inflicted on me, the fear, I still loved you. Even when you'd done this," she said with disgust, "something I could never forgive, there was a little piece of my heart that refused to let go of those feelings. I wish it had, Adam, but it didn't. Not even this killed my love for you."

Eve hissed as she spoke. "Sullivan didn't do it. You did it. When you look at me the disgust is barely concealed in your eyes. The tremor in your hands when you dare to touch me is so noticeable that I wonder why you even try. Now you want to behave as though you're hurt that I find comfort in Sullivan's arms. Not only doesn't he look at me as though to touch me would soil him, he loves touching me and he thrills in making love to me. He wants me, Adam."

"And what about you? Eve. Do you want him also?"

Eve steepled her hands. "If I did not want him I would not go to him." She closed her eyes, fighting her useless blood tears. How dare Adam question her? She bit back the angry words, not wanting them to give Adam power over her, to know that his revulsion of her cut deeply.

"This is not the way I want it," Adam said sadly.

"Nor is it the way I want it." Eve replied. "I love you. You know it, Sullivan knows it and I know it, so why pretend that it's any different. I want you to want me, to be able to make love to me as you did before you changed me. But it's not going to happen. I know that now."

"Still, I don't wish for it to be like this." Adam held her gaze for a long moment.

"But it is the way it is." Eve looked at him and then willed herself away. She found that she was in Sullivan's home for the second time.

❖

Things were much different in Sullivan's home than in Adam's. She was legally married to Adam, lived in his home and as he'd said, she only had to sign the name *Mrs. Omega* and the world opened up for her. Still, with all of that she didn't really feel Adam's home was hers. Sure, she spent Adam's money, but she didn't feel ownership.

Eve walked around the rooms of Sullivan's home trailing her fingers along the backs of furniture, then sat to wait until Sullivan returned. She wondered if he were out somewhere feeding or like Adam, satisfying his lust with someone else. He'd warned her in the beginning that vampires were not monogamous. They lived far too long to think of spending eternity with one person.

Still, Sullivan was the only friend she had at the present. Her mortal friends were better off staying away from her. Even though she now had a way to control the terrible hunger, she didn't trust herself to be around them.

"Sullivan," Eve moaned, finding herself sliding down on his bed, a bed that didn't have decorative bats and vampires. *A bed, just a bed.* She lay back, for the first time in months allowing the tears to fall, hating that she was staining Sullivan's sheets, but knowing he wouldn't mind and feeling indebted to him that he wouldn't.

A few seconds later she sensed Adam's presence and looked up.

"You will not do this, Eve. Do not push me. Now come home with me." Adam held out his hand and waited.

"Sullivan doesn't even know that I'm here, Adam. I just came here because I needed to get away from you."

"That's understandable, but you will not take refuge here."

"It's the only place I've been able to bilocate to."

"Then it's time I taught you how to find another place. Come." This time when he moved closer to Eve, she took his hand and Adam sighed in relief. Once again he would be able to allow her to live.

❖

Adam walked into Eve's bedroom and looked down on her. When she opened her eyes he smiled. "It's your first anniversary," he said and handed her a box. When he saw the anger rise in her eyes he sat on the bed. "Open it, Eve."

"Raw amber?" Eve blinked. "Adam, thank you."

"You're welcome, wife." He rubbed the amber ring that sat on his finger. "When you gave me this ring you told me the importance of amber. Do you remember?"

"No."

A sad smile played around Adam's mouth. "No matter. This is Baltic amber, the most powerful of all amber. You told me it has great healing power. I want you to find a cure, Eve, for what I've done." He saw a tear slide down her cheek and reached to wipe it away. "This wasn't meant to bring on tears."

For a moment Eve could only stare. A full year as a vampire. It seemed much longer. At first the idea that Adam thought she'd find reason to celebrate angered her. But his gift touched her.

"I've tried every crystal and healing stone that I know of. I hadn't been able to locate genuine Baltic amber, at least none that's truly powerful. Thank you. But you know, Adam, amber is also used for protection." She watched him for a moment as he lovingly touched the ring she'd given him so long ago. A flicker of remembrance touched her. "Perhaps that's the reason I gave it to you, to protect you."

"It didn't do that, did it? I still became a vampire."

"And you made me one. Maybe I should have taken that necklace."

The moment the words were said Adam reached into his pocket and pulled out his gift to his wife. As he fastened it around her neck he whispered, "Let's call a truce."

And they did.

Month after month after month, Adam brought gifts of amber to Eve. He'd changed his mind for the moment about turning her again if she found a cure. He needed her to be mortal again as badly as she wanted to be.

❖

Adam studied Eve as she examined the amber bracelet he'd given her. "No luck with the amber potions?" he asked.

"None," Eve sighed. "Six months ago when you gave me the first amber I was so hopeful. Sure, I'll admit I found no reason to celebrate having been a vampire for a year but that day you gave me hope. Now here it is six months later. I've lived like this for eighteen months. No number of potions have helped. I'm still a vampire."

"Maybe the amber is helping after all," Adam said, running a finger lightly down her arm, stopping at the bracelet on her left wrist, wondering as always what she was wearing beneath the bracelet, knowing that more than likely it was some amulet. He smiled. More than likely she'd found a way to keep him from kissing her.

"Your skin is much softer than that of a vampire." He sniffed the air. "And you smell of lemons again. What's going on?"

With a shrug Eve smiled. "I got tired of you sniffing the air when you came near me. I've been using potions to scent my body."

"For me?"

Eve didn't answer.

"Are you still sleeping with Sullivan?"

"Are you still sleeping with whomever you chose?"

"When I want."

"Adam, the truce has been working nicely. I've managed to not try and kill you in your sleep and you've managed to not kill me in mine.

Adam chuckled and reached for Eve's hand. "What are you hiding, wife?"

Snatching her hand away from him proved Adam's suspicions that Eve was wearing something beneath the bracelet that she didn't want him to see. "Aren't you going to try on the gift I bought you?" He watched as Eve slid the amber bracelet over her right hand and positioned it on her wrist.

"Why not the left wrist?" Adam asked.

"I have one there, Adam." She leaned close to him and suddenly threw her arms around him, hugging him tightly, knowing within a moment he would move. This time she wanted that.

"You're more like me than I thought," Adam acknowledged, moving away. You're shrewd and cunning. I'm going out for awhile. I'll see you later."

"I might go out as well," Eve admitted.

"Where?"

"Don't ask questions you don't want the answer to. And, Adam, I have no plans to find you and drag you home so for once would you give me that much respect and do the same?"

"Don't go where you shouldn't and I'll have no need to drag you home. You know, Eve, I receive no pleasure in always having to find you and bring you home."

"Liar," Eve laughed. "We both know you get off on having that kind of control over me. But, Adam, I'm getting stronger. My natural powers are returning so if I were you I would remember that."

"You're right, I do enjoy throwing my weight around. It's the least I can do since I have decided that I can't kill you." He shrugged, "Well, I can kill you but then I'd be forced to take out my sorrow over your death on the good Christians who flock to Father Keller's church. Since he's a friend of sorts I can't do that, now, can I?"

"No, Adam, I don't suppose you can." Eve fell back on the bed exasperated, tired of the same old fight. "Yes, my lord, I will remain in tonight," she bit out sarcastically and turned on her pillow and fell asleep.

❖

Sometime later a finger brushed across her cheek and her hair was pushed away. Eve opened her eyes slowly, blinking, trying to remember where she was. Sullivan was grinning at her and she grinned in return.

"Hello," he said.

"Hello."

"Did Adam cause you to come to me again?"

"Would it matter?"

"Just a little."

Eve stared at him. "How so?"

"Well, I'm always happy to see you no matter what, but I would love to think you came not because Adam angered you, but because you had a need to see me."

"It's funny that whenever I need a safe haven you're the one I think of." She smiled. "I fell asleep in my own bed. When I woke I was here."

"That doesn't tell me that you came here strictly on your own choice."

"In answer to your question, yes, I fought with Adam."

"What about this time?"

"Same story."

"Do you still love him, Eve?"

"Yes, I still love him, but the question you should be asking me is this: Am I holding out hope that things will change. My answer to that is, less and less."

"If he could finally get over his revulsion what would you do?"

"Nothing differently." Eve stared at Sullivan. "I was serious. I'm not mooning after Adam, waiting for him to make love to me."

"Eve."

"Okay, sure, a part of me wishes that it could be different. I love him."

"I've never known him to bed a vampire and many have tried. You're going to get hurt if you're waiting for him to change his mind."

"Sullivan, why do you care? You told me yourself that vampires don't form attachments; that includes me."

"It's true in most case and most of the time." Sullivan shrugged. "Seems that I forgot my lesson. I've enjoyed our friendship. I've enjoyed our months of making love even more." He sighed and looked at her, deciding to tell her what he'd promised himself he wouldn't. "I've fallen in love with you, Eve, against all odds, knowing that you love Adam."

He held up a hand to stop her protests. "I fell in love with you knowing that your heart belongs to him, that he's broken it and that pain will be with you. I knew exactly what I was doing and I allowed it to happen anyway. There is something about you, something that Adam saw in your spirit many centuries ago. I can see why he tried so hard to get you to love him again. I can also see why he wants you to love him now. You're very easy to love."

"I don't place a lot of stock in love, Sullivan. I've only gotten hurt by the ones who claimed they love me."

"I won't hurt you."

"Can you make me a promise that you won't?"

"Can you make me the same promise?"

"Where are you when you're not with me, when you're not working? Are you feeding, are you in another's bed?"

Sullivan smiled and touched his finger to her cheek. "Would you care?"

"Yes, Eve admitted, "I would care."

"So you care about me?"

"Didn't you know that?"

"Nothing is ever a sure thing." He sighed. "What about love? Do you think you could ever love me?"

"Sullivan, you haven't answered my question. Where do you go?"

"Here and there." He smiled. "And no, it's not always for feeding. My need to feed is minimal. As for my personal habits, I am not making love to anyone other than you. I have not wanted to."

"So where do you go?"

"Vampires have solitary natures, Eve." He smiled, then turned serious and shrugged. "I visit graves searching for my ancestors. I go to places where I am rarely noticed and I watch, remembering the days when I had a family, when I had someone who loved me. We all need it, Eve, even me. But I will not beg for it."

"You don't have to," Eve said and pulled him into her arms. "I am with you because I want to be. It has nothing to do with Adam, I promise you."

"And the love?"

"I do love you."

Sullivan closed his eyes and held her tight. This was not part of the vampire nature, this urge to bond, to have everlasting love, for surely it would be the one thing that could kill them all.

"Then leave him, come live with me. If you're no longer waiting for Adam to claim you as his wife you no longer have need to seek revenge."

"I've stopped seeking that long ago."

"Then live with me."

"Let me think about it," Eve said as she touched her lips to his. "I promise I will think about it." She pushed her tongue into the warm crevice of his mouth and she shivered. None of this was as she'd thought. She'd thought vampires would be cold, but then again with all of that human blood pumping through their veins, she should have known that was a lie, if of course she'd ever believed in vampires. Until Adam, it had all been horror movies and books that scared her.

"But you believe in vampires now, don't you, Eve?"

"I believe," Eve answered, hating that her mind was open for Sullivan's probing and closed it against further invasion. Thoughts of Adam were there. A great sadness took hold. She would probably always love him. It seemed she had no choice in the matter.

Sullivan made love to Eve slowly and tenderly. He had not expected to fall in love with her, had not wanted to, but it had happened anyway. *What a crazy old fool I am*, he thought.

He felt the heat from her tears as he was kissing her. He pretended that he didn't notice, just as she pretended that she no longer wanted to be with a man whom fate had brought back into her life. Despite all of that, Sullivan loved Eve. It was an easy thing to do.

"Sullivan," she moaned, "I'm so glad I found you."

A deep shudder went though him and a sigh of satisfaction. For now this would have to be enough. He poured everything he had into his loving of Eve's body, hundreds of years of pent up passion, and when they came, it was together and it was his name Eve screamed as she climaxed and her nails made deep rivulets in his skin. As for him, he nipped her skin lightly, not allowing his fangs to pierce her flesh, not allowing her blood to pass his lips. The bruises and abrasions they left on each other's body were many. It was their nature. Lucky for both of them they would heal quickly.

❖

Eve lay with her arms around Sullivan, her head on his chest, deeply satisfied. "We're good together." She laughed softly.

"I agree," Sullivan answered. "I thought we made a very good team."

She winced. He was talking about her working with him to betray Adam. She didn't answer. There was nothing else to say but it wasn't lost on Eve that for the second time she had betrayed Adam with Sullivan.

"Don't."

Eve felt her body being shoved away from Sullivan. "What?" she asked, truly stunned. "What's wrong?"

"You will not think about him, not in my arms, not in my bed." Sullivan stormed from the bed.

In utter amazement Eve stared. "I was thinking-"

"I don't want to hear explanations. You came to me, Eve. I didn't go looking for you. I wasn't the one who started this. If you want Adam, stay with him. He can't stand the feel of you, but maybe if you beg him, maybe if you plead and cry, he will allow his love to rise enough so that he can make love to you."

Eve saw the redness of fevered anger descend on Sullivan, turning his sky blue eyes to the hated red. His fangs descended as his anger rose. She felt waves of pain coming at her. She'd hurt Sullivan. "I'm sorry."

"Don't be sorry, Eve. It isn't your apologies or your pity that I want." In the blink of an eye Sullivan was dressed and gone. Eve fell back on the bed, wondering if she'd ever get used to the fact that every thought, every feeling she had was easily read by others. Hell, she was doing it herself.

She pulled the covers around her and bundled up as the weakness pulled at her. She'd expended a lot of energy making love with Sullivan. She had to replenish her blood. For the months since Adam's return she'd been using less and less of the AB-5 blood substitute, afraid Adam would somehow find out about the pump or spot the Picc line in her wrist, afraid that Sullivan would notice how much time she spent in the bathroom. Now she left the pump in the lab when she left work for the day. So far it was doing the job, just not as well. Luckily, she'd never needed to wear it full time.

Eve sighed and contemplated her life and how she'd ended up here in this lifetime as a vampire. *A ripple which we cause may not bounce back at us till many lives later—but bounce back it will.* Eve repeated the words from The Witches' Bible over and over, wondering what ripple she'd made a thousand years in the past that had led her here.

Chapter 15

Eve smiled as she walked down the corridor of the lab. It felt good to be respected in her own right. Matter of fact, her accomplishments had earned her more respect than Adam's name. In the twenty months she'd been working there the things Adam had feared had never materialized. She was in fact happy that the other vampires knew she was a vampire.

Here in this building Eve marveled that for the most part the vampires behaved no differently than mortals. Sure, in the break room the fridge was stocked with bottles of chilled human blood and a bowl filled with the pills the scientists had concocted to quench their thirst. But other than that, working conditions seemed more or less ordinary. It didn't bother her as much that people could disappear at will now that she was finally getting the hang of it.

"Hello, Dr. Meah." Eve grinned at the doctor before looking around the lab. "Have you seen either Sullivan or Adam?" She frowned when the doctor didn't answer her.

"What's wrong?" she asked quietly, fingering her crystal necklace, glad that she'd made one for the doctor to block his thoughts, even more glad she'd insisted that he wear it. It seemed they were going to need the privacy.

"Get in here quickly. I think we may have a problem." Dr. Meah looked out the door of the lab, then slammed the door shut and locked it. He began pacing back and forth wringing his hands nervously.

"What kind of problem?" A ripple of fear rose before she could stop it. "Does Adam know?"

"It's not him. I've been having some difficulty." His eyes darkened. "I can't believe it. It's damn near impossible." He paused, then wrung his hands again. "There's something wrong with me. I think it's a virus."

"A virus? Are you kidding? How on earth can a vampire contract a disease?"

"Do you think everything is known about vampires? I can give you the end result, but I can't begin to tell you the how of it. There should be nothing in what we've been using that should cause these symptoms. The samples are clean."

"Could someone have tampered with them?"

"Of course not. We don't have mortals working in here who have unsupervised access to my lab. We have a couple that clean but that's it. Besides, even if we did, why would they tamper with it? If this works it would benefit us all."

"I'm just saying if there is nothing that should have caused this, then how did it happen?"

"I don't know. I've been monitoring it for a week now to see if I was imagining it, but it's real." He began pacing even faster, stopping to look out the glass door, then looking frantically back at Eve.

"What are we going to do?"

"We both need to stop using the AB-5 or at least using it exclusively." He caught the look that crossed Eve's face. He was aware she'd never fed on fresh prey. "We have blood, Eve. The fridge is constantly stocked; there is no danger in the supply running low." He was trying to get the words out, trying his best not to send her into a panic but that was impossible to do since he himself was in a panic. If Adam found out what he'd done...

Eve blinked, staring, opening her mouth to speak. Almost two years she'd been a vampire and this life still disgusted her. A shudder worked its way down her body and she tried to stop the shakes that followed. Pouring blood into crystal decanters didn't make the prospect of drinking it any more palatable.

"There is nothing wrong with drinking the blood we have. We all do it, including Adam on occasion." He rushed that explanation. It wasn't exactly a lie but it was far from the truth. Adam had not drunk from the blood banks in many years. He found it disgusting.

"I just don't want to." A shudder ripped through her, "I don't want to."

"I can give you daily transfusions. I'll figure out a way to use the whole blood that we have. You can still use the pump; I can modify the bags for it. Or you can use the pills in combination. There are other alternatives. You can even feed until we're ready to start again. There is Mark, and if not him any human will do. You're more controlled now. You'll know not to take too much."

"How would I know that when I've never fed on them?"

"It's instinct, Eve."

"And what if you're wrong?"

"Eve, is it really so wrong to feed from mortals if it will keep us alive?"

"You know I'm not going to feed on mortals. That's the reason I've been allowing myself to be your human..." She stopped. She wasn't human any more. Eve shivered. "I want to continue with the experiment. It makes me feel almost normal."

Eve knew some of her reasoning was vanity, but the fact that the AB-5 was clear and so thin that it easily flowed through the micro thin tubing made her think she was perhaps a diabetic getting insulin. Somehow it was the clear color that allowed her to use it. It kept her from thirsting; it enabled her to take in occasional food and endure the burning, the acid that flowed into her body when she did.

Adam had told her the burning was all in her mind and had attempted to feed her drops of holy water but she'd been unable to accept them. Even if she could take holy water without harming herself she still found she needed to believe that there was something, even one thing, that would kill her. She'd fought with

Adam several times concerning her negative thinking. He'd told her she had nothing to fear, that it was her wanting to remain human that kept her fears alive. He'd told her that if she kept looking for trouble eventually it would find her. And she'd agreed. Of course if she thought something could harm her it would. That kept her tied to her humanity.

"Eve, where are you? Come back." Dr. Meah snapped his fingers in her face. "This is serious."

"I know," Eve answered. "I was just thinking of some things Adam told me. He is right about so many things, but I wouldn't dare tell him." Eve laughed. "His head is big enough as it is. He's the most arrogant being that I've ever known."

She saw the doctor's gaze slide away and she laughed. Of course no one else would dare call Adam arrogant with the exception of Sullivan and Sullivan had his own reason.

"I don't think you should continue with the AB-5 until I have more time to test it. Let me transfuse you. I can make sure no one knows I'm doing it."

"Transfusions only last a few hours, not nearly as long as the AB-5." She saw the quirk of his brow. "Sullivan gave them to me in the beginning, right after Adam turned me." She saw him shake his head as realization dawned.

"Maybe if you use the pump you can get the continuous feeding that you need."

She looked at him, alarm going through her. "Both Adam and Sullivan were getting suspicious about my clothing. With the AB-5, I don't have to use the pump all the time. With whole blood I more than likely will. I don't want to chance either of them finding out. I liked that I only had to slip in the AB-5 when I needed it, that I could get away for long periods of time without using the pump at all. I don't want to use it all day everyday."

"But, Eve…"

Eve shook her head. "Don't you see it's not just that. I just…I…" She licked her lips. "I can't explain it."

"I think you already have. You want to be human, a healthy human." He held her gaze. "I wish I could help you. I so much wanted to see this work for you, and in a way it has. Look at you, almost two years and you've never bitten anyone."

Her face flamed. "That's not quite true. I've bitten Adam."

A smile spread across Dr. Meah's face. "He made you. A transference is common in those cases."

"Is that the reason I feel so powerful when I've bitten him?"

"Not exactly. Adam's blood is old and powerful. He's done things a lot of us haven't dared to do. If you had to be made, you were made by the best." He shrugged. "If you had to be made," he repeated.

Eve shook her head. "It's ironic, isn't it? The one thing I don't want is the one thing I need more of. Only Adam's blood gives me a complete feeling of life." She smiled. "Maybe I should convince Adam to give me weekly blood donations."

"You do have another option. A free feed is almost as exhilarating, whether from a mortal or a vamp."

"No," Eve screamed, "no, I won't."

"Then would you like for me to modify the pump for regular blood? Or I could let you nick me," Dr. Meah teased.

"I want to continue using the AB-5."

"Why, Eve? There is nothing wrong with transfusions. If you were still a mortal you would be given one if you were in need of it."

"But I'm not mortal and it just seems to me that constant transfusion is still feeding on mortals."

"But you're not. We have other blood substitutes we could try, things that have a lot more data. You could try those."

"I want the AB-5." Eve walked toward the secure location to retrieve her pump.

"I'm not going to continue giving you the samples. Actually, I'm going to stop working on the AB-5 altogether. There won't be any more for you to use."

"You can't do that," she sputtered, spinning around.

"I can and I will. Eve, listen, I'm going to stop taking it myself." He paused and bit his lip. "Actually I stopped taking it two days ago and I think you should also."

"No." She watched the man, unable to read him because of the crystals she'd given him. "Are you worried about Adam?"

"That's not the case, Adam isn't the reason." He began pacing once again, sighing every few seconds. "I don't want anything to happen to you."

"Like what? Everything bad that could happen to a person has happened to me. This is my life, such as it is. I intend to live it my way."

"But don't you understand that I have no way of knowing what this can do to you? It could prove fatal in the end."

"Are you saying that it could be a way to rid the world of vampires?" She smiled. "I should have used you on my team."

"I'm not out to destroy vampires, Eve, I'm out to make us independent. And don't get any idea of using it for that purpose. You're strong and well liked, but no vampire is going to stand for what you want to do, not even one that loves you. Sullivan will stop you, if not Adam."

"And you?"

"I would also stop you."

Eve looked around the lab, knowing she didn't have long. Someone would come into the lab soon. She had to talk reason to the man. Damn, she thought, he behaved more like a human doctor than a vampire.

He was grinning at her. "I'm a scientist, Eve, not a moron. Yes, I want to invent something that will have lasting value. Do I want to sacrifice you to do it? No."

"But you've experimented on mortals. You put some of this into their blood supply."

"But I had a way of controlling that. This, well, there are unknown things at work."

Eve took her pump from the locked case and filled her refrigerated pouch with the life-giving fluid. "If you really mean what you say, that you're not out to destroy lives, then you will not stop me from using this."

Eve wasn't being foolish or a martyr. If it became necessary she would revert to the blood collected at the blood bank. She just didn't want to answer Adam's questions if he found out.

"Eve, I repeat, after this batch is gone I will not make any more."

"If you don't, you should think of a good reason to give Adam when I suddenly fall ill. I used to be a pretty good actress."

"You're bluffing."

"Would you care to try me?"

"This is blackmail. If something happens to you Adam will kill me, again," he grunted. "And if I don't keep you supplied you will make sure Adam destroys me."

Eve smiled and waited. "I hate using Adam in order for you to keep your bargain with me, we're friends."

"Yet you had no problem stating it. I wondered how long it would take you to play that trump card. You're the mistress of this place, my boss." He tilted his head. "And if you order me to continue making it, then I will. But that will be our new relationship, Eve, not friends, but boss and employee. What's it going to be?"

"Keep making the samples," Eve ordered and walked from the lab without looking back. She hoped the doctor would continue with the trials. Even if he'd stopped she intended to keep going. It was the best idea she'd had so far.

❖

Sullivan stood at the end of the corridor watching Eve walk away from the lab looking worried. She had not even noticed that he was near. That wasn't a good sign. She needed to have her antenna on regardless of where she was. And in a building filled with vampires she definitely needed to keep her wits about her. He materialized in the lab, taking Dr. Meah by surprise.

"Sullivan, you usually walk through the door."

"But I don't have to. I am a vampire."

Sullivan watched as the doctor nervously moved away from him.

"Something is wrong. What's going on? Why was Eve looking so worried when she left you?"

"Listen, you're making me betray her and I don't feel comfortable about it."

"You're going to be a lot less comfortable if something happens to her."

"Who are you threatening me with now, yourself or Adam?"

"Which do you fear most?" Sullivan watched as the vampire swallowed.

"Look, I tried to talk her out of it. She's stubborn, she won't listen."

Sullivan was getting worried. "What did you attempt to talk Eve out of?" He grabbed Dr. Meah by the wrist, heard the jangle of the crystals as the necklace bounced around his neck, and held out his hand.

"Give that to me," Sullivan ordered. "You won't be needing it." He watched the man carefully and felt it when his mental blocks clicked into place. Sullivan grinned. He was almost as good as Adam at getting around people's psychic barricades. The only thing that had defeated him was those darn crystals of Eve's.

"Okay, spill it," Sullivan demanded as he eyed the vampire sharply. "What have you and Eve done?"

"I've noticed some problem with the new blood."

"Did something happen to Eve, is she all right?"

"For now. Besides, it wasn't just Eve." He moved away. "I was taking the AB-5 also."

The tense didn't escape Sullivan. "*Was*, meaning you've stopped?"

"Yes, two days ago." He rushed on, seeing the anger in Sullivan's eyes. "I'd tried to contact her for two days to get her to come in, but since this is private it was hard. I had to wait until she came on her own to pick up more formula."

"Isn't she still working with you?"

"Not every day."

"Get on with it. What happened to you? Get to the point." Sullivan was trying hard to keep the alarm from his voice, yet he was snarling. "Tell me what happened."

"It's like some kind of virus. I'm not sure. I've tried it on humans with no problems, no complications at all. But I've being feeling strange, tired, little things. My mind wanders at times for a second or so. As strange as it sounds, there are variations in my body temperature. I'm ice cold one moment, burning up the next."

"Can you fix it?"

"Are you asking can I take a pill, an antibiotic? We don't have such medications for vampires. We've never needed them before."

"Adam is going to be pissed."

"I thought Eve was with you," Dr. Meah said, looking away.

"She's his wife, he loves her." His look dared the man to ask any more personal questions.

"I tried to get her to go back to the regular transfusions or pills, or even to try some of the other substitutes that are more stable." He licked his lips, bringing his bottom lip inside his mouth. He looked down. "I suggested that she use Mark until…"

Sullivan rolled his eyes. "Did you think that I actually believed Eve was feeding from Mark? What do you take me for?"

"Well, she's with him often."

"Of course she is, as a shield. She never has even a hint of his scent on her body." He looked squarely at the good doctor, once again daring him to question his statement.

"Do you think Adam knows?"

Sullivan took in a breath. Adam was not a fool and Sullivan had never thought him one, but it was obvious that he'd not gotten close enough to Eve to notice that she didn't reek of Mark's foul scent.

The thought made Sullivan smile inwardly. In spite of the paperwork, Eve was his.

"Adam will not be fooled about any of this and I would not venture to guess what he knows and doesn't know. But if something happens to Eve you'd better believe he will know about it and quickly."

"But her crystals?"

"Don't put too much faith in them." Sullivan nodded at the necklace he held in his hand. "I know this keeps your thoughts private, but we're talking about matters of the heart. If something happens to Eve, I don't doubt that Adam will be the first to know of it."

"Do you think you can tell her to stop taking the AB-5?"

"I don't know about it, remember?" Sullivan groaned. "But I will do my best to get her to confide in me and then I will set about encouraging her to stop. But like you said, once she's made up her mind about something…" He grinned. "She's the most amazing mortal I have ever known."

"But, Sullivan, she's…"

"I know, but her soul is still human. She has done everything she can to hang on to her human nature, to keep her vampire nature at bay. I want it to work for her. I want it to work." He looked up from his thoughts. "How many more days do you think I should wait?"

"I have no idea."

"Give me something. A day, a week, a month?"

"I don't know. I stopped taking it and I think my constitution is better prepared than hers. I've lived like this for almost six hundred years. She's hasn't even completed two."

"Where did Eve say she was going?"

"She didn't."

Sullivan sighed and walked away. That damn crystal was keeping him from picking up on her thoughts. Then he smiled. He hadn't talked to Eve in three days, not since he'd blown up at her. Still, he had an idea. When Eve was upset he was the one she thought of.

Sullivan disappeared in a puff of mist and reappeared in his home. Eve was sitting with her feet curled under her. She blinked as though she wasn't expecting him and he smiled, liking that he was the one she turned to for a feeling of safety.

"Hi," Sullivan said, walking up to her.

"Hi, I didn't know you had left work."

"Well, I might say I didn't know you had left. I take it you weren't looking for me."

Eve couldn't help smiling though Sullivan sensed the worry in her.

"It seems lately I just pop up here."

"Can you do it anywhere else?"

"Here is the only place I've come and I don't try. It puzzles me."

"Maybe you find this a safe haven."

"Maybe," Eve answered.

"Any reason you're feeling in need of a haven today?"

He watched for any tell-tale signs. She merely shrugged her shoulder and he decided to push a little more. "Are you in trouble?"

Eve was nervous, not willing to hold his gaze. "Are you going to feed me another lie?" Her head snapped forward and Sullivan winced, knowing that had gotten to her. He hated using that, but he needed to keep her safe. And it wasn't worry about what Adam would do to Dr. Meah or even to him that caused it; it was worry about what the AB5 could possibly do to Eve.

"I haven't lied to you," Eve whispered softly.

"Yes, you have, but I wish you would not continue to lie to me."

"Sullivan, I don't know. You're going to either get angry or try to talk me out of it…"

"I'll do neither unless you tell me that you're not going to be with me."

"That's up to you. You've been avoiding me for the past three days."

"You're changing the subject."

"Give me a moment to work up to it." She tweaked her finger toward him and patted the cushion near her. When he came she hugged him and gave him a look. "I know you feel it," she said. "Go ahead and ask me what it is."

Instead, Sullivan lifted her top and stared at the slim machine that was so small that it was easily hidden within her bra. *Very clever*, he thought.

"I haven't been feeding from Mark or any other humans."

He smiled for her to continue.

"You told me that the first time I did, it would be over for me. Adam was adamant that I didn't use the blood from the blood bank or the pills as a continuous feeding source. Besides, the other vampires would have found me weak."

"But you're still…"

"I know but no one knew about it, only Dr. Meah."

"Does Mark share your secret? Is he pretending?"

"Of course not." Eve looked at Sullivan as if he'd taken leave of his senses. "I do listen to you. I have been trying to help Mark to…"

"You want to save him?"

"I don't want him believing this is a glamorous life, that he should allow anyone to feed from him." She shook with disgust.

"So what's the problem?"

"There is something wrong with the samples. Dr. Meah and I have both been using the AB-5 for over a year. I'm sorry I didn't tell you but I knew you wouldn't approve. Anyway, it was fine. He said there's a problem. I haven't noticed any."

"Do you plan to stop using it?"

"No."

"Eve, do you know what will happen to Dr. Meah if something happens to you because of this little experiment backfiring? Adam will not be forgiving."

She glared at him. "He's forgiven you."

He smiled sadly. "Are you trying to hurt me? Were you hoping I would become angry and leave you? This is more important than your thinking about Adam. This is about your life. I don't want anything to happen to you."

"But you will not stop me."

"You're an adult, Eve, I won't stop you. But I will ask that you use caution and that you stop if you begin to notice any problems."

"Are you going to tell Adam?"

"He's your husband. If you want him to know, then I'm sure you're more than capable of telling him."

"You're angry."

"Disappointed."

"Don't be."

"Then give me something."

"What do you want…that I can give?"

"Give me a promise that you will not keep anything from me, that you will tell me what's happening."

"I'll give you that promise if you will promise not to try and take over my life and attempt to take my choices from me." She stared at him for a long moment. "I won't allow you to do it. With everything that's in me I will do what I can to stop you. I'm not weak little Eve any longer and I'm not without power. I can do things I never believed possible, so don't misjudge me or my abilities. Don't betray me, Sullivan, or I will never forgive you."

"I never have," Sullivan said and held his arms open for Eve. "And, I never will." She entered and snuggled against him.

❖

Now what the hell am I supposed to do? Sullivan paced from room to room. Pacing was better than what he wanted to do. He wanted to beat the crap out of Dr. Meah, then go to Adam's home and demand he give Eve up. Sullivan wanted to tell Adam what dangerous toys Eve was playing with and ask for his help. He wanted to put Eve over his knee and paddle her. Then he wanted to make love to her again and beg her to behave as a normal vampire. But he wondered if he would feel the love for her that he did if she were like anyone else. That, he knew, was part of the allure.

Damn, he muttered. For the past two weeks he'd kept Adam busy. When Eve went to the lab to have her blood drawn, Sullivan had heaved a sigh of relief. When Dr. Meah began once again to take the AB-5 Sullivan hoped that meant the doctor thought the blood was safe and he thanked the powers that be for looking out for Eve, for keeping her safe.

As a scientist, Dr. Meah had a need to find the answers. He couldn't understand why he was being affected and Eve wasn't. It was that need that drove him, not Eve's threats or Sullivan. Sullivan knew and respected his reason and was grateful that the attraction the man had to Eve wasn't likely to ever be reciprocated.

❖

"Sullivan, I believe I've figured out part of the problem with the AB-5. At least I think I have."

Sullivan didn't know if that was good news or bad. With scientists he'd learned they were happy just to have the answer. They didn't do as much worrying about the consequences.

"What is it?"

"Well, I've done samples of my blood and Eve's and of just the sample. It seems some sort of mutation takes place when it mixes with the blood in our veins. It's a corrosive action that's wearing down the veins and arteries. It appears to be working at a much more accelerated rate on me than Eve."

"Why?" Sullivan asked, puzzled.

"Who the hell knows? Maybe because she has so far only had what's here and hasn't taken any fresh blood except Adam's. Then of course we do know Adam's blood is strong.

"Is anything happening to Eve?"

"There is a slight change, not much, and I don't know if it will kick up a notch or continue as it is. I wish she would stop until I figure this out completely."

"Have you stopped again?" Sullivan asked suspiciously.

"I know what I'm looking for now. I'll stick with it for a couple more weeks, but that's it."

"Does Eve know?"

"Of course she knows. She doesn't seem to care."

Or she doesn't believe, Sullivan thought. After all, she did have Adam's blood running through her veins and she was behaving more and more like him, thinking that what she believed would happen.

"Does Eve know that you know?"

"She knows, but she told me on her own. Your name never came up, Doctor."

"May I ask a question?" Doctor Meah looked across the lab, not allowing his eyes to rest on Sullivan.

"You might as well," Sullivan said and looked down. "I can read your thoughts anyway."

"Why is Adam allowing you to live?"

Sullivan felt insulted for a moment that everyone thought Adam could so easily get rid of him. In all probability he could, but still, it was insulting. "We've had a talk and have put our differences aside. What makes you so sure that Adam can so easily defeat me?"

"It isn't that I think it would be easy, but, Sullivan, when he gets angry I've seen him blow up, and I would not want to be the one who pissed him off, especially about Eve. He growls if anyone so much as mentions her name." Dr. Meah shrugged his shoulders. "I just wondered. I know it's none of my business, but hasn't he ever…tried to get you to back off, to harm you in some way?"

Sullivan couldn't help laughing. "As a matter of fact he has."

"And you went against him anyway?"

"He had something that I very much wanted."

"Eve?"

"Yes, Eve." Sullivan smiled. "I believe I love her as much as Adam, and I would do anything to make her happy and even more to protect her." He narrowed his eyes. "I would never want any harm to come to Eve."

"Nor would I."

"You have a crush on her, don't you?" Sullivan smiled. "There's no use denying it. Just keep it as that, a crush and nothing more."

"You didn't."

For a second Sullivan wondered if the vamp was serious. Then he noticed the grin and knew the man was teasing. "It wouldn't do you any good to go after her. I stood a chance because Eve cares for me," Sullivan said, his chest swelling with pride.

"Adam doesn't mind his wife caring about you?"

"Adam doesn't want to do anything to cause Eve any undue pain."

"In that case I think she cares for me also." Dr. Meah laughed while Sullivan smiled. "Listen, I have no such arrangement with Adam about being friends with his wife. If it will make him go easy on me, then I want him to know his wife is fond of me."

"Just keep working, Romeo, and keep your eyes on your test tubes."

"Got it." Dr. Meah laughed.

Sullivan laughed also. He suddenly felt a need to see the smile that always came across Eve's face when she saw him.

Chapter 16

Eve observed Mark as he studied his neck in the mirror. He ran his hand repeatedly over his carotid artery before he turned toward Eve and smiled.

"You're so gentle. You never leave a bruise or anything. If I didn't feel such exquisite pleasure, I would think you never drank from me."

"But we know that I do, don't we?" Eve asked, wondering if Mark was aware of her deception.

"Why have you kept me for so long?" Mark asked, not bothering to answer Eve's question. "It's almost like you're protecting me."

A smile curved her lips and she wondered if Mark knew. "You're loyal to me, Mark, and I reward loyalty."

"I know that you've given orders that others are not to feed from me."

"How?" Eve asked.

"I tried to get a few to bite me. I wanted to test my theory."

"And exactly what is your theory?"

"Nothing much, but I'm not a complete moron. At first I thought that you might have been in love with me." He grinned. "But I knew better. I realized that you're just nice, that you were nice as a mortal and you're a nice vampire, not so much like…"

"Be careful, Mark, the walls have ears."

"Thank you."

"What are you thanking me for?"

"You have to care about me even if you're not in love with me."

For the first time in over eighteen months, Eve looked at Mark in wonder, and she thought now as she did then, why would any mortal willingly do this?

"Mark, please tell me why you want this life, to be my consort."

"I want to be one of you, to be immortal, to never have to worry about dying, about pain, about anything."

He shrugged his shoulders and Eve felt an immense stab of pity. "So you think I don't have any worries, any pain, Mark? I never wanted this. In fact, I pleaded with Adam not to do this. If I could I would trade this in a flash for my old life. What I wouldn't give to be human again, even to have a cold, or to sit around with my friends and not feel the thirst, the intense burning hunger as I imagine their blood filling my mouth and giving me the life that I don't want.

Don't you understand, Mark? We vampires need blood to live as much as a mortal needs air. The one difference is you don't have to harm anyone to get air."

"But you never harm me, Eve."

She sighed. She had thought she was getting through to him. "Don't you want more?"

"I want to remain in your presence whenever you allow me. I want to feel connected to your world."

"What's so wrong with being a mortal?"

"Look at me. You're a vampire and you find me disgusting. What do you think other mortals think about me?"

"If that bothers you so much, clean yourself up, bathe, Mark, comb your hair, brush your teeth." Eve was angry. "You don't have to be this way. I've offered millions of times to give you money for a better life. Why haven't you ever taken me up on it?"

"Because you wanted me gone."

Eve groaned. This wasn't going well at all. "Mark, I will open an account for you; I will deposit funds. Get yourself a decent place to live, clean yourself up. Bathe, for God's sake. Please bathe. I won't kick you out, just do something for yourself. You're disgusting because you choose to be. I've offered you a way out. Now be a man and take it."

"You could just hypnotize me and have me the way you want me."

"I don't want a robot, Mark, I never have."

"Then what do you want from me?"

"Yes, Eve, what do you want from him?"

A tremble started in her feet and she stopped it. She was a vampire now. Eve would not give in to fear. "Adam, if you must know, Mark and I were having a discussion on his hygiene. She tilted her head toward Adam and waited until she saw the smile on his face, the light in his purple eyes.

"You want him to bathe, I take it."

"Yes."

"Then just order him to do it."

"I don't think I should have to order anyone to bathe, Adam. That's my point."

"But he's yours to command."

Eve bristled at Adam's comment until it occurred to her he was being deliberately crude to test her.

"You're right," she answered after pretending to think about it. "Mark, you will cleanse yourself and never present yourself to me in this manner again. Understood?"

Eve could not help noticing the way Mark cringed around Adam. She didn't blame him. Adam evoked fear in the strongest of vampires, let along mortals.

"Mark, leave," Eve snapped. "Stop concentrating on Adam and do as I told you. Go now and don't return until I call for you." She waved her hand and Mark scampered like an obedient little mouse toward the door.

"Bravo." Adam clapped, coming closer to Eve. "So, my wife has teeth."

"Sharp teeth," Eve added.

"Is that a warning?"

"Yes," Eve answered and challenged Adam with a direct stare. "What is it that you want, Adam? I'm busy.

"This is my home and you are my wife," he snorted, "even though you spend most of your time in the arms of another. Yet every time I see you, you have the same words. 'What do you want, Adam, I'm busy.' Don't you tire of telling me that? Why don't you try something else? Try, 'Hello Adam. How are you?'"

Eve looked away before snapping her head around to face Adam head-on. "Hello, Adam. How are you?'"

"I'm fine, dear wife. Now back to my original statement. I've noticed you spend fewer and fewer nights here and more and more of your nights in the arms of another."

"As you do," Eve answered. She opened the door to the patio and picked up the crystals she'd placed there to be recharged from the sun. Placing them in a bowl of spring water, she smiled, stopped and looked at Adam. "I'm making a new potion. Would you like to try it?"

"Why are you still spending so much time on your herbs and potions? You're a vampire. Must you be a witch also?"

"I am what I am, Adam. Nature made me a witch, you made me a vampire. Besides, you keep bringing me gemstones that you think will help me revert."

"But you always look so sad when they don't work. I want you to be happy, Eve. I want that almost as much as I want—" He allowed the words to drop. They were both aware of what he wanted, to be with Eve as he'd been before he'd turned her.

"Adam, if you really want me to be happy you'll need to commission your scientists to build a time machine and send me back to before I met you in this life. And you would not seek me out."

"Why must we spend so much of our time fighting?"

"Because you irritate me, Adam."

"But I see so little of you."

"Enough to irritate me. Where have you been?"

"Oh, around." Adam sat in a chair and pulled it directly in front of Eve. "I'm going to have a drink. Would you like one or have you poisoned the liquor with your crystals?" He accepted the glass Eve handed him. "Why am I trusting you?"

"I have not attempted to poison you, Adam. I gave my word that it would not happen again. As for your trusting me, you really have no choice. I am the creature of your making. I could care less if you trust me."

"Yet you can't stop loving me."

"You accuse me of sleeping in the arms of another and still you think I love you."

"But this is the place you call home. This is where you return to make your witches brew. This is the place you come because you know sooner or later I will return."

"Adam, you're always so sure of yourself. Have you ever thought that maybe, just maybe, I don't want to inconvenience a lover, *if* I have one, with all of my things, that it's easier to leave them here and work from here? Has that thought ever occurred to you?"

"I know you love me, Eve. I can feel your breath quicken as I come near. Your blood momentarily stops flowing in your veins and your heart pounds. I know you love me and I know there is a secret you're keeping from me."

Eve made herself smile, then laugh. "For a vampire you're a paranoid, jealous male, more human than vampire, don't you think?"

"Don't mock me, Eve, and don't try to change the subject. There is something going on with you and that mortal, some connection that you shouldn't have."

"You gave him to me. Are you worried that a mere mortal will replace you?" Her smirk dared him.

"I've put up with this nonsense for way too long. It's been almost two years, Eve. Your dependency on him should have worn away." He walked closer, swallowing his desire to slap away the look of annoyance on her face.

"Why do you care about my relationship with Mark?"

"Why now are you asking him to change, to bathe? You should have done that the first time you fed from him." Adam noticed something flicker behind Eve's eyes and her blocks became stronger.

He shrugged casually, then looked at her squarely, his skin prickly, his senses on alert. "Are you feeding from him, Eve?"

"I'm alive, Adam. Isn't that answer enough?" Eve was doing her best to hold it together trying to not let Adam see her sweat.

"Are you still taking the pills, Eve?"

"On occasion," she answered, noticing Adam was moving even closer to her.

"And the transfusions? Are you using those as well?"

"Sometimes." Adam had now stopped directly in front of her.

"Sullivan, are you feeding from him?"

"Adam, I do believe you're jealous. There was a slight tremor in her voice, one she hoped Adam didn't hear. "No, I've never fed from Sullivan."

"Eve, there was a time when we were friends, when we talked and laughed together. I miss that."

She blinked, he'd surprised her. But then he'd always had the ability to do that. "It's been so long since that time, Adam, I don't know if I remember."

"Do you remember my making love to you?" He waited. "Do you remember telling me that you loved me?"

"I remember that I asked you to let me die."

"Do you remember how much I love you?"

"I remember that you have to leave for months at a time because you can't bear to touch me. I remember that you think I'm making love with Sullivan because you won't. I remember that I've lived this life now for almost two years."

"Do you know what your being with Sullivan does to me?"

"Evidently not enough." Eve's mouth felt dry. This was the last conversation she expected to have with Adam. For months they'd had no conversations, merely fought, then a truce and Adam's never ending stream of gifts.

"I want to kill him," Adam said. He took a breath. "And I want to kill you."

"Then why don't you?"

"Guilt."

"Adam, you remain a contradiction. You present this evil front, and you do evil deeds but deep, very deep, there is a part of you that," she sighed, "I can't quite figure out. It's like maybe you haven't lost all of your humanity."

"Is that your thanks for my not killing you or your lover?"

"First off, I haven't admitted to having a lover. I'm not crazy. But since it's Sullivan you want to kill, I want you to know that I don't think it would be so easy for you to kill either of us. We're not afraid of you, Adam, and it's a dangerous thing to underestimate your opponent."

"Sullivan I did underestimate. I never thought he'd have the balls to oppose me and to sleep with my wife." Adam shook his head. "Do you think he's loving you to get even with me?"

This time it was Eve who laughed. "I can honestly tell you, Adam, that if I am making love to Sullivan, when and if we do you're not on his mind." She laughed again, "Or mine."

"I have always liked your laugh."

Eve didn't miss the wistful look that colored his violet gaze. "I suppose since we're playing nice there are things I like about you." She smiled.

"What?"

"Your eyes, Adam. From the moment I saw you in the church I think that they more than anything else alerted me to the fact that you were a danger to me. No mere mortal has eyes like yours. And definitely not a brother."

"I'm not sure if that's a compliment or comment about my evil nature."

"Evil nature?" Eve stepped away. "I don't think you truly have an evil nature. As you told me long ago, you're a vampire. You have a vampire nature."

"And what of you, Eve? You're also a vampire, but I don't see the true vampire nature in you. You grow more beautiful every day. Your skin is softer, your scent is back. No, Eve, I see nothing of a vampire in you. "

"Not even the fangs?"

"Well, there is that. But tell me, Eve, how have you not had any other physical changes?"

"Perhaps I am able to hold the baseness back. I do have your blood that runs through my veins."

Eve turned toward the sink. They were becoming too pleasant, too much like friends and they both were aware where it would lead. Eve opened the cabinet and began throwing spices into a large bowl. She glanced at Adam, toying with the chrysanthemum for her potion that she'd brought in from the garden. She took it from his fingers and put in a little extra. She shook in the dill, then the fennel.

"Could you pass me the garlic and the myrrh?" she asked.

"Myrrh? What are you making?"

"Oh just something to banish evil spirits." Eve laughed and reached for the sage.

"But I'm not an evil spirit."

"Then you don't have to worry." Eve smiled at him as she added the jade and jasper. She smiled once more and added the malachite.

The last smile had been too much. She should have known it. The playful look was gone from Adam's face; fire replaced the amusement and she could smell his lust. She glanced down briefly and saw his arousal. "Adam, you know it won't work," she said softly, wishing the regret wasn't in her voice.

"I love you, Eve," he said a moment before he crushed her in his arms. She waited for him to push her away, hating the emotion he could still invoke within her soul. For the past two years he'd done nothing but hurt her, yet the flame of love she had for him refused to die.

"Adam, don't," she moaned. "We both know what's going to happen. I don't think I can keep sane playing your yo-yo."

She knew it was no use when he stared for a long moment at her. He was going to kiss her and she was going to let him. "I love you, Eve," he whispered and then he kissed her so slowly that the blood sizzled in her veins and created a raging inferno of lust.

She tried, she really did, not to wind her arms around his neck. But it was as if she had no control. Her body trembled under his touch. He brought her even closer and deepened the kiss. And then as she had known it would, it happened. Adam was clutching her in desperation. She felt the shudders ripping through his body and dropped her hands.

"I love you, Eve," Adam repeated. "You have no idea how hard I'm trying to make this work. It perplexes me to no end that I, Adam Omega, can't conquer this."

"I get the feeling you're trying so hard because you don't like being defeated. Is that it, Adam?"

"For a thousand years I have done any damn thing that I've wanted. None have been able to stop me. I walk in the church and dare anything to happen. I conquered the frigging sun. Hell yes, not being able to conquer something in my own damn mind bothers me. It bothers the hell out of me. And it's part of the reason that I keep trying, that I will continue trying until I succeed. I do not like being defeated even by myself."

Eve laughed and attempted to pull away. "You're crazy, Adam, if you think I will keep allowing you to use me. You either bring it and let's do it or you leave me the hell alone."

Good, Adam thought. That's just what I need. I need her to defy me. I need to show her who's in control.

"You will leave my arms when I give you permission. I control the elements and I will control my damn mind."

"Then do it, Adam. I dare you. Make love to your vampiric wife."

With the challenge trust in his face Adam bent Eve over the back of his arms and plunged his tongue into her mouth, ravaging her with his kisses. He felt her sharp fangs descending and struggled to ignore them. Damn it, he could do this. Then he shuddered, once, twice, three times and then the shudders turned violent as he attempted to hold onto her and she backed away.

Eve swallowed and closed her eyes before turning away, hating the thought of the tears that would surely course down her cheeks, hating that Adam would know.

He opened his right hand, flicked his fingers and the sound of glass shattering filled the room. Perplexed was no longer the word for what Adam was feeling. "Damn…what the hell…I'm so sorry."

She put her hand up to stop him. "Don't be sorry, Adam. You can't help it that I repulse you. I should not have allowed this to happen again. It's me, I'm a fool. It seems that the power of your mind has indeed worked against you, Adam."

"Don't."

She wiped her hand across her cheek, smearing the blood. A bone deep sorrow entered her body. She turned to Adam. "*Eve*," she heard Sullivan calling her. It was then she realized her mind had been open. Sullivan had apparently picked up on her pain. She blinked.

"It's Sullivan," Eve said in a panic and rushed for a wad of paper towels to wipe her face.

"Why are you worried about Sullivan? Does he hurt you?"

She rolled her eyes and gave a glare of disdain over her shoulder. Eve knew Adam was searching for a way to replace his anger at himself. He was trying to transfer it to Sullivan. She wouldn't even dignify that.

"Your mind is open to him. Why isn't it ever open to me?"

"Would you shut the hell up?" Eve said between clenched teeth.

"Answer him."

"Give me a minute."

"Tell him to come here." Adam ignored her glaring. "Oh, the holy water and the crucifixes. I'll get rid of those."

"That's not the reason he won't come."

"Are you saying he no longer fears them? Then why won't he come? Is it me that he fears?"

"Adam, it's out of respect. He's not trying to deliberately make you angry."

"So then he's not sleeping with my wife?"

Eve groaned and closed her eyes. When she opened them Sullivan was standing in front of her. She couldn't believe it and apparently neither could Adam. "Is there something wrong?" she asked Sullivan, unable to meet his gaze.

"You didn't answer me. I wanted to make sure no harm had come to you."

"You came to my home to rescue my wife from me?"

Oh damn, Eve thought, some psychic she was. She should have predicted this and she definitely should have known Sullivan would hone in on her if she didn't answer.

Sullivan's hand came up and he touched Eve's face. "You've been crying." He looked at her, waiting for an answer. Then he turned to Adam. "What did you do to her?"

"You are getting bolder every day. First you sleep with my wife and now you enter my home to be her champion. I would rethink this if I were you. If you value your existence you should leave."

"I will leave when Eve is ready to accompany me."

"Eve will not be joining you tonight. Tonight Eve will sleep in my bed."

I don't believe this, Eve thought and moved between the two vampires, both of whom gave her dirty looks.

"Now you think to protect Sullivan." Adam said. "Were you thinking of

Sullivan a few moments ago when you kissed me with all the passion that was in you?"

Before Sullivan turned to her, she felt his pain, saw him swallow and she swallowed as well. Eve had not wanted to hurt Sullivan, but she should have known Adam would have no such feelings.

He stared at her face, at the sticky residue of her tears, and she knew her pain was written all over her face.

"Are you leaving with me?" he asked quietly.

"She's staying," Adam said but Sullivan didn't bother to look in his direction. Instead, he continued to stare at Eve. He held out his hand to her. "It's time for us to go."

A volt of electricity slammed into Sullivan, so strong that it knocked Eve into the cabinets and she slid to the floor. When Sullivan bent at the knees to assist her up, another volt hit them both, scorching Eve's fingers.

For a moment she was dazed. Looking upward at Sullivan, she saw the fury mount in him as he placed his body in front of her. His teeth clamped tightly together in anger and pain as Adam leveled another volley at him.

When Eve was safely out of the way, Sullivan turned with speed and agility and leveled his own volt of electricity toward Adam. "Don't you even give a damn that you injured her with your childish behavior?" Sullivan's voice was no longer the soft gentle tone that Eve was accustomed to, but a roar. In fact, both their voices reminded her of the roar of tornadoes. She trembled and covered her ears knowing some of this, if not all of it, was her fault.

In the blink of an eye Sullivan had sprung from his position and had his hands around Adam's throat squeezing, choking him. His normally pale skin had reddened in anger, his blue eyes made an even deeper shade of blue by his fury. "Damn you, Adam."

A sneer curved Adam's face as he twisted from Sullivan's grip touching his hand to the vamp's face laughing when the spot he'd touched sizzled and burned. "Thank you, Sullivan, I've been waiting for this. Now I'm going to kick your ass."

Shit, Eve thought racing toward the two out of control vampires. She reached for Adam to pull him from Sullivan then stumbled and fell when Adam backhanded her.

"That's the last straw." Sullivan yelled, hitting Adam with a volley of electricity. He turned toward Eve and yelled, "Go home and stay there." He snapped his fingers, transporting Eve to his home.

"Hell no! Oh no you didn't." Adam slammed an elbow into Sullivan's face and snapped his fingers, bringing Eve back into the melee.

From her vantage point she could see out to the lake in the distance. She blinked. It had to be a mirage. Then she remembered the last time the water had looked so ominous. That had been when Adam had discovered that she was Eyanna reincarnated. A horrible roar filled the night and Eve froze, covering her ears at the noise from the elements. Then she blinked and looked at the two vamps in battle. The noise wasn't coming from the elements but from the vampires. *Damn*, she thought.

Eve watched in horror as the waters rose higher and higher. Surely not even

Adam had such powers, she thought. But even as she thought it, she knew he did.

"Sullivan, look," Eve screamed, pointing toward the quickly cresting waves. "Maybe you should go. I'll be fine, Adam won't hurt me."

Fire poured from Sullivan's eyes. "Are you crazy? Do you think I will leave you here with this maniac. I leave when you leave."

"Then you will leave as dust," Adam roared even louder.

Eve was once again forced to cover her ears to protect them. Tornadoes, she'd first assumed. Adam had brought forth a tornado. Now she wasn't so sure. She didn't think any force of nature could pack this kind of punch. The beautiful Italian tiles were popping up from the floor and the bulbs in the lamps were shattering with an intensified clatter. Adam raised his right hand and the house began to splinter at the seams from his fury.

"Stop, this is crazy," Eve shouted and ran with her hands outstretched to stand between Sullivan and Adam. She couldn't have picked a worst moment to referee a fight. Both vampires were simultaneously shooting fire at each other and both hit her with it.

When Eve screamed out in pain, Sullivan glanced toward her, lowered his hand and shook his head as if to clear it. "Eve, move," he said, racing for her. "Go back to the house and wait for me."

"I can't leave you here with Adam. You go."

"You know that's not going to happen." Sullivan turned them both, deflecting Adam's next volley, angered that Adam had once again burned Eve with his powers. He groaned, knowing she wouldn't leave him. He lifted her hands and kissed them quickly. "Don't worry, it will heal," he said softly as he shoved her around a corner. "Stay there. Please," he commanded, then looked at the anger on her face. "I'm sorry." Then once again his own fury matched Adam's.

"Aim at me, Adam, not Eve. Surely you have more control than that. But no, wait," Sullivan snarled. "Isn't that the way you killed Joanna, lack of control?"

Eve came to stand beside him but Sullivan pushed her aside. "Get out of here," he screamed at her. "Damn it, how many times do I have to tell you? Go home."

Then to Eve's surprise Sullivan shot a beam at Adam that she could have sworn carried as much voltage as Adam's.

"She is home and home is where she will remain," Adam retorted.

"This was settled, Adam. I came to you as a man and told you my intentions. I love Eve and she loves me. I am not leaving without her. So come on and give it your best shot because I can take it." Sullivan glanced briefly in Eve's direction. "Just make sure you aim at me."

"Fool, are you insane? You don't want to keep trying me. I'll annihilate you permanently. It's enough that I've allowed you to live, ignoring that you were bedding my wife. But your coming here to my home to challenge me? I've been too soft. On both of you." Adam spoke sharply, his glare taking in Eve as well as Sullivan. "Now you think you can come to my home and take my wife from me right in front of my face." This time he used both hands and sent a volley of electricity at both Sullivan and Eve.

A roaring wind whipped about the house, sending bricks from the massive fireplace flying in all directions. Eve glanced out the window from the floor where Adam's power had sent her and saw the lake swell and waves rising higher into the air than she'd ever seen. She saw the look in Adam's eyes and knew his next volley would be lethal. He wasn't kidding. He was going to kill Sullivan. His eyes blazed with blood and his body shook as both of his hands pointed in Sullivan's direction.

"Adam, don't hurt him. Stop please," she pleaded and turned just in time to catch Sullivan's glare.

"Don't ever do that again," Sullivan said angrily. "I'm a vampire, Eve, a damn eight-hundred-year-old vampire. I do not need a less than two-year-old fledging to protect me. You're my woman, I will protect you."

Adam turned briefly toward her and for a moment the red rescinded from his eyes and the purple she loved was back. Then he laughed and looked again toward Sullivan. *Oh hell*, Eve thought, wishing she had time to pray.

At that the roof flew off the house and the waters from the lake came rushing in. All Eve could remember was human science. Electricity and water didn't mix. When Adam shot his bolt across the room, he was met by two that sent him flying backwards into the far wall.

Adam looked up, dazed. Pain flicked in his violet eyes before they turned red. His mind reeled as he acknowledged that there were two volts from two different sources. Eve had used the powers he'd given her against him.

"You said you'd never betray me again." He held his hand toward her and was immediately knocked aside by Sullivan.

"You will not touch her again," Sullivan roared. "She's mine and I will not allow you to keep hurting her."

Enough, Eve thought, raising both hands and sending electric shots out at both vampires. "You will not fight over me as though you're two dogs fighting over a bone. I'm a woman. You will not decide my life for me. I will do that on my own."

Thunder sounded in the sky and flashes of lightning covered the horizon. This had to stop. This madness wasn't about anger anymore, but about love and pain and loss. And so much loneliness that it crackled with the energy of the three of them. They were all afraid of being alone. That was what was at the root of all of this madness.

Eve looked at Adam, believing in her heart that she was Eyanna reborn. Adam had allowed himself to be turned into a vampire in order to save her life and as Eyanna, she'd died once to save Adam's soul.

And now right before her eyes his soul was turning black. She couldn't allow that, she had to stop it, end it somehow in a way Sullivan would neither understand nor approve. But she had to do it just the same.

Adam's ego was bruised beyond repair and this night would end with the three of them dead if she didn't do something. She no longer feared Adam but she didn't want either man hurt and she didn't want to be their prize. She would do her own choosing.

As the cracks of thunder became louder Eve glared at Adam. "Stop that nonsense this instant."

"You're my wife," he declared, "my wife. How dare your lover come in our home to claim you."

"You're right," Eve said, glaring now at Sullivan. "He should never have come here."

"You're my wife," Adam repeated, blind fury making him unreasonable.

Eve watched as the waves became fiercer and more water poured into the house through the now open roof.

"You're right," she said softly, going up to Adam. "You're right, Adam, I am your wife."

"You disrespected me," Adam growled.

"It wasn't my intention. I didn't know that Sullivan would come here."

"You're not leaving this house with him." Adam glared at her now. "I will kill you before I allow that to happen."

"She will leave with me," Sullivan growled behind her, his hand extended to send another volt.

"I won't," Eve said in a hiss to Sullivan. "Leave us." She turned back to Adam, ignoring Sullivan. "Adam, what you say is true. I am your wife, this is my home, our home. Sullivan and I both disrespected you by his coming here. You've been gracious in not bothering us about our relationship. I appreciate that, I know you did it because you love me."

"You're trying to twist me around your little finger, Eve, I'm not having it. I should have never listened to your sweet talk. You made me feel guilty about what I did. I'm a vampire, the best in the world." Adam turned his glare on Sullivan. "And yet you flaunt him in my face. That was wrong, Eve."

"It was wrong, I should not have baited you."

"You're still doing it. Where is the fire, the I-don't-give-a-damn-Eve? This woman you're pretending to be I don't want."

"Adam, I'm trying to get you to stop before the things you do become irreversible."

"What? Are you still tying to save my soul?"

"Yes, Adam, I am. You're not completely lost and I don't want you to become so, not if I can prevent it."

"Why do you care? You make love with Sullivan and you despise me. All you ever have for me is vile words and evil glares."

"I care because I love you." She heard the low moan, felt the empty spot and knew Sullivan had vanished. She couldn't stop, not even to link with Sullivan telepathically. She had to continue because she meant what she said. She didn't want to see Adam's soul dammed.

"Adam, you can't have it both ways. I know you love me," she said walking toward Adam, ignoring the dangerous glint in his stance, the red in his eyes deepening even more.

"Adam, if you kill me you and I both know you will regret it. I fear what will happen if you do that. Yes, I fear for your soul and I fear for the world if you're truly alone in it, without me or even the thought that I might one day return."

"You're trying to save your life."

"Of course I am. But I'm also trying to save you." She touched a hand to his cheek and caressed it. "Adam, I need to live in order for the good in you to live.

Don't you understand that?"

He groaned and covered her hand with his own. "Eve, you make me insane. We both know that if I were seeking salvation that my salvation lies in your love. But I'm not seeking salvation. So tell me now while I'm in a mood to listen. What is it that you want me to do?"

"I think for both our sakes we need to part. I'm no fool. I know that you've reined in your anger concerning what I was doing. I've tried my best not to flaunt it." Her arms went around him and she felt the coiled tension in him. "Adam, what I'm going to say will be hard for you to believe. I think the best way for me to save you, to save myself, is for me to leave. As much as you don't want that you will have to make the decision to allow me to live even if I no longer live here."

"You're alive."

"For now." She pulled back and stared at him. "I need for you to allow me to leave and to wish me well. I need you to love me enough to want to see me happy."

"You think that will save my soul."

"It's a beginning, Adam. Selfless love requires sacrifice. You will hurt but you will heal. And I won't have to worry about you descending into darkness."

"I think if you leave me that will happen."

"No, my love. If I stay it'll happen."

"I do want you to live."

A smile curved Eve's lips. "Thank you. And?"

"I do want you to be happy." He growled. "But I don't want you with Sullivan." He walked away from Eve and began pacing. "God! I want him dead. Why the hell did I give my word to allow him to live? He's pissing me off big time. I want to be the one you're making love to. I want to sleep in your bed and hold you in my arms every night."

"You've tried repeatedly, you know that, so have I. I do love you, Adam. I always will."

"I want you to be happy," Adam said.

"Then stop this macho Grand Master vampire act. Stop tearing up things whenever you become angry."

She walked closer. "I didn't know all of the elements were at your control. Look at this mess," she said. "It's going to cost a fortune to repair."

"Adam," she said, throwing her arms around him, knowing he wouldn't shudder, wouldn't push her away. He never did when he was angry, only when he wanted to make love to her.

"Adam, for nearly two years you haven't been able to touch me. How long do you want me to wait?"

"He came to my home."

"I know he shouldn't have but I'm not talking about Sullivan now. I'm talking about the two of us."

"You used your powers against me, powers I wasn't aware you had. You betrayed me."

"No, Adam, I stopped you from hurting Sullivan."

"Sullivan was doing fine on his own."

"But I didn't know that."

"So you chose to help him?"

"I chose not to allow you to do something you would regret. You're not this monster, Adam, and I understand. You don't want to be this way. You want to be with me. I know that, I do. I grieve with you for that, but I don't want to keep hurting and you're hurting me, Adam. You're killing me with your constant rejection. If you truly love me, release me before you kill me, before your soul is truly unredeemable."

"How can I? For a thousand years I searched for you and waited for your return. I've had many women, Eve. But not once in all this time have I had anyone to love."

"I know that, I know that you've been lonely. I would give anything if I could change that for you. But our fighting…too many innocent people are getting hurt." Eve swiped her lips with her tongue. She wanted to tell Adam that Sullivan was hurting as well, that he'd spent hundreds of years waiting for love and being lonely, but now that Adam was finally listening, she would not mention Sullivan to him now.

"How do you think I can release you? Even if I wanted to I couldn't. I am what I've been for the past thousand years because of my love for you."

"Then at least learn to restrain yourself." Eve saw the waters recede. Then the thunder dropped to a rumble. Still, Adam's eyes remained red.

"Adam, I love you," she moaned, holding him tighter. "I will always love you, but I need to find someone who can hold me when they are not filled with fury, someone who will hold me when they want to love me."

"I want to do that, Eve. I want to hold you, I want to make love to you so badly that I would give up my damned soul and gladly go to hell if I could make love to you once."

"Don't ever say that."

"But it's true."

"I know but still…"

"Eve…" Adam shuddered. "When I leave you, when I hold other women I'm thinking of you, always of you."

"That doesn't make me happy to know, Adam. I know you think this is something that you're doing for me but think about it for a moment. You want to kill Sullivan because I'm sleeping with him. How do you think your sleeping with others makes me feel? Adam, it's not my fault that we aren't together. I've been more than willing a dozen times. And to hear you tell me that you can hold others and you're still unable to hold me, how do you think that makes me feel? Sure, I know your aversion to female vamps, but it still doesn't help me. It hurts. You ask if I remember our making love. Of course I remember it. I treasure that time. I didn't know that would be all we had. A part of me wishes with everything in me that your aversion therapy had worked, but then what? Adam, our entire relationship has been so volatile. It's easy with…"

"He's using you to replace Joanna."

"And you're using me to replace Eyanna."

"But you are Eyanna."

"I am, but then again I'm not, I'm me. True, I came into this life with some knowledge of you, but to be honest with you, I don't know how I still love you. You've caused me nothing but pain."

"Even when I made love to you?"

She smiled then and her eyes flickered as she remembered. "No, Adam, that one night you gave me nothing but pleasure. But baby, you turned me into a vampire and it's been downhill from there. You said I will live for eternity. I don't want to live an eternity like this. I would like to find a way for us to at least be friends."

"I can't make you any promises."

"I know that but you can try."

Adam tried for a smile. "You know how I am. I will allow it to fester and then I will have to do something."

"I would expect nothing less. But this, this massive show of power, I don't think it took all of that. You've completely destroyed our home."

"So this is still *our* home?" He smiled at her. "At least I haven't destroyed that." He held her for a long moment and rocked her. His body shook as he remembered. "Eve, never pit me against Sullivan again; he will not win."

Ignoring that comment she decided to ask him what she should have asked her husband two years before. "Adam, what really happened with Tarasha? Did you make love to her? Please tell me. It's been so long, can't you talk about it?" She moved back to stare deep into his eyes. He breathed hard and Eve knew at last Adam would tell her what had happened.

His beautiful violet eyes filled with shame and pain was etched into every cell. "Adam, I'm not here to judge you. I think you need to talk about this."

"Therapy, Eve?"

"Yes, why not? You've carried this pain for too long, it's time to let go of it, tell me please, what happened with Tarasha?"

"You already know, she turned me."

"That's the quick version, tell me the whole story."

The shame intensified and covered her mind as she linked with his. He was staring at her, but Eve knew he didn't see her.

"They were going to kill you," Adam said quietly. "I couldn't let that happen." He sucked in his breath. "Yes, I made love to her. I betrayed you with her."

"But to save me, Adam."

"I was a priest, Eve. I left the church to save you, and then I did this, made love to another woman, a vampire." A shudder claimed him and he shook his head, trying to will away the image.

"Adam, don't stop, please."

"While I was making love to her, she bit into me right as I…" He stumbled over the words, avoiding her eyes, "At the moment of my orgasm, she bit into me and drained every drop of my blood. And while she was doing it, I was begging her for more, until with my dying breath all I remembered was the foul smell of her, the repulsive taste of her and her fangs buried deep within my flesh." He shuddered again and stopped speaking.

Pain radiated through him, making the link painful. Eve massaged his arms gently, crooning softly to him to encourage him. "Its okay," she said, "I forgive you for going to Tarasha." She was surprised at the relief that rushed through her.

Adam pressed her hands to his lips. His eyes moist, he drew in a shaky breath and continued.

"She brought me back and I came back with a vengeance, thirsting for blood, for her blood. I couldn't believe it. First shame and then guilt filled me but I drank from her knowing I needed her blood, her strength, knowing I had betrayed your love. She thought I would make love to her again. She thought wrong. It was the last thought she had." Adam looked at Eve. "Until I found you in this lifetime, I'd told myself that I had not made love to her, that I'd resisted, but I hadn't."

Eve rubbed her fingers lightly against Adam's temple, not afraid that he would pull away. For whatever reason Adam was not only willingly accepting her touch, but appeared hungry for it. "And then what happened?" Eve asked.

"And then I killed her and I became this. If only you had loved me enough..." His lids fluttered and closed.

"I did love you, Adam. I loved you enough that guilt made me do what I did. I wasn't running from you, but I could think of nothing else to do to save you. You left the church for me, you became a vampire for me. You were giving up your soul for me. I couldn't handle that, Adam. The guilt was too much. You were and are a good man with a good soul. I had to save your soul the same as you had to save me. I love you. I begged God to take my life and allow you to redeem your soul.

"That's why I can't allow you to throw it away. If you killed Sullivan you would kill something in me, and if you kill me, you will kill something in yourself and your soul will be lost forever. Don't you see, Adam, my being with Sullivan is best for both of us."

Adam sighed, then sighed again. "It appears that your methods for saving my soul are always the same—to leave me."

"For whatever reason, it seems fated that we remain apart. I would rather we have that and the love than allow hatred to invade our hearts. I don't know if things can change, if you can ever make love to me, but I know you love me.

"I know that it hurts you that I'm with Sullivan but believe me, I'm not with Sullivan to hurt you. I really do love him, Adam, and if you think about it, I know you would much rather think of me being happy and loving Sullivan than miserable and hating you. As hard as it may be to hear the things I've said, it's no harder than your wanting me to believe that you sleep with other women for me. We both sound crazy, yet I know what you mean and I know you understand what I meant."

"I do."

"Then what are we going to do?"

"I've had a dream concerning you for many years. Do you want to know what it is?"

"Do I dare ask?"

Adam laughed. "That vampire bed, I've always wanted to sleep in it with you, with you wanting to be there with me, not your getting up and lying on the floor, not your remaining out of fear. I want one night with you in that bed."

"But you know you can't make love to me."

"No, but I can love you. I can lie there with you in my arms and I can ask for your forgiveness. Let me hold you in our bed, Eve. Give me this one night to love you."

The heat from his tears scorched her and mixed with her own. His hand swiped the tears from her face and he brought her fingers to his lips, kissing them, and then he kissed her. "One night, wife, give me one night. You're asking a lot of me. Give me something in return."

"How can I resist you, Adam? I've never been able to. And she didn't resist. Eve spun with him in the breeze he created, allowing the wind to take them to their destination. If she could have told Sullivan with a link why she was doing what she was doing she would have. But there wasn't time. Adam was hurting also, and a pacified Adam was much better than an enraged one. Besides, she didn't want him to hurt. She'd thought she did but she didn't. He was lonely and he'd given up everything that he was and had ever been for her. One night was not too much to ask. She would make this up to Sullivan. They had the rest of eternity to be happy. Eve stayed in Adam's arms knowing in a way this would be their parting.

"I need you to know how much I love you, Eve. Can I show you that at least?"

"I already know."

"You only think you do."

"Then show me, Adam," Eve answered, knowing he meant to bite her. She steadied herself.

"Have you given yourself to Sullivan in this manner?"

"No," she replied, "never." Then she felt his fangs as they sank into her carotid artery.

At first there was pain, brief and hot. Then came the images. A thousand years of suffering, a thousand years of Adam calling her name, only to be followed by his unbearable sorrow, loneliness, ache.

And then came his love. The love consumed Eve and filled her, and her soul joined with his. She loved him too. Oh, God, she loved him and nothing and no one would ever compare with it.

When he'd given her his images he turned his neck and Eve bit into him, gently at first, ignoring all of Sullivan's warnings. She poured her own images into Adam, all of her love. She allowed him to see her pain and her loneliness, how much it hurt her that he was repulsed by her.

What she couldn't tell him with words she told him by blood. Eve gave Adam her heart and soul. She shuddered as his blood filled her mouth and she drank. This had never been about any of the things they'd fought about. It had been and would always be about their love.

When she had given him all she had to give she gently licked away the remaining drops of blood and swiped his marks with her tongue, sealing the area.

"You are still my wife," Adam whispered.

"I know. I will always be that."

"When I find a way to be with you I will come for you. I will reclaim you."

Eve didn't have an answer for that; she just held him.

"If he ever hurts you, Eve, or allows harm to come to you I will kill him. And if he ever challenges me for you again, there will be no stopping my wrath, no sweet talk from you. Nothing in heaven or hell will save him."

"I know."

"You're being so agreeable because you sense you're winning."

Eve smiled. "Yes." She felt Adam smile back.

"I mean it," Adam said. "When I find a way, a cure, I'm coming for you. It doesn't matter how long or where you are. One day you will be with me where you belong."

"And until that day?"

"Until that day, I will try and do as you ask. I do love you and now you finally know that." He smiled in satisfaction. "I will allow you to have a private life."

"Allow?"

"Don't push me, Eve."

And for once she decided not to push him. She lay in his arms and played with his raven black hair, pulling back to look at his now purple eyes. "I always did love your eyes," she said, nestling into the curve of his arms. *One vampire down and one to go.*

"What if after tonight Sullivan doesn't want you?"

"He'll want me." Eve spoke with confidence. "He loves me. Oh, there is no doubt in my mind he'll be angry, or that he's hurt, but he will forgive me."

"You know I'm hoping you're wrong about that."

"I know you are," Eve laughed, "but I'm not. Adam, tell me about Joanna. Who was she to Sullivan and to you and why does Sullivan hate you because of her?"

"I think I will leave those questions for Sullivan to answer for you if he will. He hasn't spoken of it in over three hundred years, not until you."

Adam shrugged his shoulders. "I guess now he feels I have something that I want to keep and he wants to take from me."

"I'll ask Sullivan, but he's not using me to get back at you. I know the difference."

"Let's hope so." Adam narrowed his eyes. "Will this still be your home?"

"This will always be my home, just as you will always be my husband."

"I want your promise, Eve. You will not bond with Sullivan in the manner you just bonded with me. Agreed? This is your home and I am your husband and that will always remain true."

"And if I did how would you know?"

"Do not be flip. I would know."

"Not if I wore my crystal necklace. It continues to keep my thoughts hidden from you."

A moment of uncertainty claimed Adam. He'd never explained the bonding ritual and apparently neither had Sullivan. From this moment forward there would be nothing she could hide from him if he wanted to know.

"Eve, this is serious. Do not test me on this. As for your crystals, they've never given you the power you thought they did. Granted, they seemed to work but if I had chosen to break through your barrier I could have at any time. I choose not to." He smiled at her. "Give me your word."

"You have it."

He pushed a stray hair from her face and caressed her gently. He studied her for a moment deciding not to tell her exactly what a bonding bite was.

"Adam stop worrying." Eve smiled. "I gave you my word." She leaned into him, gave him a quick kiss, then moved away before her movement could cause either of them pain.

"Do you think this is my curse, to have wanted you with me for so long and not be able to have you?" Adam said wistfully.

"No more so than it was my curse to die trying to save your soul and be reborn trying to save my own. Now look at us. I do remember being Eyanna. Adam, I do remember loving you then as well as now. I'm sorry that I hurt you in that lifetime and sorry that I've hurt you in this one."

He pressed her to him. "I'm sorry that I've hurt you," he said. His fangs pierced her skin again, but only about a quarter of an inch. "This is between only the two of us, Eve. I will never allow anyone else to feed from me and neither will you. This alone is ours. "This I can give you," he said, "my strength and my power. If you ever need it or me, Eve, just whisper my name and I will come."

"Like you did when you locked me away in the coffin?"

He chuckled. "No, I'll come. I promise I'll never ignore your call again."

For the rest of the night and morning Adam linked with Eve, nicking her flesh, drawing on her blood, feeding a lifetime of memories into her mind and her heart. And likewise Eve took Adam's blood, creating a bond that could never be broken. And when they were done talking they fell asleep, still linked.

Chapter 17

^LEve looked around her ruined home. *What a mess*, she thought, then shook her head. She was alive, so were Sullivan and Adam. They all had another chance to get it right. And she had to do just that, get things right with Sullivan.

Adam materialized beside her and she nodded toward the mess. "You've got a busy day ahead of you, Adam. I suggest you get on the phone and get some people over to fix the results of your latest temper tantrum.

"I could do it all myself," he boasted, "but another time." He narrowed his eyes and allowed a hard breath to escape. "So, you're going to go make nice with the other vamp?"

Eve brought her eyes upwards but didn't answer.

"There is one thing, Eve, that I made no promises about. You're keeping secrets from me, secrets that have nothing to do with Sullivan. You and that mortal, that excuse for human flesh. What is it between the two of you?"

She shrugged her shoulder. "No more questions, Adam. I need to go and repair the damage in my relationship, while you repair the damage to our home."

With that, Eve closed her eyes, wondering if it would work. It would be the first time she'd consciously done it. *Sullivan*, she repeated over and over in her mind and opened her eyes to find herself standing in the middle of his bedroom. He was sitting at his desk glaring at her.

"You stayed the night with him and most of the day."

"He's still my husband," Eve said, slowly walking toward him.

"What did you do, trade your body to save me?"

"You didn't need saving." Eve studied Sullivan for a moment, then smiled. "I forgive your crudeness."

"Don't forgive it, I meant it."

"It was a kiss, Sullivan, it meant nothing," she lied.

"Then why the tears? Because once again Adam shoved you away and hurt you and once again you turn to me on the rebound. I know you still love him, Eve. I've never asked you to stop because I know it's not that easy. But I would ask this. If you want to live with what he gives you, then please stop returning to me. Like you, I hurt also, and like Adam, I love you. But I think it's time you made a choice."

"Wouldn't my being here now with you tell you my choice?"

He pulled back her collar and saw the faint remnants of the marks on her neck. Then he examined her body, seeing the marks all over her. He was enraged and closed his eyes against the onslaught of pain.

"What did you do?" Sullivan all but moaned.

"I wanted to stop fighting with Adam. I gave him something he needed, and I accepted the things he wanted to show me. It was necessary."

"You bonded with him," Sullivan roared.

"I was already bonded with him."

"You've never allowed me to..." He crushed her to him, held her neck between his hands and allowed his fangs to descend. He pierced her skin lightly and tasted her blood before she shoved him away.

"Are you crazy?" Eve shouted, wiping the blood from her neck with her fingers.

"Why him, why not me?"

"Because I gave him permission." *Men, vampire or otherwise*, Eve thought. "Look, Sullivan, Adam has no other way to communicate with me. Do you understand? This is all he can give me, his memories of us together. My God, man, stop being so damn blind. Adam loves me, we both know it. It wasn't until yesterday that I truly understood how much he loves me.

"Sullivan, he's given up everything for me and it kills him that I'm with you. If you think I'm going to apologize to you for giving him that, then think again." She marched away from him, fuming.

"What are you doing to me?" Sullivan asked Eve at last.

"I didn't mean to hurt you."

"Yet you did."

"Sullivan, listen to me please. Adam had nothing else he could give me. He asked that I do this one thing for him. I bonded with him because it felt right. I wanted to save the three of us from this madness. Surely you can see that. Isn't the fact that I'm here with you now proof?"

"No, it's not going to be that easy this time. I'm your safe haven, the place you come to lick your wounds. Adam is the place you go when you want to bond."

She wanted to be hard, cold, a true vampiric witch, but she felt Sullivan's hurt clear down to her bones. "Sullivan, I did what I had to do."

"No, Eve, you did what you wanted. You enjoy both of us wanting you." He stopped and smiled a little. "I can't say that I blame you. Who wouldn't want all of that attention, two vampires calling on the forces of nature to fight for the right to love you?"

"Do you think I wanted it?"

"You could have prevented it."

"Now you're saying that whole thing was my fault?"

"I'm saying that you never should have kissed him. You never should have given him a reason to make you cry. And then to refuse to answer me when I called..." He sighed again and looked at her hard. "If I had not felt your sorrow

I would never have gone after you."

"Sullivan, it's over, I'm here."

"But you weren't here when you should have been. I didn't know if you were dead or alive."

Eve stared at Sullivan and then laughed out loud. "You liar, you entered my mind. Did you think I wouldn't know it? Of course you knew I was alive."

"I wasn't going to completely leave you with that maniac, no matter how angry I was with you."

"Did I tell you that you're my hero?"

Sullivan smiled. "No, you didn't." The tension began to lessen in his shoulders. "Would you tell me why?"

"You fought for me, Sullivan."

"So did Adam. Is he your hero also?"

"No."

"Why, because you expect heroics from him?"

"You're my hero because your main concern in the midst of battle was making sure I was safe. That makes you my hero." She saw the way he preened and knew her words were making a place for her again in his heart. "Thank you, Sullivan."

"I didn't know you'd developed all the powers you demonstrated."

"Neither did I, until yesterday."

"You were protecting me." He put his hand to her chin. "But that's not your job, understand? I take care of you."

Eve moved closer to Sullivan, allowing her hand to trail up his arm. "But I love you. I will never be able to stand by and see anyone harm you, not even Adam. I know you can handle yourself, you did so quite nicely, but still, Adam pissed me off, he was playing dirty. I didn't like it."

"Then why did you choose to stay there with him?"

"Because I realized that it was not about his anger, but his frustrations. I have tired of playing the game, pretending, when we all know the way it is. I had to settle things with Adam before I could come to you."

A sigh long and weary came out of Sullivan and for a moment longer he allowed himself to be distracted by Eve's touching him. He loved the gentle way her hand found him and made him hard in an instant. "There is one thing in my favor," Sullivan said. "You were faced with a choice of whom to protect and even though I neither needed nor wanted your protection you chose me."

"Doesn't that count for something?"

"It does. It means a lot and I want to thank you for that." He smiled at her, thinking of her sending an electric current toward Adam. But then he thought of the blood bond between her and Adam and caught her fingers in his hand and brought them away from his crotch.

He shook his head no, then wagged a finger in her face. "Bonding is a serious thing, Eve, not to be taken lightly." He spoke gently but with authority so there would be no mistaking what he meant.

"I gathered that much, Sullivan. But neither you nor Adam has ever explained the significance of all the different bites. Bites given in passion and a bonding bite, what's the difference?"

"A great deal. Bonding is more like a pledge, a marriage, freely giving of your love. It's given to that one special person. I've never given or received a bonding bite, many passion bites, never one of bonding. Passion bites are as common as one night stands. You haven't been in this world long, Eve, I'll grant you that. But I'm not a fool. You knew what was happening between you and Adam. Please respect me enough to admit to that much."

"Yes, I knew," Eve admitted at last.

"Did he force you?"

"He didn't force me."

"If you're not here when I return, then I will have my answer. If you are here, then I hope you know that it means I will not accept your going between the two of us. It will mean you want me and only me. Do you understand?"

"I understand that I am not one to be talked to in that manner, neither by you nor Adam. I'm sick of both of you and you can both go to hell." Eve wasn't answering any ultimatum. No, she had not intended to hurt Sullivan, and no, she'd not intended to kiss Adam. The kiss…well, the kiss had been a long time in coming. As for the bonding, she wasn't going to lie to herself. For in that bonding with Adam more past life memories had come soaring back. She swallowed, wanting to scream, and when Sullivan disappeared she did scream out to the cosmos.

"Give me back my life."

❖

Her voice was calling him. Eve was desperate. He heard her desperation. She had not had time to decide. He would give her that time.

Sullivan held his hands to his face and wondered what he would do should Eve decide to remain with Adam. He supposed there really wasn't anything he could do. The choice was Eve's to make, not his. Now she was unsure, perhaps a bit sad, thinking that she'd hurt him. Well, there was something in that, not what he wanted, but something.

He unwrapped a fresh package of his Turkish cigarettes. The plastic wrapping caught and stuck to his finger despite his efforts to dislodge it. He wondered at the mundane things he was trying to divert his attention, as if giving up Eve would be that easy. It would never be that easy.

In that moment of clarity Sullivan thought he understood how Adam must be feeling. He'd loved Eve for a thousand years, first as Eyanna, now in her present form. And Sullivan would admit loving Eve was addictive. He was almost tempted to answer her voice, to plead with her to remain with him but he would not. He'd forever wonder about her love, as if he didn't already. But at least before he'd known Eve came to him out of need. If she came out of pity, he would rather not have her.

Sullivan sighed and looked around at the grave markers. This was where he came to think. The times when Eve wondered where he was, this was where he was. He found solace of sorts in the stillness of the graveyard and as always he wished that somewhere along the way he'd had the courage to end it, to call it quits, to rest. He thought of Eve. No, he would not like her leaving. Now that she walked the earth as a near immortal he would walk it also. No one was a true immortal. There were so many ways in which a vampire could die and maybe in a thousand more years Sullivan would join their ranks.

"Sullivan." Eve's sweet voice called to him again and again. He wanted to answer her and say, "Here am I," but he did naught. He would return home when the time was right and if Eve was there he would make love to her and if she was not… Well, if she was not, he would return here to this place of solitude and he would ponder his life.

❖

Rage filled Adam and threatened to get the better of him. In the beginning his love for Eve had caused him to turn her when he'd strictly forbidden anyone to create any more vampires. And now his desire for Eve had turned him into something he wasn't. He'd caused her more pain in two years than she'd ever experienced.

As Adam sat alone in the pew of St. Michaels, he reflected on his life. He thought back to a thousand years ago when Eve had been Eyanna and he'd been married to her. He thought of how much he'd loved her, how much she'd loved him. He remembered how he'd in essence given his life for her and how she'd given her life for him and neither of them had been happy for the sacrifices.

The bonding last night, that had been about more than sharing memories. It had been sharing exactly who and what they were and who they'd always been. He couldn't believe after what they'd gone through that she would leave him.

Yes, he'd given her his word that he'd allow it, but the mere fact that she'd left him so easily added a new hurt to the constantly growling mountain of pain she'd given him. He wondered why he'd ever pestered the Almighty all these years to return her to him. Nothing was as he'd thought it would be.

But this damn indignity. Before he could talk himself out of it, he raised his hand and sent a volt of energy toward the pulpit shattering it into splinters. He sighed, not enough. He again aimed a finger and destroyed several pews. He breathed deep, not feeling better. He'd not relieved enough stress. Adam left the church and returned home. He walked about his home, their home, and a shudder filled his soul. Despite her promise that this was her home Adam would have to be a fool not to know what was coming. Walking to the kitchen he breathed in the scent of Eve's forgotten potion. With a thrust of his hand Adam shoved all of Eve's herbs and crystals to the floor and then he roared and roared some more. This nonsense had to stop. He could barely see through the red haze but enough to wreak considerable damage. The carnage he wrought in his home was nothing compared to what he wanted to do.

He'd promised he'd try and control his rage. He sighed, wondering if it was a promise he could keep. At least he could clean up the mess before Eve returned. Only his immense guilt stayed his hand from taking revenge on Eve and on Sullivan. It wasn't his love for her that stilled him but his guilt for having forced on her a life she did not want, a life he didn't want for her.

"God," he pleaded, "is this my hell? You brought her back to me and refuse to let me have her. If ever I were in Your graces, help me, let me show her how much I love her. Let me make love to my wife before the last vestige of humanity is gone from me.

"Eve doesn't believe I'm truly evil. If I have to continue in this life knowing she's warming Sullivan's bed I will go mad. Please, if You're out there, if you've ever been out there, find a way to right this wrong. I can not exist with her loving another man. I can not. Would that I were not immortal, for if I were not, surely I would seek an ending to my existence." *And in those days shall men seek death, and shall not find it; and shall desire to die, and death shall flee from you. Revelation 9:6*

Then Adam shoved the remaining items off the table and listened as they broke. He couldn't believe that he'd just prayed for Eve to stop loving Sullivan. Adam laughed out loud at the ridiculousness of his request. He was begging God to help him find a way to make Eve stop loving another man.

"And yes, while you're at it, if you're not too busy, find a way to make me get over my revulsion."

He brought out the unbroken bottle of scotch and downed drink after drink. *Why the hell not*, he thought. God owed him one.

He'd never asked to be turned into this. He'd prayed for a way out, for a way to protect his wife and when it became evident that God wasn't answering his prayers, Adam had been forced to deal with the matter himself. So now he was a vampire. He'd only done the best he could with the hand he'd been dealt.

Adam drained the last drop from the bottle. He needed something with a little more bite. The call of fresh blood was whispering to him. It wouldn't be making love to Eve but it would be more than what he had now.

Chapter 18

"I need your help. Do you know about four or five strong men who can help you?" Eve waited for Mark's answer.

"I know some men," he finally answered her.

"Do not tell them anything except they will be well paid, understand?"

"What's going on?" Mark asked.

"I'm moving in with Sullivan."

Silence followed her declaration. "I need you to meet me at my home in two hours with a truck. Can you do it?"

"I'll do it," Mark answered, and Eve closed the phone and smiled, now glad of her decision to provide Mark with a cell phone so she could reach him. Both Adam and Sullivan had chided her for not establishing a telepathic link with him. That Eve hadn't wanted; she had enough people in her head as it was. Having a man whose sole purpose on earth seemed to be to become fodder for vampires… Well, that she could do without. He definitely didn't deserve a place in her head. A phone was good enough.

❖

As the men loaded the truck Eve watched, supervising the movement of her carefully wrapped crystals into the truck. Eve shivered at the vast amount of energy that emanated from the crystals. She noticed that the stones had an effect on the men as well.

When the stones were resting comfortably in the truck Eve went back into the house and took another look around. She even ventured into Adam's bedroom before returning to hers. She gazed at the vampire bed and smiled before lying across it for a few moments just to be sure.

When she rose she was sure. Adam's essence covered the sheets and the pillow. Taking a deep breath she sighed. *Yes*, she thought, it was time for her to move on, to let go of Adam. She wouldn't deny loving him, but it was time to move on. She wanted to be with Sullivan.

Light glinted from the violet ring Adam had placed on her finger. He'd said that it would give her the power to find him wherever he was. Eve didn't know if it were true because she'd never tried. In the beginning when Adam had left her for months at a time, she'd rubbed her finger across it and had felt an instant connection with Adam but had always thought it had more to do with their blood bond.

Natural curiosity had been shoved to the back of her mind because of what her using the ring to contact Adam would mean. Begging him to return wasn't something she wanted to do. Now she ran her thumb across the smooth surface of the ring, took it off and laid it in the middle of Adam's vampire bed. "Goodbye, Adam," she said softly and walked from the bedroom for what she knew would be the last time.

She glanced around the house. The evidence of Adam's anger spilled into every corner of the place, as did his immense wealth. She'd noticed the gleam of greed that had filled the men's eyes and had read their thoughts, that a home so empty would be prime pickings for them.

What kind of men had Mark brought to her home? Eve wondered, then immediately reprimanded herself. She had always known the kind of man Mark was. What else could she expect of a man who wanted to be her personal blood bank?

Though a vampire, Eve valued human life. She knew if the men ever attempted to return to the house to rob Adam they would be dead before they could enter his home. Since she had hired them, it was her job to keep them safe.

"Mark," she called and waited until he was near enough to her that they wouldn't be heard. "Have you told the men anything?"

"Not a word," Mark declared, looking offended that she would even question him.

She smiled and took a better look at him. "You bathed. And you've changed your clothes. You look very nice, Mark. What made you do it?"

"The way Adam looked at me."

"He wouldn't hurt you."

A snort came from Mark before he could stop it. "He gave me my orders when he gave me to you. He said my life was yours and I was to protect you. He also said I was to obey your will without question. I figured I'd better clean myself up."

Eve laughed a little. "Don't you feel better? I mean, why on earth would you want to be covered with filth?"

"Because no one noticed me when I was, no one expected anything from me." He walked away from Eve, leaving her wondering even more what had happened to make Mark into what he was. Her determination to rescue him from this craziness was renewed. She would have to show him that mortal life was a good thing.

❖

When the last crystal was placed in Sullivan's home, Eve peeled off bill after bill and handed the money over to the men. She took her time shaking each of their hands, the time needed to make sure they would never remember her or the job they'd done.

She planted an innocent story of a lottery win on a number the men shared. She didn't worry whether they would question it. They had money, that was all they needed to know. Then she looked at Mark.

"I won't tell anyone," Mark said softly. "I already know where Adam and Sullivan live."

"I'm sorry," Eve insisted, "this time I have to make sure. You saw the condition Adam left the house in. I can't have a slip that might cause your friends to return there. I have to tie up all loose ends. I'm trying to keep all of you safe." She held Mark's hand and wiped his mind clean of the event before sending them all on their way.

❖

Sullivan had given Eve more than enough time to make up her mind. He'd ignored her call until he no longer heard it and then he'd waited some more. When at last he'd returned home, he'd found the house empty and Eve gone. So it was done. She'd chosen Adam.

For an hour Sullivan had roamed the rooms of his house touching things, that belonged to Eve, at last picking up the pump she used for the AB-5. He wondered if she would remember she'd left it, if she would come back for it or if he should take it to the lab and leave it for her.

Sullivan's throat closed with unshed tears. In time he knew he would get over it. They'd made no commitment to each other. What choice did he have? In the meantime he would be grateful for the time he'd spent with Eve.

He closed his eyes and found himself back in the graveyard facing the monuments of relatives long dead. He should make himself return to the company. He shivered. After the battle he and Adam had had, he knew the time had come for him to strike out on his own. He'd start his own company.

As Sullivan sank deeper into despair he knew he should seek out the company of other vampires to talk to. He should do anything other than mourn the loss of Eve. But somehow it seemed fitting that he mourn her in this place where there was nothing but loss.

When he'd become so morose that he could no longer take it, Sullivan returned to his home. He felt her presence and a surge of energy shot through his heart. She'd come back. Then he remembered her pump; perhaps she'd come back for it. His thoughts scattered as he fought the quick hope that flared in his chest. He wouldn't assume anything. He had to ask and hope the answer would be the one he wanted to hear.

❖

This was it, Eve had made her choice. She waited for Sullivan to return and the instant he did she was aware of it. She hesitated a moment, waiting for him to come to her before realizing that he needed her to come to him.

She moved slowly as she went to where he was waiting for her and she smiled at him. "I hope your invitation is still open."

"Which invitation?" Sullivan asked, but she could see the joy in his eyes. She watched as his chest heaved with anticipation. He was waiting, not expecting, just waiting.

"Can I still move in with you?"

She didn't have time to think or move before Sullivan pulled her into his arms. She could feel his heart thudding in his chest.

"You've made your decision?"

"I had already made my decision."

He pulled back to look at her. "Then why did you kiss him? If you'd never kissed him more than likely the bonding would have never occurred. Tell me, Eve, why the kiss?"

"I guess I couldn't help myself. Maybe I wanted to know. I don't know. For a little while we'd stopped fighting. We were talking, then laughing and when he kissed me I kissed him back. I won't lie to you."

"The tears? Why did you cry? Did he push you away?"

"No, I moved, but he would have pushed me away if I hadn't."

"Did it still hurt?"

"Yes, I wish I could tell you that it didn't, but it did."

"Is that the reason you're moving in with me?"

"No, Sullivan, you're the reason. I believe together we can have a life of sorts, that we can be happy. I want to be happy, Sullivan. I want to make a commitment to you, to us, if that is what you want."

"What does a commitment mean to you Eve?"

For a second Eve thought about it. Then she answered. "It means that I love you, that you're aware that for some crazy reason I can't rid my heart of the hold Adam has over me. Maybe it's his blood. I don't know, but I do know that I like being with you. I like the way we are together. I like knowing that I can trust you and I want you to be able to trust me also. When the chips are down, I want you to know I will be there for you."

He played with her hands, allowed a little fang to show, then nipped her lightly, not breaking the skin. "I do trust you and I see you trust me. You didn't even flinch."

"Why would I?" Eve said, winding her arms around him. "I know you would never do anything against my wishes."

Sullivan laughed. "It doesn't mean that I don't want to, just that I won't."

"That's what I meant. Regardless of your feelings you always take my needs into consideration." She gave him a huge grin. "And you wonder why I love you."

"No, I wonder why I can't be the only one you love."

"Maybe someday, Sullivan. Until then I would like to try to build a life with you, such as it is. Can you live with that?"

"Can I live with knowing that your heart doesn't fully belong to me?" He looked away, then back at Eve and smiled. "Welcome home," he said and drew her into his arms. "This is our home now, Eve, yours and mine."

He held her for the longest time, then pulled away to ask, "What is it that you see in Adam? What possible redeeming quality does he have?"

"Actually, Sullivan, he has lots of redeeming qualities. But those aren't the things I like most about him. Believe it or not, I like the way he flaunts what he is, that he doesn't hide it. Sometimes I even like his display of power. I like the irony of his vampire mobile and his vampire bed."

The tension had returned to Sullivan's shoulders but this time Eve knew it wouldn't be for long. She would dispel any doubts he had. She pulled Sullivan closer.

"Are you sure?"

"If I were not sure, I would not be here with you."

"Adam is going to go ballistic when he learns you've moved in with me."

"When hasn't he gone ballistic? You should see what he did to the house. He practically destroyed it. He broke all of my jars and tossed out my herbs. I'm surprised he didn't crush the larger crystals."

"We can get you more of everything you need."

"I still plan on spending Adam's money."

"No."

"Why not, Sullivan? He owes me this much."

"No, Eve, you're with me now. I'll take care of you."

"That's just it, I don't want to be taken care of."

"What's the difference? If you use Adam's money won't it be him taking care of you?"

"With Adam I feel I've more than earned every dime." Eve's eyes had turned red and she was aware of it. "From the moment he first fed on me, I earned it. That's why I want to spend his money. It's mine as well. I earned it. Besides, Adam's the one who destroyed my things. He should pay for replacing them."

"I can see your point," Sullivan answered. "But it doesn't mean I have to like it. Now hear me out before you fly off the handle and call me awful names." He grinned. "I would love to replace all of your things Adam destroyed. It would really tick him off. Will you allow me to do that for you? Let that be my commitment gift to you."

He was asking for more than that. Sullivan was asking her to trust him, to give him a reason to trust her, and she would. Eve knew Sullivan was not thinking of angering Adam any more than they already had.

"Yes, Sullivan, I will accept. Now don't you think it's time you told me about Joanna? You're familiar with my entire life, won't you share that with me?

He rubbed his finger over the base of her throat, looking at it, making shivers chase each other up and down her spine. "Sullivan, if it hurts still…"

"It hurts. Still." He smiled at her. "But you're right, I know your pain, you should know mine as well. The vampire that made me, I was in love with her, Suzett." Sullivan grinned and shook his head. "I still see her occasionally."

"Oh."

"No need for jealousy, though I like it. What we had was in the beginning. Before I knew what she was, we were lovers. I would wake with bites all over my body. I would be sore as hell but I'd just had the most incredible night of passion any man could ask for, so who cared what my body looked like when she was done. Huge bruises covered my legs, my torso."

Centuries old memories tugged at Sullivan and he laughed as he remembered. "Then one day I got sick, a high fever, and it wouldn't go away. Suzett bathed me with cool towels. Nothing worked. She asked if I wanted her to make me feel better. As sick as I was, I was thinking sex, and she did that, the most mind blowing…" He caught Eve's look and stopped. "She asked me if I would like to have something that would make sex a thousand times better."

"Of course you said yes," Eve interrupted.

"I was shivering from the fever and the other things she had done to me. I couldn't even answer her, just looked at her, praying she would understand the pleading in my eyes for her to do more and she did. Sullivan stared at Eve. "She turned me."

"Was it worth it?"

"I have to tell you, the rush was so mind blowing that while it was happening, yes, it was worth it. I didn't know what was happening until I felt my heart seize. I tried to get her to stop but she wouldn't and I died. When she brought me back I was feeding from her, disgusted but unable to stop myself. For three days we stayed like that, making love, my getting sick and going into the full turn."

"You didn't hate her?"

"Not immediately. I was so...the feeling was... He shook his head. "I was a goner. It wasn't until we came up for air and I learned my new nature, that it wasn't a dream, that my family was gone from me forever, that I couldn't go out in the daylight, that I understood what I was, what Suzett had done to me, what I had allowed her to do. I think then I hated her, but only a little."

"But you fed?" Eve asked. She watched as his jaw clenched.

"There was no other way for me to live and I wanted to live."

"I wasn't judging you, Sullivan."

He glanced at her. "Maybe I was judging myself. You're the first that I've seen who didn't give in to the thirst or the nauseating hunger, the very first. I envy you that. You've been so brave through this whole thing. It's been almost two years and you've done something we have all been told was impossible. Sure, the older ones don't have to feed as often, but we still have to feed."

"Like you said, Sullivan, I have other options. You didn't." She kissed his cheek. "Was it hard for you the first time?"

"A little, but Suzett stayed with me. She showed me how to use finesse."

"Did you turn anyone?"

"Of course. At first I didn't know how not to, but Suzett taught me well. I had human servants who would gladly go out and get me a body or give me their blood, and I had... We would have mind blowing sex and we'd drink from each other and..." Sullivan shook all over.

"Then what?"

"Then I started to hate her more."

"Why?"

"She taught me the most valuable lesson of all. Vampires are not monogamous. We live too long to be. After a time she tired of me and moved on and I hated her because I wanted her. She came back from time to time until finally I no longer hated her and after that I no longer wanted her. I hated the life I was living but found it fascinating that I could continue to live.

"But what about Joanna. Adam said she was the love of your life. Why did you tell me about Suzett?"

"Because I can't tell you about Joanna without telling you about Suzett and how it all started and the reason I was with her." He narrowed his eyes at her. "Understand?"

"Yes."

"Adam killed Joanna. She was a mortal." Sullivan spoke with coldness, not looking at Eve, moving slightly away from her.

"I thought you didn't like mortal women."

"She's the reason why. After Suzett, I made love to many women, some mortal, some vampire, but none were like Joanna. She was so fragile, so different. She needed me with her. I felt…" He swallowed.

"Almost human," Eve said.

He caught her gaze and held it. "Yes, almost human and I was madly in love with her."

"Did you bite her?"

"That I couldn't help, not in the throes of making love but I never drank more than a little, never wanting to turn her, or kill her."

Eve was shaking, guessing what had happened. "Adam?"

"He drained her dry, made love to her and killed her. He looked at me as though I was insane and told me to get over it. He even brought me a dozen mortal women one night and told me to choose, that I could have one or all of them. He had no way of understanding my loss. I wanted to make him feel that pain, the same pain I felt."

Eve couldn't help it, she moved way. "So Adam was right. You've used me to hurt him."

"Do you believe that, Eve?"

"I don't know. I hear the pain in your voice even now and I feel your loss, so it's not a long stretch to believe that you wanted to hurt Adam, that you don't really love me."

"Yes, I've wanted to hurt Adam for hundreds of years. I've hated him for Joanna's loss, and yes, when I learned who you were I wanted him to know the pain of betrayal, just as I'd known. But after the first time I kissed you it no longer had anything to do with Adam."

Sullivan moved toward Eve and she moved backward. "How can I be sure now? How will I ever know the truth?"

"There is one way to know, Eve, but that is your choice, or you could believe me and trust that I love you."

Eve stood trembling, shaking her head no. "I want to be sure, Sullivan. I love you and I want to be sure."

His eyes closed. "It will create a bond, a permanent one, the same as you have with Adam."

"Shouldn't I have the same bond with you? You're the one I want to be with."

"But before you've never allowed me to show you."

"Before I never needed proof of your love."

"Now you do?" He smiled at her.

"Now I do," Eve said and felt the tears slip from her eyes.

"You're not in competition, Eve, with anyone. There is no other woman I desire, mortal or vampire. I promise you that. I love you and the bite is not necessary."

"You wanted a commitment between us. This is it, Sullivan, this is what I want."

"Is that all that you want?"

He turned to her, the desire burning within his eyes the love for her apparent.

"For now," Eve said as he kissed her and she kissed him back and wrapped her arms around his neck as he carried her to bed to make love to her. And in that moment Eve was aware what it was she loved about Sullivan. He lived like a mortal, moved like one, ate like one, and he made her feel human. Only the way he made love could be classified as superhuman. He took her to the brink of orgasm.

"Not tonight, Eve," Sullivan whispered.

"Why?"

"Tonight is for us and our love. I trust in that and so should you. The bonding will come when you're no longer worried, no longer doubting." With those words he took them over the edge of lust and landed them firmly in sweet blissful release.

What had he expected? Adam didn't feel the charge of the crystals nor did he feel the vibrations they gave off. And he didn't feel Eve. He'd shoved her into Sullivan's home with his revulsions. He'd forced Eve to make a stand.

For the first time in months he'd held her in his arms. They hadn't fought, well, at least not toward the end. And he'd kissed her, tasted the sweet nectar of her mouth and then he'd felt the sharp fangs though they had not descended, and he'd known he was kissing a vampire.

If Adam could change one thing in his miserable life it would be that. He would give all that he was, all that he had to be with Eve the way he wanted, the way she deserved. At least since their bonding she now knew how much he loved her. Sullivan might have her for the moment but he would never have the bonding that was his and Eve's alone. They had both promised. He waved his hand righting the house, repairing the damage.

For several weeks Eve had worked and lived in a daze half expecting Adam to fly into one of his rages and drag her back to his home. But he didn't. She'd seen him once and he'd behaved as though nothing was wrong, smiling at her, walking past, but not speaking. Still, Eve wasn't taking chances. She'd tripled the amount of research she was doing with her crystals, trying potion after potion. She searched the Internet and every metaphysical store she could find. If the word magic was in or on anything she bought it.

In spite of the turmoil there was one area of her life that was looking up. She was beginning to feel safe with her new life. She no longer had to hide her actions. Sullivan didn't necessarily approve but he wasn't trying to stop her from using the AB-5. He was leaving it up to her to stop if she thought the situation ever called for it.

Things were pretty good for them with one possible exception. Eve had not been able to get her mind off the experience Sullivan had told her he'd had with Suzett. Every night when they made love she badgered him and every night he refused. Now Eve found herself once again begging him for the bonding. This time she could tell he was weakening.

"Are you sure," he asked. "Yes, I'm sure," she whispered throatily and readied herself for his bite, surprised when she felt no pain. She looked up, wondering what had stopped him.

"Eve, you've only done this with Adam are you really sure?"

"I've never asked Adam to bite me, Sullivan, you're the only one. Adam asked me to bond with him. Now I'm asking you to bond with me. This is something I'm giving to you that I've never given to Adam. You're the first one I've asked."

Eve shivered, falling over the edge as Sullivan bit into her. She felt slight pain that was immediately blotted out by pleasure so intense that her bones melted. She was becoming one with Sullivan, a part of him. She screamed his name as a spasm of pure hot lust invaded the marrow of her being and washed over her. And then she was bathed in love, pure simple adoration. She searched Sullivan's mind and his heart and found only herself there. "Sullivan," she moaned.

"I'm right here, baby."

"I love you," she moaned over and over.

"And I love you, baby. Now you know what I wanted to give you, all of me."

"Is this as good as—"

"Better," he said, cutting off her question, "much better." He suckled her, leaving her breathless, then suckled her again, drawing just enough of her blood into his throat to create pleasure beyond belief.

Eve felt his hips rocking. He was shivering so hard that the bed shook. There was one thing more he wanted, one thing he would never ask her for. She bit gently into him, felt the crush of his arm around her and bit a little harder.

His blood touched her lips and she tasted it with the tip of her tongue. She tasted Sullivan's passion and his fulfillment, then did as he'd done her, suckled and drew back, suckled and drew back, drinking his blood, him, his life. Eve found no distaste in it. She was a vampire and she was making love with her man, giving him the kind of pleasure he gave her. With that thought she went deeper and pulled for all she was worth, swallowing his blood and feeling his plunge into her body.

And she came, his grip on her so tight she felt his sticky tears on her cheek, felt hers on his. She had at last become one with him.

Adam no longer mattered. And as they spiraled toward completeness, in the centre, a dark force sputtered angrily, reeling and pushing through Eve's head, trying to crowd out the pleasure of what she was experiencing. She refused to allow it.

"Sullivan," she called in wonderment. "I love you." Even as the force gathered momentum, it was Sullivan's name Eve called, Sullivan's face she kept in her mind. And when they twirled downwards, lying in the quietness she almost told him what had happened. She trembled, remembering Adam telling her that he would know if she bonded with Sullivan. She'd thought he'd been joking at the time. Now somehow she knew Adam was aware of what they'd done. But the way Sullivan was touching her, kissing her, no, she would not spoil that for anything or anyone. Probably her worries were groundless anyway. Adam had to know despite her promise that eventually she would want to bond with Sullivan.

❖

"Nooooooo, Noooooooo, Noooooo," Adam roared and dropped to his knees.

Both palms were open facing the sky. With each finger a line of electrical energy shot out destroying what ever was in it's path. He couldn't believe it, he should have tuned in sooner. What a fool Eve had taken him for.

Rage darker than anything he'd ever experienced, even when Tarasha had turned him, built within his skull, taking his breath with it. Scream after scream tore through his throat as he furiously pushed everything from around him. With the speed of thought he was at the lake and walking into the center. He needed to cool his body or he would spontaneously combust.

With each breath the water rose higher and higher, parting in the middle, covering Adam yet doing nothing to cool the heat of betrayal. "Eve," he roared, his voice shouting through the cosmos. "You've just put the seal to Sullivan's death. I'm going to kill him."

He felt a jerk, a connection, heard her frightened whimper, her saying his name. Then as if he were of no consequence, Eve dismissed him. Adam was in her mind, heard her murmurs of love to Sullivan as she pushed Adam out. The knowledge that Eve was aware that he knew she was in the middle of bonding with Sullivan and deliberately pushed him from her thoughts in order to continue enraged Adam even more.

Adam spit as the taste of Sullivan's blood filled his mouth. He could taste what Eve tasted, feel what she felt. "Nooooo," he screamed again.

Tremors went through every cell of his body and shot out through the tips of his fingers. The locks of his hair sparked with electrical energy. Adam roared and lightning split the sky, thunder crackled.

Adam's eyes were shut tightly. Blood poured from beneath the lids and his rage was divided and came again, coalescing into thoughts and the thoughts became matter touching every corner of the globe.

He brought his anger from the pits and became the lava that flowed from every volcano known. Even the ones declared dead became alive, filled with his fury. Adam's anger fueled the winds as they whipped over continent after continent, creating tornadoes. And then the earth split wide and still Adam wasn't cool. The fire came from inside and would not die. The pain engulfed him, twisting him and tearing away at the last link he had to humanity.

He didn't remember how long he stood in the middle of the lake, only that the water had spewed up its inhabitants and the sand was covered in dead fish, Adam looked around at the downed trees.

"*Adam, please give me until tomorrow. Let me talk with you.*" Adam heard Eve's voice and shouted back to her. "Not this time, Eve. I warned you, no sweet talk. He's dead. You're making love with a dead man." The irony of the situation hit him. "The bonding was for us, Eve, that's all I asked. Now you will pay for this. I warned you, I am not a mortal man to be toyed with. I am Adam, the alpha and the omega and you will know it."

"*Don't Adam.*"

"Too late. You're dead both of you," he muttered back to her and closed his mind off to her. Adam walked back to his home. Something had died inside him, not just hope but something more vital, something he didn't know if he could survive without.

Shimmers of rage surrounded Adam's body. His aura for the first time in a thousand years was completely black. The power that emanated from him was not tempered with thoughts of Eve to take off the rough edges. Now the edges were jagged and he intended to keep them that way.

He would still leave as he'd planned. Killing Sullivan at this moment would provide no pleasure. No, that he would save until the time was right. But he would not leave without knowing what it was that Eve had cooked up and he didn't feel inclined to enter her mind to gain the knowledge. No, this time he would call that mortal to him.

Adam had no compunction against linking with the little weasel. He could have traveled to him, but he preferred to make Mark come to him. He rather enjoyed the mortal's fear when in his presence. And he indeed planned to make Mark fear. And now before he left, he could find out what secrets Mark's mistress was keeping from him.

In less than an hour Mark was ringing his bell, looking down, his eyes not quite meeting Adam's.

"So you helped Eve move," Adam glared at him.

"I didn't help Eve move, Mark whimpered, still looking down.

Adam turned his wrists slowly and applied a little pressure on Mark's throat without touching him. "Do not lie to me."

"I'm not lying." Mark clutched at his throat. "I didn't help her move."

"Her crystals, how did she move them? If it were not you, then who?"

"I don't know."

Adam reached for the mortal, saw his fear but increased the pressure. He held him tightly until the man lost control of his bladder. Still Adam did not loosen his grip. He snarled, allowing the fangs to descend, inch after inch. He felt the foulness increase, knowing Mark had now lost control of his bowels. Adam threw the mortal from him in disgust.

"Clean that up," Adam growled and walked away, "and for heaven sake's when you're done, clean yourself and then meet me in the garden. I want to talk to you."

Mind control, Adam thought. Eve had used mind control to wipe Mark's memory clean. That wouldn't matter, he was a master at the game. Eve was just learning.

So my darling treacherous wife, you are becoming more like me than you would care to admit. You have covered your tracks very well, very well indeed, but I will find out all that I need to know.

Adam sat in the garden and waited. Tonight he would know the truth. And twenty minutes later he did. As he sank his fangs into Mark's neck he was connected to everything that had happened to the mortal. It all went in reverse order; first, Eve's wiping his mind clean as well as the minds of Mark's friends. Eve's exerting mind control over the mortal to make him think she was feeding from him. The mortal's disgusting thoughts that Eve was in love with him. Adam shoved him away. Did they all want his wife? Did no one fear him or his reprisal?

"How long has she not been feeding from you?"

"Eve," Mark whimpered, "she feeds from me."

"Fool, don't you know she's giving you a pretty picture."

Mark blinked as though trying to remember something. The action was pitiful but made Adam furious. Imbecile, he thought.

"Not all the time." Mark shook his head. "I know she has fed on me."

Adam would be able to tell if that were true. Eve's scent was nowhere on the man. He didn't find a trace of her blood in his bloodstream and if she had fed even once, her essence would have been imprinted there.

"Try again." Mark offered his neck and Adam almost killed him then and there. There was perhaps a slight chance that he was wrong, that she had fed from him in the beginning but Adam had no intention of tasting any more of the mortal's blood. It was now colored by his foul excrement. There was no way he could continue to feed on the mortal. He didn't want to know that badly. He knew for sure he didn't need to hear any more of the mortal's simpering thoughts of love for Eve.

For now Adam would take Mark at his word and believe that it had just been recently that Eve had not fed from him and that was a good thing. She needed to have more than one idiot consort to go to anyway.

"Here," Adam said in disgust, giving Mark the violet ring in the black velour bag. "You keep this, do you understand? You even think of pawning it and I will fry you, got it? I want you to watch Eve while I'm gone, stay near her and report to me. If she feeds from you I will taste the stench of your foul blood. And if she isn't feeding from you I want to know why."

Adam pulled back as the man's eyes bulged from the sockets. "And if Eve needs me, you give her this ring and tell her to contact me."

"I thought you could do that mind thing and know her thoughts," Mark said quietly, not daring to look at Adam.

Blind fury took over and Adam squeezed his palm into a fist. With his other hand, he slowly crushed Mark's windpipe. How dare this foul-smelling mortal question him?

"Adam." Eve's voice popped into his head and he released Mark. "Eve, I saw heaven in your arms. I saw hell in your betrayal. I give you your freedom. You're no longer my wife or my responsibility. I take back my love. You are closed to my thoughts," he answered her back. As filled with hatred as he was, he wished he could close out even that little place in his heart she still occupied, but not yet. Maybe someday, but not today.

"If anything happens to Eve and you don't make me aware, you will live to regret it." Adam grinned at Mark, a grin that he knew put fear into the man's heart. But he pulled back. He didn't need the man losing control of his bodily functions again.

"I mean it. If anything happens to Eve and I'm not notified you will die regretting it."

"Eve has given orders—"

"Do you think Eve orders me? That she can tell me what to do with you? Her orders extend to others not hurting you, not me. Do you forget who and what I am? I'm a vampire, Mark."

Adam laughed. "What is it your mistress calls me, a Grand Master? I'm a Grand Master vampire and after two years Eve is still playing at being mortal. Choose your allegiance well. And if it is love you seek with my wife that will never happen. I would kill her first and then you."

"You told me to be loyal to Eve. Now you want me to spy on her."

What was this world coming to? Now he was being questioned by a mortal. Adam couldn't believe it. What was it about Eve that made the weak male species turn into brave men of valor? First Sullivan, now Mark.

Adam roughly reached for Mark again and bit into him with vengeance but did not drink.

"Do you feel that, Mark?"

"Yes," Mark whimpered.

"Is it pleasurable?"

"No."

"Does it feel like what Eve does?"

"No, she doesn't hurt me." Mark squeaked the words out between the pain.

"But I will, Mark. I will strip the skin from your body an inch at a time and I will allow you to heal and repeat the process for the remainder of your life. And I will revel in your pain. Do you understand?"

"Yes, I understand."

"Then you will do as I order. You will call me with any information." Adam sent Mark's fear into Eve's heart. She wouldn't link with the mortal on her own but he would do this for her. She would feel the mortal's fear and pain and she would not know where it emanated from. And when she did she would fear herself. Good, he thought, and took his leave for another country.

A deep ache filled the blackness in Adam's soul and he mourned. He didn't believe distance or time would ever heal this ache. His world had been shattered. All that he was or had ever been or had ever hoped to be was lost. His hopes had died when Sullivan's blood flooded Eve's mouth and his. His sacred bond had been sullied. How did he go on from there? He turned into mist traveling at the speed of light, not able to witness the devastation his fury had wrought but feeling it on the wind. This time Adam was truly lost.

A chill wiped out Eve's thoughts. She closed her eyes, glad she was lying on the bed, glad that Sullivan was with her, making love to her.

"Eve, are you okay? Is it the blood?"

"I don't know it's just…I felt strange for a moment, like I was going to be sick to my stomach. Do vampires continue to throw up, Sullivan, even after two years?"

"I haven't seen one that did. Then again, I've never seen one like you. Would you like to go to the lab or have Dr. Meah come here?"

"And interrupt our lovemaking? I don't think so." Eve smiled. "Besides, it's passing."

"I think there's a storm brewing." Sullivan grinned at her as she shivered from the violent crack of thunder.

Eve snuggled deeper into him.

"Are you sure you want to continue?" Sullivan asked, licking her ear lobes and sending delicious sensations through her entire body.

"I'm sure." She reached her hand between their bodies and felt for his arousal. "I'm positive."

Yet at the back of Eve's mind something refused to budge, something that told her that there was trouble brewing. Right now, though, she didn't want to think about it. She only wanted to do as she was doing, forget her past life and make the best of this new one she had.

When they were done Eve lay in Sullivan's arms. "You make me happy," she said softly, "and I'm so glad that my stupidity didn't lose me your love."

"Like you, Eve, I don't stop loving so easily. I'm afraid I will love you for all eternity. Long after you have grown tired of me, I will love you."

Eve smiled at him. "You know, in your arms I find it easy to fantasize a future. I can pretend that nothing for me has changed, that I'm still mortal and that I can still have mortal dreams, that there can be a happily ever after for us. I can even fantasize about marriage and fidelity and babies and family gatherings and parties with friends. I can pretend that I'm truly alive and that you're alive as well." She smiled then.

"You make me want the same things and if it were within my power to grant it for you, I would." Sullivan raised Eve's chin and stared directly into her eyes. "I love you and I would give my immortal life to spend just one mortal lifetime with you."

"I know," Eve snuggled closer, "but at least I have the next best thing. I have you and I have the illusion of being mortal."

Again the strange panic filled Eve and suddenly she knew what it was. She saw Mark's face, his fear, and she felt someone's fangs sink into his skin and his blood flow into that being's mouth. In that instant Mark's blood entered her and she coughed. "Adam," she moaned. She felt Sullivan pull away. "No," she held him down. "Adam has done something to Mark. He bit him. Mark's blood was in my mouth. I can still taste it."

"Eve, you must have been dreaming."

"I felt it."

"But I thought you didn't have a blood connection with Mark."

"I don't. Adam must have wanted me to know he hurt him." She shivered. "Adam knows that I've bonded with you, Sullivan. What if he killed Mark?"

"Are you worried that Adam knows we've bonded?"

Eve blinked, so much pain just because she wanted to be happy, just because she wanted to love. Her answer to Sullivan now would be the way of their future together.

"I wanted to bond with you. Now that I know what we've been missing I have no intention of stopping." She saw Sullivan's chest heave with relief and she smiled a little at him for a moment. "What about Mark?"

"If Adam did kill Mark, there isn't much that you can do about it, now is there?"

"But I promised I would protect him." Eve made a mad dash for the cell phone and dialed Mark, going into a panic when it wasn't answered. The drone from the television caught her attention and she stood and stared, not believing what she was seeing and hearing. Devastation covered the entire world, something Eve had never known to happen and it had all happened at once, an Armageddon of sorts.

Eve stood before the television, trembling as news of floods, hurricanes, tornadoes, and earthquakes came from every channel.

"Oh my God." She covered her mouth and stared in awe at dead volcanoes in Hawaii spewing lava. "Adam." She looked again toward Sullivan. "He did this."

"Even Adam is not that strong."

"You saw what he did with the lake, with the thunder and lightning."

"But you're talking worldwide." Sullivan attempted to hold her and stopped as a picture of St. Peter's Square, flooded, came into view, then destruction in Amsterdam, China, Japan. He swallowed hard. "It's all a coincidence, Eve. Adam couldn't do anything of this magnitude."

"Are you sure?" Eve asked, wanting his assurance, knowing it didn't matter what Sullivan said in the end. Her heart told her it was Adam's doing. He was that strong. *Damn. What had she done?*

Sullivan drew her into his arms. "I'm sure baby. Adam doesn't posses that kind of power, no vampire does." He held her close, not wanting her to know that if any vampire did possess that kind of power it would be Adam. And if he had been angry before and unleashed the power of nature, Sullivan didn't want to hazard a guess what Adam was capable of doing now that he knew Sullivan had bonded with Eve. *Damn, what had he done?* He'd have to find a way to protect Eve, to keep her safe.

To say Eve was terrified would be putting it mildly. Adam's face was seared into her brain and she couldn't shove the image away. He was coming for them, the two of them, and he was going to kill them.

With speed she'd not known she possessed, she leaped from the bed, throwing on her necklace, adding several, running around the room for more to put on Sullivan. She was crying as he swatted her hand away. "Please, Sullivan," she begged, "put them on." She saw the look of anguish on his face but couldn't stop her actions. "He's going to come here, Sullivan. He's going to kill us." She gazed around the room, her glance falling on her most powerful stones that were small enough for her to carry. She swooped them into a bag and returned to Sullivan. "Please, let's go. Take me to the place where you go when you leave me."

"No, we will not run."

"Sullivan, don't you understand? Adam will kill us. Please, let's go."

"No, Eve, I will not run from him. I will protect you."

Eve wrapped her arms around him. "Oh, God," she moaned. "Sullivan, please... Please, please take me away. Please. Please," she cried, the tears coming faster and faster down her cheeks. "If you love me—"

"It's not fair to use my love for you."

"Please, Sullivan."

With a sigh of resignation he enveloped her in his arms and took her to his secret place, hating the very idea of running.

Chapter 19

Rage dark and ominous filled every single cell in Adam's body. He'd thought he could leave the killing of Sullivan and Eve for another time but this couldn't wait. In a dark mist he appeared inside Sullivan's home, knowing the moment he entered they weren't there. "Eve," he screamed out to the cosmos. "You broke your promise. Sullivan is dead and you are dead also. I warned you, Eve. Now you shall truly know my wrath. I am a damn vampire and you keep forgetting that. I'm not mortal, Eve, and I will not be treated as a mortal man."

❖

A shudder of disgust rippled over Sullivan's spirit. He was enclosed in a damn tomb, naked, watching the woman he loved come unglued enough so that she was treating him as if he didn't matter, as if he were powerless against her crazy husband. Did she forget that he was a vampire? He was furious with her. It mattered not whether she sought to protect him or believed he'd be unable to protect her. It all boiled down to the same thing. She had no respect for him first and foremost as a man. She couldn't, or she would have never asked him to run, to hide away.

He saw her trembling. That alone made him furious for he knew how the ordeal of being in a coffin had weighed on her mind. She'd been afraid and now for her to agree to hide from Adam in this place of death and decay told him more than mere words ever could. She was more afraid of Adam's wrath for the both of them than what she imagined in the grave. He'd refused to speak to her from the moment he'd brought her here and watched as she'd placed her stones around the door of the tomb. He watched as she whispered an incantation putting a spell around them. He was shaking in fury as he watched her standing there nude. She was staring pitifully at him while her hated blood tears continued coursing down her cheeks. With another snort of disgust Sullivan clothed the both of them. His eyes narrowed as her hand slid down the sleek material and her gaze met his. Did she think he was so impotent that he couldn't even provide clothing for her?

He turned away from her and every time she attempted to speak he held up his hand. His fury at her was so great that he couldn't and wouldn't talk to her now. His fury at Adam for always causing such chaos was even greater. But his greatest fury was at himself. Over six hundred years he'd known Adam. Three hundred of those years as a friend and three as an enemy. And never, not once, had he run in the face of Adam's power, not one damn time. This hiding was more than an insult to his sprit. It ripped apart everything that was him. His entire blasted doomed existence had been ripped away and he was left without a shred of dignity. All for love. Sullivan couldn't believe he was in the predicament he was in because of love. His very essence demanded that he leave, go and confront Adam, but as he watched Eve struggle with her fear, he knew he would never leave her because first and foremost he loved her. And whether she believed he could defeat Adam or not he would remain with her and he would protect her with his last breath. Like Adam he was a damn vampire and it was high time Eve be made aware of that fact.

❖

Eve once again was wishing for death but it was too late. She was already dead. She glanced at Sullivan. If she were really seeking death, all she'd had to do was wait with Sullivan at his home and she would now be dead. Adam was definitely going to kill her when he found her. She should have told Sullivan of her promise to Adam. She'd not meant to endanger Sullivan because of her own selfish wants. She'd asked things of him that she'd been unable to give to him. She wanted his love for her to be first in his heart when they both knew that Adam was first in hers. "Sullivan," she whispered, "please let me explain."

He wouldn't and she had known that he wouldn't. She'd done to him what no woman had a right to ever do to a man, vampire or mortal. She'd taken his pride and shredded it like so much paper. She'd not allowed him the dignity that he deserved.

As time passed Eve longed to be cradled in Sullivan's arms. But he was having none of that. She tried from time to time to lift the necklace to communicate with Adam, to beg him to…to what? She didn't know. There was no forgiveness for what she'd done to him or to Sullivan and she knew this. She lifted the necklace an inch and searched for Adam, knowing Sullivan was watching her. She took a breath. Adam was no longer in the vicinity. How did she know that? she wondered. More than likely that damn blood bond that they'd talked about. She removed one necklace at a time and waited. Nothing. It was safe to return home. Once again her gaze landed on Sullivan and she knew if she so much as uttered the words that it was safe to return he would leave her. She did the only thing she knew to do. She bilocated to Sullivan's home, hoping he would follow.

❖

Eve sat with her legs tucked under her and waited as Sullivan paced from room to room glaring at her, huffing, growling, still not speaking to her. With a shake of his head he finally disappeared, leaving her alone.

She was awakened by Sullivan shaking her gently. "Are you speaking to me?" she asked.

"I have to tell you this and I want you to listen, Eve. What happened with your begging me to run will never happen again. I will not run from Adam or anyone. I am bonded to you and I will protect you." He narrowed his eyes. "If you don't believe I can do this, then you need to return to your crazy ass husband for I will have no need of you and you will have less need of me if you do not believe in me.

"Sullivan—"

"Do not interrupt me. I am an eight-hundred-year-old vampire and you treated me worse than a fledgling. That I am not, Eve, make no mistake about that. I behave as a mortal man for you. You want to remain mortal and it is for you that I have this persona. It gives you pleasure and it give me pleasure to see you happy. I allowed myself to be turned into nothing. I will not ever do that again. Eternity is much too long to feel inadequate. You will not ever again use my love for you against me. I love you every bit as much as Adam does."

"Sullivan, I love you."

"Don't, Eve, not now. I have wished this, but I know it will never happen. Adam is the one you love first and foremost. Yes, I wish it were different but I can do nothing about it and apparently neither can you. I've decided to live with that. But the rest I cannot and will not live with. Do you understand?"

"I understand." Eve looked down, her body trembling, trying her best to prevent the tears that wanted to spill. "Forgive me, Sullivan, please. I love you and I should have told you of my promise to Adam."

"What promise?"

"I promised him that I would not bond with you, that I would not move in with you."

"Yet you did both."

"I wanted to. I love you and I wanted to give all of myself to you. I wanted to stop running between the two of you. I wanted only you." She felt the tears begin their slide. "But I should have asked you first or at least told you of the promise I'd made to Adam."

A smile lit Sullivan's feature. "You broke your promises to Adam because of your love for me?"

"Yes."

"I forgive you," Sullivan whispered and held out his arms to her. "Just don't do it again, okay?" He held her in his arms kissing her, loving her. "I will protect you, Eve, I promise. I will never leave you alone."

"I know that, Sullivan."

"Then why are you still worried?"

"Mark." Eve shivered. "Something's happened to Mark." She swallowed. "He isn't answering my calls." She looked again at the phone on the table and picked it, up dialing him once more.

❖

Mark looked at the ringing phone, afraid to answer, afraid not to answer. Adam would kill him if he disobeyed but he wondered what Adam would do to Eve if he did. This was one assignment he didn't want, not to spy on Eve, she'd been so good to him. He feared Adam with every fiber of his being but even so, he felt something trying to take life within him, an urge to protect Eve. He was fighting it with all the strength he had. He was not a man of bravery.

Mark did not want to endure whatever punishment Adam would mete out, yet he found himself not answering the phone. He had known somehow without Adam's telling him, that Eve would be aware of his pain.

Tears streamed from his eyes. He'd always wanted this life the vampires led, now he no longer did. Mark wanted out and only one person had offered him a way out, Eve. He had to find a way to protect her. He couldn't answer her until he could convince her that nothing had happened to him. He didn't want her attempting to protect him, he didn't want Adam's wrath to be on Eve's head.

When the phone rang again and again, Mark covered his ears, forcing himself not to answer. God help him, he loved her and he would willingly give his life to protect her. And by not answering at all he suspected that he already had. Adam would know and Adam would not be so forgiving. Terror racked his body and he curled into the fetal position and shivered against the chills that assaulted him.

Chapter 20

"Vatican City under water." Evan narrowed his eyes and stared at Adam. "Wasn't that a bit much?"

"It wasn't nearly enough," Adam snarled.

"Well, you know all the reports call it a global warming of dangerous proportions. They were shocked that no one saw it coming." Evan smiled. "How could they? Unless of course they know about you. You've been here for three days now. Do you care to finally tell me what the hell is going on with you? First you attempted to destroy the word, and then you came here and went into a feeding frenzy--a very sloppy one, I might add. What's up?"

The anger made Adam's blood boil and his fangs descend. There had been no let up from the pain. What the hell? He'd waited centuries for this. Adam snarled and looked at Evan hard before answering. "Eve and Sullivan." A low roar slipped out and Adam glared at his friend. "She's sleeping with him."

"You did all of this for a woman?"

"Not a woman, my wife."

"Adam, she's been sleeping with him for a long time now. Why are you just now going off your rocker over this?"

"She bonded with him."

"Oh." Evan sat back.

"*Oh?*"

"Don't bite my head off. I'm probably the only friend you have left on the planet."

Adam glared at Evan. "What?"

"She's been sleeping with him, they're both vampires, they've been making love. Do I have to spell it out for you, man? It's a natural reflex when we get off, it's part of the thrill. I have no idea how Sullivan held off for so long."

Fire shot from the tips of Adam's fingers and he downed several trees.

"Did that make you fell better?" Evan asked.

"No."

"Adam."

"Leave me the hell alone!"

"Adam, you need to talk about it."

"I don't bond when I make love."

"Didn't you do it with Eve when you turned her?"

"No, not while we were making love. I did a turn bite."

"Are you saying you could give her a turn bite but not a bonding bite?"

"Yes, she was too weak to know what the bonding would mean."

"And the passion bite, you didn't do that either? I can't believe it. But you could give her a turn bite. You're crazy, Adam."

"I couldn't bear to let her leave me, especially after what we'd just had. Three hundred years, Evan. Eve was the first woman in three hundred years that I allowed myself to let go with."

Evan looked at him in disbelief. "You have done nothing but talk about your wife for a thousand years and when you finally found her and made love to her, you held back the passion bite. Why?"

"I haven't since…"

"My word, since Joanna? It all boils down to that. You should have told Sullivan the truth three hundred years ago. You've taken the heat for her and there was no need."

"I'm going to kill him."

"Don't you think before you do Sullivan deserves to know that the woman he has been carrying a torch for for three hundred years was nothing more than a vampire groupie, a slut, going from vampire to vampire begging them to bite her, to bleed her dry?"

Adam glared at him. "But I was the one that did it. Until then Sullivan and I were friends."

"So why did you sleep with Joanna?"

Adam tried to stop the smile. "Because she was beautiful and she was begging." He glanced sideways at Evan. "You slept with her also."

"Yes, but Sullivan wasn't my friend. All of these years fear of your reprisal has kept everyone's lips sealed. Why were you trying to protect him from the truth?"

"I killed her, Evan. Do you think he would have believed anything I had to say after that? Besides, how could I drain her and then speak ill of her? Besides, Sullivan would have undoubtedly tried to take me on and I would have had to kill his dumb ass." Adam sighed at descending to the use of the modern slang.

"So you thought it was better that he believed you deliberately stole her from him, that she loved him and you killed her because you were jealous of him having someone to love."

"Call it atoning for my sins. Besides, fighting with Sullivan for the past three hundred years has given him a purpose. And his constantly trying to dethrone me has kept me amused. At least until recently. Killing the vampires he managed to talk into his foolishness always gave me a charge. I must admit I have enjoyed our battles."

"You're strange, Adam, you always have been an enigma. You protect Sullivan's feelings for hundreds of years and now you plan to kill him for doing what comes naturally. That's crazy, he couldn't help himself."

"She's my wife. He should have helped himself."

"But, Adam, Sullivan bonded with Eve. His intent was not to drain her but to show her his love. I'm sorry but it seems he pledged himself to her. The last we talked of this you were worried he was using Eve to get back at you. A vampire doesn't bond with another for fun, Adam."

"Have you bonded with your wife?"

"No, though I love her, bonding is meant to last for an eternity. I will have her for only one lifetime. I have no plans to do as you've done and mourn one woman for all of eternity. I think you and Sullivan are fools to bond with Eve, knowing our nature is to love many and make love to even more."

"It has never been like that for me. It was only when I found Eve again that the thought of bonding overrode everything else. I wanted her to know I'd never forgotten her, that I never would. I wanted her to know I would love her always."

Evan stared quietly a moment before he spoke. "You could hold her to you to bond but you couldn't hold her to make love to her. Adam, she's a vampire because you made her one. She's not Tarasha. She didn't turn you. Stop this nonsense. Go to her, take her from Sullivan, forget what she now is and remember her as she was and make love to her. Release your passion for her, give her many bites of passion for many years. She's now a vampire. But, Adam, that's a good thing. She can take your bite. You will not kill her."

"Don't you think I want nothing more than to make love to Eve and feel her blood run down my throat as I find my release?" Adam's eyes shuttered and he felt the stab of pain and saw Joanna's lifeless body and felt Sullivan's grief. "Evan, because of all the horrors you have known me to commit you might not believe this. But that is truly one deed that I did not plan. I didn't mean to do it."

For a moment neither of them spoke. Then Evan glanced at him. "I know you never meant to. Hell, Adam, I came close to draining Joanna several times myself. She was wild." He looked down. "How in the world did she convince Sullivan she was this puritanical virgin, this untouched paragon of virtue? Sullivan was blinded by love for that woman. Everyone knew but him."

"I think maybe he didn't want to see it. Would you want to see flaws in your wife?"

"Do you see flaws in Eve?"

"Yes," Adam spat bitterly. "She's a liar and a betrayer and I warned her."

"Maybe she loves Sullivan also," Evan said softly. "Adam, you've given her a much extended life span. You can't love her exclusively. She's probably going to have many men that she loves. It's what we do. Are you going to kill everyone that she loves?"

"Yes." The bitterness rolled through him. "She made me a promise. I told her the bonding was only for the two of us. What if…" Adam shook. "What if…" He swallowed, unable to complete his words.

"What if Sullivan had drained her the way you did Joanna? Is that what has you so worried?"

Adam refused to answer, choosing instead to glare at Evan.

"But he didn't, Adam, he didn't drain her, he didn't kill Eve."

"And you think I'm going to wait around until he does? I have to protect her as much as I want to wring her beautiful neck."

"So you're going to kill Sullivan?"

"Yes, I'm going to kill Sullivan. I will not allow him to take revenge on me through Eve. One day when he tires of her, he just might."

"And he might not. It could be possible that he does love her."

Adam's glare was lethal. He aimed it at Evan, scorching his hand before he could pull it away in time. "I will not take chances with her. Sullivan is dead. He just doesn't know it yet."

"We're all dead, Adam, and believe me, we all know it."

Adam's head cocked to the side and he glared at Evan. "Whatever word you want to use, Sullivan has a short time to walk this earth."

"Well then, I guess that's that," Evan said. "Want to go feed?"

❖

Panic had built up to maximum level in Eve. Her fangs descended and she knocked several crystals from the corner of the table. She hated she had to have crystals. She shouldn't have to have blood, shouldn't have to surround Sullivan's home to prevent a vampire from coming after her.

Crystals to prevent the most powerful vampire she knew from entering the house? Laughable. Eve didn't even know why she was doing it. There was no place Adam couldn't enter. Besides that, he was in her head. She couldn't stop thinking about him, calling to him, knowing he'd done as he'd said and tuned her out.

Adam was planning on killing Sullivan and she wanted to plead with him not to. Eve shuddered. She didn't know what living the next hundred years without Sullivan would be like. Tears hot and bloody filled her eyes. A hundred years of not being human. She wondered if by that time she would remember what being human even felt like.

"Adam, please don't kill him. Answer me, damn you."

She turned quickly. Sullivan's eyes were on her, drilling through her. That damn bond, she thought. It was both a blessing and a curse.

"Sullivan, I…I…I…"

"I know what you're doing, you're calling Adam."

"But not because—"

"You're pleading for my life with him. Did you not hear me when I told you, not asked but told you not to do that?" He glared at her for a moment, then turned away. "You truly have no idea how that makes me feel. And you think I can't protect you. Eve, I'll protect you with my dying breath."

"It's not me I'm worried about. Adam plans to kill you."

"Then I'll just have to make sure he doesn't, won't I?"

"Sullivan, you don't understand. Since we bonded…"

He tried to smile, tried to be angry with her, but he couldn't, not when she was so obviously worried for him. "I know the things he's done, Eve. I'm not a fool. The entire world fell into chaos at the precise moment that I delivered the bite. I knew it was no coincidence. He was in my head too."

"Did he threaten you?"

"He said he would kill us both." Sullivan saw the frightened look on Eve's face. "Adam will have to kill me first before he ever has a chance at you."

"I don't want anything to happen to either of us."

"Are you planning on moving back in with him?"

"No."

"Are you planning on our not making love again?"

"Of course not."

"And our bonding, do you want to stop?"

Eve smiled. "I don't think I could even if I wanted to. When we make love and we…" She shivered. "The atoms in my being mingle with yours and we're complete."

"That's a different bite, baby. That's a passion bite. Couldn't you tell the difference?"

"I guess not." She grinned. "I have so much to learn about being a vampire. I wonder if you'd teach me."

Sullivan pulled her to him and held her close. He sighed as he tried to think of a solution to their problems. Adam was not going to just let it go, eventually he would return to do as he'd said. "Eve, because of your bonding with Adam he will always be ale to feel everything that you feel if he chooses. You need to know that before we make love again. You need to know that when we deliver a passion bite Adam will feel it the same as he felt the bonding one. That might anger him even more."

"I love you and I've never had that feeling before, not even with Adam. But what about you? Maybe if we don't do it any more he'll get over it."

"He's not going to get over it. Besides, I feel the same way and dying for your love is not a bad way to go."

"Stop it," Eve said, screaming at him. "This isn't funny."

"It's not meant to be but I told you once I don't want you trying to intervene on my behalf. I'm not afraid of Adam." Sullivan looked sternly at Eve. "I will protect you, Eve, I promise."

"I never worried about that, I've always known you would." She fell into his arms. His lips covered hers and she shivered, hoping her love for Sullivan would not get them both killed.

Funny, Eve thought, they were both dead, yet they worried about dying.

❖

Eve paced the rooms. Her hands were shaking and when she tried to stop the tremors they shook even more. She felt truly ill. The thought flashed through her, that maybe it had something to do with the pills or the AB-5 she was taking.

'*Ask and it shall be given*,' she thought. Hadn't she just told Sullivan that she almost felt human with him? Now she felt more human than she had in two years. All at once Eve felt herself slipping to the floor. With her last lucid moment she called out to Sullivan.

❖

A smile played across his lips. He had to tell someone or he would burst. "Eve doesn't have to hide the AB-5 anymore," Sullivan began, "she's now living with me." He noticed the way Dr. Meah stared at him.

"I'm not worried about Adam. I'm a vampire also and I'm not without resources. Eve and I will build our own company, you can come and work for us."

Dr. Meah blinked, moving his lips without issuing any words.

"What's wrong with you, man?" Sullivan asked as feelings of dread begin inching their way up his spine.

"Maybe it's not a good thing for Eve to leave the company right now," the doctor said softly, "or to leave Adam."

"I love her and I want her. She is free to choose whom she wants and she chose me. You don't have to leave the company, I'm sure Eve will still work with you to help you find just the right formula."

Sullivan's excitement was starting to wane. It was impossible for him not to notice that the doctor did not share in his earlier joy. He'd been in such a euphoric state earlier that he'd failed to notice the doctor wasn't answering him. Now Sullivan sensed sadness coming from the vampire in waves. "What's wrong?" he asked, knowing what was coming.

"Eve needs to stop taking the AB-5 or it's going to kill her."

"Just her? Am I to assume that once again you've stopped taking your concoction? That's becoming a nasty habit with you." Sullivan stared. "What is it this time? I thought you said when you put the formula for the AB-5 in the gelatin capsules that the effects would be a lot less caustic. You were so excited a month ago. You said it was working. Are you aware how excited Eve has been since she no longer has to use the pump? When you took the Picc line from her wrist you said she wouldn't need it anymore."

"I tried, I did, but the results…" Dr Meah stared at Sullivan. "The side effects have increased dramatically. I've fed and that helps to slow down the damage but Eve won't feed. Since I came up with the capsules she won't even take an occasional transfusion."

He blinked rapidly, not wanting Sullivan to see the moisture building in his eyes. "Sullivan, she wants to be mortal so badly that…" He stopped and licked his lips. "If she doesn't stop taking the AB-5 I won't be responsible."

"Who the hell do you think will be responsible? I warned you about trying out your formula on Eve."

"She threatened to tell Adam."

With a low growl his hand shot out and swept the counter he was sitting next to clean of all objects. Glass crashing brought Sullivan's gaze to land on the vampire sitting in front of him. He forced the tension from his body as the human janitor rushed to clean up the mess, flipping his hand 'no' at her when she asked if he needed anything for the cut on his palm. "No," Sullivan said as politely as he could, considering the mood he was in.

When the mess was cleaned away, Sullivan gave the other vamp a hard look. "I warned you what would happen if this didn't work. I warned you it wouldn't be Adam you had to worry about."

"I no longer care about your threats or Eve's to tell Adam. I've dumped the remainder of the formula. She can't take it even if she wants to."

Sullivan stood dumbfounded. "What have you done? You've taken away the one thing she wants to use without even talking to her."

"I'm trying to save her life. I love her too," Dr. Meah admitted at last, and then looked sharply at Sullivan. But I only love her as a friend. Having Eve live her life practically as a mortal was as much my dream as hers. I wanted to give that to her, to give it to all of us. Her success at not having to feed was what I was hoping to achieve, but it didn't work. I can't continue with the experiments. I'll try something else." He shrugged his shoulders.

"She's not going to do anything else. Your damn pills make her feel human, she told this to me." Sullivan shook the doctor and would have continued shaking him had he not heard Eve's voice calling to him.

His face drained of the little color he had. "Something's wrong with Eve," he said and disappeared, not worrying about behaving as a mortal.

❖

"Eve," he called to her before he even reappeared in his home. He scanned the rooms quickly and rushed toward their bedroom where he found Eve stretched out on the floor.

"Sullivan," she whispered when he was by her side. "I knew you would come. You're always there when I need you. Something is wrong."

"I know, baby."

"Maybe this batch of the pills, I don't know. Maybe we should ask Dr. Meah to come and bring me a different batch."

"Eve, there are no more," Sullivan said. "The AB-5 is killing you, he got rid of it."

He heard the gasp, saw her look of shock, then her resignation. "Sullivan, I thought I was ready to die, but I'm not ready," she said, looking into his eyes. "We've just now truly found each other."

"Don't worry, baby, I'm not letting go of you that easily." He lifted her into his arms and carried her to the bed. "You need blood, fresh blood."

The bell rang and Sullivan saw the look of panic in Eve's eyes.

"That's Mark," she said. "I found him, he's alive and, Sullivan, I intend for him to stay that way."

"I didn't ask you to kill him, Eve. I said you need fresh blood. Hell, I'll bite him and give you the damn blood."

"If you do I will never speak to you again. No, you will not harm Mark, understand? I'm getting him out of this life if it's the last thing I do."

How the hell could Sullivan promise her that he wouldn't take Mark's blood in order to save her? He couldn't, so he didn't. He just went to the door and let Mark in.

"She's in there," he growled and pointed toward his bedroom.

"Mark, I'm so glad to see you. Thank you for coming."

"You don't have to thank me," Mark said. "I belong to you."

"You do not belong to me, Mark. I have something I want to give you, something that will make you independent. I've been waiting for the right time to give this to you and I guess this is about as good a time as any."

Eve attempted to sit but the room began to spin and again she thought of being mortal. She closed her eyes and summoned Sullivan. When he appeared beside her she ignored the look in his eyes that was telling her to take Mark and instead sent him a telepathic message of her own. She couldn't help sensing the fear in him. From the way he was looking at her, she knew her condition was bad. "Sullivan, the package I asked you to keep, would you get it for me please?"

When he disappeared in a mist she really knew it was bad. Around humans, even Mark, Sullivan never broke character. His behaving according to his true nature told Eve more about her condition than any words he could have used. When she had the package in her hand she gave it over to Mark. "It's $250,000," she said.

Mark whistled. "Does Adam know?" The smile was genuine.

"Why should he know? Adam took something from both of us and I just took a little something from him in return. Don't worry, Mark. It's my money, too, and Adam won't be able to trace the money back to you. Take the money and leave and start learning to appreciate the life you have. Don't go looking for vampires or other monsters that go bump in the night. Don't go looking for trouble, Mark."

"What's wrong with you, Eve? Why are you trying to send me away?" Mark looked at Eve, then at Sullivan. "Something is wrong, isn't it?"

"Eve needs human blood," Sullivan said without fanfare, "fresh human blood."

"I'm here, Eve, I'm human and my blood is fresh."

Mark sat on the bed, moving closer, baring his neck for Eve to bite. She touched his skin, gently running a fingernail down his carotid artery. Her stomach knotted in pain and the thirst threatened to suck the life out of her. She drew in a deep breath, inhaling the scent of human blood, then shook her head. She saw the bruises that had not faded but lingered still around the base of Mark's throat.

"Who did this?" When Mark didn't answer she nodded again. "Take the money, Mark, go away and never come back."

"If I left you, he'd find me. Besides, I don't want to leave you."

The last thing Eve wanted to do was argue. She watched in silence as Mark moved to the side. She heard him plead with Sullivan to use his blood for her.

When Sullivan kneeled beside her, Eve gripped his hands in hers. "Don't do it, Sullivan, no matter what happens to me. Give Mark a shot at a better life. He deserves it, all humans deserve to live." She lifted her hand to caress his face. "We would do it, if we could. We can't, but Mark can. Do it for us."

Eve's lids fluttered and she looked up as she felt Dr. Meah's essence in the room. "You too. What is this, a death watch? Come on, tell me the good news."

"There are some things we can try, Eve. I can give you a transfusion or we could try the old pills." He looked hard at her, his gaze narrowing. "Or you can go natural. I don't even know if that will work but at least it's your best shot. I brought some blood for you and I brought some pills."

"I don't want the blood," Eve said.

"You said you weren't attempting to be a martyr. You're taking the blood or so help me I'll rip your veins open and pour it in," Sullivan roared.

The thought of Sullivan ripping her veins open to pour in blood amused Eve. It didn't make any sense. She started giggling like a kid and the giggles turned to laughter. She couldn't stop. Pretty soon Mark saw the humor and started laughing. Sullivan was trying not to laugh, but when the doctor broke down, Sullivan joined in. Then he gathered Eve in his arms.

"I'm not losing you. Do you understand, I'm not losing you. I've waited far too long to find love and I can't just stand by and not do anything. So whatever the doctor has in mind we're going to try it. "Agreed?"

"We?" Eve stroked Sullivan's cheek and resumed laughing. "I agree," she answered between laughs. "I don't want to give you up either. Believe me, I'm not looking forward to dying."

"But you all are already dead," Mark said and continued laughing.

Eve sobered and stared at Mark, then Dr. Meah, before allowing her gaze to rest on Sullivan. She swallowed and waited. It seemed an eternity passed before Mark realized he was the only one laughing.

"What's wrong?" he asked.

"We're not dead," Eve answered for all of them.

"But you're vampires," Mark argued.

"That doesn't make us dead. I never died. I was dying and Adam turned me. I didn't die, Mark."

"But still, you're not mortal."

Again Eve looked at Sullivan. She closed her eyes.

"How does drinking his blood sound to you now?" Sullivan asked telepathically and Eve laughed once more.

"It sounds better than it did two minutes ago," she joked back in the same manner. Then she sobered and reached for Sullivan's hand. "You do know that I'm kidding. If anything happens to me, take care of Mark for me, look out for him and try to get him to give up this idea of his."

Sullivan held onto Eve's hand as tightly as he dared. "You'll look after the moron yourself. You're not going anywhere."

He turned to his left, glaring at the other vamp. "What are you waiting for, Doctor? Get started with the transfusion."

After six units of blood and a dozen of the old pills Eve felt refreshed. "Thanks," she murmured. "Sorry for the scare." She glanced at Sullivan and held his gaze. He wasn't convinced that she was feeing better. Her gaze landed on Dr. Meah and she knew the reason why. The doctor's look was somber and his eyes held a look of despair.

"Neither transfusions nor pills are the answer, Eve," Dr. Meah said and shook his head. "Even with our miraculous healing powers this thing seems not to care. I've been working on this for weeks. The corrosive effect was halted only for a few hours. You're going to need massive amounts of blood continuously unless… I think you're going to have to reconsider. I do believe it's time to try more drastic measures."

"What?" Sullivan asked.

"Adam made her. He could give her his blood. It might heal her."

"She already has his blood. Why didn't it stop her from developing a virus in the first place?" Sullivan snorted.

"And it would keep me bound to him and he would kill the three of you for being involved. What would I do without you?"

"What about my blood?" Sullivan asked. "Would it work? Eve, you already have some of my blood in you. Do you want to try?"

She saw the hope in Sullivan's eyes. He loved her. "Yes, I'll take your blood."

"That's not a good idea."

Eve held Sullivan back. He'd turned so viciously on the doctor that his fangs were bared and his muscles rippled with fury.

"Why can't I give her my blood? Hell, don't tell me it won't match because we don't have the same blood type." Sullivan was furious, not waiting for an answer. "That's nonsense," he shouted, not waiting for the doctor to give his reason. "We drink blood from everyone and it doesn't matter."

Eve read his thoughts even though he wasn't sending. He would give the rest of his immortal life to save her.

The doctor's face flooded with color, the same as it must have been in life, but he was determined to finish what he had to say. Eve had to give him credit for that.

"Go ahead, Dr. Meah," she said softly. "Tell us why I can't use Sullivan's blood."

"The blood of any two Masters resists residing in the body of one vamp, even from passion bites. The system will love the one and hate the other. There is no middle ground."

"How do you know it will be my blood that Eve's system will reject?"

"Adam's her soulmate." Dr. Meah backed up a few inches. "I know neither of you wants to hear this but he is. They have the connection of a thousand years. I don't think you can beat that, Sullivan. Not only that, Adam's blood is different—from any other vampire's. I've tested it."

"And you're telling me that our bonding may have hurt her?"

"Yes, that's exactly what I'm saying."

Sullivan groaned and reached for Eve's hand.

"You didn't know, neither did I. It wasn't deliberate on your part." Eve held his gaze. "I wanted it, Sullivan." He refused to look at her, the pain in his heart forcing its way into her own. Both of their hearts were breaking.

"All of these years," he told her through telepathy, "three hundred years, I've hated Adam for killing the woman I loved, and now I may have just killed the woman we both love." He bit back the angry tears. "Eve, I never meant for this to happen. You've got to believe me."

"I do, Sullivan, there is no doubt in my mind. I love you and I know that you love me." She put her arms around him, holding him close, forcing him not to vanish in a puff of smoke.

Dr. Meah continued, "I don't know what makes Adam's blood different, maybe it's all the holy water he's drunk. But Eve's blood is so polluted by this damn corrosive virus that Adam's blood in her isn't protecting her. Besides, Adam keeps his blood strong by feeding, which Eve refuses to do, damn it."

Both Sullivan and Eve stared at the doctor as he stalked about the room. He'd very much wanted the pills to work, so had Eve.

"Still, there has to be something that I'm not seeing, something else Eve is taking and for the life of me, I don't know what it is."

"I've been taking the elixir I make from my crystals." Eve looked around the room at the three male faces staring back at her. "But that won't hurt me; it will heal me."

"What elixir, Eve?" The doctor was at her bedside, his face excited and alarmed at the same time. "What have you been taking?"

"A general tonic," she answered, puzzled.

"Where is it?"

"It's in the fridge." Before she could say more Sullivan and Dr. Meah ran together to the massive kitchen and returned with the elixir.

Dr. Meah held the bottles toward Eve. "What crystals did you use in making these?"

"I'm not sure, give me a second to think."

"You're not sure. You're not sure what's in this stuff? It could be the thing that's killing you and yet you're not sure? Crystals can be toxic, fatal mixed with the things I was using in the AB-5. I want to know every crystal you used and I want you to stop using the tonic immediately."

Eve looked at the men standing in the room yelling at her, two vampires and a mortal. She shook her head, wondering for an instant if she were delirious. "What has happened to the three of you? Why are you all yelling at me? Have you all gone mad?"

Sullivan kissed her hard, holding her body close to his. "We all love you, Eve, and we're angry that you may have done something to take you from us."

What could she say to that? They all loved her. She looked into their eyes and knew Sullivan's words were true. They did love her and she loved the three of them.

"I'm going to test Eve's potions," Dr. Meah said, more excited than Eve had ever seen him. "Sullivan, I'm leaving more blood for her if she needs it. For now, Eve, take it easy, rest."

"Sure," Eve answered and looked toward Mark. "And you think I'm not alive. I'm being told by my doctor to stay in bed and rest, so that proves I'm alive." She grinned, then closed her eyes and slept.

❖

Sullivan didn't like the frown on the face of the other vampire. Sullivan had thrown caution to the wind and had gone to the company just to be there when Dr. Meah came up with an answer. Right now Sullivan didn't give a damn if Adam did come back. He was staying with the doctor until he found a cure for Eve.

For two days now the doctor had been checking each of Eve's potions and frowning. Sullivan was becoming irritated by the man's actions and lack of words. Finally Dr. Meah spun around.

"All of her potions are toxic."

"Do you think she knew that?" Sullivan asked.

Dr. Meah shrugged his shoulders. "The ingredients are meant to be deadly."

"Are you sure?"

"As sure as I can be and mixed with the ingredients I was using, the effect has been even more deadly."

"But what about you? The AB-5 was having the same effect on you."

Dr. Meah slapped his head, wishing he had thought of it sooner. "That was undoubtedly from the crystals Eve gave me to wear. When you took the crystal necklace from me that was about the time I started to get better. That's why I started using the AB-5 again."

"But Eve didn't have effects when you did."

"That's not quite true, Sullivan. Remember, I told you that there were only trace amounts in her blood, unlike mine. I thought at the time that it was because she wasn't taking human blood." He shrugged again. "Maybe it was just Adam's blood giving her protection. I'm not sure what went wrong. We didn't ask her how long she's been taking the potions and that puzzles me."

"It puzzles you?" Sullivan hissed and brought his fist down on a metal cabinet, renting it in two. "Man, do you have any idea how badly you're pissing me off? You've given her this stuff now for way over a year. You should be able to tell me more at this moment than that it puzzles you."

"The AB-5 wasn't a complete failure. It's kept her alive all of this time. She's done what she wanted, and she didn't have to feed."

"But if she had just fed all of this time and had not bothered with your AB-5 she would not now have this problem, right?" Sullivan asked, advancing on the doctor, seeing his fear as he moved away.

Dr. Meah stopped backing away then glared. "It's not all my fault. I was trying to help her. I was trying to help all of us and I was so close, Sullivan, so close."

"Close doesn't win the game and it doesn't give me a real answer."

"I'm telling you what I think, man, not what I know."

"You're guessing!"

"Yes," Dr. Meah shouted back, this time moving farther from Sullivan's reach. "I'm guessing. But I do believe the AB-5 worked more slowly to break down her system since she had not taken in human blood. Then something triggered it. Eve's tonic and something else produced a massive amount of adrenaline. Just a few weeks ago the side effects for her were minimal but I still advised her to stop using it." He glared at Sullivan. "I wasn't trying to kill her, I was trying to help her. I don't know…" He raked his fingers through his hair.

"Would stress do it?"

"Do what?" Dr. Meah asked. The irritation that Sullivan had been showing him was now clearly in his own tone.

"Would stress have caused the extra boost of adrenaline?"

"Stress creates its own chemicals and that is one of them, yes. Has she had undue stress lately, an overabundance of adrenaline?" He stared at Sullivan. "This speed up didn't happen to Eve until recently, until…"

"Until she moved in with me, until she fought with Adam. That was her stress. Do you think it's because she's regretting it?"

"I don't think so. She looks too happy to be with you. She loves you, Sullivan."

"Then why the stress?"

"Adam has caused me a ton of stress just by being in the lab and looking at me. I can't begin to imagine how much stress she was under to cause her to move out. I'm sure she was worrying about… He looked at the frown on Sullivan's face and changed direction.

"I'm sure she was worrying about what Adam would do to her. And she must have worried about Mark. She loves you, Sullivan, probably as much as she loves him. That would be more stress than anyone could handle."

Sullivan's mind flicked on Adam. It was always Adam who was at the source of problems. If Adam had not kissed Eve, if she had not kissed him back, if he had not been able to hold her without the revulsions… Sullivan's throat closed. And if Adam had been able to hold Eve, then Sullivan wouldn't have her.

He thought of Eve's tears, her pain and his ultimatum to her. Yes, she'd had a barrel load of adrenalin mixed in with the crystal potions and the AB-5. It had made for a deadly cocktail.

Sudden fear claimed Sullivan. "Didn't you say that Eve's not taking human blood even in transfusions was probably why she'd not had the effect when you had?"

"Yes," Dr. Meah answered. In the same instant they realized that giving Eve the transfusions and the old pills might have very well been the last straw.

Rage overtook Sullivan and he reached for the doctor. "You did this to her, you with your constant experimenting. You've killed her."

"It wasn't just the AB-5," Dr. Meah defended. "It was like a house of dominoes. One thing triggered another. It wasn't just me. Your biting her and bonding with her didn't help either, Sullivan. Did you ever think of that? If you don't think her blood created a load of adrenaline when you did that, think again." He smoothed out the wrinkles from where Sullivan had twisted his lab coat. "From here on out, keep your hands off me, or I'm going to start fighting back."

"I'm sorry." Sullivan looked up. "I can't lose her. Do you really think Adam can save her?"

"I don't know, but I do know he's her best hope."

"No one knows where he is. Eve has tried to contact him and he's closed his thoughts to her." Sullivan squeezed his eyes tightly. "And you can bet he will have blocked all of my thoughts."

Dr. Meah looked away. "No matter how furious Adam was with Eve, I don't believe he would leave her completely, not without a way for her to reach him even in his snit. I'm sure Eve can reach him if she wants."

"She doesn't want to," Sullivan said between gritted teeth, "but I want to. What about the blood you've given her already?"

"The virus has already taken over. It was the only thing I had available to use. It's like a blessing and a curse. It can keep her going for awhile but using it will accelerate the virus and kill her that much sooner."

"Damn!" Chills rampant and strong froze him, making Sullivan remember he'd only been playacting. He was dead, not alive. He was a vampire and without Eve there was no possible joy in his vampire heart. The thought of the impending loneliness shook him and he called out to Adam telepathically. When the tears stained his cheeks red he didn't bother brushing them away, knowing more would come. His gaze landed on the doctor and he saw the other vamp's cheeks stained as well.

"What are we going to do?" Sullivan asked quietly.

"Find Adam. Eve can reach him, she has the blood connection. I think she had the connection with Adam even before… She has to be able to reach him," he said and shook his head sadly.

"I'll tell Eve. It will be her decision." The gazes of the vampires locked and held before Sullivan vanished.

❖

Eve listened to her options. It was rather like learning she had a mortal disease that would kill her. She would try all of the treatments with the exception of one. She would not call out to Adam.

"Sullivan, I made my decision when I left Adam. I severed my ties. That's the end of that. How long?"

"Don't talk how long. I don't want 'how long,' I want forever."

"Well, you're out of luck. Even if I wanted to I don't know how to reach Adam. I told you, he's closed his mind to me."

"I don't believe you."

Eve shrugged her shoulder. "If you choose to waste what time we have left fighting over Adam, I don't. I would like to do as we said, live like mortals. I'd like to take a vacation with you, pretend that we're just a normal couple in love."

"Eve, this is important."

"I don't know how to reach him," Eve yelled and hopped from the bed, ignoring Sullivan's outstretched arms, his warning that she was not to exert herself. "I can't reach him, Sullivan, and as I said, even if I could I wouldn't." She walked away, turning her back to him.

Sullivan looked after Eve. This arguing with her was probably not doing her any good. With every word she shouted the poison was probably racing through her body. He sighed and looked across the room at Mark who was staring at him with a look of worry. The mortal had not left Eve's side since she'd found him.

"Don't look so worried, I won't hurt you. Eve wouldn't like it."

"I know how to reach Adam," Mark croaked.

"You? How?"

"He gave me something to give to Eve, told me to tell her that if she needed him, he would hear, and he would come."

Sullivan wanted to throttle the mortal for not having spoken sooner. "Give it to me," he said between clenched teeth that showed an inch of fang because he was angry.

"Adam told me to give it only to Eve."

"You will give it to me or I will forget my promise to Eve." He reached his hand out toward Mark. "Adam is not the only vampire around who's willing to inflict pain on others to protect the woman he loves. Now hand it over."

Sullivan stared at the ring. He was familiar with it. Eve had worn it when he'd first known her. He remembered when she'd threatened them with the ring, saying that Adam would be at her side in a microsecond should they attempt to harm her.

He closed the ring in his fist. This would be the end of his relationship with Eve. He would have to give her up in order for her to live. He knew that, yet he wanted more time with her.

"Don't you say a word," he warned Mark, "not one word. You remain here with Eve until I return."

❖

"How long can Eve survive without Adam's blood?" Sullivan stared at Dr. Meah, probing the vampire's mind. He didn't want any fancy words or deception. Now was not the time.

"I have no way of knowing," Dr. Meah answered. "Now get the hell out of my head. This is uncharted territory. A vampire having a virus…" The doctor laughed in spite of his wanting to cry. "I truly don't know. I think for a couple of months the old pills and regular transfusions will keep her going."

"But you said—"

"I know what I said," Dr. Meah interrupted. It was killing him that he couldn't find a cure for Eve. "We're talking the reverse of what I said before, Sullivan, two, three months tops."

"Time to take her on a trip, a vacation?"

"You want to take a vacation? We're talking about her life, man."

"She wants to go on a vacation. I want to take her on one. Do we have the time?"

"You're both crazy. You're vampires, not mortals. Vampires don't take vacations."

"That's just the point. She wants to live as one, and I want to give that to her. Now do we have the time? Will my taking her away for a month make her worse?"

"No."

"Good, now we're getting somewhere. Will you still be able to use Adam's blood to save her?"

"The sooner you call Adam the better her chances." He tilted his head to the side. "Have you found Adam?"

"No, but I've found a way to reach him."

"And you don't plan on telling Eve?"

"Of course I'm going to tell her," Sullivan spat out in disgust, glaring at the man. "I would never withhold information from Eve, even information that might take her from me if that was what you thought."

"Now it's me who owes you an apology. I'm sorry," Dr. Meah said, "but I know how much you love her and since you no longer work here at the company I just assumed after your last fight that things were not so good between you and Adam."

"You assumed correctly," Sullivan answered, "but still…" He waved his hand. "Enough of that. As I said, I have a way to reach Adam and I'm going to insist that we do it. But I know Eve. She's going to refuse and I want to know if I give her a month of pleasure whether Adam will still be able to save her."

"Perhaps," Dr. Meah said, "but I'm not giving any guarantees. I don't even know for sure if he can save her if he appears in the next hour."

"So my taking Eve away will not be putting her in any more jeopardy than she's already in."

"No, it won't."

"Thank you," Sullivan answered, "that's all that I wanted to know."

Chapter 21

Eve twirled in the field of yellow, purple, red and orange tulips. Turning toward Sullivan, she said, "You've given me something I've always wanted. I didn't know I'd have to be a dying vampire to get it," she joked.

When she saw the flash of pain on Sullivan's face she tugged on his arm. "Come on, Sullivan, don't be so glum. I'm happy."

"So am I." He smiled at her. "You've also given me something, a gift I can never repay you for. You've given me the sun, the daylight hours. For hundreds of years I believed I could not go out in the sun. Then you came into my life, a ray of sunshine, and gave it all back to me."

"And you've given me a taste of what it's like to be a mortal again. I love you even more for that." Standing amidst the flowers she went up on tiptoe and kissed Sullivan. "We're like any other mortal couple. The only difference is that each night and each morning I need a transfusion of blood to start my day." She grinned. "It's nice having friends in high places, and nice that vampires control the blood banks the world over. It makes traveling a lot easier."

Sullivan swung her upward and nuzzled her neck, careful not to nick her. He remembered the taste of her blood hot in his mouth and the perfume of her essence.

"You know you can. I miss it," Eve whispered.

"So do I but the thought that I could take away a second from your life…"

"Don't be sad, don't ever be sad. You've made me happy, Sullivan. I know you want to give me your blood, that you're willing to allow Dr. Meah to bleed you dry to give me life. I also know that as much as you don't want to see him, you want me to call Adam. I thank you for not trying to override my decision, for not being like Adam. He would have taken over and ignored my feelings. But you respect me and my feelings. For that I love you and trust you. As for living, the here and now are enough. I want to be in your arms. I want the passion bites."

She looked at him and smiled, kissing him with all the passion that was in her, nipping his lips, nicking his neck, tasting lightly of his blood until he pulled away. Then she snuggled in the nest of his shoulder and laughed at him.

Something in Eve's words worried Sullivan. He looked down into her face.

He had to know. "Did you know the potions you mixed were toxic? Have you been trying to kill yourself?"

"No, Sullivan, I wasn't trying to take my own life. Even though I've complained about it for the past two years, I didn't poison myself deliberately."

"But you've been working with crystals for a long time, Eve, you had to know something."

"I miscalculated. I thought that if the crystals were harmful to humans they would have the opposite effect on me as a vampire. I didn't do it deliberately. Besides, the tonic made me feel better. I thought it was helping me."

"But why did you start taking it in the first place?"

"I was trying to shock my system into turning back into a mortal. Ironically, it seems I succeeded."

"But your life doesn't have to end this way."

"What better way than to live out the remainder of my life loving you, knowing that you love me, being with you in all of the wonderful places we've been to, pretending that the last two years never happened. Sullivan, this trip is for you as well as me. When you think of me I want you to think of the joy we've shared. I don't want you sad and mourning. Well, not forever anyway. I want you to find someone else and give her all the love that's in your heart."

"You can't truly love me if you want me to find someone else." He was trying to joke with her but the thought of losing her was ripping his heart out.

"I do love you. I'm not saying I don't want you to mourn me, just not for a thousand years. I don't want you turning into Adam and wasting your life. I don't want you turning bitter and sad."

"And what would you like for me to do with the enormous guilt I feel for my part in your condition and for not calling Adam?"

"I want you to let it go right now in this beautiful field of tulips. It was my choice, Sullivan, my choice not to call Adam. Can you imagine the scene if you had called Adam, his rage? It would end with Adam doing what he does best— he'd just cause more chaos by throwing his thunderbolts."

Sullivan held her in his arms. "Is it that you're afraid that Adam will push you away again? Is that the real reason you don't want to call him?"

She smiled. "Just the opposite. Adam is tortured over what he did to me. No, calling him would heap more guilt on him, give him more reason to cause trouble in the world, more of a reason for mortals to fear him. I don't want that laid at my door. I've forgiven Adam for everything. I still love him, Sullivan, and I don't want the two of you to be enemies."

As Sullivan swiped his lips with his tongue, Eve caught his tongue in her lips and bit lightly. "My love for him doesn't dilute my love for you. If you would bond with me you would know it." She bit down on Sullivan's throat and sent him the information, feeling his shudders as the knowledge flooded him. "You never have to doubt my love for you. You're in competition with no one." She smiled, giving him back the words he'd given her months before when she'd questioned his love for her.

"What will happen when you die? He made you, Eve, he will feel it. It's his blood bond with you. That's different than what we have. Don't you think he will still take out his hurt on the world?"

"For a little while, but then he will be relieved. I won't be a constant living reminder of what he did."

"I don't want you to go."

"And I don't want to go but we were never meant to live forever, Sullivan. We were never created to be vampires, to live off of the blood of others. Come on, let's go back to the hotel and make love. I need to feel that oneness with you." She smiled up at him. "But we will return to the hotel in the mortal way. We will walk."

❖

"Eve," Adam said softly. He blinked.

"What's wrong," Evan asked, looking at him strangely.

"I have this weird feeling that Eve is close by and she's in trouble. It's like I can feel a flutter in her heart, like she's dying. I could swear I heard her speak my name and it sounded as though she said she'd forgiven me for everything I've ever done, as though she loved me still."

Evan didn't answer, only continued to stare.

"You're looking at me as though I'm insane," Adam growled.

"No, I'm looking at you because you're sounding like a lovesick mortal. Make up your mind: Either you love her or you hate her. You're going to kill her or let her live. I personally don't care what you do. But you're so damn conflicted, no wonder your wife has no idea how you feel about her. It seems that you don't even know."

"I've always known how I felt about Eve. I love her."

"Yet you cut off communication with her for months at a time. You close your thoughts to her, put an energy barricade around yourself so she can't get through, and now you worry that because you've done it she might need you and can't find a way to reach you."

"Why am I friends with you?"

"Because no one else believes they can stand up to you. I don't worry about it, and I can't help it if the truth I tell is not to your liking."

"Eve has a way to reach me should she really need me."

"What?"

"I gave a ring to that mortal she's befriended. It's the same ring I gave to Eve when I first claimed her, back in the beginning when we were friends, way before I knew she was Eyanna. I gave her a ring so she would be able to call on me, before I made the blood connection. And I warned the mortal on the threat of severe and long lasting pain that if Eve needed me, if she were in trouble, he was to give the ring to her."

"Did she ever use the ring when you first gave it to her?"

"She used it a couple of times, briefly." Adam had felt the sensation of Eve's fingers trailing his skin as she'd touched the ring. He shivered.

"But each time she touched it she stopped." He closed his eyes and swallowed. "She wanted what she knew I couldn't give."

"I was right, Adam, you do need therapy."

"You're right and if you can point me in the direction of a good one I might just take you up on that." Both vampires laughed, knowing that would be the last thing Adam would do.

❖

"Adam." Sullivan rubbed Eve's ring and felt intense energy emanate from it. He breathed in hard and felt the tremor of time and space as he linked with Adam.

"Sullivan, how the hell did you get the ring?"

This was it, the moment he'd waited for and dreaded. The vacation was over and he was doing as he'd promised Eve he wouldn't do. He was calling for help. She would never forgive him.

But now Sullivan thought he understood what Adam must have felt. He could not just stand by and allow Eve to die without trying everything at his disposal.

"Adam." Sullivan swallowed hard. How could he ask what he'd called Adam to do? He closed his eyes and felt the tears run down his cheeks. Then he opened his eyes. "Eve is dying," he said at last. "She needs your blood."

Chapter 22

There was no denying the tension in the lab. Adam's anger crested and became a living force. His energy pulled at Sullivan and Sullivan could feel a band of steel close around his throat though Adam had not moved a muscle.

"I don't care what you do to me," Sullivan croaked out, resisting the urge to strike back. This humiliation he would take if it would keep Eve alive.

"Help Eve, Adam. If you love her, help her."

Slowly the pressure eased and Sullivan opened his eyes to stare into Adam's blood red eyes. He saw the grief on Adam's face. He'd somehow hoped that the revulsion Adam felt because Eve was a vampire had weakened his love for her. It had not.

"What have you done to her?" Adam asked, "Have you hurt her?"

"For over a year now she's been taking the new formula Dr. Meah invented, the AB-5."

"You fools tested this on my wife?"

"Eve wanted to take it. She asked the doctor for it. He didn't want to give it to her but she insisted."

"And now what has it done? It's bad or you wouldn't have used the ring to contact me."

Sullivan couldn't hold Adam's gaze because there was so much hatred in it mixed with fear for Eve. Damn, he didn't blame Adam for hating him. Still, he needed to tell him exactly what was wrong so he could help.

"Dr. Meah said it has a virus effect. He told her to stop but Eve refused. Now the virus is killing her and he has no way to stop it. He's tried."

"Tell me this." Adam stepped closer. "How could she keep getting the samples if he didn't continue making it?"

Adam stared hard at Sullivan. "How long have you had this information?"

"About six weeks."

"And you just now decided to contact me?"

"Eve wanted to go on a trip. I took her."

"She's dying and you took her on a vacation. I see," Adam said, rubbing his chin with his thumb. "Did you take her to Amsterdam?"

"Yes, how did you know?"

"Because I felt her there, damn it. I should have done something then."

Adam clenched his fists at his sides, snarling as his incisors came down two inches then two more. He roared as several inches of fangs ripped through his gums. A black cloud covered him and his dark energy whirled around him.

"You've killed my wife because of a tramp?" he asked through the red haze. "For three hundred years I have protected your feelings. Your Joanna was not the pure virgin you thought her to be, Sullivan. Evan was right, I should have told you centuries ago. She was a whore. She came to all of us begging us to bite her, to drain her and turn her. She came to me, Sullivan, and I did as she asked. I drained her, only I didn't turn her. I thought I did you a favor. Who the hell would have wanted her around forever? She was a whore. Do you hear me? A whore! Every vampire had her," Adam roared louder and louder.

Adam wrapped his hands around Sullivan's throat, the urge to kill him obliterating everything, even his vow to allow him to live. Sullivan's pasty color turned a cherry red and Dr. Meah ran up to Adam.

"Adam, Adam, let him go."

Releasing one of his hands from Sullivan Adam reached for the doctor and began choking him also. A roar of anger rolled throughout him splitting the walls with its intensity.

"Please, Adam. Stop. We want to help you help Eve. You need us."

"I need no one," Adam roared again but released his hold on the doctor, twisting his fist and watching as the doctor dropped to the floor. He shoved Sullivan away, and twisted his heart. He watched as both vampires clutched their chests.

"Adam, I've always been loyal to you, you know that.

The words came out in a choked whispered but it was enough. Adam stopped his torturing of the vamps and took it out on inanimate objects, destroying everything in his path. "A whore. I can't believe you did this because of a whore."

"This is not about Joanna. I did nothing to Eve in order to get back at you."

"Don't you dare speak, Sullivan, or I swear you are going to die here and now." Adam paced from one end of the room to the other for several long minutes, aiming a finger at anything that came within his vision. Two vampires came to investigate what the problem was and Adam sent a beam at them, turning them to ash before they had a chance to speak. He shook with anger, so much so that the mortal janitor who ran into the room behind the vampires was the next to go.

"Damn it! Now look what you made me do. Speak, Sullivan, and you'd better damn well make me believe what you have to say. Tell me why you attempted to kill my wife over a whore. A whore who didn't love you. You had nothing, Sullivan, do you hear me? Nothing. I had love. Real love. Eve came into this lifetime remembering me, loving me, wanting me. Do you think your whore would have ever come back for you?"

Adam became enraged again, unable to allow Sullivan a moment to answer him. He paced again and raised his hand toward the ceiling causing more lights to blow. He saw Dr. Meah moving toward the corner, cringing. He took in a deep breath and went to stand in front of Sullivan. "I said tell me why a whore is worth my wife's life."

"I love Eve." Now Sullivan's eyes blazed.

"That's your damn answer?" Adam reached for Sullivan and sank his fangs into his neck. "You stupid fool. I want you to know what Joanna was." He bit harder, drinking Sullivan's blood and sending him image after image of Joanna with him, of her begging him to turn her, of her calling Sullivan a fool. When he was done Adam tossed Sullivan aside.

"You did this to Eve for that piece of trash, that slut? She didn't love you, Sullivan. Damn. Evan was right. I should have told you that years ago instead of thinking it best that you continued living with the illusion that you'd had love."

"I know she didn't love me, Adam. You're not telling me anything I didn't know. I haven't fought with you all of these years because of that. I fought with you because you killed her, Adam. You killed her and whore or not I loved her. Hell no, she was not worth Eve's life. But I'm not you. I would never use one woman to make up for the wrongs either you or Joanna did to me. I know what Joanna was. I knew three hundred years ago but still I loved her. And I didn't need the pictures you showed me. I saw them when I bonded with Eve, I saw them there in your blood."

"I don't believe you, Sullivan. I believe you planned to poison my wife with your foul blood and I think eventually you would have drained her dry."

"Believe what you want, Adam, we can sort this out later. Regardless of what Joanna was, it still stands that you're the one that killed her."

"And because of that I have allowed you to live well beyond your time. I have allowed our past friendship to be a factor, my guilt for hurting you, my guilt over Joanna. I told you not to allow harm to come to Eve."

"Do you think I did this deliberately?"

"You bonded with her."

"That is not uncommon, Adam, not when you're in the throes of—"

"Finish that sentence and I will kill you where you stand. I made her, Sullivan. Your blood tainted her and killed her."

"Adam, it was the AB-5 and a potion Eve made."

"It was your blood!" This time when Adam roared both Dr. Meah and Sullivan were forced to cover their ears and run for cover as huge sections of the roof caved in.

Adam's rage was not to be contained. Windows were flying out of the building by the force of his thoughts. More than a dozen vampires went up in flames, vampires that were not even near the lab.

"Adam, stop, not now please. We can do this later, after you heal Eve. She needs you now, there's not much time. Go and see her," Sullivan pleaded, hating that he had to plead with a maniac. But he was the only one who could save Eve.

"Someone will pay if Eve dies. Do I make myself clear?" Adam spoke through clenched teeth, his body continuing to shake in fury.

"Adam, you can save her."

"Someone will still pay for it. Where is that mortal she was to feed from?"

"Mark is at my home with her. He's heartbroken. Eve has a fondness for him."

"But not a blood connection, I take it," Adam asked, baiting, Sullivan, wondering if at this juncture the vampire would dare lie to him. As a plan began to form, Adam forced himself to take it down a notch.

"No, not a blood connection. She has never fed from him but she put the pictures in his mind and he thinks that she does."

"I know she never fed from him. Maybe tonight she will."

"She will not feed from him, Adam. Her life in exchange for a mortal?" Sullivan smiled slowly. "Perhaps you don't know Eve as well as you think. She would rather die than do as you commanded her. Adam, in all of this time she's never fed from a mortal."

"What the hell," Adam roared. "I can't believe she's been a vampire for over two years and never fed from a mortal." Adam tilted his head, "You, Sullivan, you knew this. You knew she needed to have fresh blood in order to survive. Why did you allow her…"

"Allow? Have you forgotten she is a vampire made by you? She shares many of your traits and I didn't have the power to allow her anything. Besides, Adam, I could refuse her nothing. I love her."

"Love her," Adam laughed. "I don't believe we're having this conversation. You've done the unthinkable. You tried to kill my wife. And you speak to me of loving her."

"What are you going to do? Kill me because I love her, or save her knowing that she loves me."

"I'll save her, and then I'll kill you so she can watch and then I'll do the job right and kill her myself." Adam glared at Sullivan. "Did you not think Eve would have to pay for her betrayal?"

"Sure, Adam, whatever you say, just let's go to her." Sullivan was flabbergasted. Adam was beyond reason, talking of saving Eve in order to kill her. In case he didn't know it, once he saved Eve, Sullivan was going to make sure Eve stayed alive. This was one promise he'd made to Eve that he would not break. He would protect her with his dying breath. He was going to kick her crazy husband's behind from one end of Chicago to the other when this was over. For now he'd put up with this, act the punk until he got what he needed from Adam.

"Get Dr. Meah, I want him with us. We will all take part in this. Go get him now," Adam roared and Sullivan vanished. Adam went to Eve, coming to her in a rush of wind. He saw her on the bed lifeless, her color dusky, the brown drained away.

"Eve," he said softly and went to her. "What have I done?" he asked.

He saw the mortal sitting near her bed and ignored him. He touched Eve's skin. It was soft, pliant and cool. "Eve." He attempted to connect with her. "I love you, Eve," he whispered.

"I know. I love you too."

Adam felt a fist closing around his heart. Eve was delirious. She didn't know it was him. She must think he was Sullivan. For a moment he thought to keep her words of love, but only a moment.

"Eve, it's Adam," he said instead.

"I know," she answered.

"I love you, Eve."

"I know that also, Adam, and I love you. I love you enough to forgive you. And I want you to forgive me for all I've done to you. It's over."

"It doesn't have to be."

"Yes, it does, Adam, this time it does. I have an illness almost like a mortal. Don't interfere, Adam, not this time." Her hand reached up and she caressed his face. "Give me up, Adam, let me go."

He brought her hand to his lips and kissed her fingers. "I can't, I love you too much." Adam ignored Sullivan watching him, concentrating only on Eve.

A lump formed in Sullivan's throat and his chest filled with pain as he watched the tenderness between Adam and Eve. He attempted to blink it away. Underneath it all he'd always known that Eve had never stopped loving Adam or him her. Hell, she'd admitted to it. What would make him think that near death she wouldn't reach out to her soul mate?

Still, this was not about him or his feelings for Eve. This was about begging Adam to save her life, to do what he couldn't do.

Sullivan wanted desperately to go against what Eve wanted and in a way he was. Only it wouldn't be his hand that saved her. He'd promised her he wouldn't. He hoped that she would at least forgive him that much.

Sullivan's eyes flicked upward as Dr. Meah materialized. The room was silent for a moment. They both watched as Adam turned. He moved his head in slow motion between Eve and Sullivan. "Sullivan is here, Eve," Adam whispered in her ear.

Sullivan dropped to his knees beside Eve and clasped her hand in his. Adam moved back and allowed it, swallowing this, knowing that it was his fault that his wife was getting what she needed from another, what he'd failed to give her. He shivered and probed both Eve and Sullivan.

Adam felt the sadness in Eve, felt the love she had for Sullivan. His heart twisted as he watched her hand entwine with Sullivan's and then he heard Eve's words.

"You'll keep your promise?" she asked Sullivan. And Adam heard Sullivan's promise to Eve. "I'll keep my promise," Sullivan answered.

What promise? Adam wondered and probed Sullivan's and Eve's minds deeper and without detection. When he'd learned what he needed to know, Adam drew out of their minds. He'd heard more than enough of their private bonding conversation and what he'd heard filled him with unbridled fury. *So this was how Sullivan thought to keep his hands clean.*

He wanted Adam to do the dirty work, to bring her back when she wanted to leave, to keep her a vampire. Adam lifted his eyes to the doctor and saw the man cowering in fear. Then for the first time he observed the mortal, the one who should have kept Eve alive so she would have had no need for any experimental blood. This crime rested on their shoulders, the three of them, not Adam's and they wanted him to fix it.

Of course he could and he would but not without the blood being on their hands also. If Eve was going to hate Adam for once again keeping her alive, then she would hate them as well.

"Adam," Sullivan called to him softly. "She's slipping away."

"I know."

"You can save her."

"So can you, Sullivan. Give her your blood."

"My blood isn't as strong as yours."

"But it's strong enough to save her, especially if we drain her body of the tainted blood first and you give her what she needs."

The vampires locked eyes, neither speaking for the longest time. "I can't," Sullivan roared. "I promised her that I wouldn't give her my blood to save her. I love her, Adam, and she loves me, she trusts me."

Sullivan's words more than anything else angered Adam. How dare this vampire speak of his wife trusting him to his face, as if to say Eve did not trust Adam. How dare he? "Do you think she no longer loves me, Sullivan? Ask her, ask her whom she loves." Adam glared as the color drained from Sullivan's face. "Okay, if you won't, I'll ask."

"I already know that she still cares for you but I'm the one she's in love with."

"Care to make a little wager on that?" Adam bit into his wrist and sucked the blood into his mouth. Then he went to Eve and lifted her in his arms. His lips came down over hers and he parted them, allowing the blood in his mouth to fill her. Adam felt the moment when the faintest stirring of life returned to Eve's body and her whisper, "Adam, not again."

"Eve, this is just for a moment. Sullivan is here and so are Dr. Meah and Mark. Do you understand me?"

"Yes, Adam, I understand."

"Do you love me, Eve?"

"Yes, Adam, I have always loved you."

"What of Sullivan?" Adam waited and waited and waited. He could hear the heartbeat of the other two vampires and of the mortal as they all waited for Eve's answer, the deathbed confession. At last the words fell from her lips.

"I love him too."

"How can you love us both?" Adam asked.

"I don't know, but I do. My soul is connected to you, Adam, and I still have a soul. I love you even though I have wished a million times that I didn't."

Adam swallowed. "You've wished not to love me?"

"If there were a way for me not to love you, Adam, I wouldn't. As for Sullivan, he loves me and I trust him. He would never hurt me. He would never do anything against my will. Besides, he's been a good friend to me. How could I not love him? I've freely given him a part my heart. I love Sullivan because I want to and I love you because I can't help it."

Now Adam was wishing he'd left well enough alone. He'd thought to show Sullivan up, to show him that he would never replace Adam in Eve's heart but she'd made a liar out of him. "Eve, if you have all of that for Sullivan, what is the love you have for me?"

"It's a sickness, Adam," Eve said softly, "Apparently something I have no control over. If I had known how to stop loving you I would have."

There was so much Adam wanted to say to Eve. He wanted to beg her not to give up on him, to stop loving Sullivan. He swallowed but the pain and humiliation would not go away. He would not speak to Eve of intimate matters, not here in front of the others.

"You need to rest now, Eve." He kissed her again and felt her weakness as her arms attempted to hold him.

"Adam?"

"Yes," he answered, turning back.

"Don't harm Dr. Meah. He was only doing as I asked. He was trying to help me."

"I will not touch him. I will give you my word on that, Eve. I will not put a finger to him."

"And Sullivan?"

Adam laughed.

"Adam?"

"I will make no promises to you about that but Sullivan can take care of himself."

"Adam?"

"Rest now, Eve, save your strength." Adam turned to the ones assembled. "I want the three of you to remain here with Eve until I return."

"But—"

Adam turned toward Sullivan. "There is time," he said, and just like that he vanished. He could not keep his promise to Eve if he remained there a microsecond longer. He would rip Sullivan into shreds and he would kill the doctor by the most vile means he knew. And he knew a lot of despicable methods. After he took care of the doctor it would give him great joy to drain the mortal dry for not doing as he'd been ordered.

But Adam had promised Eve and it would be one of the few promises he would keep. At least he would keep them until he had a plan. He didn't like knowing that his wife truly loved Sullivan, that she trusted him. Until today he'd thought she was merely sleeping with Sullivan to make him jealous. That he could have understood, that he could have forgiven. But to actually love another man was more of a betrayal than the bonding. This affront could not go unpunished and it would not.

❖

His heart breaking, Sullivan sat beside Eve, holding her hand. What if Adam didn't come back? What if he didn't save her?

"Don't worry, baby." Eve opened her eyes for barely a second and smiled at him. "I'll see you again in a few hundred years. "Don't be sad." She attempted to lift her head but Sullivan leaned down into her and kissed her.

"Did you call Adam?" Eve asked.

"No, he just sensed you were ill and came back," Sullivan answered without looking into her eyes, knowing that if he did she would know he was lying.

She opened her eyes again. "You're wearing my crystals. Why?" Eve asked.

"To feel closer to you," Sullivan lied again. The crystals had aided Eve in hiding her thoughts from him. Now he was using them to hide his thoughts from her.

"Thank you for not asking Adam to help."

Eve closed her eyes and Sullivan watched as her breathing became labored and she fought for each breath. He didn't know how long he could bear it. Everything in him was crying out for him to order the doctor to transfuse her with his blood and Adam be damned.

He waited while Eve slipped into a vampiric coma and his own heart stopped. "Damn you, Adam, when do you plan to help her?" He sent the words to Adam and sensed the massive energy as Adam materialized beside him.

"I'm right here, Sullivan." Adam looked to the side where Dr. Meah was waiting, the fear making his face rigid. "Go to the lab and bring back what you need to transfuse Eve. We're going to do a direct transfusion from my veins to hers, understand? And, Doctor, if you're gone for more than thirty seconds I will stop your heart and pull it from your chest." Adam smiled. "Now go."

"Theatrics, Adam, even in this? Can't you just do what you came here to do?"

"Sure." Adam gazed at Eve. "But first I think we need to have a little talk."

"She doesn't have much time, Adam."

Adam glanced down again at the face of his wife. "Like I said, we need to have a talk."

He walked away from Eve as though he didn't give a damn and heard Sullivan's muttered curses. *Good*, he thought. Sullivan was afraid for Eve's life, just as Adam had been once before. But this time Adam would not be the only force of evil in saving Eve's life. When this was done he wondered if either of them would brag that Eve trusted Sullivan.

"How badly do you want Eve to live?" Adam turned to face Sullivan, ignoring his glare, his look of unadulterated hatred. Sullivan didn't answer, merely looked at him.

"Would you give your life to save her?" Adam asked.

"Yes," Sullivan said without hesitation.

At that Adam smiled. That one had been easy, anticipated. They would both give their lives to save Eve. That was already understood. Now for the harder question. "Would you take a life in order to save her?" Adam's eyes slid over to Mark. He saw the hesitation begin. "What is it, Sullivan, you don't think Eve would like it?"

Adam glared, his eyes blazing, but this time his fury was contained and he was in control.

"Hear me and hear me well, Sullivan. Do you think when this is over she's going to still love you? That you are going to live out eternity as this happy vampiric couple? You're a fool. She's my wife. Do you understand, mine. Did you think I would agree to being the only one that she hated?"

A stab of pain twisted through Adam, making him jerk his head stiffly. He didn't have time to play with Sullivan. Eve was slipping away, but still he wanted to finish the game, to end this as it should be ended. Eve he would save if he had to fight hell itself for her soul. She was not leaving him again.

He laughed cruelly and pain filled his entire being. Her essence soaked into his skull and he heard his name in the deep recesses of her mind. "*Adam, you're my husband and you'll always be my husband. I have always loved you. I want you not to grieve this time.*" He blinked. There was no way in hell he would shed one tear in front of Sullivan.

"This time, Sullivan, I will not be the only one who will betray her." Adam shuddered, not knowing if he could continue this charade if he were in the room with her. With his hand he opened a portal and both he and Sullivan gazed at Eve two rooms away.

He looked down at Eve, the woman whose soul was linked with his and his with hers. Her life once again was slipping away. Adam knew he would not let that happen but Sullivan didn't. Adam saw the question in the other vamp's eyes of how he could be so cold.

Adam knew the answer to that question. He hated that Sullivan was able to give Eve what Adam wanted badly to give her. He'd seen the look that passed between them and it had filled him with a jealous rage. "Time is running out, Sullivan," Adam, said closing the portal and looking toward the door. "Would you kill to save Eve?"

Both of their eyes fastened on Mark before Sullivan managed to get the words out. "Yes, I would kill to save her."

"And would you let me feed on you to save her?" Adam waited.

"Why do you need to feed on me?"

Adam tilted his head and laughed. "How the hell do you think I will give her all of my blood if I don't take in more? I will give to Eve, you will give to me and Mark will give to you."

Adam saw the understanding of his plan beginning to form in Sullivan's mind and he smiled.

"So that's how you plan to do it," Sullivan said softly, realizing that Adam was extracting revenge and at the same time ensuring that Eve would no longer trust him. She would live but she would not live with Sullivan at her side. A hard shudder racked his body and he shook his head. "Adam, you're a cold-hearted bastard. You promised Eve that you wouldn't harm Doctor Meah. What are you planning for him?"

"What I promised Eve was that I would not put a finger to the good doctor and I won't. He will drain the tainted blood from Eve's body."

In a flash Adam disappeared to reappear at the doctor's side.

Dr. Meah was trembling, the tubing and container to drain the tainted blood from Eve's body he held at arm's length. One look in Adam's direction and he knew he wouldn't need the bags. Adam's look was lethal and it was apparent he was looking for payback. Dr. Meah swallowed when Adam pointed toward the bags and shook his head no. Still, he had to say the words.

"I have everything we need to drain Eve's body of her blood," Dr. Meah said from parched lips.

"Oh no, this is your fault, Doctor. You made the poison that you fed to my wife. Now you will rid her body of it. You will drink her blood, and you will not spill a drop."

"But her blood is tainted, Adam. It could kill me."

"And so could I. You will drink it," Adam said with authority, ignoring the wave of terror that rode the man's blood. Adam clenched his fist. All of these challengers for Eve's affection would be dealt with. They all thought they had her trust. When this night was over none of them would.

Dr. Meah turned to run and Adam laughed. Predictable, he thought, the man wanted to play God where others were concerned, giving Eve things he shouldn't have. But now when it was time to pay the piper he no longer wanted to experiment.

Adam had to give the vampire credit, though, for attempting to escape. He laughed as he forced the vamp toward Eve. He held him in his powers and growled, "Stop that nonsense or I will snap your neck this moment. At least this way you stand a chance at living."

Still, Adam had to force the vampire's body to bend over Eve, force him to allow his fangs to descend and pierce Eve's skin, to drink that damn tainted blood he'd poisoned her with.

Adam snapped his fingers for one of Dr. Meah's assistants. When Dr. Carleton appeared, his frightened look made Adam smile. Damn, when would they learn to behave as vampires instead of frightened mortals? "Dr. Carleton, I have no plans on hurting you. Hook up the tubes from me to my wife so that I can transfuse her. Seated, Adam watched the doctor's shaking hands finish the task he'd given him. "Dr. Carleton, you may go." Adam waved the vampire away, then turned his attention to the other scientist.

"Doctor Meah, you're a scientist. Remember that you like experimenting."

With the tubing in place Adam put his finger on the ballcock. "When all the players are in place we will begin. Doctor, if you please." He saw the man's fear as his fangs descended even further and he bit deeper into Eve's neck. He tried to resist but Adam had no plans to allow that to happen. A moan of pain escaped Eve's lips and she tried to push the doctor away from her. Adam flinched inwardly as the vampire's incisors tore through her flesh. She recoiled in pain. Her lids flickered and she opened her eyes and looked to Adam. He saw the fear there and wanted to soothe her, to tell her there was no need to fear, but he couldn't break character, not now.

"Drink the blood, Doctor. We don't want to waste it. Now, Sullivan, you."

Adam glanced at the mortal, almost stopping as he noted Mark didn't have the scent of fear on him. Adam probed his mind briefly, surprised to learn that this mortal thought he was going to die and he was glad to do it to save Eve. Disgusted, Adam ended the probe. So they all thought he was a monster? So damn what?

As Sullivan's fangs bit into the mortal's flesh, Eve's lids fluttered open again and she moaned. Turning her head slightly to the right, she found Dr. Meah feeding on her. Then her gaze left him and fell on Sullivan feeding on Mark.

Her eyes filled with tears and disappointment and recognition of Sullivan's betrayal claimed her features. "Sullivan, no, don't do it," she whispered softly. Her head rolled to the side and she saw Adam. She took in the tubing that ran from his arm to hers and the blood tears fell. "Adam, I beg of you, not again," she pleaded. "If you love me, not again."

Her gaze swung to connect with Sullivan. Mark smiled at her, unafraid. He should be, Eve knew that. "Run, Mark," she said softly, "get out of here." His answer that he wanted to help her didn't matter. It was as if he wasn't aware of the death grip he was in. There was no way for him to escape.

"Sullivan, you promised me. Don't let him do it." She caught Sullivan's grief and was weighed down by it. He loved her and was going back on his promise because of that love—the same as Adam had done.

"I believe," she mumbled to Adam, "I believe my powers are as strong as yours and I believe I can end this for myself. You're not going to use the people I love for your evil purposes." Then she closed her eyes, willing herself to die before Adam could stop it.

"You need me, Eve, you need me in order to feel alive. You've been waiting your entire life for me. You knew it when you were wasting your time with that would be priest, trying to become pious and all the time you were, my love. And you've known you belonged to me the entire time you've been with Sullivan. You know I'm the only one for you. You need someone who can touch your soul. Sullivan can touch your body, maybe even your heart, but whether you want to admit it or not, only I can touch your soul. You need me to touch your soul, Eve."

Adam's gaze connected with Sullivan's and he saw the hatred there. Sullivan had never truly hated him before but now he did. That didn't matter. Sullivan's hate was of no consequences. He'd warned the vampire. And now he'd have to pay the price; they all would. Adam grabbed Sullivan in a steel-like vise and sank his fangs into him. Sullivan twisted his neck in an effort to look at Adam. For a moment he attempted to resist but just for a moment for Adam sent words with stern clarity into Sullivan's mind: "Eve will be dead soon unless she receives my blood. Prove this love you have for my wife. Prove it or she dies." Then he turned the ballcock.

Not all of them would survive this little experiment. Adam was as aware of it as were the others. He sank his fangs deeper into Sullivan and felt the blood flow into him as his own blood flowed out of him.

"And this too shall pass. I love you, Eve." Adam sent the words to her. "Everything I've ever done in my life was because I loved you."

When it was all done Adam lifted his eyes to survey the damage. It was the first time in a long while he allowed the blood tears to flow from grief.

❖

Dear Mortals,

I have been receiving your communications. Alas I regret that I cannot allow the mortal F. D. Davis unlimited access to me. She wears on my nerves. She has however promised to get each installment to you as quickly as possible. In the meantime I have devised a plan by which you may speak to me and receive answers. I have been keeping an Internet diary of sorts for sometime now. Recently it was suggested that with my immense knowledge who better than I, Adam Omega should solve all of your mundane mortal problems. I will also tell you truthfully if your lover could have vampiric tendencies or whatever you might need to know. Write me and if you are respectful I will answer. AdamOmegaVampire@AOL.com. Until then you may read and enjoy the musings from my diary and advice column.

Adam Omega
Vampire

Diary Entries

Entry for January 07, 2007

I find that it pains me still to think of Eyanna. I loved her with my very breath. I gave my life for her and in the end she betrayed me. This is too painful at the moment to continue, even to annoy Eve.

Adam

Entry for January 06, 2007

I am growing tired of this nonsense. I am at the point where I almost don't care if this mortal woman feelings are injured. Eve keeps trying to tell me that I should care. And that's another thing...she's really beginning to annoy me.

I remember and believe I liked her better in many ways when she was Eyanna. Now I will be the one daring her. Let her dare read my words why not? I have suffered her disdain long enough. Yes, I do believe I will start reliving happier memories, those of my wife adoring me. Of course that was over a thousand years ago but so be it.

Let's see how you like it Eve. Let's see if my talk of Eyanna burns a hole in your spirit as your disdain has done to mine.

Entry for January 05, 2007

What was I thinking? A dumb wager, a challenge from Eve. She has little belief in me as a vampire, or as a man it seems. And I, the fool that I am gave into her because of her smile, and because I do remember how I have loved her for almost a thousand years. When I make love to her it had better be worth it or I might just…

Well no matter, for now I've given into the silliness. I could very well use my powers and help this silly mortal girl that I've hired. Where she came from I have no idea. Why Eve recommended her, and then insisted that I allow her to help me is beyond my comprehension. But when her eyes misted over, I was a goner. When she told me that I could accomplish nothing without my powers, my blood boiled. Eve had already won that round. I could have conceded, but no, I allowed her taunts to get to me, now I'm forced to do this web business without any powers.

Which brings me again to that mortal. Can you believe she put the pictures of babies up on my site, my kingdom, my domain. What idiotic nonsense. But of course you know Eve finds it sweet. Sweet. Can you believe that nonsense? I'm a vampire. Sweet is not what I am, nor what I desire. I desire, and do in most cases strike fear into the very marrow of mortals, male or female.

Challenge me please. I relish the opportunity to sink my fangs into your body to drink until I'm filled.

Damn, that smell. It is Eve's scent. I must go now. I must have that human show me how to keep Eve from reading my diary. She already thinks she has me by the… You thought I was going to say it, didn't you? Maybe later.

Eve, my love…there you are.

Entry for January 12, 2007

I had a dream last night and when I woke this morning it bothered me so I decided to write about it. For more years than I care to remember I have been attempting to bring my kind into the light with me. There is an old superstition that the light from the sun or the touch of a cross will kill them. I know better. But then as usual I digress. This is a time I really need to journal to figure out what is gong on. I feel bewitched.

I was sitting in St. Michael's listening as usual to the sermon. Okay if I'm to be truly honest I was scoping out the place for new blood. The faithful are more than accommodating and I am more than satisfied with my finds there.

Anyway, I found myself walking from the pulpit taking the bible and looking out on the audience as I begin to preach. That in itself is not what worries me. It was the ease with which I was accepted. That made me wonder. I have long lost my need to spread the word as it were. And even though my home is adorned with religious things it's mostly for the fear my enemies have for these inanimate object. They protect my home while I slumber.

My actions in my dream are what have me dismayed. I have no wish for absolution no need of forgiveness. I enjoy my life. I love being a vampire. I love the power. So why would I dream of nonsense?

Humans!! that can be the only answer. My wanting of Eve has infected my system. I am behaving strangely dreaming of things I do not want. The one thing I desire I have denied myself. Were it not for the three beauties that went home with me from St Michael's. I would think this dream was induced by hunger. My thoughts are not making any sense and neither are my words.

EVVVVVVE, what are you doing to me?

March 10, 2008

So my dear mortals, it seems that while the vampire's away the mortals will play. I have heard rumors that some of you do not fear me. It's even been said that I, Adam Omega have brought sexy back.

Do you think I see myself as this billionaire playboy vampire, handsome beyond belief and more powerful than... dare I say it? Of course I dare. More powerful than he who created man. I've been wondering lately what would have happened to this world if I had come in it sooner.

I've been working on many things with the psychic. I always knew that magic could be controlled by the right person and I am the right person. I've decided that being a vampire is no longer enough. It doesn't matter if I'm the most powerful vamp in the world. I've decided I will become a warlock. Yes you heard me a warlock. That my dear mortals is a necessity. I intend to keep one step ahead of the love of my life.

Darling Eve, hopefully you're as nosey as most females and you're reading this. This will serve as your warning that there is nothing that you can do, no trick, nothing that that I can not defend because beloved I love you and wish you well.

P. S. Little Debbie Thank you. Some vermin came and destroyed my words.
Adam Omega
Vampire
(The witch's husband)

March 05, 2008

I am so psyched. I never dreamed that anything could increase my powers. What the hell my powers didn't need any increasing. But I have learned that there are certain things that even I can use to my advantage. And my beautiful traitorous wife has not been as vigilant with her thoughts as she should be. I know the knowledge she seeks. She is unable to hide her thoughts from me.

There's the rub. Sometimes I wish she could. But no matter, I can easily conceal from her that which I do not wish her to know. When the time is right I will spring my surprise on Eve. I can barely keep from rubbing my hands together with glee.

Poor Eve, my poor misguided naive wife. To think she could learn things that I could not. She will be taught many lessons before I'm done with her.
Adam Omega
Vampire

March 02, 2008

I can barely believe I did this but what a rush. I went to see Lora, that psychic I promised Eve I would not visit. The woman was so frightened that it gave me tingles. I've been so charming as of late, okay, as charming as I Adam Omega can be to mortals. Anyway, like I was saying I've been so charming that I had forgotten how much fun it is to scare the hell out of mortals.

Damn that was fun!! The woman was so damn scared that her eyes grew large. She looked like something out of one of your mortal horror movies. I couldn't help it, I laughed in her face and not just a regular laugh but one that would chill the blood in the bravest vampire. So you know what that did to this puny mortal woman.

It felt good. It felt damn good to instill fear in her. First I walked around her hovel and gave her a smile every so often. Then I informed her that I wanted her to teach me to become a psychic. She opened her mouth to tell me that being a psychic was not something that was taught. I allowed the blood to fill my eyes and I stared at her. She pushed a button and several bodyguards ran in. That made it even better. I like nothing better than kicking the crap out of burly bodyguards. I stretched my hands and smiled at them then I beckoned them with the middle finger of my right hand to come closer. The smell of fear that covered their bodies, the sheer terror in their made my visit to Lora worthwhile. I will carry that picture for a few days it gave me such joy. They ran away and left Lora behind for me to do what I would do anyway. I couldn't stop laughing. Blood tears coursed down my cheeks from the amusement.

Did I care that the woman was frightened? Hell no. I looked at it like this. If she were truly a gifted psychic she should have known I was coming.

And guess what? Tonight I'm in such a good mood that I'm ready for a taste of my favorite little Debbie. Don't you love me…little Debbie?

Adam Omega

❖

Adam Omega's Advice Column

Tuesday, March 11, 2008
Dear Adam,
I read of your most recent desire to become a warlock. Whether I believe in warlocks and such is irrelevant. However, I wonder, is it really necessary for you to become the second most powerful being in creation? As it is, you're already the most powerful immortal walking planet Earth. Is this overload of power really necessary? And just so you don't show up at my home when least expected, the most powerful being is of course you, Adam Omega.

Besides, what's your plans for all of this power? Are you planning World Peace? To end poverty or hunger? The abuse of the weak and innocent?
Ethical Ethel

Dear Ethical Ethel,

What I wish to do with my increased powers is none of your concern. AS to who's the most powerful being, your comment was not to my liking so I edited your words. Besides, what you said is debatable. The need for more power is my business as I've stated. Absolute power corrupts absolutely. I am absolute power incarnate.

And so it is written, the first man ADAM was made a living soul; the last ADAM was made a quickening spirit. 1st Cor. 15:45

Need I say more? I will however give you something to ponder. If Eve is becoming a vampiric witch should I not also do likewise?

Adam Omega

Vampire

Friday, March 7, 2008
Dear Displeased Vampire,
Yes, I have lost my mind, I have finally come to my senses. I Beg you to forgive me, don't take your love away. I will be your most willing and humble servant for the remainder of my days. Please accept my apologies. I forgot that you are Adam Omega, Vampire. My mind is so filled with thoughts of you and my love so deep that I forgot my place. I promise if you will continue to visit me I will never forget again. As for that promise of pain the next time you visit. Sounds interesting.
So Crushed

My Dear So Crushed,

You have begged admirably and have been properly chastised. Though I received your letter a day ago I still felt that you needed more of a lesson. Your groveling however has given you a reprieve and your anticipation of the pain I will inflict on you interest me. There is hope for you yet mortal. Wait patiently

and reverently for My return.
    Adam Omega,
    Somewhat appeased VAMPIRE!

Tuesday, February 19, 2008
Dear Adam
Since Eyanna had bled on the amulet that she had given you, would Eve be able to use that with her crystals to make both of you mortal again? What is your biggest fear? Is it that Eve had the power to destroy you, or that you had already destroyed her soul?
    I had tried to post this question on the blog page but was unsuccessful.
Amanda Ortega

My Dear Amanda Ortega,
    First I must commend you for your brilliant questions. As to why you were unable to post on my blog. I have no wish for mortals to comment on my words. I am the last authority so I disabled that function. Oftentimes I tend to go into a rage and kill before I think. Not allowing mortals the freedom to comment is strictly for their safety.
    Now as to your questions: Know this, F. D. Davis has decided to belabor the point and take twelve books to tell my story but let me see if I can answer your questions honestly without giving away too much.
    As to whether or not Eve will be able to use her potions to turn the both of us human only time will tell. I have no such wish to return to my mortal state. But of course we both know that Eve is a stubborn woman. Now that she's remembering her own powers given to her by nature she no longer fears being called a witch. Add that to her dislike of this lifestyle and who knows what she might attempt. But my dear much to Eve's chagrin there is no cure for Vampirism. I am Immortal. I am Adam Omega.
    Again, I must say for a mortal you are indeed quick of mind. Which is my greatest fear? This I answer honestly for they are both true. I fear what I've done to Eve as much as I fear that she has the power to destroy me. I sometimes wonder what will happen when she realizes that. Will I do what I don't want and destroy her? That I cannot tell you. I won't know until that time comes. I do hope this answers your questions sufficiently. If not please rephrase and resubmit.
    Adam Omega
    Vampire

Thursday, January 24, 2008
Dear Adam,
How does a powerful vampire spend his day?
Curious

Dear Curious,
    Have you ever heard the phrase curiosity killed the cat? It's true. It's also true that curiosity kills the curious.
    Adam Omega

Vampire

Dear Adam,
Is Eve aware that you're online threatening those who dare to ask you questions that you don't want to answer with promises that you will drain them dry...and making them like it? I've got the feeling that she wouldn't be too happy with your treatment of everyday mortals.
Tattle-tale

Dear Tattle-tale
Let me assure you. Though Eve is the love of my life, she does not control me. I will admit there are many ways that Eve can persuade me. But she has not been using those methods as of late.
Now as to my issuing threats. I have never done that. What I have done is to make promises. A threat is meaningless and usually the one issuing it has no power to fulfill it. I on the other hand have much power behind my words. That my dear Tattle-tale is a promise.
Adam Omega

Dear Adam,
I am an old woman. I long to be young. I've heard that drinking vampire blood is like having a drink from the Fountain of Youth. Is this true? Or don't you share your blood.
Victoria

Dear Victoria,
What you believe is indeed true. A vampire's blood is the font of eternal live. One drink from this fountain and you would again be young and vibrant. But alas, you're right a second time.
I do not share my blood with any besides my wife.
Perhaps there are other things I can give you. I can give you dreams of youth, nights of passion. I can make it so that when you look in your mirror you will see the face that looked back on you from your youth. Would you like that my dear, Victoria?
Adam Omega

Dear Adam:
I have a question about sex. My boyfriend wants to do it in a casket at midnight under a full moon. The trouble is he wants the casket closed, and I want it open. Which is best?
Thanks for writing "Ask Adam." I wouldn't know who else to ask. Can you help us?
Emily

Dear Emily,
My dear what games are you playing with your lover? I do not brag. There is no need. I am Adam Omega and I am without a doubt A GREAT LOVER!!

That said, I would never make love to a woman in a coffin, closed or otherwise. What nonsense. A woman's body should be laid on a bed of pure silk. And I don't mean that crap that undertakers tell the family the coffins are covered in.

No I mean real silk. A woman should feel free when making love. How could you if you're enclosed in a tiny container. You need room to allow your legs to wrap around your lover's body, for him to travel up and down yours pausing at his leisure to place kisses on your satin flesh, to nibble you and make you scream with the wanting, to touch you and make you...

Are you with me? If your lover can't find such accommodations for you allow me to show you the way to heaven. Eve has no objections to such matings.

Adam Omega

Visit Adam's website at www.adamomega.com. You can write him and he will answer your questions. Write Adam at adamomegavampire@AOL.com

Author's Information

F. D. Davis also know as Dyanne Davis is writing under a pseudonym for her new vampire series. Award winning author, F. D. Davis lives in a Chicago suburb with her husband Bill, and their son Bill Jr. An avid reader, she began reading at the age of four. Her love of the written word turned into a desire to write. She retired from nursing several years ago to pursue her lifelong dream. Her first novel, The Color of Trouble, was released July of 2003. The novel was received with high praise and several awards. More nominations and awards followed with preceding books.

F. D. Davis has been a presenter of numerous workshops. She has a local cable show in her hometown to give writing tips to aspiring writers. She has hosted such notables as USA Today Best Selling erotica author, Robin Schone and vampire huntress L.A. Banks.

When not writing you can find F. D. Davis with a book in her hands, her greatest passion next to spending time with her husband Bill and son Bill Jr. Whenever possible she loves getting together with friends and family.

A member of Romance Writers of America, Dyanne is now serving her second term as Chapter President for Windy City. Dyanne loves to hear feedback from her readers. You can reach her at her website.